THE W... CHILD

Book Three of
THE WHITBY SERIES

Titles by Robin Jarvis

THE DEPTFORD MICE ALMANACK
  (Available Autumn 1997)

THE DEPTFORD MICE trilogy
  The Dark Portal
  The Crystal Prison
  The Final Reckoning

THE DEPTFORD HISTORIES series
  The Alchymist's Cat
  The Oaken Throne
  Thomas

THE WHITBY series
  The Whitby Witches
  A Warlock in Whitby
  The Whitby Child

On Audio

THE DARK PORTAL
  Narrated by Tom Baker

THE CRYSTAL PRISON
  Narrated by Martin Shaw

THE FINAL RECKONING
  Narrated by Jon Pertwee

THE WHITBY WITCHES
  Narrated by Julia McKenzie

A WARLOCK IN WHITBY
  Narrated by Siân Phillips

*With thanks to Penny Walker for all her
encouragement and infinite patience.*

THE WHITBY CHILD

Book Three of
THE WHITBY SERIES

Written and Illustrated
by Robin Jarvis

First published in Great Britain in 1994
by Simon & Schuster Young Books

Reprinted in 1995 and 1997
by Macdonald Young Books
an imprint of Wayland Publishers Ltd
61 Western Road
Hove
BN3 1JD

Photoset in Palatino in North Wales by
Derek Doyle & Associates, Mold, Clwyd
Printed and bound in the Channel Islands
by the Guernsey Press Co Ltd, Guernsey,
Channel Islands

British Library Cataloguing in Publication Data available

ISBN 0 7500 1581 0

CONTENTS

The broken ruin of the abbey appeared dark and ugly against oppressive black clouds. Its ancient stones were stained by the rain and it seemed as if the jagged pinnacles of its remaining windows had punctured the low ceiling of mist which hung threateningly above the cliffs.

The day belonged to the drizzle. Since the bleak dawn, dismal rain had poured from a slate-coloured sky. Relentlessly it streaked through the chill air, teeming down chimney pots and hissing on the sputtering fires beneath. Drumming on the terracotta rooftops it sluiced through the guttering in a frantic chase to gurgle and rush from the spouts below.

On to the one hundred and ninety-nine steps the drizzle fell until they glistened like black glass and the few muffled figures that dared to climb them slithered and skidded their way to the top.

The narrow streets of the East Cliff were filled by the incessant music of the deluge. Drain-pipes flowed as fountains – gushing into the rivers that churned like rapids beside the pavements, whilst an echoing chorus sang from every gargling grid and grate. The small town was thoroughly drowned, and that bleak morning gradually seeped into an equally drab afternoon.

The month of February was glumly displaying its sourest humour and all hearts grumbled and prayed for the rain to cease.

No, not all, for in the drenched town there was perhaps one who did not care whether it poured for forty days and forty nights. Whitby could be submerged beneath the sea for all she cared, the world outside might be swept down the cliffs forever and what would it matter to her?

Through eyes every bit as watery as the day itself, Alice Boston gazed morosely from the window of her cottage and gave a bored yawn.

Almost a month had passed since she had been discharged from hospital, yet the old lady was compelled to wonder if her life was now worth living.

A pale shadow of her former self, the once vigorous ninety-two-year-old now suffered each and every day of her great age. Her weariness was compounded by a recent birthday which had brought her to the grand total of ninety-three and she felt that she could bear the endless drudge of her dreary existence no longer. For someone who had always been a tireless and sprightly figure, her present condition was a bitter and repugnant one.

Ever since November of the previous year, Alice Boston had been close to death. Her valiant battle with Nathaniel Crozier – the vilest man ever to have sullied the world – now seemed distant and difficult to believe. There were times when she even forgot the horrific spectacle of Morgawrus, the monstrous serpent, whom she had sent back to the caverns beneath the cliffs to perpetual slumber.

Now, sitting in the armchair hour after hour it was easy to let the mind drift and allow fragments of memory to melt away forever. Could that terrible confrontation really have taken place? Was her tragic situation really due to the forces that she had unleashed? Had they drained her energy or was it merely her age? What if she had merely imagined it all? None of it seemed real any more – the threat and menace was over and she found herself regretting it.

The only life she knew now was experienced within the four walls of her sick room and anything beyond their bounds was difficult to comprehend or believe in. The life force that had once burned so fiercely within her soul was almost entirely quenched.

For many weeks she had been in the intensive care unit of the hospital and everyone feared that her time had come. But the thought of Jennet and Ben left alone in the world had kept one last ember of her indomitable spirit glowing. Miss Boston had not allowed herself to submit to that final peace, yet as the days wore on she became ever more despondent.

The old lady was trapped, chained inside the prison of her own crippled body. Propped against pillows in her armchair, she was a frail and wasted figure. Her left side was completely paralysed and she could neither walk nor dress herself. So drawn were the muscles in her face that she could not speak and when she struggled to make herself understood Miss Boston mumbled and grunted as unintelligibly as a new-born baby.

It was a humiliating end to the life which she had always embraced to the full. To think that the person who had saved the world from the threat of Morgawrus was now incapable of going to the toilet unaided.

The thought rankled in the old lady's mind. Never had she known such despairing frustration; her brain was still alert and active yet her body was almost useless.

Of course she was not left to fend for herself. Her good, but irritating friend Edith Wethers had retired from the post office and moved in to tend to the invalid's needs and wants.

For much of her spinster's life, Edith had cared for her own sick mother and was delighted to be of service once more. How she loved to fuss and cosset; tucking in the blankets around the bed, patting the pillows, brushing Alice's white woolly hair and wiping that oh so lined and poorly looking face with a brisk wet flannel. Never had the ex-postmistress felt so needed. What with seeing to Miss Boston and the children she hardly had time for herself and was thoroughly enjoying every last second.

As Miss Boston stared at the drizzle, she repented of those occasions on which she had bullied and bulldozed her tireless nursemaid. She could not help but wonder if this was some divine retribution for those times. If Edith Wethers had indeed sought a terrible revenge upon her then nothing could possibly have been more painful than this.

During the past few weeks, she had learnt to dislike Edith quite considerably and could not fathom how that sick mother of hers had ever endured such suffocating care for so many years.

With these sombre thoughts simmering impotently within her, Alice Boston waited for the hours to roll by. The afternoon grew old and the light began to fail. Across the window, raindrops drew slanting lines and their streaming shadows scored the invalid's wrinkled face.

A ruddy glow in the hearth signalled that the fire too had given up and the room became lost in a dim gloom. Curled up before the fading heat Eurydice, the cat, stretched her three legs and dozed contentedly – dreaming of the many suitors that had pursued and caught her.

Very gently, Miss Boston's eyes closed and her many chins were flattened against her bosom as she nodded and slipped into a fitful slumber.

"Alice Boston!"

Her head jerked and the stern voice snapped again.

"Good Lord, look at the state of you! Wake up, woman!"

With a hiss, Eurydice dug her claws into the carpet as every hair bristled and spiked upon her back. Then, emitting a frightful mewling shriek, she raced from the room and tore upstairs to hide beneath one of the children's beds.

Miss Boston stirred and her tired eyes blinked drowsily.

Suddenly she drew in her breath and the invalid's eyes grew round with wonder and amazement. Then her lop-sided mouth gaped wide open.

"Don't gawk, Alice!" said the familiar voice. "Do you have any idea how foolish you look? A shrivelled baboon, that's it exactly."

Miss Boston clapped her mouth shut and one corner of it twitched into a joyous grin. There, standing by the half open door was someone whom she never dreamt she would see again – Prudence Joyster.

But Prudence was dead, and it was several moments before Miss Boston realized that what her eyes beheld was merely a phantom of her departed friend.

Mrs Joyster's silvery hair was scraped back into the usual fist-sized bun and over a linen blouse she wore her comfortable grey cardigan decorated with embroidered roses. Yet like a reflection upon gently rippling water, the unforgettable figure shimmered. Very faintly Miss Boston could see the outline of the bed and the deep cherry glow of the fire through the shadowy form.

The ghost of Mrs Joyster, however, behaved exactly as she had done in life.

Clicking her tongue brusquely she looked with undisguised disdain around the sickroom. Then, folding her arms, she dismissed the whole sorry sight with an impatient shake of the head and before saying another word perched herself upon the other armchair.

"Confined to barracks," she archly observed in her crisp, military manner. "What has that dithering numbskull of a postmistress done to you? I never could bear her, you know. Never did like silly women and she's one of the silliest."

If Miss Boston had been able to speak, she wouldn't have known what to say.

Fortunately this did not seem to matter, for Prudence was quite prepared to do all the talking herself.

"Well, to be brutally honest, Alice," she rattled on briskly, "I am compelled to admit that I am disgusted with you! Such an abysmally wanton display of self-pity and wallowing apathy! You might as well be in one of those homes you always detested. Bed baths and bingo – that's all you're fit for!"

Miss Boston had always admired her friend's direct and incisive comments but now she smarted beneath the withering criticisms.

"Just look at you!" the phantom continued crossly. "Your legs are like spindles, and stop pulling that ridiculous face – it makes me want to slap it! How can you have surrendered to the ministries of that ludicrous Wethers woman? No wonder you look so dreadful. Pull yourself together!"

Finally Miss Boston could take no more and she gave a pitiable grunt.

"Don't you 'oink' at me, Alice Boston!" retorted Prudence indignantly. "If you want to make pig noises you can go to a farmyard. Have you heard yourself? Why, you're even dribbling!"

Miss Boston gazed at her despairingly. Why could she not understand? This was simply being cruel.

The phantom raised her eyebrows and leaned forward in the chair.

"Where did the Terror of Whitby disappear to?" she demanded, "Whatever happened to that Godawful nuisance who badgered and berated everyone? That's right, I'm talking about you, Alice Boston! You were the staunch campaigner, the leader of our ladies' circle, the one who made things happen. Always you were there to sort things out. Remember Mr Lomax, that shiftless plumber who drove Tilly to distraction? Who was it blacked his eye and bullied him to repair the mess he had made? When Howard died, who did I lean on? He sends his regards, by the way. You were always there for us, always ready to come out fighting, colours flying and wits as sharp as knives. So what has happened?"

Tears welled up in Miss Boston's eyes and trickled down her corrugated face. Prudence was right, she was no use to anyone like this.

"Stop snivelling!" the spectre snapped. "That won't solve anything. Why aren't you trying to conquer your disabilities? Where did all that fight and bluster go?"

The old lady blinked the tears away and looked steadily into Prudence's face. The challenge was unmistakable but some things were simply beyond her strength.

"Come on, Alice," Mrs Joyster barked, "you have never shied away from anything – why start now?"

Using all her concentration, Miss Boston tried to move her right arm. The withered limb twitched and trembled as it gingerly rose but she could do no more and after a few moments it flopped limply at her side again.

Prudence was not impressed and sniffed loftily. "Well, if that's the best you can do you might as well forget the whole thing," she uttered. "Oh honestly, have that idiot doctor and that twittering birdbrain really convinced you? I never realized that Edith's dithering foolishness was contagious."

Miss Boston frowned, wondering what Prudence was trying to tell her. The phantom clapped her hands in exasperation then gripped the arms of her chair as a peculiar smile spread over her dead lips.

"What was it you used to boast?" she asked. "You

never suffered from colds or pains in the joints like the rest of us. Oh no, you had your own little methods, trifling remedies for this and that. It was no small feat for a woman of ninety-two to climb those abbey steps every morning."

A gleam appeared in the phantom's eyes. "What have you been waiting for all this time? You know what I mean. So what if the doctors have told you to accept your fate – to blazes with the lot! You never paid any heed to them before. Modern medicine has failed you, so throw their pills and lotions down the drain and use your own special talents."

Miss Boston shifted in her seat, for Prudence was talking excitedly now, inspiring her with her words.

"Remember who you are," she continued. "Remember *what* you are. You have a skill far beyond that of ordinary people; use that knowledge now – heal yourself."

The white woolly head shook in despair; her condition was too severe for those humble ways.

Mrs Joyster slapped the arm of the chair and sprang to her feet in annoyance. "Don't be ridiculous, woman!" she cried. "I don't expect you to do it all by yourself! Have you utterly forgotten what you brought from London? That most precious thing Patricia Gunning entrusted to you?"

An expression of complete bewilderment passed over Miss Boston's face as she finally remembered – the Book of Shadows!

"There!" Prudence exclaimed. "How could you have neglected such a treasure as that? Use the book wisely, study it and make yourself strong again…"

The spectre paused and looked up sharply, as if she had heard something that alarmed her. Miss Boston strained to listen but the only noise was that of the rain.

"So soon?" Prudence gasped in a voice fraught

with dread. "But there is still much to tell!"

A concerned look, almost one of fear, now fixed itself over her ghostly features and when she next spoke, her words were hurried and filled with urgency.

"Listen!" she said. "My time here is almost over. I have not yet explained the real reason for my presence. Oh, damn them – I feel His thought reaching out to us! Alice, there is great danger, I came to warn you. Plans are being laid – terrible, evil plans."

Prudence shuddered as she spoke, twisting her head the entire time, and those pale blue eyes darted from side to side as though she expected some frightful horror to spring at her from the shadows. Evidently her fears were growing for her voice quickly rose until she was practically shouting.

"Alice!" she shrieked. "A day will come when you will need all of your strength. You sit there, thinking that the hazards and nightmares are over – well, they are not. I promise you, the worst terrors are yet to come. You have no idea of the peril that is creeping closer with every passing day."

At that moment the rain beat more loudly upon the window and Prudence jumped in fright. Reaching out her ghostly hand, she tried to clutch the gnarled arthritic mitten that was Miss Boston's.

"Against the forces which are mounting," she cried, "little can survive! There will be no salvation – no refuge! Think of yourself and those children that are so dear to you!"

The old lady glared at her. What did she mean by that?

"If you are not able to defend them," Prudence warned, "then Jennet and Ben will most certainly die!"

Miss Boston uttered a pitiful whimper but outside

the cottage the rain was torn aside as a sudden gale whipped through the courtyard. Plant pots crashed to the ground, scattering their earth into the ferocious wind which hurled it against the window panes. Prudence gave a yell of panic and leaped backwards as an unseen force flung her across the room. Like a cornered animal she stared wildly at the storm and cast an anxious look at her stricken friend.

"Don't give up, Alice!" she wailed. "Use the book – but above all, beware!"

Then, carried upon the squalling gale, came the roaring sound of the sea. Its effect upon Prudence was startling. Covering her ears, she shrieked and her terrified voice rose above the thunderous weather.

Suddenly, from the fireplace, came a blast of freezing, salty air and the room was at once filled with dust and ash.

With a final, agonizing scream, the ghost of Prudence Joyster crackled and vanished.

Almost immediately, the storm subsided and the gentle drizzle resumed its monotonous drumming upon Whitby. But in the cottage, Miss Boston shook and trembled as she stared fearfully around her.

Covering the now dead embers, the hearth was filled with wet sand and more of it was still trickling down the chimney. The old lady lifted her eyes to the dark windows and uttered a cry of shock, for pressed against the glass and obliterating the world outside was a solid wall of dripping seaweed. It was as if the ocean itself had tried to invade the cottage and Miss Boston shuddered, remembering Prudence's ominous words.

1

A SECRET FOUR
MONTHS OLD

Ben pulled the hood of his coat over his dark mousy hair and hurried along the shore. It had been several weeks since he had last visited the fisherfolk, for Miss Wethers was not keen to humour this fanciful notion of his and kept him indoors as much as possible.

"How could there be such creatures living in tunnels beneath the cliffs?" she had asked, not wishing to listen to any more of his nonsense. "And you shouldn't encourage him, Jennet. I don't like him wandering on the beach alone and nor should you. He's only eight, remember."

The boy pulled a wry face; he had tried to explain about the fisherfolk but she would never understand.

For countless years, the aufwaders had dwelt in their vast warren below the town. Once there had been many different tribes, but over time their numbers had steadily dwindled until only one was left, made up of the gleanings of the others.

Yet the ancient home of the fisherfolk had been destroyed by Morgawrus and since then the tribe was forced to seek shelter in other, more shallow caves set in the East Cliff.

All of the aufwaders mourned the loss of their former homes. Now they were exposed to the worst ravages of the weather and shivered inside the dank new holes. It had been a severe and biting winter and for one of the eldest members of the tribe it had proved too much.

Lorkon was the only survivor of the ancient ruling triad and his death was taken as an omen of their impending doom and extinction.

Sadly, Ben remembered that cold night when the funeral boat containing Lorkon's body had sailed out to sea in a blaze of fire. The aufwaders had gathered upon the shore and as they sang the Song of the Dead the boy had wondered what would become of them.

It was difficult for that proud race to accept this new life, for now they were like refugees in their own land. Even Ben's friend Nelda had grown disheartened and he sorrowfully recalled that she had hardly spoken to him on that solemn occasion. Perhaps she, like many of the other aufwaders, had started to feel bitter towards mankind.

It was with some trepidation therefore that he approached the towering cliffs.

"Nelda!" Ben called. "It's me! Nelda! Can you hear me?"

There was no answer, and the boy stared up at the sheer wall of shale that reared above him. The fisherfolk had been extremely busy disguising the entrances to their new caves – even his eyes could not see them.

Rain splashed on to his face, and irritably he wiped away the water with his sleeve.

Nothing stirred, no large eyes stared down at him and no voice was raised in greeting. All was strangely silent and Ben realized that there were no gulls flying overhead. It was an unnatural calm and he shuddered and almost fled, for in the fading light the place took on a sinister aspect and the cliffs seemed threatening – with menace lurking in every shadow.

"Don't be silly," he told himself. "You're too old to be scared of the dark."

Eyeing the boulders before him, Ben tried to recall the route he had taken on his last visit. The rocks were wet and slippery, but undeterred, the boy began to climb.

Very slowly he made his cautious way upward, though not at all sure of the correct path; he found the going exceedingly difficult.

The knees of Ben's school trousers were quickly soaked as he scrabbled over wet moss that stained them a livid and indelible green. A shameless grin lit his face as he imagined Miss Wethers' face when she saw the state of them; he enjoyed inflicting little upsets upon Dithery Edith.

The trousers became greener and dirtier as he ascended, but after a while he paused to catch his breath and inspect how far he had clambered. The boy was disappointed to discover that he had hardly made any progress at all and he put out his bottom lip in annoyance.

"Just have to try harder," he said aloud.

Standing upon a narrow shelf of rock, he saw that to his left a series of treacherous looking footholds were notched into the cliff face. Confident that he recognized them, Ben pushed the toe of his shoe into the nearest and warily continued.

But the rain had made the way perilous and it was not long before the boy wished he had never attempted the dangerous climb. Twice his fingers slid over the shale and he pressed himself desperately to the rock, breathing rapidly and longing to be standing upon the shore once again.

"Why do I always get myself into these messes?" he fumed. "You really are a Cret, Benjamin Laurenson!"

With an effort, he lifted his right foot and placed it

into the next cleft. But this one was shallow and
when he put his weight upon it he slipped.

Out into the empty air his leg swung and the boy
lost his balance. Shrieking, he struggled to cling on
but his fingers were torn from the rock and he knew
that he was going to fall.

"Help!" he wailed as he fell backwards.

"Up tha comes!" bawled a gruff voice. A strong
brown hand flashed from the shadows above and
caught Ben's wrist. "What addled daftness be this?
Weer did tha reckon tha wert headin'?"

Tarr Shrimp, present leader of the fisherfolk tribe
and the grandfather of Nelda, hauled the boy to
safety with one hand then clipped the back of his
head with the other.

"Th – thank you," Ben gasped. "I nearly…"

"Aye, yer girt gawby mad allick – tha mun be
witless a comin' out on such a day as thissun. Get
thee inside afore tha catch a death."

Taking the boy by the arm, he led him up a gently
rising ledge then mounted a rocky outcrop that
served as a natural flight of steps.

Now Ben was sure of the way; the entrance to the
Shrimp dwelling was just a little distance ahead.

Up to a tall and narrow crevice, Tarr went and
waited for the human child to follow.

"Skip to it, lad!" he snapped. "Ah doesna' wish
t'chase Lorkon t'grave."

Ben squirmed into the seemingly shallow gap, then
twisted sharply to the left where the rock behind him
suddenly opened out and he found himself standing
inside the cliff face.

At once Ben's eyes began to water as they were
filled with woodsmoke and it was some moments
before he could see clearly.

The cave was small and its walls were roughly
hewn. Hanging in great swathes from the rocky

ceiling were many fishing nets and from these, two tiny lamps were hung. The steady flames that burned within them threw confused criss-crossed shadows into the furthest corners and in their light, Ben saw the cause of his streaming eyes.

In the middle of the meagre chamber, a pathetic fire was burning, and the damp wood that had been placed upon it gave off a continual thread of steam and smoke. Sitting before these miserable flames, with her back turned towards the entrance – was Nelda.

The aufwader girl was staring into the fire, lost in her own thoughts, and so intense was her concentration she did not hear Ben or her grandfather enter.

Over her huddled frame the lamplight danced, rejoicing in her large sea-grey eyes and glowing in the soft curves of her lined, leathery face. Nelda's dark, tangled hair trailed over her shoulders and as the waving tresses flowed down the back of her gansey, the lanterns picked out hidden strands of copper and made them glint and shine.

The youngest of the fisherfolk was undoubtedly one of the fairest ever to have graced any tribe, yet she was also the unhappiest.

In silence she gazed into the heart of the flickering flames and brooded upon the deadly secret that she had not dared tell to anyone. For months now she had kept it from even her grandfather, not knowing what to do or where to turn. If only her Aunt Hesper was still alive, she would have listened and hugged her.

A solitary tear of despair fell from Nelda's lashes, as she realized that soon her secret would be all too obvious. For inside her, the unborn child of Esau was growing and eventually her swelling stomach would betray her.

"Stir thissen, lass," barked Tarr gravely. "Us've got usselves a visitor."

Nelda hastily wiped her eyes and turned around.

"Hello," Ben said. "Thought I'd come and see how you are, before Miss Wethers realizes where I've got to. It's pouring down outside."

"Take thy drippin' coat off," Tarr told him. "Ah'll put it near t'fire. Sit thee down."

Nelda managed a faint smile for the boy as he wormed his way out of the sodden coat and handed it over to her grandfather.

"It is good to see you again," she said, glad to be distracted from her dismal thoughts. "Come, sit by me and I shall put more wood on the fire to cheer us."

Mechanically, she thrust another piece of driftwood into the flames whilst Tarr settled himself upon a low stool and took up his pipe.

"Reet fain am I t'sithee," he remarked to Ben. "Our Nelda's been no company. Fair mardy she be gettin'. Ah nivver did think it o' the lass. Nigh on a month she's been a mopin' wi' 'er face a draggin' on t'floor."

No reply came from his granddaughter. Throwing him an angry glance, she stared sullenly back at the fire.

Ben said nothing but felt horribly uncomfortable. He had obviously walked in upon some family squabble and wondered how long it would be before his coat was dry enough to wear again.

From a pouch at his belt, Tarr pulled out a hunk of dried fish and began to chew it, offering a piece to Ben.

"Womenfolk!" he mumbled, scratching his white whiskers. "Nivver knowed wheer ye be wi'em. Either chelp or chunter, ain't no middle track."

Ben sniffed the morsel of dried fish and tasted it dubiously. It was like eating a stringy piece of carpet that grew no smaller no matter how long you persisted in gnawing and biting. He felt that it would be too impolite to spit the offensive lump from his mouth, even though the amount of salt in it made him want to retch. For a long time, he occupied himself in trying to swallow but this was impossible so, like a hamster, he tucked it inside his cheek to dispose of later.

"How are the rest of the tribe?" he finally asked. "Are they a bit more settled now after Lorkon's funeral?"

"Settled as them can be in these pokey holes," Tarr grumbled. "Most of 'em found it too harsh and found a way in to th'old caverns."

"I thought all those were destroyed!" Ben cried.

"Aye, that's reet enough, them was. But the main entrance chamber is still theer behind the girt doors which are sealed ferivver, and a new way were delved to enter it. The death of Lorkon put the wind up 'em, see. So now them sits in that one place, crowded t'gither like skeered sheep. A sorry sight 'ave us become."

Tarr drew on his pipe and gazed across at Nelda but she would not look at him and he puffed out a ring of blue smoke that drifted past her eyes, yet still she said nothing.

"Well, then, lad," Tarr began, "how's thy aunt farin'? Any tidings theer?"

Ben shook his head. "No," he sadly replied. "Aunt Alice is just as poorly as she was before. I don't think she will ever get better and there are times when she looks … terrible. It's so awful, I don't know what me and Jen would do if she died. If only I could do something. Miss Wethers doesn't help either; she treats her like a baby and I can tell Aunt Alice detests it."

"Aye," agreed Tarr sombrely, " 'tis a sore trial for

all. Much does we owe that aunt o' thine. She'll allus be remembered by us; so long as the tribe lasts, her name'll be honoured."

The old aufwader reached for his staff which was leaning against the wall and nudged his granddaughter with it. "Now theer's one wi' summat t'despair of – not thee, lass. What ails thee? Nowt so bad as that, ah'll be bound – so buck up."

Nelda had to bite her tongue to keep from telling him there and then and with a tremendous effort changed the subject.

"What of your sister, Ben?" she asked through clenched teeth. "She is well, I trust?"

Ben shrugged. "I don't know what's got into Jen," he replied. "She isn't the same as she used to be. She just isn't any fun these days."

"None of us are the same as we used to be," Nelda muttered grimly. "Both you and Jennet have grown, you have seen and learnt a great deal since the death of your parents."

"I suppose," the boy agreed, but he was reluctant to talk about his mother and father and said no more.

Nelda, however, seemed strangely eager to hear all she could. "Is it really three winters since they were killed?" she asked.

Ben gave the slightest of nods then fidgeted with his school tie.

Tarr scowled at his granddaughter but she would not be silenced.

"Do you know how they died?"

"Stop it," the boy said in dismay.

"Was their passing quick?" she morbidly persisted. "Do you think they suffered much?"

"Yes!" Ben cried. "They must have. Mum and Dad were drowned – all right? The car ran off the road and crashed into a river. They couldn't get out in time so – yes, they suffered."

"Nelda!" shouted Tarr angrily. "Why badger the lad? See how he is upset!"

"Forgive me, Ben," she said, putting her hand over his, "but you and I are alike. We are orphans we two, yet at least you know the manner of your mother's end. It is best to know all, not be left to conjure up demons in the mind to feed on ignorance and fear." She spoke the final words for Tarr's benefit but her grandfather slammed his staff furiously upon the floor and rose to his feet.

"Enough!" he demanded. "Will tha not cease? Ah've told thee many times – ah shall not speak of that time! Nivver!"

Nelda glowered at him. "How did my mother die?" she shrieked. "Tell me!"

"NO!" he yelled, pointing a trembling finger at her. "Ah warn thee, dunna pursue this. Them days were evil – ah forbid thee to speak on it!"

"Why will you not tell me what her final hours were like? Have I not that right? It was for me that she died – I demand to know!"

"NIVVER!" he bawled, and such was the force of his voice that she knew it was pointless to continue.

Ben sat awkwardly between them. He had never seen either Tarr or Nelda so impassioned before and to witness them now with their tempers boiling alarmed him greatly. Each aufwader glared at the other, the elder positively quaking with rage and the other near to bursting with a frenzied obsession that the boy found weird and macabre.

"I ... I think I'd best go home now," he uttered quietly.

Tarr held his granddaughter's eyes for a moment longer then whipped round and stood with his back to the pair of them.

"Remember me t'thy aunt," he said curtly.

"I will, Mr Shrimp. Er ... goodbye."

"Aye."

The boy took up his coat; it was still damp but he was only too glad to put it on. The atmosphere in the cave was unbearable and he pulled on the garment as fast as possible.

Nelda fumed at her grandfather's back then sprang to her feet. "Wait," she called to Ben. "I will walk with you – the air here is stale. I stifle in it!"

When they had gone, Tarr kicked the stool across the floor. "What divil has seized hold o' the lass?" he ranted. "Why rake it all up now?"

Fumbling for his pipe, he thrust it into his mouth and waited for his temper to cool. "Womenfolk!" he spat. "Won't ever reckon 'em."

Standing in the open air Nelda breathed deeply and pulled her woollen hat down over her ears. The daylight had faded completely but the rain was still flooding from the sky.

Ben stuck his hands in his pockets and waited until she had collected herself. "What was that all about?" he ventured.

"My grandfather thinks of me as a bairn and naught beyond," she said. "Sometimes I fear the gulf between us is too great."

"He is very old," the boy said carefully, "and in the eyes of your kind you are practically the same age as me – even though you are seventy."

"Perhaps," she muttered, "yet I was considered age enough to wed with Esau Grendel."

"Only because he was barmy and none of the others dared oppose him! Nelda, you're still only a child – don't go all funny like Jennet."

The aufwader glanced past him to the dim edge of the great dark sea and shook herself. "I am sorry," she said. "Times are grim, yet it is wrong of me to inflict my woe upon you."

"Won't you tell me what's the matter?" he asked

10

gently. "You've done it before, remember?"

In spite of herself Nelda smiled, then she looked down at the sands and began to descend the cliffside.

"It is nothing," she said unconvincingly. "Let us leave this high place and wander by the fringe of the tide awhile."

Bowing their heads beneath the drizzle, the two of them slowly made their way downwards, then side by side, they strolled over the level rocks towards the shore.

Between the great weed-covered boulders that had ripped into the bows of many ships, they carefully stepped. Where possible, they avoided the shallow pools in which the rain splashed but neither of them spoke and the silence began to prey upon Ben's nerves. Twice he caught an odd look stealing over Nelda's face as if she was plucking up the courage to say something. But each time her resolve failed and she cast her eyes to the ground to avoid his gaze.

Eventually, the boy could bear it no longer. "Look," he said flatly, "just tell me – I know you want to."

Nelda raised her eyes. "My troubles are now four months old," she began in a wavering voice. "You recall the nature of my late spouse?"

Ben shuddered; Esau had been a vile and grasping creature.

"Just so," she sorrowfully agreed, "yet from him I did buy the knowledge of the third guardian and brought it safe from the clutches of the Mallykin."

Ben had no idea where this was leading but nodded encouragingly.

Nelda pulled the neck of her gansey up over her chin and turned shamefully from him. Her tears mingled with the rain and she covered her eyes as finally she blurted out the awful secret which so terrified her.

"None have I told," she murmured, "no one knows the heinous price that accursed Esau placed upon that knowledge. Nor do they suspect that I, Nelda, was fool enough to pay it – but what else could I have done?"

"What did you do?" the boy asked, a horrible suspicion beginning to form in his mind. "Listen, Nelda," he said gently, "without the guardian, Nathaniel and the serpent would have destroyed everything." He stared at her reassuringly and pressed her cold hands in his. "Esau is dead," he whispered. "Let him be forgotten – no one will ask how he died, nor will they blame you."

Nelda pulled her hands away and a chilling, mad laugh erupted from her small mouth. "You ... you think I killed him?" she cried in disbelief. "You think that in fear for his own wretched neck my husband told me where the guardian lay? Oh Ben, did I then slit his throat or throttle the breath from him? Tell me which – for dearly would I have done that deed and regretted it never. No sleep would I have lost and no meal turned aside if that were the happy truth. His very blood would I steep myself in if I could undo what I have really done!"

Ben took a step backwards; she was almost hysterical and he looked over his shoulder to the cliff face, wondering if he should fetch her grandfather.

"Ha!" she wailed. "Can it be so repugnant and contrary to nature that you really cannot guess? Alas, I see that it is, and poor Nelda is damned with the doom she has brought upon herself."

Hiding her face in her hands, she threw herself against a rock and wept desolately.

Ben did not know what to do. He did not have the faintest idea what she had done and clumsily tried to console the unfortunate aufwader girl.

"Don't worry," he said. "I'm sure it will be all right,

Nelda – please don't cry."

"Blether, blether, blether!" snapped a sharp voice from the surrounding shadows.

Ben looked up, but it was too dark and he waited for the stranger to approach.

"What's that scrawny whelp squawkin' fer now? Always makin' a racket and squeal, squeal, squeal!"

From the gloom a small, round figure emerged. Old Parry narrowed her sly eyes and wrinkled her spiteful face up at Ben. She hated all humans but despised him especially because he had the favour of the Lords of the Deep.

She was the most vindictive and downright nasty member of the aufwader tribe, whom the boy always avoided if he saw her upon the beach. The viciousness of her tongue was well known to him and he had learnt that she was always eager to speak poison about others. Tarr barely tolerated her and she always drove Nelda to distraction with her sneaky and malicious ways.

The girl stirred as she heard her and dried her eyes. The last thing she wanted was for the creature to go spreading tales among the rest of the tribe.

Tentatively, Old Parry sniffed the air around Ben and pretended to choke in disgust.

"Consortin' wi' the landbreed again," she observed through tight lips. "No wonder yer blubber so."

"I wasn't crying," Nelda retorted defensively. "I merely caught my foot on a stone – it pained me, that's all."

The other waggled her head in amusement. "Tell it to the sea," she huffed, "only make it quiet – I've a mind to go pool wading this night and I'll not be disturbed by your screeching! Can't a body have any peace? There's cramp and clamour enough in the great hall without any pesterin' from the likes of you!"

Nelda drew herself up and thought of a good many things to say to the interfering old nuisance, then she had a different idea and her angry face became wrapped in smiles.

"Oh," she exclaimed with feigned interest, "what are you wading for?"

Old Parry eyed her uncertainly. "Just shells," she mumbled, "to tie in my hair, and ought else I find, though it don't concern you."

"It's been such a long time since I foraged in the pools," Nelda enthused. "May I join you?"

"You," uttered Old Parry in complete surprise, "wade wi' me?"

"I should love to."

The astonished female shrugged, then glanced back at Ben. "But no stinkin' landbreed!" she warned. "I'll not share the waters with none of that race! Tell him to crawl back to his hut!"

Guiltily, Nelda looked across at the boy and bit her lip. "You would not mind if I tarried here?" she said.

"I thought you wanted to tell me what the matter was," he answered, puzzled as to why she would want to spend any amount of time with that hatchet-faced crone.

With a shake of her head, Nelda dismissed the notion that she had been upset. "Don't worry so," she told him. "Is it not time for you to return? I shall see you soon, no doubt."

Ben could not understand her behaviour and felt hurt at the way she was treating him. Rejected and miserable he gave a sulky grunt, spun on his heel and made for the town.

Feeling worse than ever, Nelda watched him leave.

"Thought you'd tire of human company," Old Parry said haughtily. "They're not worth the water they bathe in. It's well to see you come to your senses at last. 'Tain't proper for us to mingle; look what happened to Oona."

"Yes," breathed Nelda, "it was she who brought the wrath of the Deep Ones upon us by wedding one of the landbreed."

"And sealed our fate with the laying of the Mother's Curse!" added Old Parry. "Naught but trouble and grief comes of mixing wi' them."

"A terrible punishment for so simple and blameless a crime."

The old aufwader waited until the figure of Ben had disappeared in the dark distance before she began to hunt among the rocks for a suitable pool to dip into.

"Ooh yes," she agreed as she peered into the water, "a fouler end them Lords of the Deep could not have devised."

Nelda followed her to the next rockpool, trying not to betray the anxiety she felt. "What ... what exactly happens under the curse?" she murmured.

Old Parry bent low over a dish-shaped stone and whirled her fingers through the water it contained. "Death o' course," she burbled.

"Yes I know, but how exactly?"

The scourge of the fisherfolk lifted her eyes to the girl and her eyebrows twitched curiously.

"So," she crooned, "you want to know the full extent of the Mother's Curse?"

"I ... I want to know what happened to my mother."

"Tarr not told you? Nah, he wouldn't, but I was there – I know."

"Will you tell me?"

Old Parry's eyes glinted. " 'Tain't no pretty tale," she muttered darkly, "but I can see there's no denying you. Sit here."

Stiffly, Nelda sat upon the cold wet stone beside her and the crone chuckled horribly to herself.

"Never had I seen such pain," she began, recalling that hideous time. "Your mother was a headstrong, foolish creature who listened to no counsel but her own. We all told her it was in vain but still she tried to give her husband a child. Not for many centuries had an infant been born to our kind, not one that lived, that is.

"Determined and wilful she was, and stubborn as the cliffs themselves. Strong was the bond 'twixt she and your father and for his sake she bore you. But as the time went by and her belly swelled, her agonies steadily increased.

"Every time the moon waxed and was full in the heavens, you could hear her screams rent the night and echo through every tunnel and chamber. Now, as you know, few wives survived beyond the first three months so when she lingers on past the eighth, with only four more remaining we all wondered if the curse had lost some of its power.

"But the Lords of the Deep and Dark showed their displeasure in ways various and plenty lest any other wife dared flout their might. Shoals of rotting fish were washed ashore and storms raged at sea so that no boats could set sail for many weeks. 'Twas an evil time full of such signs and portents and your mother was to blame."

Old Parry paused to gauge the effect her tale was having upon Nelda. The girl looked pale and ill so she gladly resumed the tragic story, revelling in the gruesome details.

"No one living can describe the torture that your mother endured for your sake and that of Abe your father. For when her time came it was beyond aught I had yet seen. As soon as you were born she began to die."

"How?"

"By the most evil of means. For when it became

16

apparent that by some miracle you were to live, your mother let loose a sickening screech. Such is the fell manner of the curse that the very blood in her veins did change and under the enchantment of the Deep Ones, it turned to brine."

"No!" Nelda gasped, stricken with horror and disgust. "It cannot be true!"

"On my Joby's watery grave," the other swore, spitting into the rockpool, "that was the way of it.

"Into a blazing fever your mother swooned, the salt water creeping through her body, burning and blistering through her flesh until her very wits were eaten away."

"She ... she went mad?"

"Raving!" came the cackling response. "An agony of madness was hers, and not even her own husband's father did she know. Wounded to the heart was Tarr and he stumbled through the caverns like one blinded. Yet not swiftly was she taken – oh no, for nigh on two whole weeks did your mother linger and by the end she was like a salted slug. No black boat carried her into the sea. There was naught remaining – only a briny sludge with Abe weeping over it."

Nelda staggered to her feet. It was worse than she had dreaded. For now she knew the precise nature of her mother's demise whereas it had only been hinted at before, and she wept for the parent she had never known. Yet more bitterly did she weep for herself, for that same fate would undoubtedly wreak its terrible vengeance upon her.

"Don't go," Old Parry sniggered as Nelda hurried unsteadily away. "Let me tell you of others that perished and of the countless bairns that did not survive. How their first sweet cries were changed into shrieks as they crumbled into dust!"

But Nelda was too distraught to hear her and the

spiteful old crone clutched her sides at the sight. Her brutal and raucous laughter echoed over the shore, rebounding off the cliffs, as if they too mocked the poor aufwader girl.

* * *

"Oh come on, Jennet! It'll be a good laugh."

"I said no, all right?"

Sarah Wellings tried one last time. "Martin Gravsey will be there."

"So what?"

"He fancies you!"

"Oh leave me alone – I don't care what you do, just leave me out of it!"

Sarah flicked her damp fringe from her eyes and pushed Jennet savagely. "If it wasn't for you we wouldn't have had that detention!" she said. "I'm not going to have time to put some make-up on now. God, Laurenson, what's up with you anyway?"

"Look, I don't want to hang round the arcade or be chatted up by a group of spotty lads with bad breath who wear too much cheap aftershave. Is that so hard to understand?"

Sarah sneered at her. "You're mad, you!" she shouted. "Tracey and Clare were right, they said you'd gone as loony as your brother. Well I've had it, okay? From now on don't bother speaking to me."

She stomped off over the wet cobbles and chanted at the top of her voice, "Laurenson, Laurenson, lordy, lordy what a loony!"

Jennet rubbed her arm where Sarah had punched her. She was a pretty girl with dark brown hair and a pleasant oval face. At first she had been popular at school but that had all changed. Over the past few months the friends she had made in Whitby had gradually abandoned her. She knew it was her own fault; she was indifferent to them and hated their incessant, ridiculous talk about boys and music. Jennet was interested in neither of these, not since she had come under the influence of Nathaniel Crozier.

For a twelve-year-old girl whose thirteenth birthday was only a matter of months away she seemed old before her time and withdrew into herself a little further every day.

Glumly, Jennet walked along Church Street towards Aunt Alice's cottage. At last the rain had ceased and the narrow road glistened in the lamplight. Overhead, the window-sills and projecting signs dripped amber jewels but the girl was oblivious to the beauty of the clean, washed world. Through the puddles she traipsed, scattering the reflections and dwelling on the idiotic night her former friends would have.

"Who wants to do that anyway? I certainly don't. Boys are stupid!"

Passing one of the shop windows, Jennet came to an abrupt halt and stared through the glass. It was a photographer's studio and examples of his art were on display to entice prospective customers inside.

A large print of a surprised baby sitting amongst a quantity of pink silk met Jennet's eyes but she ignored it and looked at the one by its side. There, upon textured paper to make it resemble a painting on canvas, was a photograph of a bride and groom. The girl studied it thoughtfully as her breath fanned out over the window-pane. It reminded her of a picture she had of her parents' wedding day.

"Oh Mum," she uttered in a hoarse whisper, "why aren't you and Dad here?"

The couple before her beamed back, and the girl dragged herself away. Swinging her school bag over her shoulder Jennet resumed the short walk home.

Just as she was about to turn into the alleyway that led to the cottage, she saw Ben trudging along the street from the direction of the shore.

Jennet did not need to ask where her brother had been.

"How was Nelda?" she asked.

Ben made no reply but brushed past and tramped through the courtyard to the cottage door.

"Charming," Jennet remarked. "I don't know why I bother."

Hungry for his tea and keen to be rid of the dry, salty taste in his mouth, Ben leapt up the doorstep and knocked loudly.

At once the door was torn open and the courtyard was filled with yellow light. A woman in her fifties, with greying hair that looked as though it had been sat on, was framed in the doorway. With one hand clinging to the handle and the other positively squeezing the life from a bunch of tissues which she dabbed to her nose, she let out a squeak and ushered the children inside.

"Oh where have the pair of you been?" she twittered in distraction. "What a day to go roaming off. Look at the state of your clothes, Ben – oh dear!"

The boy dragged his sopping coat off and sniffed expectantly. "What's for tea?" he asked, unable to detect any of the usual smells.

"Oh dear!" Miss Wethers exclaimed again. "Your teas, I clean forgot!" And she threw an agitated glance at the door of the sickroom.

Jennet was watching her closely. Dithery Edith seemed more preoccupied than normal and she sensed that something was wrong.

"What's the matter?" she asked. "Aunt Alice! Has something happened to her?"

Miss Wethers flapped her hands as the girl made

for the sickroom and only just managed to pull her back in time.

"You can't go in there yet," she told her, "not until the doctor's finished."

"The doctor?" Jennet cried. "Is she all right?"

Desperately, Ben stared at the closed door and his empty stomach turned over. What if the old lady had died?

"Alice is fine," Edith hastily explained as she saw the colour rising in the children's faces. "She got a little agitated this afternoon, that's all – over-excited herself for some reason."

Before she continued, the tissue flew about her nose like a fat butterfly. "I had only popped upstairs for a little lie down," she trilled, "when suddenly the storm awoke me and I heard a crash from downstairs."

Here she paused to catch her breath as if reliving the moment when she tore down the stairs. "When I entered the sickroom I found Alice sprawled on the floor. The silly old thing had tried to stand, can you imagine? Lord alone knows what got into her! Oh it was awful, and do you know what else? Sand! Everywhere there was sand. It dripped from the chimney and made a fine mess all over the place. How do you account for that? I'm sure I don't know! And covering the windows was a heap of seaweed. It was like one of those uncanny events you read about – when it rains frogs or sardines. Took a long time to be rid of it too. Anyway, there Alice was – sprawled."

Her report complete, Edith gulped the air exhaustedly then added in a respectful whisper, "Of course I ran to telephone Doctor Adams immediately. He's just finishing his examination; shouldn't be too much longer."

The children looked at one another nervously, and wished they had both been here sooner.

Within the sickroom, Doctor Adams closed his medical bag and shook his head at the patient.

"You are nothing but a stubborn old nuisance," he told her in his most professional voice. "Getting up from your chair indeed! You should have a little more consideration for the people who care for you than to persist in these foolhardy ventures. You're not a young woman; people of your age should do as their physicians tell them."

Doctor Adams had practised in Whitby for nearly twenty years and was nearing the age when his thoughts turned towards taking an early retirement. He was a tall, pink man with rather too much flesh on him than was healthy. His thinning hair was swept over his domed head and slicked down by generous applications of pomade so that no sudden gust of wind could send the long wisps flying.

Miss Boston stared at him, and if looks could maim then he would have been the one in need of medical attention.

She was now lying in bed with the pillows properly fluffed up by Edith and her coverlet neatly tucked in all around.

"You should be thankful there's no damage done," the doctor concluded. "Old bones are very fragile, you know. One of my patients in Bagdale had a hip replacement last week and he's thirty years younger than you. Just don't think you can gad around any more."

Giving Miss Boston a final, disapproving look, he went to the door and told Edith that he had finished.

At once, Jennet and Ben pushed past him and put their arms about Aunt Alice's neck.

"Careful," the doctor scolded. "She's an invalid, remember, and it's been a tiring day for her. She needs as much rest as possible and plenty of peace and quiet – don't excite her."

Miss Wethers drank in the doctor's words and privately resolved that she would try harder as a nurse.

"Is there anything more I should be doing for her, Doctor?" she squeaked.

Doctor Adams gave her a pleased smile and revealed in the expansive pink face were his little, perfect, pearly teeth.

"I wish all my patients were so well tended to," he praised her. "Alice Boston should count herself lucky to have such a good friend. If she were a little less selfish and reconciled herself to her infirmities she mightn't put you under this unnecessary strain."

On the bed, Miss Boston snorted, but Edith blushed and nervously rushed into the kitchen to make the doctor a cup of tea.

"Now then," he said to the children, "remember what I said, no excitement for her." And with that he followed the flustered ex-postmistress from the room.

As soon as she was rid of him, Miss Boston urgently tried to speak to Jennet and Ben. But all that issued from her paralysed mouth was a series of incoherent grunts.

"What are you trying to say?" Jennet asked her. "I can't understand."

"Do you want something, Aunt Alice?" guessed Ben.

The old lady puckered her face into a scrunched-up mass of wrinkly skin as she battled to force the words from her mouth.

"Careful," Jennet warned her. "Remember what the doctor said."

The old lady's head flopped against the pillows and tears of frustration sprang from her eyes.

Ben's heart went out to her. "Perhaps if you pointed at something," he suggested, "we could work it out from there – a bit like charades."

Miss Boston's face brightened at once and again she summoned her feeble strength.

Her right arm twitched and for a brief second she managed to indicate one of the shelves in the alcove.

"Is it up here?" Jennet asked, jumping from the bedside and running to the collection of bizarre objects that Miss Boston had gathered about herself over the many years.

The old lady nodded and Jennet quickly ran through a list of all she could find upon the shelf.

"Corn dolly, jar with – pooh what's in there? Not that? Carved piece of stone, bird's nest, three old bottles – no? Lace pin cushion, candlestick, another little jar, (I'm not looking in that one), row of books..."

Miss Boston raised herself from the pillow and her eyes grew large with excitement.

"One of these, then?" breathed the girl as she began to read what was written on the spines.

"*Greek Legends and Other Myths, Translations from the Celtic Manuscripts, Is Anybody There?, The Spirit Guides of the Ancients, Passion on the High Seas* – I think that's one of Miss Wethers'. I can't read this one, it's too tatty. The next is *Legacy of the Witches, Angelic Messengers of the Old Testament, Magic and Superstition in the Modern World...*"

"Jen!" Ben called. "Stop!"

The girl looked round and saw that Miss Boston was tapping her hand upon the bedclothes and nodding her head frantically.

"Which?" asked Jennet. "The last one or the one about angels?"

"No," said Ben as Aunt Alice shook her head, "it was that scrappy one she wanted."

Jennet eased the volume from the shelf but the binding had deteriorated and several loose pages fluttered to the floor. Picking them up, she handed the untidy sheaf to the old lady, who spread her arthritic fingers over the cover and gave a grateful sigh.

Ben peered at the jumble of yellowing pages sandwiched between the two faded covers and pulled a puzzled expression.

"It looks as though it's been ripped apart and thrown back together," he said. "Is it an old diary, Aunt Alice? There's handwriting on that bit, and a funny drawing there."

"Ooh, Doctor Adams," Edith's fluting voice twittered towards them from the kitchen. "I'll make sure she doesn't exert herself again. Do you know it's just like when I was looking after Mother – quite nice to be caring for the sick again. I'll see you to the door, Doctor. Thank you so much for coming over. Yes, I'll see to it she takes the new medication."

Miss Boston and the children listened as the doctor and Edith left the kitchen and padded down the hall. Quickly Miss Boston lifted her hand and Jennet, catching her intention, picked up the book and hid it beneath the bedclothes by the old lady's side.

"Here we are, then," said Miss Wethers as she returned to the sickroom. "Doctor Adams is just off, Alice, and you children should let her get some rest. Come on – out you go. Oh Ben, your trousers! They've made a horrid wet patch on the coverlet. Go and change at once."

The children kissed Aunt Alice goodnight, but as they filed through the doorway Ben glanced back at her and to his delight she gave him an encouraging wink.

Briskly, the doctor bade his patient farewell then Miss Wethers showed him out and flitted back to the invalid.

"I imagine you feel much better now," she cooed, bending at the knees as if she were talking to a three-year-old. "Isn't he marvellous with his little black bag? So solid and reassuring, don't you think? Now then, it's medicine time for you before bobos."

Vanishing into the kitchen for a moment to fetch a glass of water, Miss Wethers returned carrying two tablets between her fingers.

"The doctor's given you some new pills. He says they'll keep you a little bit more settled, stop you getting fractious and fretting so much. 'The carer's friend' he calls them, isn't that lovely? Now open up, Alice."

The old lady gave her attendant demon a mutinous glare then was forced to open her mouth when Edith pinched her nose.

"Be a good girl," admonished Miss Wethers. "We must take our tablets, mustn't we? There, now have some water to wash them down. Mother was just the same, she hated taking the medicine but I knew what was best for her. All done! Who's clever then? I'll leave you to doze while I make the children's tea, then I'll turn the light off."

Edith tiptoed from the sickroom and gently closed the door behind her.

Miss Boston gave a contemptuous grunt, then she spat the tablets from her mouth and laboriously hid them in the pocket of her bedjacket.

When this was done, she slowly drew the tattered volume from under the blankets and held her breath. Here it was, the most precious thing in a witch's possession – the Book of Shadows.

Patricia Gunning had entrusted it to Miss Boston with her dying breath, but since her return to Whitby she had not given it a single thought.

Now the old lady's hand trembled with excitement. If this really did hold the key to her recovery then Patricia had been more powerful than she had ever suspected.

Holding her breath, she felt a thrill of expectancy

and wonder tingle throughout her entire being. Carefully, she lifted the cover and turned the first page.

Written in silver ink, in a familiar, ostentatious style that took her back to her lecturing days at the ladies' college, she read the following inscription:

I, Patricia Eliander Gunning, do commit to these pages all the lore I have learned in my lifelong study of the Craft. I pray that the powers of light keep it from those who pursue the dark road, for contained herein is much secret and sacred knowledge. In the name of the great Mother Goddess I devote this work and charge you who read it to bring neither hurt nor harm to any other.

Blessed be.

Miss Boston smiled sadly as she remembered her former pupil. The voice of that exuberant young girl seemed to call to her from the distant past and the old lady hesitated before she studied the Book of Shadows in greater detail. She had no idea what it would reveal to her – Patricia had been one of the most powerful and respected white witches in the country.

With her heart fluttering in her breast, she began to read.

* * *

Later that night, red and glowing after a hot bath, Ben wrestled into his pyjamas. With the main light still switched on, he crawled into bed and stared thoughtfully at the sloping ceiling.

"What was bothering Nelda?" he drowsily murmured to himself. "And why did she want to talk to that awful Parry?" The boy yawned, then rolled over and reached across to the chest of drawers where he picked up a small piece of stone.

The ammonite that Ben had found in the first week of his time in Whitby had become one of his favourite possessions. To him, it symbolized a steady continuity, a permanent thing in a world that was always changing. Some nights, when he felt especially vulnerable or if he had rowed with his sister, he would go to sleep with the fossil grasped tightly in his hand. Tonight was one of those occasions. Nelda's curt dismissal was troubling him and Ben traced the snake-like, spiral pattern of the ammonite with his fingers to reassure himself.

"Ben," Jennet's voice suddenly hissed from behind the door, "are you asleep?"

Before the boy could answer she was in the room and Ben noticed with some surprise that she was carrying a photograph album. He recognized it at once but said nothing, for an odd look was spread over Jennet's face.

"Mind if I sit down for a while?" she asked, already sitting upon the end of the bed.

There was a pause as Ben waited to hear what she wanted but the girl seemed reluctant to mention the album and chattered instead about Miss Boston.

"She was very keen to get that book," Jennet remarked without any real enthusiasm. "It's been on that shelf for months now – why the sudden interest?"

The boy made no answer; they both knew that Jennet had not come to talk about Aunt Alice.

Jennet gave a nervous cough. "I was leafing through this," she mumbled, indicating the album that was still clutched tightly in her hands. "I just wanted to see them – you know."

A deep furrow appeared in Ben's forehead as he

tried to guess what his sister was up to. She never let him see the family photographs – why was she doing it now?

Jennet hesitated before she opened the album, then a peculiar smile fixed itself to her face as she turned the first page.

"There's Mum and Dad when they were married, there's the honeymoon, me when I was a baby – my first birthday ..." Her voice began to tremble and the girl lowered her head so that her long hair curtained off her face and Ben knew that she had started to cry.

Patiently, he waited until she had recovered before saying anything. Even after all this time the grief could take you by surprise; he had experienced it himself and there was nothing to be done except let it pass.

Presently his sister composed herself and swept the hair over her shoulders again. Her eyes were redder than before but she continued as though nothing had happened.

"And there you are," she uttered in a husky voice. "Do you remember that holiday? How young we both were!"

Throughout all this, Jennet had kept the album close to herself, hugging and guarding it jealously – hardly letting Ben have so much as a glimpse. Not once did she look at him; all her attention was focused upon the photographs, but now she shifted her gaze to her brother.

A moment passed as she stared. It was obvious that she was troubled by something and did not know how to tell him. This in itself was unusual, for Jennet had always been the direct one who made her views and opinions known.

"It's good to have the pictures," she eventually said. "It's nice to be able to see them, isn't it?"

Ben wanted to say that he rarely saw the

photographs. When he did it was only because he had sneaked into Jennet's room whilst she was out. But he kept silent and waited for her to continue.

"Sometimes," she said, "sometimes I get confused – do you know what I mean? Their faces – Mum and Dad's – they sort of fade and get jumbled in my head. I forget what they looked like." The girl shuddered at this admission and cast her eyes down as though she had betrayed her dead parents.

"That's … that's why I have to open the album now and then," she breathed, "just to reassure myself and remember."

"I know that," Ben finally managed to say. "I like to see them too, but you hide the album from me."

Jennet snapped the pages shut and reared her head, determined to ask what had been burning there for many months.

"I want you to tell me," she began. "I want to know and this will be the only time I'll ever ask." She took a deep breath. It was difficult for her to broach this subject; she had always hated her brother's second sight, because it made him different and had only caused them trouble in the past. But this was important and the girl had to know for certain.

"Tell me," she said again, "do you still see them? Do you see the ghosts of Mum and Dad?"

There, she had said it and the relief she felt once the rush of words had tumbled out was immense.

Ben could only gape at her. She never willingly talked about his "visitors" as he called them, and the question took him by complete surprise.

"Well?" she demanded. "Do you? Do they still come to you at night like they used to? Are they concerned about us? Have they changed in any way? Do they look the same as on the day they died – the same as they did in these photos?"

Jennet was shivering now and her eyes shone with

a wild and frantic light that alarmed and bewildered her brother.

"I ... I don't know," he stammered.

"What do you mean?" she snapped back. "Have you or haven't you? Do they still care about us? Do they care about what happens? What about me – do they ever mention me? I must know! It's important – tell me!"

"No!" the boy yelled. "No, I haven't seen them. The last time was that night Aunt Alice had a seance when we first arrived and I saw Mum."

"But that was ages ago!" she shouted back. "Are you trying to tell me they haven't been back since? I don't believe you! Mum and Dad loved us – they loved me! They'd want us to know they still cared. You're a liar! You have seen them! You have!"

Tears streamed down her face but her heart was filled with anger. Fiercely, Jennet seized Ben by the shoulders and shook him violently.

"You're a foul, spoilt monster!" she bawled. "Is it because I won't let you see the album? Is that why you're telling me these lies? I hate you! I hate you! I hate you! I wish you'd died with them!"

"Jen!" her brother wailed. "You're hurting! Stop it!"

"What's all that noise?" called Miss Wethers from downstairs. "Go to sleep the pair of you!"

In disgust, Jennet threw Ben against the pillows, snatched up the album and stormed from the room.

Ben winced as the door slammed shut and rattled in its frame. From Jennet's room there came the sound of her stomping, then the bed groaned as she cast herself upon it, followed by a flood of bitter and miserable tears.

As the night deepened, sleep washed over both children and they were lost in fitful slumbers.

Whitby grew dark; only the buzzing street lamps

shone in the town, for every house light was extinguished as all inhabitants sought their rest. The small houses that balanced upon the brink of the river now stared with unlit windows down at their reflections and silence spread through the swaddling night.

The mouth of the River Esk was calm and still. In the harbour, countless fishing boats bumped softly against each other, bobbing languidly upon the high tide. A group of gulls lazily rode the swollen waters and with mournful voices they gossiped and jeered.

The water of the harbour was dark, black as jet – yet beneath the waves something far blacker was moving.

Between the two piers that stretched far into the sea, a rush of bubbles suddenly shattered the smooth face of the tide. Waves began to foam as from the deeps something surged, passing beneath the shadows of the lighthouses and drifting towards the distant town.

Floating contentedly, the chattering gulls washed their beaks and shook their weary heads. With a peevish peck at its closest neighbour, one of the larger ones stretched its wings and prepared to take to the air.

Abruptly it was surrounded by a frothing mass of water and the bird let out a terrified screech as it floundered helplessly.

At once the entire host of gulls rose from the river, shrieking down at the bubbling surface in frightened alarm. Their comrade was still flapping in wild panic but its cries increased as it saw a dark shadow pass below the waves. Only when the trail of bubbles moved away was the gull free and it shot upwards to join the others.

Hovering on the night airs, they watched the gurgling path advance towards the quayside until it came to a seething halt by the harbour wall.

Above the rippling waves a black shape rose and the

air darkened around it as shadows gathered to conceal what the sea had sent forth.

From the river, the creature climbed. It was a formless horror like an immense and tarry amoeba that extended a thick, snaking arm to heave itself up the steps. With a vile squelching sound it slowly moved through the narrow cobbled streets, and where the great flabby bulk passed a stinking path of slime was left in its wake.

Beneath the bedroom windows of snoring townsfolk it crept, with only one purpose filling its black mind. Towards Miss Boston's cottage it went, squeezing through the alleyway and oozing into the courtyard beyond.

At the front door, the thing stopped and the snake-like limb melted back into the quivering body. Rolling forward, the creature pressed against the wall and glued its hideous shape to the brickwork.

Clinging to the mortar, the bloated nightmare began to crawl and with a faint sucking noise, it stole upwards. Like a great black leech it slithered past the window of the sickroom and drew closer to its goal.

Pulling itself to the upper window, the slimy horror spread out two strands of dank flesh and gripped the sill firmly.

Within the bedroom, Ben muttered in his sleep and rolled over, kicking the blankets from him and pushing his head deeper into the pillows.

The hideous shape pushed itself on to the window-pane, revealing a dim grey mass of liquid muscle like the underside of a snail. Flattened against the glass, frills of pale flesh parted and two clusters of eyes pushed forward to spy into the room.

Glittering balefully, the fragmented eyes peered long at the sleeping boy and in the swirling fronds of slime a ghastly mouth fell open.

Three tentacles stretched from the damp glistening

skin and their sensitive, squirming tips began to feel all around the window, tapping and groping for a way in.

Trapped in a gruesome dream, Ben whimpered. He felt as though a great dark cloud was smothering him, pressing itself against his nose and mouth. With an unhappy groan he turned on to his back, flinging his arm over the edge of the bed, and one by one his fingers fell open.

On to the carpet rolled the ammonite and from the vileness that clung to the window ledge like some hellish fleshy spider, there came a gurgling and a contented sigh.

2

THE BITTEREST
OF HERBS

Brandishing a large umbrella high above her head so that it afforded little protection from the inclement weather, Sister Frances marched over the swing bridge as though she were charging into battle. In her other hand she gripped the handles of a capacious brown shopping bag that had seen better days and was bound around and patched with various coloured tapes.

It had been another wet morning, yet she was not one to mind a little bit of rain. The nun enjoyed the feel of the drops plopping on to her upturned face and would often hold her mouth open to try and catch them.

Into the centre of every puddle she stamped her enormous feet, smiling broadly to herself with each satisfying splash.

She was a bizarre figure: of all the nuns in the convent of the West Cliff, Sister Frances was undoubtedly the most unusual. Attached to those great, gauche feet were a pair of long, stalk-like legs that were perpetually hidden within thick black woollen stockings, through which her lumpy knees protruded like a couple of gnarled and bulbous potatoes.

The nun's body was straight as a plank and from the collar of her habit her neck stretched and tapered up to a long gawky head which always seemed to be grinning like a laughing mannequin at a fairground.

This strange, spoon-shaped woman was in her early forties and there was no one in Whitby who had not heard or been made aware of her. When she galumphed by, the sight of her brought smiles to many, but to others the merest glimpse could bring only dread.

It wasn't as if she was a bad person – no one could be sweeter. Frances was an innocent and had all the eagerness to please that a faithful terrier possesses.

That was in fact her main problem: Sister Frances utterly exhausted people. She would rush headlong into situations without stopping to think of the consequences. So anxious to be of service, she would be deaf to any refusals until satisfied that her duty had been well and truly done.

Many times the Mother Superior had gritted her teeth to endure the nun's unasked for assistance, but what to do with her was a complete bafflement. For an order which devoted itself to visiting the sick, it had been extremely embarrassing to receive that snarling telephone call from the senior registrar. In no uncertain terms he shouted that Sister Frances would never be permitted to enter the hospital again – from now on the building was barred to her.

Unfortunately, Frances' visits to the wards had been rather too frequent and rather too long. The recovery of the patients had been hindered by her over-zealous desire to help. Finally, when a man who had only been admitted with an ingrowing toe-nail had to be treated for three fractured ribs, a broken arm and aggravated stress, enough was considered to be enough.

Everything the nun ever did stemmed solely from

her willingness to give aid where she thought it was needed. Yet, in spite of her intrepid endeavours, she never accomplished anything and blustered through life oblivious to the mayhem that erupted around her.

Even that fateful banishment from the wards failed to dampen her lively spirits. Seizing this God-given opportunity she had taken it upon herself to visit those in need of her special skills in their own homes.

However, it seemed the only beneficiaries of her new devotions were likely to be the owners of Whitby's china and crockery shops. As Sister Frances invariably outstayed her welcome, when she finally departed the helpless invalids she left behind felt worse than before her arrival. So exasperated were these victims of her eager bounty that they hurled whatever came to hand at the door through which she had recently departed. Hence many vases and tea cups were smashed to pieces and needed to be replaced.

That morning, with the rain running down her long straight nose and plopping in large droplets on to her chin, she was ready for anything that God might throw at her, and breathing in the clean sea air rejoiced in all He had created.

As she made her ungraceful way into Church Street, Sister Frances gave her ungainly salute to everyone she knew. But for some reason, the owners of those familiar faces broke into furtive trots when they saw her and rushed by with only the briefest of exchanges. The nun waved after them but evidently the rain was too severe or their hats too tight over their ears and they did not hear her.

With large, irregular strides she passed The Whitby Bookshop, whose proprietors hastily immersed themselves in the stock-taking which they had been putting off for weeks.

Frances stared in at them. Madeleine, the willowy

woman with strawberry-blonde hair, was desperately trying not to notice her, and Michael her partner had deviously hidden behind one of the bookshelves.

The nun rapped teasingly on the window and in her overgrown schoolgirl voice called, "That's it! Nose to the grindstone!"

"Go away!" Michael droned. "If she comes in you deal with her – I'll have to go and lie down."

"Don't you dare leave me to cope on my own!" Madeleine hissed through teeth which were still smiling at Frances' grinning face. "Last time she tried to reorganize the local interest section. No, it's safe – she's gone."

"Thank God," he muttered, shuffling cautiously into view. "You know, we should really take that offer on the shop. We could always open up in Scarborough."

Madeleine chewed her lip thoughtfully. "So long as we don't tell her where we've gone to," she said at length, "I agree."

As Sister Frances walked, her oddly-shaped head pushed and pecked at the air as if to counter-balance her unusual gait and in her black habit she resembled an ostrich at a funeral. Her unfaltering progress was checked only when she attempted to enter one of the small alleyways, for she had forgotten the width of her umbrella and the instrument became well and truly stuck.

"Simply too dippy of me," she laughingly chided herself. The nun heaved at the wooden handle and the spokes of the umbrella scratched and squealed over the bricks with a nerve-fraying shrillness.

"Gracious!" she exclaimed, yanking the now broken contraption free. "Clumsy old thing I am. Whatever will Sister Clare think – her favourite brolly!"

Giving the damaged article one futile waggle just to

make certain it was beyond repair, Sister Frances thrust it under her arm then marched up to one of the cottages and pressed the bell.

With a honk of mirth, she playfully pressed it again, then kept her finger jammed firmly on the button.

The front door was flung open and a jangled Edith Wethers peeped crossly out at her.

"Couldn't resist," the nun explained. "Well, it's another Thursday and here I am – how's the poorly patient?"

"Not herself, I'm afraid," Miss Wethers informed her, taking the disfigured umbrella from the nun as she bounced inside. "Got a trifle overwrought the other day. I had to call the doctor."

Sister Frances' face assumed its startled, yet sympathetic expression. "How rotten!" she puffed glumly. "I would have come yesterday had I known."

"Well you're here now," Edith said quickly, "that's the main thing. You'd best go and sit with her – Alice has been acting most oddly since her fall and keeps poring over a fusty old book which I've a good mind to throw in the dustbin."

"Don't you worry," the nun assured her, "I'll bring the colour back to her cheeks."

"I'm sure you will," Miss Wethers whispered to herself as she opened the door of the sickroom.

Mr Gregson, the next-door neighbour, had already been in to carry Miss Boston from the bed and place her in the armchair with a blanket covering her lap and tucked in below her knees.

Usually the old lady would sit there, lamenting her condition, and wait for the hours to roll slowly by. Not so today – Alice Boston was busier than she had been for months.

During the past week she had marvelled at the

Book of Shadows, and the tantalizing things she had read there inspired and filled her heart with hope. She had never guessed that Patricia Gunning had been such an adept; the book was crammed with ancient charms, incantations, faourite pieces of mystical poetry and page after page of secret knowledge.

Unfortunately Miss Boston had only managed to read brief extracts from the volume, for Edith Wethers was continually interrupting her. Sometimes the book would be whisked from her lap and a cup of tepid milk plied to her lips. One of the most infuriating acts of sabotage practised by the Wethers enemy was to switch off the bedside lamp without warning. This nauseating act had left the invalid in the dark on two occasions now and it was driving her to despair.

Yet Miss Boston had read just enough to learn by heart an obscure rhyming chant and had lain awake the whole of the previous night, speaking those esoteric words in her thoughts.

Over and over in her mind she repeated the spell, concentrating with all her strength upon the mysterious little verse and calling on whatever powers were still left to her.

Thus engrossed, she failed to see Sister Frances advance through the courtyard and did not hear the conversation in the hall.

"There you are!" the nun suddenly yahooed. "Who's been a naughty old girl then? I hear you tried to go walkabout – that'll never do, will it?"

Sister Frances peeped closely at the frail figure in the chair. "I say," she addressed Miss Wethers, "I believe she's dropped off. Shall I be as quiet as a wee mousie and tippy-toe to the other chair until she wakes?"

Edith scrutinized her sick friend with critical eyes.

"She's not asleep," she commented, "just pretending. Mother used to do that too."

"Well then!" exclaimed the nun. "We can't have that, can we? I've brought my Jolly Cheer Up Bag especially to buck the poorly patient out of those dreary doldrums."

Miss Boston continued to show no sign that she was aware of them. Her eyes were tightly closed and in the map of wrinkles that was her face, it was difficult to say exactly where they should be.

Edith took her overcoat from the stand and smartly slipped it on. "Most aggravating," she commented. "Been like that all morning. You've no call to be stubborn, Alice! Doctor Adams won't be pleased, will he?"

Fishing a plastic rainhood from her pocket, she tied it neatly over the grey haystack of her hair and said to the nun, "Just popping to the shops; won't be long."

"You shop away!" Sister Frances told her. "We'll have such a spiffy time, won't we, Miss B?"

Edith gave the old lady one final, dithering look then flitted out of the door.

Sister Frances laced her fingers together and paced towards Miss Boston.

"Come, come," she called, stooping over the armchair. "Time to open those eyes. There's sleep enough in the grave, as my dear Papa used to say."

Miss Boston did not stir so the nun put out a hand and patted her on the head.

At once the eyes snapped open and Miss Boston's concentration was completely shattered.

"Oh what a grumpy face!" laughed Sister Frances, sitting upon the other chair. "I can see I've got my work cut out for me this morning."

Indignant and furious, Miss Boston scowled but the expression faded when she saw the nun reach for her large bag and the old lady groaned inwardly.

"Now then," declared Sister Frances brightly and pronouncing each word with an exaggerated movement of her mouth as if Miss Boston was deaf and reading her lips, "what lovely things can we do today? Shall I peep inside the Jolly Cheer Up Bag and see what rays of sunshine we can find? Here I go then."

As this was not the first time Miss Boston had been visited by the nun, the old lady knew exactly what rays of sunshine the wretched bag contained and loathed each and every one of them.

Out came the home-made glove puppets that were not exclusively reserved for entertaining sick children. But thankfully the stitching in one of the heads had started to unravel and disgorge cotton wool everywhere so the nun put them to one side. Then appeared a game of Tiddlywinks, but one glance at Miss Boston's arthritic hands made Sister Frances think twice and go rooting for something else.

"Here we are!" she announced, flourishing a large cardboard box held together by rubber bands. "A lovely jigsaw. Wouldn't that be nice! I'll get a tray and pull my chair next to yours then you can watch me fit the pieces – what fun! Such a divine piccy of ducklings on a pond with a dainty bridge spanning…"

Sister Frances looked at the poorly patient and faltered. The old lady's countenance was so terrible that it quelled that idea – but not Sister Frances' unbridled enthusiasm.

"If you don't feel up to the quacky little ducklings," she rallied, "how about some nice soothing music?" In one bound she reached for Miss Boston's radio and eagerly turned the switch.

A sudden blast of painfully loud wailing screeched through the room. The windows rattled in their panes and the ornaments upon the shelves jumped and shook until a small green bottle toppled on to the floor and spilled its contents of dried leaves everywhere.

With her ear drums pounding, Miss Boston gritted her teeth and shook with rage.

Giggling, Sister Frances revelled in the clamour as she fumbled for the volume control. "What a fine voice that young gentleman has!" she shouted above the din. "But it is rather modern, isn't it? Shall I try for another station?"

Blithely, she twiddled the dial and the room settled back into silence.

"Ooh, how simply marvellous!" she gushed when voices began to filter through the ether. "A play – smashing! We can sit back and listen to it. Won't that be pleasant, Miss B?"

Smoothing out the creases in her habit, she sat down once more and turned an attentive ear to the drama.

Miss Boston closed her eyes to try and blot out the whole thing and concentrated on her thoughts.

With a charmed smile, Sister Frances let the play unfold around her.

"I can't go on, Ricky! I just can't!"

"Shut your mouth and do as you're told!"

"What you're asking me to do is murder!"

"Listen, you little tart! If it weren't for me you'd still be on the streets. If you haven't got the guts for the job I can always get someone else! Nobodies like you are cheap to come by! The gutter's full of them."

"You're a swine, Ricky! Why don't you just go to Hell?"

The smile dwindled from the nun's face. "Gosh," she muttered a trifle uneasily.

"You'd miss me then, wouldn't you?"

"Never!"

"Not what you said last night, honey!"

"I was drunk!"

"Not too drunk you weren't – come here."

"No!"

"Come here!"

"Stop it – let me go."

The voices were replaced by heavy breathing as the actors on the radio kissed and Sister Frances cleared her throat then gazed absently about the room.

"Love me, love me!"

"I need you – you need me!"

"I'll do anything for you, I promise."

"Oh Sandra!"

"Oh Ricky!"

"Oh dear!" Sister Frances squealed as she raced over to switch the embarrassing machine off before the drama went any further. "Not very suitable for a day of carefree jollity, was it?" she stated, a little pink in the cheeks. "I know what you're thinking – what can we do now? Never fear, there are more jolly sunbeams in my bag."

Out came a magazine. It was one of those dreary publications full of recipes, helpful hints, problems and short stories which always find their way into dentists' waiting rooms.

"Can you guess what I'm going to do?" she piped up. "That's right, I'll read it to you. Just relax and enjoy."

Miss Boston opened her eyes, mortified by the unrelenting torments of her visitor. As the nun turned the first page, after reading aloud the title of the magazine and what delights lay in store – she felt that truly she could bear no more.

Quivering with impotent fury, Miss Boston's hands clenched into fists and her face turned purple.

"How I grouted my kitchen tiles in one afternoon" the dreadful creature read with a light-hearted lilt in her voice.

The dastardly monologue continued and Miss Boston could feel the blood vessels thump and pound in her forehead.

" 'Dear Norma – I have an insightly blemish on my chin which is most upsetting. I am very conscious of it at social events and have taken to wrapping a scarf around my face when I go out. Can you help me? Spring is coming and I shan't be able to wear the scarf in warmer weather.' "

Miss Boston shook all over and her one good hand gripped the chair arm so tightly that her knuckles turned white. Her breath snorted down her nostrils like that of a horse and she opened her mouth to scream.

" 'Three mouth-watering ways to use red cabbage – inflame your salads and make others green with envy…"

That was it. In a voice that had not been heard for three whole months and with a trumpeting shout so loud that the windows trembled a second time – Miss Boston roared.

"GET OUT!" she yelled. "GET OUT OF MY SIGHT, YOU STUPID IMBECILE!"

Sister Frances dropped the magazine and stared incredulously at the old lady.

"You … you spoke!" she exclaimed, "Oh! How fabulous!"

*   *   *

That afternoon, when the children returned from school they were disappointed to find Sister Frances still at the cottage and even more dismayed to hear that Doctor Adams was once again examining Aunt Alice.

"Has she fallen again?" Jennet asked fearfully.

They were gathered in the small kitchen. Miss

Wethers was trying to arrange some biscuits on a plate for the doctor but she was in such a fretful state that they kept breaking in her twitching hands. She was too busy to answer so Jennet directed her question to the nun instead.

Sitting upon a stool, with her long legs stretched out in everbody's way Frances breathed a great sigh. "It really is miraculous!" she informed the children. "I feel so honoured that I was the one to witness such a momentous event."

Jennet looked across at her brother. They had not spoken since the girl's angry outburst and though she regretted it, Ben was not prepared to forgive her yet. Ignoring his sister, he screwed up his face and regarded the nun with annoyance.

"But what has happened?" he asked.

Sister Frances put a finger on her lips and signalled for them to listen.

The sound of Doctor Adams's voice floated from the sickroom.

"Well, Miss Boston," he said in a resigned sort of way, "I'm afraid there's no explanation for it. None whatsoever."

Ben held his breath. Whatever it was it sounded extremely serious. Perhaps the old lady had had a relapse, and he glanced worriedly up at Miss Wethers.

"There now," the woman soothed when she saw his concerned face, "have a bourbon. There's nothing to…"

Before she could finish, to both Ben's and Jennet's amazement and disbelief, they heard Aunt Alice's answering retort to the doctor.

"Of course you have no explanation!" she cried. "I always thought you were a quack, Adams – now I know for certain! Don't you think you should step aside and let a younger fellow take over? Well overdue for retirement you are."

Ben forgot that he was not speaking to Jennet and pushed her aside as he ran from the kitchen. "It's Aunt Alice!" he shouted. "She can talk again!"

In the sickroom Doctor Adams was preparing to flee from the vicinity of the restored voice when the boy burst through the door and rushed at Miss Boston.

"Benjamin, dearest!" she laughed, and the sound was wonderful to hear. "Oh my, what a commotion! It's nothing to get excited about. I was just telling Incompetent Adams here that from now on there is nothing to worry about. Ho – look at him, he's completely foxed! Hasn't a clue how I managed it."

Jennet entered the room just in time to see the doctor shift his weight from one foot to the other and hold his medical bag before him. He looked decidedly uncomfortable and felt as though he was back at school in the headmistress's office. Miss Boston's tongue was just as disconcerting as it had always been.

"It seems all I can do is congratulate you," he said with a nervous cough. "If you recall, I did say that you might one day speak again – only not so quickly as this."

"Pooh!" scorned Aunt Alice. "You'd given me up totally – another month or so and it would have been some home or other, to be sure. Well, you can take all your charlatan paraphernalia out of here and do whatever you like with it. I have no further need of your services, thank you very much."

The doctor knew it was hopeless to argue with the old battleaxe so he mumbled his farewells and hurried to the door, bumped into Jennet on the way, then was caught by Edith who pounced on him as he passed the kitchen.

"You're not going?" she simpered, bearing her tray

of broken biscuits. "I was going to make a nice pot of tea."

"Not today," he snapped.

Edith's tissue dabbed her nose. "Next time then," she whimpered hopefully.

Doctor Adams was out of the front door as fast as his legs could take him and Miss Wethers stared after his receding figure with a vexed and injured look on her face.

"My!" said Sister Frances, slipping into the hall. "He's in a whirl today, isn't he? I wanted to prevail upon him and see if there were any more of his patients I could cheer up."

Edith gave an angry squeak and thrust the biscuit plate into the nun's hands – much to her delight.

"Well really, Alice!" the unhappy woman whined, charging into the sickroom. "How could you be so rude?"

Miss Boston looked at her crossly. "Oh, stop fussing, Edith!" she bellowed, making up for lost time. "Things are going to change around here. Don't just stand there, I want a cup of herbal tea – there's a packet at the back of the cupboard! Then you can take that wheelchair from the garden shed. I'm not going to be cooped up any longer!"

Miss Wethers' anger dissolved before this commanding presence and she meekly hurried away to comply.

"Poor Edith," Aunt Alice chuckled mischievously. "I'm afraid she won't have a minute's peace. We'll show her and that jumped-up stethoscope twirler, won't we, Benjamin?"

The pair of them laughed and, standing alone by the door, Jennet watched for a moment before she disappeared to her room.

* * *

When night stole over the town the rain clouds finally dispersed, and in the clear heavens the stars shone coldly. A frost-haloed moon blazed pale and white, its ghostly beams shimmering a wide path over the sea and turning the sand upon the shore to silver. Below the cliffs, the world was lost in deep shadows, but between the black rocks, two small figures slowly clambered.

"The very air bites tonight," Nelda said with a shudder. "Will you tell me now? Why did you wake me and draw me from my warm bed?"

Her companion said nothing but continued to lead the aufwader over the rocky shore.

Tired and cold, Nelda was in no mood for games. "If you refuse to tell me," she said, "I shall turn back!"

In front of her, Old Parry whirled around. Her untidy hair had been brushed and pulled into a straggly, branching mass laden with newly-found shells and the occasional gull feather. This bizarre and wild formation made her shadowy silhouette weird and grotesque. It was as though some deformed shrub had come to life and pulled itself up by the roots to go roaming in the night.

Fingering her bristly nose, she regarded the youngster and shook her head, rattling the shells which dangled there. "Not wise," she warned. "Your loss would that be – hearken to me, child, I know."

"But what is it that you know?" Nelda asked. "You creep into our quarters and tell me not to wake my grandfather..."

"This ain't no business of menfolk!" Parry spat. "Them can't know all. Some secrets we mun keep to ourselves."

"You said it was important," the girl protested, "yet all we have done is climb over rock and boulder."

Coming to a ring of craggy stone that was filled with sea water, Old Parry made herself comfortable and told Nelda to do the same.

"Are you set on pool-wading this night?" the girl cried, "for if so, I have no wish to join you."

"No, child," the other answered mysteriously, "it is not shells I look for, not this time."

There was a strange edge to Parry's voice and Nelda sat upon one of the rocks, wondering what the spiteful creature was up to. From the other side of the pool the aged eyes gleamed at her and she shivered under their intense scrutiny.

"Short have been the years of your life," the cracked voice began, "and from the hour of your birth I have watched you grow. You are the only bairn to have survived the curse laid upon us. Have you never wondered at that? I have. Aye, many long nights and bitter days have I dwelt upon that most abnormal chance."

Nelda hung her head. Throughout her life she had been forced to endure the resentment of the seawives. No one knew why she alone had escaped the power of the Mother's Curse – least of all herself.

"Many times have I heard these grudging words," she muttered. "If you have brought me hither merely to assail me with them once more then I bid you goodnight!"

"Stay!" Old Parry snapped. "My words have a purpose!"

"Indeed! To gratify your base spite, no doubt! You do naught else."

"There is much you do not know of me! Aye, much – although your mother knew some of it well enough."

Sucking her peg-like teeth, Old Parry waited – she was enjoying confounding Nelda. The Shrimp brood had always been above itself and it galled her that

Tarr was now leader of the tribe, but his granddaughter at least was, for the moment, in her power.

"What do you want?" Nelda asked.

A wide grin split the wizened face opposite and a low cackle issued from the crabbed lips.

"Why, child," Old Parry murmured, "to be a mother to ye. No, hear me out. Have you never heard of scryin' the waters?"

Nelda nodded warily. Just what was the foul hag up to? "Yes," she answered, "Hesper spoke of it often. It is something I should have liked to have played with my mother."

"Ah, Hesper!" Parry clucked with disdain. "And did your aunt ever glimpse your fortunes?"

"No," the aufwader girl said sadly, "she was too absorbed in finding the Moonkelp to waste time in such trifles."

Parry chuckled, "I thought no one had scried for ye. By rights 'tis the mother's task to peer for her daughter's fortunes, but I'm willin' to undertake it."

Nelda spluttered in amazement. "You?" she asked. "You wish to do that for me – but why?"

" 'Tis as I said. I have watched you since the hour of your birth and have no offspring of mine own. Would you permit?"

The young aufwader had never liked Old Parry and she was sure the ugly crone despised her all the more. There was no reason to trust her but what harm could it do?

She knew that scrying the waters was a simple game that mothers used to play with their children. She had often heard the barren seawives talk of the dark nights when they had been led to a rock pool by their mothers. When they spoke of it they would weep and lament in the knowledge that they would never have any children to gaze the water for, but no one had ever offered to do it for Nelda – until now.

It was only ever a harmless amusement and the fortunes glimpsed would invariably include husbands and fishing nets that knew no lack. This was why Nelda was suspicious; Old Parry would not have gone to all this trouble merely to indulge in some pretended devotion to herself, yet though she racked her brains she could not see what harm it could do.

"Very well," she agreed, "look into my future. Will I be a bride again?"

Parry tutted at her mockery. "No game do I play," she muttered in all seriousness. "The frolics of gazing nights were founded in ancient tradition. In every tribe there was one who could really part the curtain of time and look beyond tomorrow."

"And you are one of those?" Nelda asked, not believing a word.

The other sniggered and took from around her neck an egg-shaped pebble threaded on to a piece of string. "No," came the unexpected answer, "but this bauble did belong to one and sometimes, if it allows, I can see days yet distant. Now be silent and still."

Twirling the string in her fingers, she held it over the rock pool and slowly lowered the stone into the inky water.

Nelda did not have to ask how Parry had acquired the stone. She was like a magpie and did not scruple to thieve anything she took a fancy to.

"There now," the crone gurgled in a sing-song voice as she swirled the trinket through the pool. "Remember thy mistress – 'tis I, Idin. Thou knowest me, my pretty stone – awake and show unto me this night. Tell thine secrets, oh stone so round and smooth. Let out thy knowledge, Idin commands."

The disturbed water remained dark to Nelda's eyes, but Old Parry crouched over the rippling surface and peered keenly into the shallow depths as she released the stone and let it sink to the bottom.

"Ah," she hissed, "it clears. I see a lone figure – a child. Why! 'Tis no other than yourself, Nelda. Yet your face is grim. Oh, is there naught merry to show me? See, a cloud of darkness and despair is closing around you – oh unhappy bride, what evil stalks you? Ever tighter it binds; you are in direst peril and ever your voice is raised in cries of pain and woe."

Slyly, her eyes slid round to look at the young aufwader and she knew she had guessed correctly. "But the sea does drown your calls," she continued with a sneering leer spreading over her face, "and you are shrouded in its doom."

Nelda grabbed a large pebble and flung it into the centre of the rock pool. The water exploded into Parry's face and the wicked hag fell backwards, coughing and spluttering on the brine.

"Harridan!" the girl yelled. "Begone before I strike you! That stone never belonged to Idin the far-seeing, though I believe you would have stolen it from the very black boat she was laid upon before it set sail. What vile glee does your twisted mind enjoy? Why taunt me?"

Parry pointed a knobbly finger at her and gloated maliciously. " 'Tis true then," she wheezed. "You have come under the curse! A bairn is growing inside your belly – 'twere your words that set me on it, asking how your mother perished. Hah! 'Tis your own death you fear. Into agonies undreamed of will you be plunged. Many other hands than mine are needed to count the mothers who have died that way. They were the foolish ones – they would not listen."

Nelda grimaced in disgust, but she was afraid of what the crone would do – would she tell the rest of the tribe? Of course she would. Old Parry delighted in the pain of others. Struggling to remain aloof and not admitting that the guess was correct, Nelda said, "I have wasted too much time in your company already. Do not speak to me again, and if you wish to remain safe and well then keep a hold on your evil tongue."

But it was an empty threat and the hag knew it. "Horror and death," she repeated coarsely, "horror and death. All them seawives a-dyin' with them infants inside them. None would listen to me – not even your mother. Oh no, not her!"

"Don't you dare speak about my mother!" Nelda shouted. "Or the next rock I throw will be aimed at your head!"

Parry took no notice. "Only the clever ones survived," she intoned. "Only those who hearkened to me saved themselves. Weren't no other way."

Nelda had begun walking back to the cliffs but she halted and turned round once more.

"What do you mean?" she asked. "How did they manage to survive?"

"I could show you," the crone suggested, "though I don't sees as why I should, you being so hostile like."

"Please yourself," the girl wearily replied. "It's probably another of your tricks. I'm too tired for any more."

"No tricks!" Parry promised. "On my dear dead Joby's life this ain't." She lifted her eyes and stared at the waxing moon that shone with an icy brilliance. "Aye, 'tis the proper time; you're fortunate, child – come."

She scrambled to her feet and hurried over the rocks towards the sand and the direction of the town. "If'n you want to live to see another winter you'd best be with me."

Nelda hesitated. She still did not trust her, but soon found herself following.

Over the steps of Tate Hill Pier the aufwaders

climbed and Nelda marvelled, for the crone loathed anything to do with the humans and would never normally walk amongst their ugly huts. But through the streets they went until they came to the foot of the abbey steps. Immediately, Parry hastened upwards, her eyes darting to and fro, in case they should meet one of the infernal landbreed. But at that late hour the one hundred and ninety-nine steps were deserted.

When she reached the summit Parry sat upon a tombstone and waited for Nelda to catch up. The breeze was strong on top of the cliff and her wild hair writhed about her head like a hundred snakes.

Whilst there, she took a leather purse out of her pocket and from this she carefully removed a small disc of sea-polished green glass and held it to one of her eyes.

Eventually Nelda appeared, but she was puffing and panting and had to rest before she could speak.

"See how the lifestealer within you already drinks your strength," Parry commented, "otherwise you would have raced to the top and left old me toiling below."

Still out of breath, Nelda leaned against the rail and looked down at the rooftops of Whitby. Somewhere nearby was the cottage that Ben lived in, but she could not recognize it from up here and shifted her gaze to the wizened aufwader upon the tombstone.

"What is that?" she asked, pointing to the circle of glass.

"Aha!" came the proud reply. "Now this truly is a useful trinket, and is all mine. I found it, I used it." She threw Nelda a quizzical glance and smirked. "Did Tarr ever tell you of the time before the Mother's Curse came upon us?"

"Of course he did – I know all about our histories and lineage."

"Bah! Not that bilge!" Parry snorted. "I'm talking of

me. Did he tell you what I did before we were doomed?'' She raised her eyebrows and laughed horribly on seeing the girl's blank face. ''I was the midwife!'' she murmured.

''Into this sorry world did I deliver the infants, yet never a one did I have of my own and then Oona disgraced us and it was too late for me. Yet brides still loved their husbands and life was made, so a new task was I needed for.''

Leaving the tombstone, she beckoned to Nelda and passed further into the graveyard.

The girl hesitated. ''Where are we going?'' she asked.

Parry gave a hissing laugh through her teeth. ''There's nowt to fear,'' she assured her. ''Only the dust of landbreed bones lies beneath the sod; the shade of no human do I fear.''

''I am not afraid,'' Nelda insisted. ''I often come here to sit and think, but why are we here now?''

''You shan't ever know if'n you don't follow.''

Nelda gazed into the gloom-ridden graveyard; the lamps that illuminated the church were dark and the top of the exposed cliff was forbidding, cloaked in watchful shadows. She could imagine all sorts of terrors lurking in the long grass that swayed and rustled in the wind. Many strange beings had dwelt in Whitby throughout the ages, many dangerous wild creatures with razor teeth and murderous hearts.

Old Parry had nearly disappeared into the darkness and feeling suddenly alone and vulnerable, Nelda hurriedly stepped from the path and ran through the grass after her.

Into the engulfing black shade of the church they plunged. The church of Saint Mary was vastly different at night and Nelda kept looking over her shoulder uncomfortably. The squat, square bulk of the building towered over her; no more the cosy place of worship, it was almost a crouching ogre preparing to spring – waiting until its victims were close enough. More than once she thought she could see something flit behind the panes of its unlit windows and her pace quickened to escape the range of their hollow stare.

Old Parry was totally at her ease however, and strolled casually between the forests of headstones.

The graveyard stretched in all directions, vanishing into the night whichever way Nelda turned. She had been here countless times before but at that moment the aufwader could almost believe she was standing in a country of the dead, and felt that she was a trespasser upon their peace.

Parry observed her disquiet and bared her brown teeth in a repulsive grin to show that there was nothing to fear. Then she held up the glass disc and tittered.

"Thirteen times has this been steeped in the reflection of the full moon," she explained, "once for every month that we carry the unborn within us. Forbidden words have I spoken over this shiny glass and with it I spared many of our tribe from their agonies."

"I don't understand," Nelda breathed, still looking around nervously. "What does it do?"

Parry lifted the disc to her eye again. " 'Tis a boon to sight," she answered. "Through this lens can be seen much that is hidden from even we fisherfolk. Beneath the moon some things grow which it is better we do not see, yet at certain times in certain places, there is a plant – the bitterest little herb which only the glass can disclose. It is the moon's gift to us, her merciful balm sprung from the tears of her compassion at our plight."

With that, she left Nelda's side and began hunting between the headstones, parting the long grass with her eager fingers, questing the gloom like a hound after a scent.

Then, emitting a crow of delight, she called to Nelda and with a bony finger pointed at the shadowy ground.

They were standing beside a grave that was smaller than the others and Nelda felt her skin crawl in revulsion at the callousness of her companion.

"Behold!" Parry cried. "Peer through this, child, and see your salvation."

With shaking hands, Nelda took the lens from her and put it to her eye.

At first there was only a green darkness, and then as her eyes adjusted to the glass, her vision cleared and she drew her breath in sharply.

There, growing from the centre of the grave was a small, sickly looking plant.

Nelda lowered the glass and stared again but she could see no trace of the ugly weed.

"The moonlight blinds your eyes to it," Parry whispered in her ear. "Not for all is the fruit of her pity."

Nelda gazed through the lens a second time and studied the weed more closely.

It was a vile and repugnant growth. The feeble stem was a pallid and ghostly grey – the colour of putrefying death and decay. Bunched around the base were clusters of tiny blade-shaped leaves and wispy threads of spiralling tendrils wound themselves about the frail stalk as though they were trying to strangle the sap from it.

But the herb's most awful aspect was the flower. It too was leprously grey in hue, yet each of the five petals was shot through with a diseased vein of putrid red. Together they formed a spikey cup and from the centre of this loathsome vessel two long stamens wafted in the breeze.

Suddenly Nelda covered her nose and mouth. From the flower a nauseating reek was rising and she had to gulp down the clean air to prevent herself being sick.

"Is it not the daintiest bloom?" Old Parry softly sang. "See how the petals strive up to bathe in the moonlight, whilst the delicate creepers attempt to murderously choke and drag it down."

"It repels me!" Nelda gagged. "I do not think I shall ever be rid of the stench! What vileness of Nature is it? What horror have you shown me this night? See how it flourishes upon that small grave – how far do the roots reach into the earth? On what soil do they feed?"

"Don't you trouble to worry about that," the crone cackled, "for this bitter weed is your friend."

"What do you mean?"

"Exactly that – this tiny herb can save you. Hither have I brought many whose fears were no less than your own. The remedy to your woes is at hand. Simply taste one drop of the plant's juice and it is done. The life-leeching infant will be cast away and you shall live."

Nelda stumbled against the weathered headstone. "What are you saying?" she cried aghast. "Stop! I shall hear no more!"

Parry caught hold of the girl's hand and pulled it towards the sickening plant but she wrenched it free and backed away.

"Be not too hasty," the crone told her. " 'Tis but a moment's work. Pluck the blossom and lay a petal upon your tongue. Others have done it before you and lived to thank me afterwards."

"Did you bring my mother here?" Nelda whispered in bewilderment.

"I did," Parry replied, "though she was too stubborn and craven to partake of the juice. Come

child, one morsel, that is all. I shall tell no one we came hither or what passed between us. Who shall know save thee and me of this night's work? Do you want to die in a torment of raving and be devoured by the salt which will blister through your veins?"

Nelda shook her head slowly. She was terrified of dying in such agony so, with a quivering hand, she reached down.

A cold sweat pricked her forehead and as the fetid odour assaulted her nostrils again she opened her fingers to take the flower from the ground.

"Why hesitate?" Parry goaded. "Save yourself. Why must you both perish instead of one? That's it. Lift the herb, lift it."

Nelda faltered; the flower was too disgusting to look at and the mere thought of actually touching it made her want to retch. A sudden gust of wind caused the plant to stir, the diseased leaves twirled and the stinking perfume blew fully into the aufwader's face. Caught in the draught, the flower swayed and its stamens whipped around and brushed against Nelda's hand.

"NO!" she shrieked, desperately wiping her stinging fist on the wet grass. "I cannot! What am I thinking of? My mother could not do this evil deed – why then should I? I cannot kill the life which is inside me. Get away, let me pass!"

With tears streaking down her face, she staggered through the churchyard, sobbing in utter despair. Appalled and ashamed of what she had been about to do, the girl lumbered away desolate and wretched.

Behind her, Old Parry shouted and snarled. "Fool! What will the tribe think when I tell them of the danger you bear? Does Tarr know? I shall tell him – you should have been rid of the bairn. I'll not help again!"

The hag spat on the ground, then a smile every bit

as repulsive as the flower disfigured her face. Nelda was still in possession of the lens.

Throwing back her head, she let loose a horrible laugh. "Better make use of the glass soon!" she screeched. "Afore it's too late!"

3

NEWCOMERS

February gave way to March and in that time Miss Boston grew steadily stronger. Consulting the Book of Shadows, she directed Edith Wethers in the application of weird ointments and poultices to her withered limbs and kept to a strict diet of her own devising.

The sickroom was turned into a veritable garden of sweet-smelling and virtuous plants that the children had picked under her guidance. Tucked beneath her pillows were dozens of sachets containing secret mixtures of dried roots and seeds, and sometimes the old lady burned an exquisitely fragrant incense which she inhaled in great gulps.

"Got to fill my lungs," she would declare. "Only way to purge all the confounded poison that fool Adams poured into me."

Following this unusual regime, Miss Boston would wake just before the dawn and sing an incantation until the first rays of the sun stole into her room. Then she would invoke the forces of life, calling on them to bestow upon her some of their vigour and energy, and would spend the rest of the day either in deep study or performing what exercises her fragile strength allowed.

During this time, Miss Wethers was kept extremely

busy. What with buying the ingredients for the poultices and following peculiar recipes, she was rarely allowed to rest.

Doctor Adams made regular visits, just to make certain that his patient was not killing herself with these strange remedies, but he was reluctantly forced to admit that she was actually making progress.

Slowly but surely, Miss Boston began to resemble her former self. The weary, haggard look that had so disfigured her face completely vanished and was replaced by a familiar robustness in those soft and wrinkled jowls.

After three weeks it was obvious that strength was returning to her wasted arms and the poor doctor was at a loss as to how to account for it. Though he plied the old lady with many questions she would only laugh at him and say that it would need a broader mind than his to comprehend.

Doctor Adams had countered with a grave warning. "If you are not careful," he told her, "you will overreach yourself. I've seen it many times – people push themselves too far. The heart can only bear so much strain, you know; yours has been inactive for some time now and you're piling on the pressure too fast too soon!"

Miss Boston's reply to what she termed his "professional jealousy" had been brief and cutting. So, with his medical tail between his legs, Doctor Adams had left the sickroom thinking that perhaps he ought to take her advice and retire after all. On an impulse, as he passed Edith Wethers in the hallway, he invited her to a tea dance that afternoon and the overjoyed spinster accepted almost before the words were out of his mouth.

Focusing her attention only on getting well, Miss Boston paid no heed to the other minor business of the town. Those small, mundane events which once would have so enthralled her now kindled no interest whatsoever.

After many years, Mr and Mrs Gregson finally patched up the quarrel with their son Peter who lived in Huddersfield and saw their grandchildren for the first time. The little bookshop was finally sold and the former owners reopened in Scarborough. This was not welcomed by most of the townsfolk, who found the new proprietor grandly aloof, unhelpful and on occasion, downright rude. Sister Frances had tried to jolly her along but not surprisingly she failed in her mission. On the West Cliff, along Pier Road, another café opened which served excellent cream teas and one of the curio shops was taken over by what Edith described as an exotic-looking woman.

None of this thrilling news aroused even the slightest curiosity in Miss Boston and she continued to bury herself wholeheartedly in the matter of her recovery.

On a rare fine afternoon that brought the tourists pouring in to the town, the old lady was sitting in her garden behind the cottage. It had been a tiring day. Impatient at what she considered to be her snail-like progress, Miss Boston had pushed herself harder than she had yet dared.

For three whole hours without any rest, the invalid had raised her arms as high as she could, flexed her fingers until the knuckles ached, rotated her shoulder joints, occupied herself with co-ordination exercises and shouted mysterious words at the top of her voice.

Now she was exhausted and realized she had done too much, for the breath rasped in her throat, her arthritis throbbed painfully and her chest felt uncomfortably tight.

"Rash!" she scolded herself. "You'll be fit for nothing if you keep this up, Alice. Let us hope the fresh air will prove beneficial."

NEWCOMERS

Sitting in her wheelchair, with the pale March sunshine beaming upon her face, the old lady gasped and struggled to breathe.

It was truly a gorgeous day. Spring had come early to her garden, every flower had opened and the colours danced before her weary eyes. She could not remember a time when they had been more beautiful and even as she sat, panting with fatigue, their scent grew more powerful.

Blown on the lightest of breezes, the fragrance wrapped itself around her form, clinging to it like a sticky vaporous cloud. The heady perfume was rich and intoxicating, stealing the very breath from her mouth and Miss Boston gave a wide, drowsy yawn.

Upon that garden alone, the sun seemed to shine more brightly than in any other part of Whitby, and through her watering eyes, the old lady saw the colours flare and become more intense than ever. So brilliant were the flowers that they dazzled and their heads became as flames turning the garden border into a river of fire that was painful to look at. Soon the lawn was entirely enclosed by this vivid blaze and even the grass shone like one enormous emerald.

Her breath still rattling in her chest, Miss Boston blinked – for everything was blurred and shimmering. But the struggle to keep awake was too much and her head lolled to one side.

The garden glowed about her, regardless of the season; every flower opened and contributed its glory to the blinding display. Overhead, the March sky was a fierce blue devoid of cloud or shade and gradually the world fell silent, only a haunting and joyful bird song floated on the warm breeze as all other noises faded and became dumb.

In one corner of the garden, from behind a rose bush that was burgeoning with immense ruby-coloured blooms, a small figure emerged. Slowly, it stepped from the border that was burning with daffodil flames and snapdragon fires and placed two small pink feet on to the verdant grass.

The spiky lawn tickled ten tiny bare toes and a happy, gurgling laugh sounded in the garden.

At once Miss Boston was awake and she stared at the figure in astonishment.

A young child gazed back at her and the old lady shook her head in surprise.

The boy could not have been more than four years old. His face was round and crowned with a tangle of curling, golden hair. Above the chubby cheeks his eyes shone with a light all their own – as blue as the fierce sky. A warm and friendly smile crinkled in the child's face which deepened every dimple and made Miss Boston gasp in delight, for the infant was the most beautiful child she had ever seen.

Never had she beheld a vision of such innocence. Untouched by the harshness of life, it was as if the pure sunlight had taken human shape.

With his merry, twinkling eyes fixed brightly upon her, the small boy took a step forward.

He was dressed in an old-fashioned nightgown made of a white, gossamer material that flowed about his form like smoke.

Miss Boston frowned with concern. Where had he come from? His parents must be terribly worried.

"Are you lost?" she asked. "However did you climb over the fence? Where are your mummy and daddy?"

The boy made no answer; he seemed perfectly happy and as he passed the radiant flowers he paused to hold a blossom to his small nose. At each new scent he would smile and in this slow, meandering way came ever closer to the old lady in the wheelchair.

"Are you lost?" Miss Boston repeated.

He lifted his golden head and the brilliant eyes

blazed at her. Then in a soft, and infinitely reassuring voice, he said, "I am not lost. I have come for you."

As soon as he uttered those words, the old lady felt the pain in her chest disappear and her breathing grew easier. A blissful calm washed over her and she knew what the strange child wanted.

"Will you come with me?" he asked.

"Yes," she answered in a whisper, "I'll come."

Smiling, the infant stretched his small arms out and approached her. "Take my hand," he said gently, "I shall guide you."

All the fears Miss Boston had ever had vanished completely and as she held out her arthritic hands towards him a perfect peace settled upon her soul.

The sunlight glimmered in the boy's hair as he stepped nearer, forming a halo of gold about his head.

"No," Miss Boston cried, abruptly letting her hands drop to her sides, "I cannot go with you – I am not finished here. There is still so much I have to do."

"Your labours are over," the child said lightly. "Please, all your earthly woes will vanish."

"But the children," she insisted, "I must be here for them – they need me."

"Do not worry, those concerns are ended and all cares are past. Come and you shall see. Joy everlasting is waiting for you."

The old lady raised her hands again and a contented smile spread over her face as the child drew close. His fingertips reached for her own and the sunshine bathed both of them in a wonderful glow.

"Yes," she sighed, "I am ready."

"AUNT ALICE!" shrieked a voice suddenly.

Into the garden charged Ben and the golden-haired infant drew back, upset and tearful at the interruption.

Ben glared at him and for nearly a minute, they stared at one another. Then the infant took a hesitant step forward again.

"Keep away!" Ben cried, guessing what the "visitor" had come for.

"Her time is done," the cherub replied, disconcerted that the mortal could see him. "I must take her."

"I won't let you!" Ben snapped angrily and he placed himself directly between them.

The child peered around him to see Miss Boston, then stared long and hard at the savage intruder.

"I must take her," he insisted. "I must."

"Don't you dare!" Ben shouted furiously. "I will not let you! I will not let you!"

Such was the force behind his voice that the infant recoiled, sensing a hidden and angry strength that it dared not challenge.

A look of thwarted disappointment appeared on the child's heavenly face.

"Go back!" Ben commanded forcefully.

The stranger pouted and with a sad shake of the head began to retrace his steps. Whimpering forlornly, he returned to the flower-bed and as the sun turned pale, the divine figure faded and was no more.

Immediately Ben threw his arms about Miss Boston's neck. She was in a deep, deep sleep and he had to shake her and call her name before she stirred.

Eventually the old lady's eyes flickered open and she glanced sharply about the garden almost as though she had lost something.

"Oh Benjamin!" she breathed. "I was having such a lovely dream, only I can't for the life of me recall what it was about. All I know is how splendidly restful it was. I do wish you hadn't woken me. What is it you want, dear?"

The boy grinned and kissed her cheek. "Just to tell you that I'm back from school," he answered mildly, and the anger which had begun to burn within him dwindled as he hugged her tightly.

"So I see," she mumbled. "Oh, do be a good fellow and wheel me indoors. It's grown so chill out here and I'm very tired. My, my, don't the flowers look cold and sad?"

* * *

March slipped into April and Jennet's thirteenth birthday drew ever closer. She had no friends left at school now; all had deserted her and she had become the brunt of their jokes. And yet the girl did not care, for not one of them could possibly understand the conflicts that simmered within her. Who could she ever tell that after all this time she still dreamed of Nathaniel Crozier?

That sadistic and callous man would often plague her sleep and, though she utterly despised his memory, she knew he would always be with her.

The dreaded birthday finally arrived and, without any enthusiasm, Jennet opened her cards before leaving for school. One was from Aunt Alice, whose handwriting was rapidly improving. Another was from Ben and the girl was glad that their row had now been forgotten. The third was from Miss Wethers who twittered around her as she slid it from the envelope, and the fourth was from the children's great-aunt who lived in an old folk's home in Lancashire.

To Jennet's dismay she learnt that a small celebration had been planned in her honour that evening.

"Do bring all of your chums round," Aunt Alice called after her as Jennet left early for school. "The more the merrier for when you open your presents."

Jennet closed the front door without answering or waiting for her brother and wondered if it was possible to stay out late. But miserably she realized that there was nowhere she could go. With a sullen look on her face, she left the courtyard and wandered through the street beyond.

It was a blustery morning, the wind rampaged through the narrow lanes and the signs which projected over the shop windows swung madly on their hinges.

Gloomily, Jennet trudged the way to school. The street was still quiet, for few businesses opened before ten o'clock and her solitary footsteps rang off the cobbles.

Outside the new curio shop, the girl paused and gazed inside. A section of the window display was full of unusual jewellery and beautifully made little trinkets. Longingly, she contemplated the silver then the carved coral and finally rested her forehead against the glass as she studied the local jet.

Jennet drooled over the brooches made of this deliciously black material and she idly hoped that when she opened her presents that evening one of them would contain something small and precious like this. It was a vain wish, however, and she knew she might as well pine for the moon. With a final, lingering glance at the unattainable, she raised her eyes and started in surprise.

Within the shop, someone was watching her.

Sitting behind the counter, a dark-eyed, exotic-looking woman with short black hair viewed the girl over the rim of her spectacles. With an air of indifference, she arched her elegantly plucked eyebrows then shifted her gaze back to the accounts she was efficiently sorting into order.

Jennet considered herself dismissed and the girl slowly resumed the boring walk to school.

NEWCOMERS

When she had departed, Hillian Fogle, new resident of Whitby and owner of the curio shop, lifted her large brown eyes once more. "So," she uttered with a faint and husky accent, "it was she."

Later that morning, the woman turned the sign on the door to read CLOSED and stepped from the shop, locking it behind her.

She was dressed in clothes more appropriate for the director of a successful company than the proprietor of a glorified junk shop. By the cut and the way it fitted her slightly plump, short figure, it was obvious the outfit had been tailored especially for her and was hugely expensive. Everything about the woman denoted her extravagant taste and style, from the immaculate make-up which lightly covered her olive skin, down to the handmade Italian shoes that tapped nimbly down the street.

Amidst the tourists, who were already ambling through the East Cliff in their weatherproofs and sturdy boots, Hillian was an incongruous sight. A few anorak-wrapped people turned to gape at her crisp, chic figure before returning to ogle the fudge bombs and enormous chunks of cinder toffee in the sweet emporium.

Briskly, Hillian opened the door of The Whitby Bookshop and passed quickly inside.

It was a small place, but every available space was utilized to the full. All manner of fascinating works crammed the shelves from floor to ceiling; carousels of spoken-word cassettes and picture books loomed in every corner, a crowd of dumpbins vied for position, almost shouldering one another aside in a rugby-like scrum, and above all this, spinning gaily in the draught from the open door was a flock of colourful mobiles suspended from the ceiling.

At first glance the shop seemed chaotic but everything was in fact well-ordered and each book occupied its own logical position, ready to be found by the prospective and gleeful purchaser.

Despite these enticing charms, however, that morning the bookshop was virtually empty. Only two customers were wandering between the shelves, stooping to peer at the titles and flick leisurely through the pages.

Hillian looked at them with annoyance then turned her attention to the woman behind the till.

Miriam Gower was a large lady of middle years. Her tall, mannish height permitted her to reach the highest shelf, but her ample bosom and matronly figure made this a comical and ungraceful spectacle. Strictly speaking she was not fat – just heavily-built like a shot-putter. To counteract her unwieldy frame, she was always attired in the most feminine clothes she could find to fit her broad size and bore herself with as much pompous dignity as she could muster.

Today she was wearing a printed cotton dress covered in pale pink roses, with a neckline that plunged so low that it verged on the scandalous. Her thinning hair was coiffed and set into a perfect confection that had been dyed a dusky shade of orange. She had a broad, heart-shaped face – bisected with a vivid slash of crimson lipstick painted over her wide mouth. A nose that was slightly too small and pointed nestled snootily in the centre of this fleshy expanse, and on either side were two permanently narrowed eyes that could swivel sharply round and glare with such arrogant force and accusation that she had already become a terror for the local children.

It was obvious to even the most casual of observers that Miriam loathed the bookshop and no one knew why she had bought it. If she had been more approachable perhaps the curious would have asked but as yet none had dared and so it remained a Whitby mystery. The only satisfaction she appeared to gain from working there was in keeping her suspicious gaze trained on her customers. With Medusan looks that could petrify a troublesome child at the furthest end of the shop, she watched and waited – hoping that one of them would foolishly commit a crime worthy of her retribution.

So far this had not happened and although she had not given up hope, Miriam became bored with the daily running of the place. When Hillian entered, she did not even bother to look up. She was too occupied in painting her nails the same garish colour as her lips so that it seemed she had dipped her fingers in fresh blood then drank the rest.

Hillian gave a slight cough at which Miriam's eyes gleamed out at her. A look of recognition passed between the two and the nail varnish was swiftly consigned to a shelf below the counter. Hillian faintly nodded at the other customers and the large woman understood at once.

Suddenly the crimson, sneering mouth became one massive smile that almost wrapped itself around the back of her head. Like a ship in full sail, Miriam Gower rose majestically from her seat at the counter and bore down upon the unsuspecting browsers.

"May I be of assistance?" said she who had been no help at all so far.

The customers were so astonished by her abrupt change of manner that they allowed themselves to be herded like sheep to the nearest shelf where, by Miriam's enthusing they were compelled to choose a book they had no intention of ever reading.

Within ten minutes the customers were ushered to the door and they stumbled out into the street clutching their unwanted purchases, shaking their heads as if emerging from a bewildering dream.

Locking the door behind them, the smile vanished from Miriam's face as she turned to Hillian.

"There is none persons above?" the smaller woman asked, peering up the spiral staircase which led to the tiny first floor area.

Miriam only snorted in response and resumed her seat behind the counter.

"Have you news?" she asked with a note of desperation in her resonant voice.

A pert smile curled over Hillian's more delicate mouth. "Indeed yes," she said. "The contact shall be made tonight. Then will we receive our instructions."

Like a huge, deflating balloon, Miriam let out a great sigh. "Praise be!" she exclaimed. "I doubt if I can stand it here very much longer – each day is a torment without *him*." Her bright fingers reached for her throat about which was strung a necklace of primitive wooden beads. The adornment jarred with everything else the woman was wearing, yet as she touched it her eyes closed and she breathed deeply as though drawing strength and pleasure from it.

"We all are feeling in the same way," Hillian told her, "but until we know what is required, waiting is all we can be doing."

"Let it be over soon," Miriam moaned. "I shall go mad submerged within these barbarian absurdities! Oh how I despise this hideously dull backwater!"

"If we are favoured, then you shall not suffer it too much longer."

Miriam's eyes sparkled. "When shall we meet?" she asked breathlessly. "Make it here – tonight."

The other woman agreed. "It shall be so, but there is many things to be done before then. I must also be informing Susannah."

At the mention of that name Miriam's face clouded over and grew hard. With her nostrils twitching disagreeably her face took on a sour and contemptuous expression.

"Tell Plain Little Susie?" she scoffed. "Is there any

point? I fear our own darling Quasimodo is lapsing!"

Hillian shook her head. "She will do exactly what she is bid!" she said firmly. "As will us all."

"Have a care," Miriam purred. "You have not been made priestess yet."

"Nor you either," Hillian retorted. "The ring of amethyst could maybe go to any one of us."

"Tuh! Not our hunchbacked little leprechaun! That is just unthinkable."

Hillian was tired of this petty feuding. "Never have you tried to like Susannah," she muttered. "Who of the circle ever had liking for the one who was our replacement in *his* affections? Yet we must be bound by our oaths and labour together. I do not doubt that Susannah will obey; her heart belongs to *him* as surely as the rest."

Miriam licked her teeth. "I shall try to be more … Christian," she said, her voice dripping with irony.

"Just be ready for this tonight," Hillian said curtly. "The bickering and argumenting must cease. Are we not splintered enough? Adieu."

"Goodbye … Sister," Miriam answered in drawling tones as the short plump woman left the shop. Then, when she was alone amongst the hundreds of books, Miriam stroked her necklace and kissed it reverently. "Soon," she silently mouthed. "Oh, make it soon."

* * *

When Jennet returned to the cottage that afternoon, she found Miss Wethers rushing around the kitchen in a cloud of flour and icing sugar.

The woman let out a shrill squeal when she saw her and hastened to the table with a tea towel to hide the cake that she had spent most of the day struggling and toiling over.

"Hello, dear!" she twittered, wiping a stray stripe

of pink icing from her nose. "Do go into the parlour, there's a good girl."

Jennet removed her coat and surveyed the kitchen with mild amusement. It looked as though every pan, dish and bowl that Aunt Alice possessed had been used by Miss Wethers and they lay in a jumbled chaos, spilling over the crowded sink and covering every visible surface.

Throwing her school bag into a corner, Jennet left the kitchen and, with some apprehension, opened the parlour door.

"Jennet!" cried Aunt Alice as the girl entered. "Oh splendid! Have you brought your friends along? Do bring them in, there's plenty to tuck into."

In the centre of the room, the round table which had once been used for Aunt Alice's seances was now covered in a clean white cloth and laden with a sumptuous spread of sandwiches and soft drinks.

Leaning forward in the wheelchair, Miss Boston clucked excitedly and shook her chins with childish enthusiasm.

"I put the sausages on the sticks myself," she proudly declared, "and cut up the cheese into cubes. Not an easy task with these infernal hands of mine. Well, what do you think? We've been dying for you to return."

Jennet looked at the humble feast and tried to be as enthusiastic as Aunt Alice, but a party was the last thing she had wanted and though she had tried to tell them no one had listened.

"It ... it looks lovely," she managed at last.

The old lady eyed her in surprise. The child didn't seem interested at all and she could not understand this unexpected reaction.

"Your friends," she muttered, "are they here?"

"No," Jennet said firmly, "I haven't brought anyone."

"Why ever not?"

"I just haven't – all right? I didn't want to."

Miss Boston slowly wheeled herself over to the girl.

"Is there something wrong?" she asked gently. "You don't seem very happy."

Jennet gazed at the kindly, wrinkled face for a moment. How could anyone so old understand what she was feeling? It was impossible to tell anyone of the thoughts and emotions which troubled and frightened her.

"I'm fine," she said at last. "Just tired, that's all."

Aunt Alice patted her hand consolingly. "You do know that I'm always here for you, don't you, Jennet dear? You used to tell me everything. Nothing's changed has it?"

"Only me," the girl replied. She hesitated for several moments as she wondered if she could confide in Aunt Alice after all. Then, taking a deep, decisive breath she began. "Tell me, is it possible to hate something – or someone, so much yet still ..."

Abruptly, the door bell rang in intermittent bursts and Miss Boston groaned as she recognized the sound which always heralded the arrival of Sister Frances.

"Confound the woman!" she snorted, wheeling around the table. "I shall be glad when I'm fit again – if only to be able to run from that blethering nuisance!"

Jennet slowly shook her head and braced herself for the nun's entrance.

"Many happy returns!" Sister Frances shouted as she burst into the parlour, gushing her good wishes to the birthday girl.

"Good evening Miss B!" the nun cried. "I say, isn't this enormous fun!"

"What on earth are you doing here?" Aunt Alice demanded. "You're not due until Tuesday!"

Sister Frances nodded. "I know," she heartily agreed, "but who should I meet on his dawdly way from school but little Bennykins, and when he told me it was sweet Jennet's birthday I insisted on joining the celebrations. Oh how delightful! What a delicious looking tea! Bags I a ham and egg sandwich!"

Aunt Alice rolled her eyes in exasperation. Sister Frances had the thickest skin she had ever encountered. "Well, you had better make yourself at home," she said grudgingly.

Like a pelican, the nun swooped upon the table and carried off a handful of food which she rapidly made short work of. Just as a sausage was disappearing into her wide mouth, Ben put his head around the door.

Without pausing to greet Aunt Alice, the boy raced forward and piled a teetering quantity of sandwiches and crisps on to a plate.

And so the party began, but Jennet enjoyed none of it. In silence, she picked at her food and solemnly watched the others. It was as though she were isolated from all of them, a separate and lonely figure who no longer belonged amongst this cheerful group. As if from a great distance, she dispassionately viewed the proceedings and the sober ticking of the grandfather clock soon became the only sound she was conscious of.

"Is that orange squash I spy?" Sister Frances enthused. "Might I partake of just a smidgen?"

Aunt Alice passed the nun an empty glass but the frown which had furrowed her brow since the unwanted guest's arrival suddenly evaporated and a mischievous chuckle issued from her lips as she casually opened a cabinet and reached inside.

Presently Miss Wethers finished her work on the cake and nipped into the parlour for a bite to eat. But she had spent so long preparing and tasting everything that she was no longer very hungry and nibbled tentatively at a cube of cheese and a small tomato.

The appetite of Sister Frances startled them all. It was as though she had not eaten for days. Ben attempted to guard what was left of the crisps and sausages, for the nun had wolfed most of them, and he glowered at her as she moved towards the table for a fourth helping.

"Some more squash, Sister?" Miss Boston beamed, handing her a third tumbler full.

"Rather!" came the eager reply and the nun swigged it down in two great gulps.

"Oh, let me fetch you another," Aunt Alice declared.

Presently, Miss Wethers slipped out and scurried back into the kitchen. When she returned, her face was aglow with the flames of thirteen candles that crowned the cake she had laboured over. It was decorated with pale pink icing and, in a deeper shade, fine fondant worms spelt out the merry occasion alongside a rather distorted yellow blob that she wistfully proclaimed to be a "darling baby bunny".

A loud chorus of "Happy Birthday" erupted but the exuberant voice of Sister Frances drowned out all others and when she had finished, the nun gave out a great and giggling laugh.

Miss Wethers and Ben stared at her in astonishment but Aunt Alice had to hide her face to conceal the guilty smirk which had appeared there.

Jennet looked at Sister Frances coldly. She had always thought the nun was stupid and the way she was tittering at the slightest thing seemed to prove she had been right.

When the cake was cut and passed around it was discovered to be one of Edith's less successful creations. At least the chewing required to swallow it kept Frances quiet, although by then she had started to sway unsteadily.

An unexpected knock at the door made Miss Wethers choke and she scampered into the hall to answer it amidst much coughing.

"Doctor Adams!" she announced in a shriek as she realized how dreadful she looked covered in flour and icing sugar. Hurriedly, she herded him into the parlour, handed him a clean serviette and disappeared upstairs to make herself more presentable.

"Halloo there, Doctor!" hailed Sister Frances. "Isn't thish marfel … marvellesh?"

The fleshy man could only blink at her, for the nun's head was waggling on her long neck as though it was about to fall off. With one eye half closed and the other fixed upon him in a defiant glare, she held her tongue between her teeth and hissed through them.

"Do have a thothage! They're the nithesht lickle porkers and sho teeny and thweet. Go on! What about a thandwij, or a wee dwinky? Don't be thuch a fuddy duddy! HIC! Oh, pardin me."

"Are you feeling quite well?" the doctor asked.

"Coursh I do," came the slurred and indignant reply. "Never felt bitter – better. HIC! Shcuse again, mosht impoleet."

Doctor Adams was horrified: the woman was drunk. "I think you had better sit down," he said sternly. "You ought to be ashamed. In front of these children too – what sort of an example is that?"

"To which are you alluding?" the nun asked primly.

"Whatever it is, you should take more water with it," he scolded, removing the glass of orange from her grasp and giving the dregs a cautious sniff.

"Hum," he mumbled. "What would your Mother Superior say about this?"

The nun's face became an exaggerated vision of wounded innocence. "How outrage ... outrageoush!" she gasped. "How could you accushe me of sutch wickednish! To imply that I am inebri ... inebri – squiffy! 'Tis you who ought to be ashamed, Doctor! Is that why your whole face goesh beetroot shometimes? Oh yesh, I've theen you quaff it down at the fête."

Folding her arms with as much dignity as she could muster, the nun turned her face towards the wall and sniffed loftily.

Doctor Adams glanced at Miss Boston. "How long has she been like this?" he asked in a low whisper.

Aunt Alice tutted under her breath and with mock condemnation in her voice answered, "Rolled up like this over half an hour ago. Disgraceful, isn't it? I don't know what to do, I really don't."

An odd twinkle glimmered in her eyes but the doctor failed to notice it, for at that moment Frances whirled around and jabbed him with her forefinger.

"Ash for Mother Shuperior," she cried, "you can tell her all you like. She'sh a rotten old ratbag and I don't give a jot!"

"I'll make you a strong black coffee," the doctor said.

"No!" Frances roared loftily. "It's time I was going anywaysh. Thank you for a mosht delightful evenin', Miss B. Ta-ta Bennykins, happy birthday Jennet – goodbye Doctor!" And she strode in a wavering line from the room, navigated to the front door and stumbled outside where she crashed into Miss Boston's rusting bicycle.

The old lady bit her lip to keep from laughing but the doctor scratched his chin thoughtfully. "Is she often like that, I wonder?" he mused. "How dreadful.

Perhaps I should have a word with someone about her problem."

"I shouldn't worry too much," Aunt Alice said, choking back the mirth. "I'm sure it only occurs very rarely."

Before he could answer, Miss Wethers came skipping down the stairs, attired in a new dress and with her hair thoroughly brushed and pinned behind her ears.

"Well, I'm ready," she said.

"Ready for what?" Aunt Alice asked. "You look as though you're off out somewhere."

"We are," the doctor smiled. "There's another old-time dance on tonight and Edith has accepted my invitation once again."

"Oh, Doctor Adams!" cooed Miss Wethers.

"Conway!" he reminded her.

In a matter of minutes they had both left the cottage and Miss Boston uttered a grateful sigh.

"At least I can get on with my studies without her twittering around me," she said. "Here, Ben, put this in the dustbin if you would be so kind."

From the blanket which covered her knees, she brought out an empty bottle of vodka. "Only had it in for when the late Mrs Banbury-Scott used to call round," she explained, handing it to him. "I thought I would explode trying to keep a straight face. Oh, what sublime revenge for all those afternoons of 'Torture by Nun'! Did you see the expression on old Adams?"

Ben pushed her from the parlour back to her sickroom and, laughing together, they left Jennet sitting alone.

The girl gazed sorrowfully around the room and slowly began to clear the table. In the distracting spectacle of Sister Frances, they had completely forgotten to give Jennet her birthday presents.

The sun was still just above the horizon and pale shadows filled the streets and lanes of the West Cliff. A cool breeze blew in from the sea and, as Sister Frances staggered unsteadily over the cobbles she felt extremely giddy.

"What ish the matter with me?" she burbled aloud. "Don't feel at all … I say, why is the street spinning round?"

Lurching against a wall, she tried to balance herself and drew a hand over her brow.

"Mosht unlike me, thish ish," she rambled on. "Wonder if it was something I ate? Praps if I sat down for a while? No – fresh air, that'sh the chappy. Get some good air in you, Frances, that'sh the ticket – do you a power of good. If I shtand on the shore for a few minutes it'll all clear."

Carefully, she made her way down the steps of Tate Hill Pier, holding on to the wall with one hand and her reeling head with the other.

The world was revolving in the most disagreeable manner and she lifted her eyes to the sky but that too was whirling. When her feet sank into the soft sand the nun halted as she tried to control her rubbery legs. Then she took several steps down the gentle slope, slithering only once, and breathed deeply.

"Aarghkk!" she coughed, wildly backing away with her fingers pinching her long nose.

The effects of the alcohol disappeared immediately as a most putrid and disgusting stench filled her nostrils and the poor woman turned a livid green colour.

"What is it?" she shrieked, the back of her throat burning from the bile that she could not keep down.

Sister Frances' eyes grew wide and round as she stared about her.

NEWCOMERS

The entire beach had turned silver. Covering the shore were hundreds upon hundreds of dead fish.

It was a bizarre and grotesque sight. The countless scaly bodies trailed right down to the water's edge where the waves relentlessly washed over them, churning up more of the glittering corpses and disgorging them on to the stinking sand.

With her hand covering her mouth as well as her nose, the now sober nun stooped to peer at the grisly shoal that surrounded her and shuddered in horror and revulsion.

The fish were the most grotesque creatures she had ever seen. They were hideously mutated, with cancerous bulges and weeping ulcers peppering the silver skin. Many were deformed monsters of spine and fin with rows of savage teeth and dead, staring eyes. Others had weird horns growing behind the gills or barbed, vicious-looking lower jaws that curved upwards over the fishes' pointed faces.

The scene reminded Sister Frances of old religious paintings that depicted the saints tormented by similar demons. No, not even they had imagined anything so vile as these foul carcasses. It was as if even the sea could not bear to hold them and had flung the unholy shoal at the land to be rid of its unclean presence.

Overhead the gulls screeched in alarm, but none of them dared alight upon the ghastly shore. No bird would dare feed off that flesh and the air was thick with their agitated flapping.

"Sweet Lord," Frances uttered as she crossed herself in despair, "deliver us!"

Yet as she retraced her steps back to the pier stairs, the nun caught sight of the most revolting malignance she had yet witnessed.

In shape it resembled the other fish but there the similarity ended. The creature was a bloated terror and halfway up the flabby body it split in two, possessing a pair of loathsome heads which lolled over the other corpses and filled Frances with nausea.

Each was coated in a phosphorescent slime that glimmered in the fading light. The wide mouths gaped up at her and the three eyes which protruded from each deformed head seemed to follow her movements.

Sister Frances backed away and to her distress she realized that the thing was not quite dead.

A clawed fin jerked upon the ulcerated side and one of the mouths gave a deep, gasping moan.

That was too much. The nun gave a distressed scream and bounded up the steps, gulping for breath as the fish had done.

Along the curving shore, sitting behind a large, weed-covered boulder, was Nelda.

The young aufwader had been there for some time. She had seen the horrific multitude wash on to the sands and her blood had run cold.

"'Tis a sign," she wept. "Thus do the Deep Ones reveal their displeasure. What other terrors will come to pass? What new foulness shall be shown before my time comes?"

Bowing her head, she brought from her pocket Old Parry's disc of polished glass and clutched it desperately as the tears flooded from her eyes.

4

THE WHITBY WITCHES

In the rugged miles of coast that lie between Whitby and the hill-hugging town of Robin Hood's Bay, the exposed clifftop path is a magnet for ramblers and the hardy tourist.

In places the dirt track disappears completely where the ground has slipped into the ravaging sea far below and the intrepid traveller is forced to cut through fields where placid cows graze and plod through the well-clipped grasses.

That evening, as the inland farms faded in the encroaching dusk, a solitary figure hurried over the pathway.

Hillian Fogle cursed her own foolishness for the umpteenth time. Unwisely she had forgotten to change her shoes and the spikes of her heels continually plunged deep into the mud, impeding her progress.

"Ninety-five pounds," she uttered, heaving the Italian leather from the mire yet again, "ruined totally."

She had left Whitby some distance behind and here, amongst the twisted hawthorn hedges and cow pats, her designer clothes looked even more incongruous.

"Preparation," she intoned, grimacing at the mud spatters that stained her skirt. "Not enough prepared – this will teach you. What did *he* always used to tell? 'Prepare and succeed, blunder and fail.' 'Tis true, I shall not let it be happening again. Those who fail do not wear the amethyst."

Pushing her spectacles further up her nose, the woman squinted along the path, then peered down at a piece of paper she held in her hand.

It was now too dark to see the map, so from the smart bag which had once matched the shoes she brought out a torch and shone it upon the paper.

"Not far," she breathed, "yet it was more distant than I was anticipated."

Waving the bright beam before her, she carefully negotiated the squelching route for a further fifteen minutes then consulted the map once more.

"Here, I am certain," she said, looking down at a large, irregular-shaped stone that jutted from the ground and was scored by three weathered lines.

Cautiously, Hillian shone the torch over the edge and saw that below her the cliff face dropped less severely to the shore and in a tight zigzag, a precarious pathway wound down the steep slope beyond the reach of the light beam.

Tucking the map back into her pocket, she began to descend, and here again she was obliged to curse her expensive footwear.

Quietly lapping the shore, the dark sea was still and at peace. Behind the lazy waves that rolled almost wearily on to the stretching sands no ripple marred the smooth surface and out into the far distance the waters merged with the smothering night.

From the shallows, a massive column of black rock

rose dramatically into the sky like a tower sacred to heaven that had been roughly hewn in the lost, pagan ages of the world.

Into this secluded place, Hillian came hobbling. When her shoes sank into the sand, she slipped her feet from them and continued the rest of the way with them dangling from her fingers.

Curiously she gazed up at the rearing pillar of rock and satisfied herself that it was indeed the correct spot, then switched off her torch.

An air of expectancy charged the salty atmosphere, as though the sea had been waiting for her arrival, and she felt a chill tingle travel along her spine.

Gravely, she placed her belongings upon the sand and stood as still as the immense rock which loomed nearby as she composed herself. For some moments she listened, but the only sounds were those of the waves upon the shore.

Flinging out her arms she stared fixedly at the invisible horizon then cried, "Hearken to me!" and the sudden noise of her voice tore the waiting peace into shreds.

"Here have I come," Hillian called. "This is the meeting place of your devising – show unto me that our efforts have not been in vain. Disclose the contact that we seek and are promised this night. In the name of he who has passed over and by the coven of the Black Sceptre I summon you!"

Keeping her arms raised until they ached, she waited for an answering sign, but only the soft murmuring sea called to her and Hillian's nostrils twitched in irritation and impatience.

"He keeps me lingering," she muttered, "yet bide here I shall. Does he test my endurance? More than this would any of us suffer."

Lowering her arms, she buttoned her elegant jacket and thrust her hands deep into the pockets, for the exposed shore was cold and it was not long before the chill entered her very bones.

When twenty minutes had gone by, Hillian lit a cigarette and sat upon the damp sand, for her feet were totally numb and she rubbed them vigorously.

"A waste of time this is," she told the empty shore. "Why delay further?"

Another half an hour dragged by and with an annoyed snarl, she finished the packet of cigarettes and threw the screwed up box into the water.

"Were we deceived?" she yelled. "What joke was this? Many months in the planning I spent – was it only for your amusement? Why do you not answer?"

Even as she uttered the last question she became aware that the wind had changed and was swiftly growing stronger.

From the blackness of the open sea it blew, whipping the foam from the waves and driving them against the shore with increasing violence.

"Yes!" Hillian roared as she sprang to her feet. "Show me, oh Mighty Majesty! Reveal thy will!"

At last it was happening. Rejoicing at the raging gale, the woman leaned into the squall and with her mud-splashed, sand-encrusted silk and linen clothes flapping madly about her she raised her arms in exultation.

From the furthest reaches of the sea, the storm came thundering. Huge waves crashed against the column of rock, venting a hellish fury about its solid bulk until it seemed as if it would topple and smash into the savage waters below. Upon the shore the sand was ripped up and hurled against the cliff, gouging deep cuts into its sloping face.

Hillian's short black hair streamed flat against her skull as the tempest screamed about her, yet she withstood it fearlessly and bawled back into the howling wind.

"Show me now!" she screeched. "Show me!"

From the wild darkness above, a torrent of hailstones suddenly pelted from the sky and pounded the tortured shore. Then from the deep, seething waters, a spout of icy water exploded to the surface as a small, square object shot from the waves.

Hillian clapped her hands as she watched it fly through the night in a perfect arc towards her.

Spinning and twisting, the shape tumbled down. Through hail and sleet it sliced a curving path until, with a tremendous thump, it hit the beach and was half buried in the sand directly in front of the gleeful woman.

Eagerly, she kneeled to dig it free with her bare hands and stared at the object excitedly.

It was a wooden box, no larger than a small suitcase, and Hillian snatched it up greedily.

"I thank you!" she cried into the wind. "Now we can begin to do thy bidding. Be assured that no task shall we balk at – for if we are granted that which is promised then there is nothing we will not commit."

The sea roared about the towering rock and Hillian put the shoes back upon her feet. With a final glance at the raging waters, the plump woman carried the box up the narrow pathway and set off back to Whitby.

* * *

On the East Cliff, situated along the Pier Road beside the gaudy, chattering amusement arcades, The Sandy Beach Café looked bright and cheerful in its clean peppermint paint and golden letters. The establishment had only been open for a few weeks but already it was luring many regular customers away from their old haunts and had proven a firm favourite with the early holidaymakers.

The new owner, Susannah O'Donnell, wiped down the last table and surveyed the shining interior of her café with undisguised pride.

She was a plain, stunted-looking woman with a dull face that held no sparkle or redeeming feature which might have lifted her from the trough of ugliness. Her eyes were small and positioned too far apart under her heavy brows where they blinked alarmingly at anxious and nervous moments. Between these a misshapen lump of freckled gristle poked into the air – it was more of a snout than a nose and burdened her with the fact that it was always shiny and on cold days looked just like a polished radish.

A mass of wiry ginger hair framed this unlovely countenance and the coarse sprouting had been cut with so little attention or skill that it seemed to grip her head like a tight-fitting helmet.

From early on in her life, Susannah had realized that she was never going to be beautiful and had taken to sinking her chin into her chest and walking with a stoop to try to go unnoticed in the world. This habit had resulted in an unpleasant curvature of the spine and now her hunched shoulders and slightly rounded back were aspects of her appearance that she could no longer control.

No, when she forced herself to gaze in the mirror, she knew that there was nothing a man might find attractive about that sorry reflection, and had resigned herself to that fact long ago. Yet every time Susannah O'Donnell opened her mouth to speak she turned the heads of everyone who heard her.

She possessed one of the most exquisitely enchanting voices ever to have sang outside a nightingale's throat. With her lilting Irish accent, every sentence that she uttered was a marvellous music that made the fortunate listener smile with pleasure. Once Susannah had harboured the aspiration to become a professional singer but her father had forbidden that, for it would never have done for his ugly daughter to make a spectacle of herself in public. And so the dream withered inside her and she retreated further into his grand house, for her family was rich, and when her father died she had become one of the wealthiest women in Ireland.

It was too late then, however, to fulfil her childhood ambition, for whatever meagre confidence she once nurtured had been mercilessly trampled and killed.

By the time she was thirty-nine years old, Susannah had become a recluse and the family residence rang with the echoes of her unhappiness.

Briskly, she shook the cloth out of the café door then pulled the rubber gloves from her hands.

"A come-down this is," she sang lightly. "To think, O'Donnell, there were servants aplenty in that rambling old house o' father's." But as she said this a smile was irresistibly curving over her mouth and she wandered slowly through to the kitchen where the cloth and gloves were consigned to the appropriate drawer.

"Ah, but you love it, sure you do," she eventually added with a spellbinding laugh, "and when were you so happy? 'Tis a time I can't remember."

As she removed her overall, the woman paused and she did indeed recall such an occasion.

"That was it," she lamented, "that first day when *he* came sailing into my life – all grin and blarney. Oh yes, that were a sunny chance and no mistake."

Susannah became lost in a fair memory, that unforgettable day when the only man who had ever noticed her confessed his adoration, and from the moment she beheld those blazing eyes she was lost. Since that time she had followed him half-way around the world, and though he had proven faithless and cruel she had remained insanely devoted to him.

"Nathaniel," her voice chimed softly, "oh my sweet, sweet love."

For six years Susannah had been a member of the Crozier coven and during those witching years the high priest had squandered most of her fortune. But she had not cared. She knew that he had never had any affection for her and only used her when it suited him, but that did not matter. Nathaniel had let her stay by him and that was all she craved.

She was not the only coven member to be so ensnared; she could list at least two others whom he had seduced merely for their wealth. Others were procured because they possessed some skill or talent that he could pervert and enslave to do his bidding. Only one of Susannah's "sisters" was brought into the coven because of her beauty, and she had heard dreadful tales from the others of how he had dealt with those who resented the lovely newcomer.

He had been a selfish and arrogant devil who made certain that he got his own way in all matters, and those who disobeyed him were barbarously punished. But that had happened ten years before she had joined and every one of his disciples since that time had remained steadfastly loyal.

As she hung the overall behind the kitchen door and began to pull on her overcoat she smiled ruefully.

"A frightful man and that's the honest truth," she chirped. "It's mad I must have been to traipse from country to country, dodging the authorities. To what end has it brought me, I ask myself? An O'Donnell waiting on tables and wiping up grease and tea slops."

A look of fright froze over Susannah's face and she shook herself angrily.

"Of what am I thinking?" she gasped, fumbling with the collar of her coat. "Ah, that's better, much better. Be calm now, Little Carrot, think of *him* – that's it, remember his eyes. Remember his voice, hear it from your heart ... ah yes, there he is – that gorgeous man."

Throughout all this Susannah had been fingering a necklace of wooden beads and as she touched it she was reassured. The obedience to Nathaniel had begun to falter but now it was just as strong as it had ever been.

"All will be well," she chanted solemnly. "We shall succeed and all will be well."

Striding through the café she placed her hand upon the light switch but hesitated for one final look around the cheery room.

"'Tis an indignity right enough," she admitted, "but mild compared to most of the things I've done these last years. Come on, O'Donnell, I said before as how you love it. Wouldn't be so bad a life running this place."

She glanced across at the menu written in large colourful letters on the far wall and wondered if she ought to change it slightly for the following week. But all such thoughts were frivolous and futile – she might not even be here then.

Quickly, she left the premises and locked them behind her. Then, hunched over more than ever, she walked along the quayside and drank in the pleasant sight of Whitby after dark.

"It's a mercy that pile of stinking fish has been washed away," she observed as she crossed the swing bridge. "'Tis a grace I had any customers at all this evening with that foul reek a-wafting from the beach. Sure, me cream teas must be improving."

Before she set foot upon the West Cliff, Susannah turned in a full circle, taking in the entire town which glittered beneath the buzzing street lamps.

"'Tis a rare place," she murmured tunefully. "A most precious community with a history as fancy and noble as any other I've seen." She lifted her eyes past the rooftops to the shadowy stones of the church and tilted her head thoughtfully to one side. "More so perhaps," she added, "a quiet dignity resides up there – hmmm."

The woman smiled regretfully then disappeared into one of the dark lanes beyond the bridge, her lovely voice humming a charming song from the old country.

Inside The Whitby Bookshop, Miriam Gower looked at her watch and pursed her blood-red lips.

"Nearly half eleven," she said tersely. "What are they up to?"

The shop was in darkness for she did not wish to invite prying eyes; besides, she was perfectly at ease sitting in the pitchy gloom. As she sipped at a cup of strong, sweet tea, the large painted woman stared out at the street and waited.

A little time ago, she had heard the stragglers leave the public houses at the foot of the abbey steps and saw them lumber past the window, clapping one another on the shoulders and laughing raucously or tottering by on white slingbacks with arms folded and moussed hair defying the breeze. Once a bony, bespectacled man who was out walking a yapping terrier had peered in at the bookshelves and Miriam drew her round figure deeper into the shadows until he and the dog had continued on their way.

Now the street was deserted and she tapped her watch grimly until the sound of furtive footsteps drew near and Miriam recognized the ridiculous noise at once.

"Dear little Quas," she snapped, "about time too."

Rising, she emerged from the gloom and unlocked

the door just as Susannah was about to tap upon the glass.

"Get in," Miriam ordered. "It's nearly midnight – what have you been doing?"

Susannah hurried inside the building and tried to peer into the darkness. "Is Hillian here yet?" she asked. "Have I missed anything?"

"No and no," came the curt response. "Oh, don't just stand there like a Belisha beacon for everyone to see – go upstairs."

From her greater height, Miriam looked down upon the red-haired woman who stood awkwardly in full view of the window and pulled her towards the spiral staircase.

"Take that horrible coat off first and leave it on the chair – don't spill that tea! Now come this way."

The cast-iron steps shivered and groaned as the owner of the bookshop stomped over them, but when Susannah followed it was as if a ghost had floated by.

On the tiny first floor Miriam had cleared all the books to one side and created a reasonable space in the centre of the carpet where three black candles were flickering.

"You have been busy," Susannah praised her. "Did you shift those shelves by yourself? 'Tis a strong arm you have."

Miriam let out an offended snort and promptly primped the frills that covered her muscular shoulders.

"I hope there's enough light up here," she said archly. "I don't want you tripping over everything, do I?"

Susannah shifted with unease and wished that Hillian would arrive soon. She never felt comfortable around Miriam – especially if they were alone together. The woman seemed to delight in making her feel small and inadequate.

"Your nose has gone purple," Miriam commented.

"'Tis mighty cold out there."

"You're blinking again, Susie darling," the other remarked, forcing a horrible smile on to her broad face. "Maybe if you tried a little make-up you wouldn't look so peculiar. I'd let you have some of mine but I detest waste in all things. You should stop biting those nails too – it looks repulsive. I'm sure it would quite kill my appetite to see those chewed-up stumps serve me an iced bun or whatever it is you sell over there."

Susannah felt as though she was being scrutinized under a magnifying glass and she could not bear it. "Have you heard from any of the others?" she blurted, trying to change the subject. "How goes it with them?"

"Each has a part to play," rapped the answer. "All will be gathered in the end – how many times have you been told this? Can't you remember anything?"

"I wish we weren't all scattered, that's all – we work best together."

Miriam waved her large hands airily. "Blame that on Hillian," she said. "This is her great plan. I only hope she knows what she's doing – I would have done it very differently."

"Ah," crooned Susannah, "but then you weren't chosen to lead us, were you?"

The large woman glared at her, but before she could spit out the gall that had bubbled inside her they were both disturbed by a knock upon the door below.

"Here she is," Miriam sneered, moving towards the staircase once more, "and I think we'll just wait until we are successful to see who'll lead the sisters."

Susannah leaned over the rail and pulled an insulting face at the great descending back. Then she heard the door open and Hillian's excited voice speaking breathlessly.

"I have it!" she cried. "The contact is made. Where is Susannah?"

"Upstairs."

Nimbly, Hillian pattered to the first floor and when Miriam caught up with her, proudly showed them both the wooden chest that the sea had given to her.

"Straight here have I come," she said, kicking off her mud-caked shoes and placing the box in the centre of the three candles.

The chest looked ancient. It was made of black wood, carved with images of the deep oceans and bound around by two wide bands of rusting iron.

Susannah did not lean forward admiringly like the others; the box reminded her of those ugly relics that Nathaniel had so cunningly acquired during his lifetime. Usually they had been foul artefacts stolen from some primitive tribe or taken from museums and her skin always crawled to see them.

"Open it," Miriam urged, "quickly!"

With the candlelight picking out a frenzied glint in her eyes, Hillian tore at the two iron clasps then carefully lifted the lid.

A musty smell filled the room and Susannah swallowed as she blinked nervously and wrung her hands together.

The chest was filled with dry straw and the three witches exchanged surprised glances.

"Is there anything else in there?" Susannah ventured.

"Only one way to find out," said Hillian, beginning to part the straw and search inside.

"Perhaps it's a snake," Miriam said, "or a nest of scorpions."

Hillian's fingers twitched gingerly as she contemplated these suggestions but dismissed them quickly. "No," she whispered, as her hand touched something round and hard. "Is it a dried gourd? No!

See, my sisters!"

Reaching in with both hands, she brought out what she had found and emitted a short, delighted laugh.

Miriam's almond-shaped eyes shone and her sharp tongue peeped between her lips and licked them in rapture.

"Delectable," she purred. "Let me touch it."

"Look, Susannah!" Hillian exclaimed, showing her the contents of the box. "What a dainty we have been given."

The red-haired woman looked at the thing which her coven-sister held in her hands and shivered.

It was a horrible, mummified creature and Susannah instantly wished she was far away. The wizened nightmare was part fish, part monkey.

Over the small ape skull a brown, papery skin still retained its features although they were shrivelled and withered by great age. Below the domed forehead two scrunched up circles indicated where the eyes had once been and a grimacing beast-like mouth scowled from the shrunken jaws.

This foul head was perched upon a spindly neck which had contracted around the bones of the spine that protruded along the creature's humped back, ending in a small brittle tail fin.

It was like a preserved freak of nature that had crawled from the pickling jar, and two emaciated arms were locked in a perpetual gesture of aggression and clawing attack.

Almost as if the abhorrent specimen were a young child, Miriam cooed and stroked the clumps of fur which still clung to the parchment-dry flesh.

"What a sweetheart," she murmured, preening the tangled hairs and blowing it kisses.

Hillian put the creature on the carpet, then took from the box three small pouches of dark red cloth.

"Incense," she commented, opening one of the

bags and taking a wary sniff. "Each one is the same and look, there is a bronze dish to burn it in."

Susannah ran her fingers through her coarse hair. "I don't understand," she muttered. "How can that dried-up thing possibly help us?"

Miriam patted the fishmonkey's head and regarded the woman haughtily. "Really!" she tutted.

"None of that!" Hillian rebuked the owner of the bookshop. "You are as puzzled as she. Even I am not certain how we are benefited by this novelty – charming though he is. Now, I think we had all best sit on the floor. That's it – form the circle."

"With only three of us?"

"It will have to do, Miriam. There, I take the dish and pour one pouch of incense on to it." Hillian closed the box and lifted the mummified creature on to the lid, then she placed the burner on the carpet just in front and lit the powder with a match.

At once the incense spluttered and red sparks spat into the air.

"A little damp perhaps," Hillian mumbled, as a thread of sickly green smoke began to rise from the crackling substance.

"It's a dreadful smell that stuff has," Susannah said. "Like rotten kippers and old seaweed – and it stings my eyes."

Miriam beamed across at her. "Now you really do have something to blink for," she leered.

"Hush!" breathed Hillian. "See what is happening!"

The fine stream of smoke rose ever upwards, yet it was not dispersed by the heat of the candle flames, nor by the draught of the three witches' excited breathing. Up the smouldering trail steadily climbed until it reached a point just above the fishmonkey's head, and then the acrid fog curled down and began to flow over the shrivelled form.

Around the frozen limbs it wound, under the spiny fins, covering every inch of wafery skin and engulfing the disfigured head in an impenetrable cloud.

Into the pinched, flattened nostrils the smoke pushed, washing over the wizened eye sockets and filling the frightening mouth.

Miriam stared in beguiled fascination, smearing her immaculate lipstick as she pressed her lips together and felt the familiar glamour of coven business steal over her.

No one dared speak, for even as they watched a rasping gasp issued from the creature's mouth whilst the smoke poured into its lungs, and soon it began coughing shrilly.

Then, inhaling the noxious fumes of the incense in one great breath, the papery eyelids snapped open and two yellow eyes shone in the candle-light.

Susannah covered her mouth in case she screamed as the hideous head twisted upon the scrawny neck and the fishmonkey stretched its puny arms to pull itself up and glare at each of them in turn.

The wrinkled mouth fell open and a vicious cluster of needle-like teeth was revealed to them. For a short while it continued to gasp and stare at its surroundings, then in a cold, sharp voice the mummified creature spoke.

"I am the mouthpiece of the Allpowerful," came the chilling declaration. "He has heard your entreaty and does consent to bestow upon you your dearest longing."

Three cries of joy issued from the witches and even Susannah forgot her fear of the disgusting apparition.

"Through this animated vessel alone," it continued, "the master can give you aid, for his hand must not be recognized in this work. Spies are all about and watchful eyes are trained on this place.

Only when the tide of fate turns shall the danger be past – till then secrecy is all.''

The fishmonkey fixed them with its beady eyes. ''Is that understood?'' it demanded.

''Perfectly,'' Hillian answered. ''None here will betray the identity of your lord.''

The creature gave a reedy hiss of satisfaction. ''Then hear me now, oh disciples of the Black Sceptre,'' it croaked. ''Thrice only am I permitted to assist you. Should you fail to complete your part of the bargain then your dreams shall be lost.''

''The coven has never failed before,'' Miriam assured it. ''Tell us what task your master asks us to perform.''

'' 'Asks'?'' the fishmonkey shrieked. ''The Allpowerful does not 'ask' – he demands. Listen to me, woe-filled children of the mortal lands, and know the commands of the great lord.''

Hillian shot her sister a warning look that told her to keep quiet and the large woman ground her teeth in silent anger as the creature continued.

''There is, in this town, great danger – a heinous threat which can throw into confusion all our designs. Here, living amongst your kind, is one who has the strength to destroy us all should he be permitted to live.''

''Then your master must destroy this menace at once!'' Susannah interrupted. ''What manner of dreadful power does this person wield if even the ...''

''Fool!'' spat the creature. ''Name him not! The enemies of the mighty one are all around us. Let not thy careless tongue give proof to their ears.''

''I'm sorry,'' she said. ''I was not thinking.''

The fishmonkey squirmed round to face her fully and the yellow eyes narrowed as it glowered at her.

''Then know this,'' it uttered in a sibilant whisper. ''The mortal wretch of whom I speak has touched the treasure of the deep kingdoms. Never before have human hands held the most precious prize of the sea and thus the old laws now protect the loathsome worm. No power of the world can be seen to cause grief or hurt to that insect and so is my master foiled."

"Then we are to be his agents in this," stated Hillian flatly. "It is no great matter for us – we have killed before."

"Many times," mumbled Susannah.

"Remove this base obstacle," the fishmonkey vowed, "and the reward is thine."

To atone for her earlier mistake, Miriam forced a sickening smile on to her face. "Honour me with this glorious mission," she begged. "Let me be the one who brings death to the upstart. I don't care what method you choose, I adore them all. But, if I might proffer a suggestion, I always find poison most agreeable. A slow, lingering agony that eats away inside or a quick and sudden end that cuts the thread of life in a moment. Both ways have their merits; in the past I've had considerable success with venomous chocolates."

"Webs and hatchings!" the creature snapped impatiently. "A poisoner! Is that the sum of thine ambition and scope of thy petty mind? There is a much simpler method of despatch, for the way has been chosen and the hand of no one shall be in suspicion in the grey light of day that heralds this timely death."

Miriam's face set like stone as her temper boiled within her, yet she fought to remain calm although she could not bring herself to curl her lips into a smile.

"What must we do?" asked Hillian, ignoring Miriam's simmering fury. "We are here to obey."

"First, join your hands," it ordered, "and

concentrate your powers. Summon what strength you possess. Let the essence of night flow through you."

"We are but three," complained Miriam through clenched teeth. "We should have all been here – Susie was right."

"Obey me!" screeched the fishmonkey. "You are but the instruments of my master! His strength shall join with you – you need no others here!"

Hillian took hold of Miriam's fat hand and the circle was complete. The witches closed their eyes and the wizened creature crawled over the box until it faced the far wall.

"There are many spies abroad," it cackled, staring beyond the plain wallpaper, "yet many have allied themselves to the Allpowerful. One has already seen how this death can be achieved – it is a fitting demise."

Baring the tiny brown teeth, it gave a shrill call then raised its emaciated arms. "Do not break the circle," it warned them and then, in a low hiss, the fishmonkey began to mutter a string of evil-sounding words.

Susannah held grimly on to the hands of her coven-sisters as the cold, chanting voice filled her mind. There was power in that incantation; she could feel it coursing through her and knew that terrible forces were gathering.

The atmosphere inside the small bookshop became thick with unleashed enchantment as the invocations increased until the high, wailing voice of the fishmonkey reverberated through the very bricks of the building and the shelves trembled before the mounting might.

Suddenly the witches gasped as each felt the breath rush from their bodies and above their heads bolts of dark energy crackled into existence. Fiercely, the vivid lightnings lashed about the room, hurling books to the floor and blistering through the posters pinned to the wall.

The three women held on to each other desperately, yet each was thrilled and the blood sang in their temples whilst gooseflesh prickled over their creeping skin.

Jagged forks of shadowy fire flashed about their wrists, burning into their hands until they cried out with pain. Every fist shook uncontrollably and they dug their nails into one another's palms so that the circle would not be breached.

The fishmonkey was shouting now, bawling out the final words of the terrifying spell – and then it was over.

Silence fell and Susannah drew her breath sharply. It felt as though she was floating, rising from the floor with her sisters, up into the empty air.

Keeping her eyes firmly shut, with her mind's eye she saw the blank wall drift towards them and then it melted, dissolving around the women like shimmering water.

A chill wind caressed her cheek – they were outside.

Out into the night the witches flew, holding on to each other more lightly now. Over the clustering yards of the East Cliff they sailed, soaring above the chimneys and riding the air like thistledown.

Susannah marvelled at the sensation and the others trilled with pleasure. Miriam had never felt so buoyant and she giggled helplessly whilst Hillian surveyed the buildings below, her small mouth pulled into an inane grin.

But the flight did not last long, for soon they began to descend, down towards the grassy slope of the cliffside, to where a white-washed cottage nestled in the shadows.

The neat-looking house grew larger as they glided down, descending unerringly to a darkened window that peeped out beneath the eaves.

The glass rippled before them and they passed through the window as though it were a sheet of smoke. Into the cottage they floated and found themselves standing upon a rag rug in a darkened bedroom lit only by a chink of grey light that poured through a gap in the curtain.

"Here doth the enemy of all our designs slumber, unaware of your presence," the voice of the fishmonkey resounded in their heads. "Behold the human worm, the insolent whelp who dares to challenge the sovereignty of our great master."

Susannah and the others stared about them; the room was tiny and they bent their heads beneath the sloping ceiling as, together, they stole towards the bed.

Beneath the blankets a small figure slept soundly and as her eyes adjusted to the inky darkness Susannah's mouth fell open in horror.

The sleeper was a child!

Staring at Ben in disbelief she shook her head mutinously. Was that young boy the one whom the Allpowerful feared so much? Was that sweet innocent life the one they were commanded to extinguish? Her mind revolted at the thought and her forehead dripped with perspiration.

Beside her, her sisters looked down on the boy dispassionately, their faces betraying no emotion whatsoever. The child was nothing to them; if he had to die then so be it; their hands were already steeped in the blood of so many others.

"This scrap of bones and blood", the contemptuous voice continued, "is all that stands betwixt your hearts' desire and the high plans of our most noble lord. Yet see how easily this impertinent mortal is destroyed – look to his left hand!"

Susannah could hardly raise her eyes. Yet she did as the creature ordered and gazed at Ben's hand that lay outside the bedclothes.

It was clenched into a fist and even as the witches peered at the curled fingers they heard the chilling voice begin to chant once more.

Upon the bed, Ben murmured in his sleep and he rolled over, his face moving into the dim light that streamed through the curtain.

Susannah wept with pity and hot tears trickled from the eyes that were too stricken to blink.

The incantation rang out sharply and, very gently, the boy's fist opened. In the centre of his palm was the solid, round shape of the ammonite, and the fishmonkey squealed in evil joy as it barked out the dreadful spell.

Susannah began to shake in terror, for as she watched, the fossil in Ben's hand began to move.

With a jerk, the ancient stone ammonite convulsed and uncurled, twitching and writhing upon the boy's warm skin.

The snake-like fossil wriggled and stretched as the power of the enchantment imbued it with life and filled it with murderous intent.

Like a loathsome worm, it pulled itself along the open palm, crawling over Ben's wrist and up his arm.

Miriam's eyes widened at the sight, but she was flushed with excitement and licked her teeth, revelling in the fiendish situation and feasting upon the macabre agony that was to come.

The living ammonite was now slithering over the boy's chest, creeping ever closer towards his head.

Susannah's wiry hair was drenched in sweat and hung lankly over her face. She wanted to scream; this was utterly insane.

Over Ben's throat the stone shape squirmed and he

muttered under his breath as it reared up to cling to his chin. For a moment it dangled there like a leech, then with a flick of its twisting tail the fossil fell on to the boy's lips.

Susannah tried to pull her hands away from the others – this was obscene.

"Stop!" she protested. "It's vile! Stop it!"

But her sisters gripped her hands tightly and she could not break free. Hillian's grasp was vice-like and Miriam's huge fists crushed Susannah's fingers, staunching the blood until they throbbed.

Malevolently, the ammonite wormed across the boy's mouth, and pushed itself inside.

In desperation, Susannah struggled against the tenacious grasp of the others, lashing out and kicking them.

Slipping over Ben's teeth, the fossil wriggled on to his tongue and in his sleep, the boy coughed.

Deeper it squirmed, reaching further into his throat.

Ben began to choke. The ammonite had lodged itself inside his windpipe and there it remained.

The boy's body contorted as he gagged and gasped for air. His hands tore at the collar of his pyjamas and his choking cries gargled piteously from his mouth.

Miriam was transfixed. She was glued to the horrendous scene and relished every despairing second. Her bosom heaved and she gazed at the dying child adoringly.

"Magnificent!" she drawled. "Exquisite invention!"

At her side, Hillian watched with cold detachment. Never had she witnessed so beautifully simple a death. No one could possibly be held responsible for this.

Ben clutched at his throat and writhed in the bed. His lungs were bursting and his heart thumped in his chest. But no air could pass by the ammonite and the boy's strength gradually began to fail as his agonies increased and a tingling blackness crept over him.

Suddenly, Susannah threw back her head and screamed at the top of her voice.

"NNNOOOOOO!" she bellowed. "IT'S EVIL!"

At once the string of beads around her neck snapped. With a clatter, the wooden trinkets fell to the floor and Susannah O'Donnell was finally free of Nathaniel's control.

Darting forward, she bit Miriam's hand and pulled herself free, then savagely punched Hillian in the ribs.

The circle was broken.

Susannah tore herself away and immediately found that she was back in the bookshop.

At her feet, the fishmonkey shrieked at her.

"The charm is ruined!" the shrivelled creature squawked. "You have destroyed its power!"

Sprawled over the carpet, Hillian clutched her aching side and glared up at Susannah whilst Miriam snarled and nursed her bleeding hand.

In the cottage, Ben retched and choked until finally the ammonite was dislodged and he coughed it up from his throat and spat it on to the bedclothes.

Gulping down the sweet air, the boy collapsed on to his back, and when he had recovered enough he examined the now inanimate fossil in his trembling hands.

It appeared the same as it had always done, but Ben flung it to the floor and leapt from the bed to look out of the window.

All seemed quiet outside and his wheezing breath quickly steamed up the glass. Yet in the misty condensation he drew a mysterious sign and snorted defiantly.

"I warned you the hunchback was lapsing,"

Miriam snapped. "Now look, her necklace is broken. She is no longer one of the sisters."

Susannah was terrified; the expressions upon the witches' faces were deadly and full of menace.

"It was only a child," she pleaded. "I could not let you do that!"

Hillian polished her spectacles and gave a brisk shake of the head. "Your oath is violated," she said in a soft, sinister voice; "this night we could have achieved everything the coven has longed for."

"Don't you understand?" Susannah cried. "It isn't worth it – can't you see that? Are you mad? Listen to me!"

Upon the wooden chest, the fishmonkey lashed out with its claws and tore long rents in the woman's trousers, gouging out a ribbon of skin beneath each sharp nail.

Susannah howled and clutched her leg as the blood welled up between her fingers.

"You have failed us," Hillian muttered, "betrayed my trust in you. You do realize that you must be disposed of?"

Susannah backed away. "No!" she screamed. "No!"

Whirling around, she fled down the spiral staircase and raced through the shop below.

Miriam sprang forward. A bestial growl rumbled from her lips as she snarled and put her hand to her own necklace. A hellish light began to blaze in the almond-shaped eyes and the varnish flaked from her nails as they quivered and grew.

"No," commanded Hillian, "there is not time for that. I shall deal with her!"

Like the wind, she hared down the staircase and found Susannah scrabbling at the locked door.

"Let me go!" she begged. "I won't tell anyone – I swear. Oh Hillian, please!"

"You are faithless," the witch spat vehemently. "Your words mean nothing and nor so do you."

"Don't come near me!" Susannah warbled. "Keep back!"

"Come away from the door, O'Donnell," Hillian told her. "Don't make this harder for yourself."

For the last time, Susannah fumbled with the lock but the key was upstairs with Miriam so, panic-stricken, she blundered into the window and banged upon the glass, screaming for help.

"Stop that!" Hillian shrieked, lunging after her and catching the woman by the hair. "Do you want to wake up the whole of Whitby?"

Violently, she dragged Susannah from the window and hauled her back into the gloom.

But Susannah fought against her. With a yell, she shoved the witch against a shelf and the books came crashing about their heads.

Hillian roared and flew at her, wrapping her hands about the woman's throat. Susannah wrenched the strangling fingers away and threw her attacker to the ground.

With papers fluttering all about her, she picked up a chair and ran towards the window with it. But Hillian tripped her and Susannah careered headlong into the counter. The till shuddered as she crashed into the panels below and the woman let out a horrible moan.

Panting for breath, and with her expensive clothes torn, Hillian Fogle seized Susannah's feet and pulled her to the rear of the shop, grunting at the dead weight.

"No ... no one leaves the ... the coven of the Black Sceptre," she breathed, stooping over the limp body and pressing her fingers into the fleshy neck.

Susannah bucked beneath her and Hillian dived helplessly into a carousel of audio cassettes that toppled to the floor and exploded in a flurry of plastic boxes and festoons of magnetic tape.

Groggily, Susannah lurched to her feet and she peered at the witch lying motionless in the heap of books and tapes. Then she spun round to flee but it was too late.

Down the spiral staircase Miriam Gower had come. Through the wreck of her shop she had pounded and from the floor she had snatched up the largest book she could find.

With a ferocious screech, she brought it smashing down upon Susannah's skull which splintered beneath it, and with a whimper, the woman sank to the floor.

As the swirling shreds of paper settled within the bookshop, Miriam gazed down at Susannah's crumpled body and moistened her lips.

With a groan, Hillian staggered to her feet and stared at what Miriam had done.

"She is dead?"

"Must be," the other replied acidly. "Just look what her blood's doing to my Dickens."

Hillian bent over their former sister and searched for a pulse.

"Yes," she affirmed, "she is no more."

Both witches looked at one another – what were they to do with the body? This was not some primitive corner of the world where death is easy to conceal.

"What shall we do?" Miriam breathed. "The police will come; we must escape while we can."

Hillian kicked a pile of books and buried her face in her hands. "After all my work!" she complained bitterly. "All that planning – for it to fade merely for this!"

Her sobs subsided and they fell into dumbfounded silence as they desperately pondered on what was to be done.

And then they heard it. Above them the fishmonkey was calling and the witches hurried up the staircase.

"Susannah is dead!" Hillian cried, climbing the final steps. "We must leave at once."

The wizened creature twisted its head and the yellow eyes became narrow slivers that glowed brighter than the candle flames.

"Listen to me!" it hissed. "Panic no more, for you are not alone. Hearken to my words and obey this instruction. The body of your perfidious sister shall be taken for you. Do not trouble over such a trifling concern. Do this only: remove the mortal remains from this place and put them in the alley without."

"What?" Miriam bawled, "That's idiotic! You can't dump corpses by the bins for collection. It will be discovered."

"Silence!" squealed the fishmonkey. "At the precise hour of three this night, something will come. The carcass shall be taken – have no fear. It will be as if your sister had never existed."

Hillian nodded her agreement. "It shall be done," she said, "but what of the boy? How are we to complete your master's wishes? Are we to resume what we have begun?"

The yellow eyes closed fully as the creature considered this and he reached out with his thoughts.

"No," he said at length, "that route is now barred to us. The mortal scum is becoming aware of his own strength. It is vital we do not arouse his suspicion any further – not yet."

"Then what must we do?"

"Waiting is all. My master must construct a new design. When the rest of thy coven is assembled, then we shall try again."

The fishmonkey's voice began to fade and its

movements became ever more laboured. "My time is over," it uttered. "Summon me only when you are ready." And with that the eyes closed and it became a lifeless preserved curiosity once more.

Hillian looked at her sister. "So we wait," she sighed.

The large woman eyed her dubiously. "Are we really going to lug Plain Little Susie outside and put her in the alley?"

"Of course. What else can be done?"

"But what if someone sees us?"

"No one shall. Now make haste – there is a shop to get back in order."

At three in the morning, a squelching darkness crept over the cobbles of Church Street and moved purposefully towards The Whitby Bookshop.

The bloated shadow flowed through the alleyway, its quivering membrane brushing over the walls and coating them with slime.

Half hidden by the bin sacks, the forsaken body of Susannah O'Donnell lay upon the wet ground, a fine dew sparkling over her face.

Taking a break from cleaning her premises, Miriam Gower realized the time and peeped curiously out of the first floor window which overlooked the alley.

A black, formless shape had obliterated the place where she and Hillian had deposited the corpse and Miriam shuddered.

"Never did like that ugly Quasimodo," she sneered. "Now at last that voice of hers is silenced forever." And she resumed the cleaning, humming pleasantly to herself.

When the dawn came, no trace of the body remained. But the plastic of the bin sacks where Susannah had briefly lain had melted and the contents were spilled over the ground.

No one ever noticed the wisp of red hair that was

glued to the cobbles by a peculiar trail of slime, for in the afternoon the rain came and the last fragment of Susannah O'Donnell was washed away forever.

5

THE HORNGARTH

With her baggy trousers rolled up to her knees, Nelda ambled slowly through the shallow waves at the water's edge and flapped the hem of her gansey.

She had walked some distance from Whitby, for that afternoon the tourists were swarming everywhere and the beach beneath the cliffs was filled with their clamour. Dozens of human children scrambled over the rocks, shrieking at one another and daring to explore the shallow caves set into the cliffside.

The fisherfolk half dreaded the fine weather which the month of May brought with it; the brilliant sunshine inevitably heralded this riotous invasion of holidaymakers. The aufwaders hated the constant noise which their cars, radios and raucous picnics caused. In the past they had always retreated further into the grottoes beneath the cliff to escape the landbreed babble but now that was impossible, and in the entrance chamber behind the great doors the human voices echoed from outside and resounded around the walls.

This, combined with the baking heat, had turned the cavern into an unendurable place in which the fisherfolk either sweltered or were driven to distraction. For many of the tribe it had proven too much and they ventured above the ground to seek a secluded refuge free from noise, hoping that the blistering weather would cease.

Yet the parched month continued and it seemed that the sizzling spell would never break. Summer had come early and showed no sign of dissipating, for today had been the hottest yet.

Beneath the thick wool of her gansey and the leather jerkin she now wore, Nelda felt as if she was melting. It was stifling and unbearable, yet she dared not remove the thick layers of clothing for she needed them to conceal her stomach, which she felt was growing larger every day. The young aufwader's condition was still a secret known only to herself and Old Parry, but Nelda knew she could not keep it from her grandfather for much longer.

"I must tell him," she muttered, patting her belly morosely. "He isn't blind and there's folk enough who'll notice even if he were."

Almost wilting from the heat, Nelda waded a little deeper into the sea and let the waves splash around her waist. She was tired, the unborn child sapped all her strength and she yearned for an undisturbed night's sleep without the constant ache that twinged and cramped in her back.

Scooping up the salt water in her hands, she threw it over her scorched and sunburned face then shielded her eyes to squint at the cloudless sky. The afternoon was nearly over and she yearned for dusk when the heat would subside and peace return to Whitby's shores.

Eventually, as the sun blazed orange and swollen above the horizon, her solitary figure padded back through the waves towards the cliffs. The familiar rocky stretch drew closer and Nelda was relieved to see that it was now deserted – except for two small shapes sitting upon the great stones, watching her as she approached.

Eurgen Handibrass and Judd Gutch drew on their long clay pipes and regarded the girl with sour expressions graven on their weathered faces. Normally they were two of the kindliest members of the aufwader tribe, but no glimmer of a smile twitched over their whiskery mouths as Nelda came nearer.

Perched upon the rocks, they averted their eyes when the youngster greeted them and concentrated their gaze upon the calm waters of the sea.

"A fair evening," Nelda said warmly. "'Tis a lovely sunset. I hope the caves are cooler this night."

Neither of the aufwaders looked at her and she raised her eyebrows in surprise at this uncommon lack of manners.

"At least all is quiet now," she persisted. "'Twas a mighty crowd afore. I did fear one of the bolder children would find our dwelling."

Judd sniffed then shuffled round on the boulder until his back was facing her. Nelda stared at him in confusion, then to her dismay Eurgen slowly removed the pipe from his mouth and spat at her feet.

"Master Handibrass!" she cried. "Why do you mistreat me so? What have I done?"

The other aufwader snorted and Nelda grew fearful at their spiteful silence.

"I ... I must find my grandfather," she mumbled, pulling the leather jerkin more tightly about her as she hurried towards the cliff face.

Eurgen cleared his throat and tugged at the tobacco-stained whiskers upon his chin.

"Tha won't find Tarr in yon cave!" he called after her. "'Im's not theer!"

Nelda turned slowly, feeling a cold dread wash over her. "Where ... where is he?" she asked.

Eurgen scratched his large ears and exchanged several low muttered words with Judd before answering. "Shrimp's in the main entrance!" he said curtly. "Tha'll find 'im theer."

Nelda clasped her hands in front of her and stared up at the cliff. Since the destruction of the fisherfolk caverns, her grandfather had only returned to the entrance chamber three times. As leader of the tribe he was obliged to sit in judgement there and listen to all complaints brought by other aufwaders. Shivering in spite of the heat, she wondered what had compelled Tarr to go there today.

A glance at Eurgen and Judd brought her no comfort.

"Tha'd best seek him," Eurgen told her. "Theer's summat to touch thee theer."

Nelda left them and walked cautiously towards the hidden tunnel entrance which led to the great chamber.

With her heart in her mouth she passed within a narrow and dripping passage, her waverings steps carrying her up a steep slope. The tunnel was dark and humid, filled with the ponderous sound of falling droplets that steadily ticked the time away like a landbreed clock. Yet Nelda wished that it would never end, for she could guess what kind of reception awaited her.

Suddenly the cramped way opened out into a much larger space and, turning a sharp bend, she found herself in the entrance chamber behind the cliff face.

The cavern was large and lit by the silver radiance of many small lanterns. Their pale flames shimmered through layers of fishing nets like the moon behind the leaves and their dim beams rippled over the high walls until they appeared as fluid as the sea. Quivering pools of pearly light shone over the stone floor and played on the faces of those who were assembled there.

Nelda looked timidly before her. Standing in the glimmering gloom, waiting in grave silence for her to arrive, was the rest of the tribe.

Every old and weather-beaten face stared across at her with accusation and reproach burning in their solemn eyes.

Footsteps behind her made the girl turn around and she saw that Eurgen and Judd had been following. The two aufwaders brushed past and joined the others without uttering a word.

Nelda eyed them fearfully, then took several hesitant steps forward.

As one, the crowd parted and there, sitting behind them, was her grandfather. His grand and stately chair of office was made of rusting cogs and pieces of the mechanism which once operated the huge doors. Flanked by two enormous spindles of corroding iron, it had become the throne of the tribe leader and he only sat upon it when a judgement was to be proclaimed.

One look at Tarr's cold and blighted face told Nelda all she needed to know. He was stiff with pain and pride but his ancient countenance betrayed no emotion. He was as immovable as granite and his steady, condemning eyes seemed to bore right through her. Across his lap Tarr gripped his staff, and only in the almost luminous whiteness of his knuckles could his inner grief be glimpsed.

A malicious hiss issued from a squat figure standing at his side, but Nelda paid Old Parry no heed. The evil crone had done her worst and she was not going to gratify her with any acknowledgement.

Fixing her eyes solely upon her grandfather, Nelda approached.

The other aufwaders backed against the rocky walls as though she carried some infernal contagion, and their mouths twisted into ugly scowls. A few of the elderly seawives shook their heads with pity as the girl passed them but they feared and were revolted by her all the same.

When she stood before the chair, Nelda gazed sorrowfully at Tarr and in a subdued voice uttered, "Is aught amiss, Grandfather?"

The leader of the fisherfolk lifted his eyes to a point just above the girl's head so that he did not have to look at her and cleared his throat to summon his cracked and faltering voice.

"Hearken to her!" Old Parry shrieked before Tarr could speak. "Brazen as you please – the foul hussy!"

Nelda winced at the bitterness contained in that harsh voice but she continued to stare up at her grandfather and waited desperately to hear what he had to say.

"Go on!" Parry urged. "Make her admit it! Then tha'll see if'n I don't speak the truth!"

Tarr threw the hag a flinty look then returned his attention to his grandaughter.

"Be this true?" he managed at last in a husky voice. "Is the poison which drips from her barbed tongue a vile fact?"

Old Parry huffed in outrage but no one took any notice.

"What poison has she uttered?" Nelda asked meekly.

"Tha knows."

"The wretch brims over with malice," she murmured. "How can I tell which deceit or venomous tale she has told? There have been so many."

"Must tha make me give voice to it?"

"If I am to know, then yes."

Tarr's pent-up rage suddenly erupted from him and he slammed his staff upon the floor. "The bairn!" he roared. "Have tha been carrying a child these past months?"

There, he had said it, and on hearing his own, violent accusation, Tarr felt a part of his soul perish within him.

Tears sprang to Nelda's eyes and ran down her burning cheeks before she could wipe them away.

"Yes," she said, her voice battling to overcome the lump which was choking her.

Disapproving and contemptuous cries echoed around the cavern as the horrified fisherfolk vented their anger. Only Old Parry appeared pleased and she lunged forward to rip aside Nelda's jerkin.

"See!" she screeched as the girl pulled away. "Her belly's already swellin'!"

Nelda pushed the crone from her and hastily buttoned the jerkin over her gansey once more. Everyone was jeering at her now and she looked beseechingly up at her grandfather but it was no use.

Trembling with anguish and fury, Tarr glared back. "Art tha mad?" he wailed, joining in the ranting cries of the tribe. "Dost tha not know the mortal peril that burden of thine puts each and every one of us in?"

"I think of naught else!" she sobbed. "I cannot sleep for the fear which freezes my blood – the same blood which will turn to brine when the time comes."

Old Parry raised her arms to address the others. "Woe and disaster!" she announced in a doom-laden voice. "That's all this whelp will bring upon us. Never mind frettin' about her salty death, 'tis the rest of us who'll suffer for her wanton stubbornness. 'Tis the tribe who'll feel the brunt of the Deep Ones' wrath long after she's withered and oozed into the sands."

"Cast her out!" one of the aufwaders demanded. "Exile the selfish fool!"

"Aye!" agreed another. "Let us prove to the Triad beneath the waters that we want no part of this base madness."

"This is why our nets are clogged with stinking weed! She is the reason our catches have diminished!"

"Let us be rid of her!"

"Out! Out! Out!"

Nelda stared wildly round at the hate-filled faces, then turned to her grandfather. "Listen to me!" she pleaded. "What am I to do? The babe is the result of a bargain I made with Esau. I had to lie with him; our very existence depended upon it."

"Yet now the fruit of thy bargain threatens us also!" Tarr snapped. "The displeasure of the Lords of the Deep will grow daily. Already are we suffering – what more evil signs are we to endure?"

"But what would you have me do?" she cried. "I am sorry I kept this secret from you, yet I was afraid. Oh Grandfather, what am I to do?"

Tarr hung his head.

"You know well enough!" snarled Old Parry. "What does it take to convince your feeble brains? Did I not warn you? Did you not scorn my advice? Advice founded on years of toiling with the labours of others."

"Leave me be!" Nelda implored her, but Parry would not be quelled. Striding up to a shelf carved into the rock, she took down a large conch shell and carried it reverently back to the young aufwader.

This was the horn of the fisherfolk, the ceremonial trumpet which few could sound and whose mighty voice boomed out over the sea – reaching even the far-off realm of the Deep Ones. It had been given to them in the beginning and was one of the few treasures that remained from the time of the tribes.

A cruel glint shone in the crone's eye as she lifted the conch to Nelda's ear and forced the girl to listen.

"This is why I told the others," she said, "for this very day I did put mine ear to the shell and this is what I heard.

As she listened, Nelda's eyes grew round with terror and she whimpered in fright.

Instead of the usual roaring of the sea, the shell was filled with screaming voices. It was as if she was standing at the gates of Hell and the tormented souls were yelling and shrieking in their agony, drowning in a cacophony of despair and desolation.

Yet even as she listened in stricken horror, Nelda grew faint. One of the tortured voices grew louder in her ear and her scalp crawled as she recognized it – the voice was her own.

Old Parry kept the conch there longer than was necessary and a triumphant leer stole over her ugly face. "'Tis another sign," she hissed. "By that unborn maggot we are all doomed. For is it not the result of a union which the Lords of the Deep and Dark themselves forbade? Did their herald not warn you against marrying Esau? Did you not flout their ban? Are we all to pay for your wilfulness?"

"It wasn't like that!" Nelda protested, looking round at the rest of the tribe. "You were all there, we couldn't stop Esau. He was the ruling elder – I had no choice!"

"Maybe!" Parry bawled. "But you have a choice now!"

Nelda stared at her blankly, then turned to her grandfather for support. But Tarr was still cradling his head in his hands, unwilling to involve himself any further.

The young aufwader felt totally alone. All around her the members of the tribe were agreeing with Old Parry and shaking their fists at the girl for placing them in such danger.

"Do as she says!" they called. "Show some wisdom at last, child! Even now it is not too late!"

From the middle of the insistent fisherfolk, Maudlin Trowker, a seawife who had arrayed Nelda for the Briding, stepped up to her and put a tender hand upon her shoulder.

"Dinna fret so," she soothed. "'Tis nothing – I should know. When I were young 'twas Parry I looked to when the curse fell over me. For the good of all, entrust thissen to her care – she knows best in this."

Aghast, Nelda dragged herself from the insidious and sympathetic comforter. "No!" she stormed, disgusted and appalled at the suggestion. She could not believe that the whole tribe was urging her to get rid of the baby and saw each one of them as if for the first time.

Through their fear, they had become callous, depraved creatures and Nelda was at once alarmed and aggrieved to witness the base transformation.

"Purge the evil from you!" they called. "Cast it aside! Kill the wicked spawn of Esau!"

As this insane uproar filled the chamber, Nelda looked once more at her grandfather, seeking one last time for his assistance and understanding.

"Help me," she beseeched him, "please."

But Tarr could not even raise his head from his hands. "Ah canna," he said flatly. "As leader ah mun look to our safety. The Deep Ones will punish us."

"What ... what are you saying, Grandfather? Are you agreeing with this mad rabble? I must know. Do you also wish my unborn child – your grandchild – do you wish it dead?"

Stung by this, Tarr lifted his face but it was set and grim. "Don't fling that at me!" he snapped. "Ah knowed what we're askin' and ah ain't proud o' it. But reckon this – what are we to eat if'n the fish desert our waters? Wheer are we to shelter if the sea crashes agin the cliff and drags it into the deep?"

"Is that the measure of your concern?" asked Nelda sadly.

"Tha know it ain't! Oh Lass – ah were theer when thy mither bore thee! Ah saw all that happened to her – ah nivver wish to look on such horror agin! For thy sake if not fer the tribe – think on!"

Nelda recoiled from him. She was bewildered and a stinging sense of betrayal tore through her heart. The young aufwader bit her lip and shuddered wretchedly.

"Come now," Old Parry piped up. "I shall look after you. Poor little Nelda, let Parry help and assist in what must be done."

At that moment a cold anger seized Nelda and all her hurt was forgotten.

"How dare you!" she yelled. "How dare all of you! What right have you to order the death of my child? Listen to yourselves! You speak of the most innocent of all things as though it were some reeking foulness! To what base level have you sunk? You disgust me – each and every one!"

Tossing her head defiantly, she whirled around, incensed and furious. "Listen now to me – I will carry this child for as long as I am able, and if it is fated that we perish together then so be it. That is my decision and no one – not even my so-called family – can deter me now! Exile me or do what you will – I have finished with you all and want no part of the tribe for as long as I and my baby live!"

Tarr clung to his staff until the wood bit into his palm as his granddaughter thundered from the chamber.

Around him the aufwaders shouted but all had been taken aback by Nelda's inflamed temper, and though they had not changed their minds about what she should do, many were already feeling guilty for the things they had said.

With her arms folded, Old Parry sneered. "She'll come to it in the end," she predicted acidly, "for all her fine talk. The bitter herb will be picked – I'll wager everything on it.''

Too distraught to say anything, Tarr bowed his head to weep, but so intense were his shame and grief, the tears would not come.

* * *

May's glorious weather continued and the tills of Whitby rang merrily as trippers continued to squeeze into the small town. Never had the souvenir shops known such business and the tea-rooms and restaurants were always overflowing. The Sandy Beach Café had reopened shortly after the mysterious disappearance of the proprietor and a tall, reedy-looking woman now ran the establishment. But she proved to be extremely unpopular with those customers who had grown to love Susannah's cream teas.

On one occasion, Doctor Adams took Edith Wethers there but they were both dismayed by the slovenly manner of Miss Gilly Neugent, the new owner. Slouching up to their unwiped table, she unceremoniously shoved two cups of tepid dishwater before them followed by a plate of walnut-like scones which were as tough as cork and tasted of cardboard. After a miserable half-hour, the doctor and Miss Wethers left the place and vowed never to return.

They were becoming closer than ever and Conway frequently brought flowers round for the delighted ex-postmistress and once, in a mad, unthinking moment of passion, she had given him a peck on the cheek.

During this time, Miss Boston continued to regain her old vigour. Her arms were as strong as they had ever been and she would often spend the warm evenings sitting in the wheelchair, bowling cricket balls for Ben in the garden.

As the month progressed, the old lady became increasingly agitated and had circled a date on the calendar. When Ben had asked her about this she had vaguely replied, "The Horngarth is approaching."

The boy had thought no more about it, assuming that Aunt Alice was talking about astrology or equinoxes as usual. Then, one Saturday morning, he awoke early and trailed downstairs in search of breakfast, only to discover that the old lady was well wrapped up and ready to wheel herself outdoors.

"Ah, Benjamin!" she cried. "I wasn't sure whether to wake you or not; still you had better change out of your pyjamas if you wish to join me. I'm afraid Edith has no taste for it – do you, dear?"

In the kitchen, her mind fixed on other matters and thoroughly out of humour, Miss Wethers stirred a pan of thick porridge and answered in an impatient tone. "That I haven't," she twittered. "It's a thing I've seen far too many times – why don't they liven it up a bit? Any change would do, just to make it interesting or mildly entertaining. It really is very dull."

Aunt Alice scowled. "Not to me it isn't," she replied.

"Oh well, we can't all find dreary little hedges enthralling, can we?"

"Had a bit of a falling out with Doctor Adams yesterday evening," Miss Boston whispered confidentially to Ben. "Be no use to anyone today, will our Edith."

"But where are you going?" the boy asked, rubbing the sleep from his eyes.

"Why! To see the Horngarth, of course!" she exclaimed, screwing up her face and chuckling gleefully. "It's the morning of Ascension Eve and there's only one place you'll find me then. Best hurry, for I shall be gone if you're not ready in time. You might pop in and see if Jennet wants to come too – I'm sure she'd find it all very intriguing."

Ben doubted that, but he dutifully ran back upstairs and peered into his sister's room.

Jennet was still sound asleep and he wondered if he dared awaken her. She had been so unpleasant to him lately that he no longer enjoyed the rare times they spent together. Eventually, however, he plucked up courage and shook her gently.

"Oh get lost," she mumbled, hiding her face in the pillow. "It's a Saturday. Leave me alone."

Ben tried again. "Jen, Aunt Alice wants us to go to see the Horngarth – are you coming? It might be fun."

Grunting with impatience, the girl rolled over and peered through the dark hair which hung untidily over her eyes. "I'm not interested, all right? I just want to be left alone. Now get out!"

Her brother did as he was told and hurried back to his own room where he quickly pulled on his clothes, then dashed downstairs.

"She doesn't want to come," he told Aunt Alice.

The old lady pulled a sorrowful face. "What a pity," she said. 'Jennet doesn't appear to want to do anything any more. I hope it's merely a phase she's going through and she will return to her normal self soon. Growing up really is a nuisance, it gets in the way of so many things – I remember how foolish I was at that age."

"If you ask me you still are foolish," Edith mumbled, then called out, "It's a quarter to nine, you'll miss it."

Aunt Alice gripped the wheels of the chair and propelled herself towards the front door. "Let us be off then, Benjamin. To the Horngarth!"

When they reached the street, Ben asked, "So

where exactly are we going?"

"To the harbour," the old lady replied, "straight down Church Street."

"And that's where this Horngarth is?"

"Exactly! Gracious me, cobbled roads were never made for wheelchairs. What a most unpleasant juddering!"

Ben fell silent. Aunt Alice was being deliberately mysterious. Once they had passed the swing bridge he could see that an immense crowd of people had gathered by the harbour wall a little way ahead.

"Into the fray!" Miss Boston barked with determination as the wheelchair shot forward.

Ben had to run to keep up with her. He was burning with curiosity now, and eagerly wanted to know what everyone had come to look at.

Hundreds of people were assembled by the railings of the harbour wall and all their faces were cast down towards the river. As Aunt Alice slowed to a halt behind them, Ben stood on tiptoe and jumped as high as he could to try and see what was so fascinating.

"I ... I can't see anything," he said crossly.

Aunt Alice winked at him. "Don't worry, Benjamin dear," she clucked, "we'll get a good view." She gave a pathetic sounding cough then called to the people in front of them. "Excuse me, can I get by? I'm an invalid."

After some embarrassed and awkward shufflings, the human obstacles squirmed aside and allowed Miss Boston and the boy to the front.

"There now," she chirped, triumphantly scrunching her face into a mass of wrinkles, "that wasn't so difficult."

"Oh jolly dee!" trilled a voice beside them. "It is good to see you out and about, Miss B."

At once Aunt Alice's pleased face vanished as she

noticed for the first time the person who was standing at her side.

"Sister Frances," she mumbled dismally, "how ... how fortuitous. Fancy bumping into you – of all people."

"I never miss the Penny Hedge," the nun gushed. "Sort of professional interest you might say, and it really is so quaint and darling. What do you think of it, young man?"

But Ben was not listening, for his full attention was commanded by the scene which was taking place below.

Upon the muddy shore of the river, a group of townsfolk were building a peculiar and flimsy looking fence. They had stuck nearly a dozen sticks into the squelching ground and were now weaving thinner and more pliable strips of twig between them. It was an extremely odd structure that hardly came up to their waists and could not have been much over a metre in length. Ben had no idea why they were toiling over such a ridiculous object. It wasn't even connected to anything – they had just planted it in the middle of the shore with only two sticks propped against each end for support.

"That'll fall down," he said, bemused by the strange goings on.

"It's supposed to," Aunt Alice whispered next to him, "but not just yet – it's got to withstand three tides first, you see."

The boy rested his chin upon the railings and breathed a puzzled sigh.

Miss Boston chuckled. "I can see you don't understand. You see, it all began long, long ago."

Ben laughed, "Doesn't everything here?"

"Just so," she agreed, "yet this ceremony is older than all our other festivals. Very ancient is this funny little ritual and totally unique to Whitby."

THE HORNGARTH

Gazing dreamily down at the figures building the fence, she laced her fingers and began.

"Like all great legends, the story of the Penny Hedge begins far in the forgotten past – a little time after William the Conqueror, when Henry the Second was upon the English throne. In those rugged days, three wealthy gentlemen were hunting a wild boar through the forest which covered much of this land. Imagine it: three arrogant nobles riding their horses through the trees, their hounds baying before them in hot pursuit of the terrified creature that they had already sorely wounded.

"Hard they bore down upon that unfortunate animal, crashing through the woods of Eskdaleside and hollering terrible oaths – wild and greedy for the kill.

"Now there was at that time a certain holy man who lived as a hermit in the forest. Upon that fatal day, the monk was praying within the chapel when through the open door the frightened boar comes charging. The poor animal is close to death. Exhausted and bleeding it collapses and dies at the hermit's feet, and the man hears the hounds draw close. Quickly he shuts the chapel door and returns to his meditation and prayers as the dogs fling themselves against the barred entrance, howling and whining.

"Then come the noblemen. They see that their quarry has escaped them and are so outraged that the monk should spoil their sport that they batter down the door, then set about the man with their boar staves.

"The holy man is mortally wounded, and the nobles fear for their own lives for the Abbot demands they be punished. Yet before he dies, the monk forgives them and spares their wretched necks but only on one condition.

"Every year, on Ascension Eve, they and their descendants must do a simple penance. With the aid of a knife costing a penny, they must build a small hedge at this appointed spot, strong enough to withstand three tides. With stakes, stout stowers and yedders must the hedge be built, and if those who come after fail in this then their lands shall be forfeit."

Miss Boston grew silent then shook herself. "Of course, two of the families have since bought themselves free of the task but it is a lovely quirky ceremony."

At her side a voice began to recite softly:

> When Whitby's nuns exulting told
> How to their house three barons bold
> Must menial service do ...

Sister Frances gave a gauche shrug and thrust her arms behind her back. "Sir Wally Scott," she told them. "*Marmion*, don't you know? Oh yes, I adore this day. Just to think, throughout all those centuries this has been going on every year – simply splendid. And what magnificent forgiveness the hermit showed. It's a lesson to us all."

Aunt Alice gave Ben a nudge. "Of course the legend is complete balderdash," she added wickedly.

"Oh don't say that," whined the nun. "What a spoil-sport you are, Miss B."

"I'm so sorry, dear," the old lady apologized without a trace of repentance, "but you see the ceremony goes back a lot further than the legend would have us believe."

Sister Frances twisted her head aside in the manner of a sulking infant. "Tommy-rot," she protested. "Where did it come from then, I should like to know?"

"Why, from our pagan past," Miss Boston uttered

with relish. "No one will ever know the true origin of the Penny Hedge, but I shouldn't wonder if it was already well established long before Hilda came. You see it seems to me that it's much more likely to be a votive offering to the sea than anything else. Monks of the Dark Ages were always attributing religious explanations to matters they were afraid of."

"An offering to the sea?" Ben murmured.

"Or a guard against it," she replied. "You see 'garth' means an enclosure."

"But what does the 'horn' bit mean?"

The old lady made no answer but pointed down at the shore where the Penny Hedge was now complete.

Ben watched as a man stepped up to it and put to his lips a curved horn of great age.

The blasting note trumpeted over the river then the man yelled at the top of his voice, "Out on ye! Out on ye! Out on ye!"

A cheer rang out from the hundreds of onlookers, followed by much applause.

"Why did he shout that?" the boy asked.

Sister Frances butted in before Aunt Alice could speak. "I always thought it was to call shame on the family of those dreadful noblemen, but who am I to comment? I'm sure Miss B has a far more outlandish interpretation, however misguided it may be."

Miss Boston chortled to herself. She was in an elated mood, and as the crowd began to disperse she came to a swift decision.

Without any warning, she lumbered from the wheelchair and placed her feet firmly upon the ground, gripping the railings for support.

"Aunt Alice!" Ben cried as the old lady turned and took two shambling steps.

"Great heavens!" Sister Frances exclaimed. "How absolutely super! You're walking!"

"Be careful!" Ben urged.

"Oh yes," the nun agreed, "we don't want you to overdo it, do we?"

"Nonsense!" Miss Boston roared, lumbering confidently against the rail. "I'm perfectly ... Oh!"

The old lady's weak legs buckled beneath her. The harbour spun before her eyes and her whole body went limp.

Ben darted forward and grabbed her quickly. Just as her head was about to strike the sharp corner of the metal railings he snatched her back and she reeled against him.

"Oh my," she spluttered, clutching the boy's shoulders, "I don't know what came over me. I think I had better sit down."

She returned to the wheelchair then patted Ben's hand. "Thank you, dear," she said gratefully. "I might have cracked my skull open back there. Let us go home; I feel in need of a strong cup of tea."

"I think you should get Doctor Adams out to see you," Frances advised. "A funny turn is nature's way of telling you something isn't right."

"Oh, stop talking out of the back of your wimple," Aunt Alice said tersely. "Haven't you got someone to annoy with your Jolly Cheer-Up Bag today?"

The nun beamed, "Rather," she enthused. "Young Mr Parks' sister has gone away for the weekend so I'm spending the day with him to keep his spirits up. He's been most unwell you know, terribly under the weather, so I've rooted out my best jigsaws and Mother Superior gave me a fabulous puzzle book, to keep me quiet, she said – wasn't that nice? We'll have oodles of fun today I'm sure."

"How pleasant for you," Miss Boston commented. "Well, come on, Benjamin; I long for a brew."

A little distance away, standing half in the soft blue shadows cast by the morning sunshine, a white-gowned infant sadly hung its curly head and retreated into a dim alleyway.

By now the crowd had almost totally dispersed,yet a few stragglers remained to gaze at the Penny Hedge and take more photographs to finish off their rolls of film.

Forming an odd trio beside an intrepid ice-cream van, Hillian Fogle, Miriam Gower and the new owner of the cafe – Gilly Neugent – lingered longer than most. With their eyes trained on the boy pushing the wheelchair back up Church Street, they waited, exchanging meaningful glances. Then they too left the harbour and returned to their businesses.

* * *

Back at the cottage, Ben and Miss Boston found Doctor Adams sitting in the parlour with Miss Wethers. At first Aunt Alice thought Sister Frances had called him, but this was not the case.

"Oh Alice!" Edith trilled, leaping to her feet and dabbing her nose with a tissue. "You'll never guess, you never will in a million years."

"I'm sure I won't," the old lady replied, bewildered. "Whatever is it, dear? Do stand still – you look as though you've sat on an ant hill."

Miss Wethers clasped her hands in front of her and let out a squeal of pleasure. "Conway," she gurgled, "Conway has asked me to marry him!"

Aunt Alice and Ben gaped at her, then stared at Doctor Adams. The fleshy man was bright pink and the top of his domed head, where the long strip of hair had slipped somewhat, shone as though it had been buffed with a duster.

"Congratulations," Miss Boston managed at last. "I hope you'll be very happy."

Edith gave a tiny dance then blew her nose. "Oh

we will," she breathed. "It's all worked out perfectly. You're getting better every day so you won't need me under your feet much longer, will you?"

"I suppose not. Will you return to your cottage or move in with the doctor?"

Miss Wethers shook her head coyly and returned to her beloved's side. "Ooh, we haven't thought about that have we, Conway dear?" she cooed. "It's all happened so fast, but love's like that, isn't it? We've both been swept completely off our feet."

Ben pinched himself to keep from smiling – it would take a bulldozer to sweep Doctor Adams off his feet.

"Well," Aunt Alice mused, "it would seem that today is one for many celebrations." With a proud smile upon her lips, she lifted herself from the wheelchair and carefully tottered over to shake their hands.

"By God!" Doctor Adams cried. "However did you do that? I can't believe it!"

Miss Boston bowed theatrically. "Oh, I haven't finished yet, Doctor," she told him. "The battle against my infirmities is far from over. There is still a long way to go, I assure you."

* * *

When the entire town had gone to sleep and the shades of night were deep and impenetrable, a solitary figure stole through the East Cliff.

Towards the harbour the muffled shape crept, pausing only when it stood before the railings where that morning so many people had watched the planting of the Penny Hedge.

Down on the shore the second tide of the day was receding and the Horngarth was just a dark smudge that jutted from the ever-increasing waves.

Swiftly the figure hurried to the stone steps which led to the glistening mire and cautiously descended.

THE HORNGARTH

Through the thick mud it staggered, sinking deep into the treacherous and sucking mire. But undeterred the figure pressed on until the water swirled about its legs and the Penny Hedge was within reach.

The Horngarth dripped with sea water; its sodden sticks were black against the reflecting river that shone with the orange light of the street lamps. Like a weird decaying skeleton it stood there, a simple bony framework of hazel wands that braved the tides – stoically waiting to be wrenched apart after it had withstood the allotted three. Yet every year would this humble barricade be renewed, every year would the horn be sounded, lest those who remembered forget ancient promises.

Here it had stood for countless ages. Before Morgawrus was born to despoil the land and before the first stone was laid in the foundations of the Saxon church, it was here. The Horngarth had passed silently through the history of the world, the symbol of a bargain made between primeval forces, enduring beyond the span of all things and edging into the endless realm of eternity.

Yet in the darkness, as the water shrank further down the shore, the Penny Hedge was a frail and somewhat ludicrous structure. Its origin and purpose was lost, continued now only to attract the tourists and perpetuate a charming, outdated ceremony.

The figure which had waded out to reach it, stretched out a hand and touched the barricade gingerly. It was cold and impregnated with the deep green reek of the limitless seas.

Stooping, the intruder grasped the stakes which fixed the low framework to the shore and pulled. After several attempts, the hedge was heaved from the squelching mud, and without hesitation was carried off into the black shadows.

6

THE CRY
OF THE GULLS

Ben had not seen Nelda since that rainy evening when she had dismissed him in favour of Old Parry's company. Although he often went to the rocks beneath the cliffs in search of her, the boy's efforts were in vain and it seemed as if she was avoiding him.

Once Ben thought he saw Tarr in the distance, but by the time he reached the place where he had glimpsed Nelda's grandfather the shore was deserted.

Gradually, Ben's visits to the beach grew less frequent and then, late one June afternoon on his way home from school, the boy decided to try one more time.

In dawdling steps he strolled over the sands, swinging his schoolbag from side to side and absently drawing wiggling patterns with the toe of his shoe. Then, as he drew near to the high pillars of the footbridge, Ben dropped his bag and stood stock still.

Sitting with its back against one of the concrete supports was a bundled and hunched figure – it was Nelda.

The aufwader was lost in contemplation; staring

intently at something in her hands she did not see the boy as he crept closer.

"Hello!" he cried without warning.

Nelda jumped and stared at him in blank surprise.

"You startled me!" she exclaimed. "Why sneak up like that?"

Ben shoved his hands into his pockets. "Thought you might have run off otherwise," he said sheepishly.

"Run? From you? Why would I do that?"

"Well, I haven't seen you for so long, and after last time, I thought perhaps ..."

"Oh Ben!" she breathed with the faintest of smiles curling over her small mouth. "I offended you – I am sorry. That was not my intent. I was troubled and alas vented my spleen on the one who deserved it least."

Ben grinned. "That's all right," he said, "Jen does that to me all the time – I'm getting used to it."

"But 'twas wrong of me. I have missed our meetings. I thought perhaps I had driven you away forever."

Ben sat opposite her and, resting his chin on his knees, he regarded her with some astonishment. Nelda's appearance had changed.

The aufwader's long dark hair had grown thicker than ever and tumbled about her shoulders in wild branching tangles that were coated with sand. Her great grey eyes were rimmed with red and the lids drooped wearily over them as though she had not slept for a week. The neck of her gansey was pulled up high to keep out the cool breeze but the garment itself was dishevelled and small twigs prickled from the woollen stitches. On top of this she wore the leather jerkin and her small hands were furtively concealing something which occasionally caught the sunlight and glittered like an emerald.

Nelda was in a sorry state and Ben thought that she

was beginning to look like Old Parry.

"Is Tarr okay?" he asked, politely ignoring her unkempt aspect.

The faint smile faded. "I have not seen him for many weeks now," Nelda told Ben. "I no longer dwell with my grandfather, nor do I speak to any other member of the tribe."

"But why? What's happened?"

The aufwader gazed at him for a moment then looked down at her stomach. "Can you not tell?" she murmured. "Does not this declare my woe?"

Ben frowned, Nelda had grown quite fat. "You been eating too much?" he began. "You should see how Sister Frances puts it away ... oh!"

"Aye," she affirmed, "'tis true, I bear the child of Esau. Forgive me, I have shocked you. If you wish you can depart and think no more of me – do as the others have done."

"Nelda!" he cried.

She covered her eyes with her hand and breathed heavily. "Again I am sorry," she said. "It is difficult to recognize friendship. Perhaps my solitude has driven me mad – either that or the curse is already at work. Oh Ben, I have spoken to no one these many weeks – shall I tell you all that has happened?"

"Only if you want to," he encouraged gently.

And so Nelda proceeded to tell him all that had occurred, of Esau's evil bargain and the anger of the tribe and her ultimate doom.

When she had finished, Ben was horrified. "I'm so sorry," he mumbled. "Is there really nothing anyone can do for you?"

Nelda shook her head. "No," she said, "only the Lords of the Deep and Dark can save me and my baby. 'Twas they who placed the Mother's Curse, thus 'tis they who must remove it. Yet I fear that is an act of compassion that they will never make. Their

hearts must be blacker than the deepest pit – they know nothing of mercy or pity."

Ben bit his bottom lip. It was difficult to believe what she had told him, but one thing he knew for certain – he was to blame. "It's all my fault, isn't it?" he whispered guiltily. "I had the chance to ask for the removal of the curse but failed."

"No," Nelda told him, "Rowena Cooper was the one. She it was who stole the boon from you – you could not have withstood her power. Oh Ben, you must stop assuming blame – did you not see Esau's debauched claim upon me as your own fault also? You are my true friend, I harbour no grudge towards you."

All the same, Ben felt dreadful. Nelda and her unborn child were going to die and he could have prevented it. Why did everyone he love always have to leave him?

"What will you do?" he asked eventually.

Nelda shrugged. "I do not know. Spend what days are left in what comfort I can. But no one shall order my life for me; whatever happens shall be on mine own terms with none saying yea or nay. My decisions are my own and I am willing to pay what price I must for that freedom."

"So where are you living? Surely not outside? What about when it rains?"

"There are many caves cut into the cliff," she explained. "I have made a new home for myself in one of their number. Do not fear, I shall not hunger nor be chill when the weather turns."

"But to do it all on your own," Ben remarked, "isn't it very lonely?"

"It is," she answered desolately, "yet what choice remains? I want nothing more to do with the others and they are of the same mind."

Ben sucked his teeth. "Even so," he added, "I'm

surprised at your grandfather – how could he be so cruel?"

The aufwader said nothing and he could tell that Tarr had hurt her deeply. Ben scowled at the ground then brightened and looked up.

"I know!" he cried. "Why don't you come and live with us? Aunt Alice would love it and Dithery Edith is getting married soon so she can't object, and as Jennet isn't able to see you anyway …"

Nelda held up her hand to stop him. "No," she said, "that is not the answer, generous though the offer may be. I am an aufwader, Ben. I do not belong in your world nor you in mine. 'Twould be a grave mistake. Is it not enough for my kind alone to be bound by the curse? If I were to dwell with humans then they too would be embroiled – the sufferings must end. I am a wanderer of the shore, descended from the many tribes which once thrived here before your kind built the first huts and populated the land. Do you not understand? My place is here."

The pair fell into uneasy silence, one contemplating her plight and the other racking his brains for something to say or do that might be of comfort or assistance.

Suddenly the heavy peace was shattered as the sky became filled with raucous shrieks and yammering screeches that cut straight through them like the bitter wailings of a hundred cats in pain and anguish.

Nelda glanced up at the cliffs. "The gulls!" she cried. "Something has happened to the gulls! Listen how afrighted they are!"

The air was swarming with white wings. It was as if every sea bird in Whitby was flocking overhead and whirling in tight circles, filled with alarm and panic. Their fearful voices croaked and screamed so loudly that Ben jammed his fingers in his ears whilst he stared up at the chaotic jumble of feathers that thrashed before the cliff face.

"What are they doing?" he shouted to Nelda.

The aufwader shivered, for the dreadful shrieks reminded her of the voices she had heard in the conch shell and she closed her eyes in an effort to blot out that hideous memory.

"I cannot tell," she finally answered, "for though my late husband knew the language of gulls, he did not teach it to me."

"Well, I hope they settle down soon; it's deafening!"

But the birds continued to scream and fly in confused and frenzied groups, and every so often their screeches would increase as though some fresh nightmare had terrorized them.

Nelda became uneasy. "This is no ordinary squabbling," she uttered; "there must be something up there which they fear."

"Well, why don't they just fly off?" Ben cried. "They must be pretty dim!"

"Come," she said, carefully scrambling from the concrete ledge, "we must discover what assails them."

Doubtful, Ben trotted after her. "What?" he asked. "Climb all the way up there? Have you gone barmy too? For one thing you're pregnant, for another I'll break my neck trying. Besides, we haven't got any ropes and stuff."

"Don't worry," she assured him, "my race know the ways of this cliff well. There is a path, not too difficult, and you will not have to climb far – see how the gulls mass just over there?"

"What do you mean *I* won't have to climb far?" Ben asked with a nervous laugh.

"As you reminded me, I am pregnant – I could not clamber up yonder. Do not look so unhappy; I shall guide you."

"Oh, thanks."

Up they went, over the first of the great rocks and then a little further until Nelda could manage no more.

"Now," she insisted, "place your foot there and hold on to that outcrop with your right hand. That's it, now reach over to that cleft and shift your weight to the other foot."

"I don't think this is such a good idea," he shouted down. "Can't we just let the gulls get on with whatever it is and leave them alone?"

But Nelda was insistent, for some dark instinct was telling her that this was her concern and she had to discover the cause of the squalling disturbance. So warily Ben edged his way up to where the screaming birds rode the wind feverishly, their demented cries growing painfully louder with each cautious move the boy made.

Soon Ben was close enough to be able to see that above him there was a narrow ledge heaped with twigs and dried grasses.

"I think their nests are up there!" he called to Nelda.

"Then that is why they do not leave," she shouted back. "Their eggs will not have hatched yet. But what is it they fear there?"

Ben had the disturbing suspicion that he was about to find out. The gulls were flapping all around him now and his ears rang with their wild shrieks. One bird flew too close and the tip of its wing slapped him in the face.

"Get off, you stupid Nelly!" he bawled. "I'm only trying to help!"

Pulling himself upwards the boy lifted his head level with the ledge and peered over.

Horrified, Ben's fingers slithered on the rock but he recovered quickly and forced himself to look again.

Inside the scruffy nest, squirming between the fragments of two gull's eggs, was a writhing knot of snakes. They were slender and long, covered in dark brown scales spattered with black diamonds, and moved constantly like animated strips of liquorice. The serpents hissed and wound their dry scaly bodies about each other as the boy peered down at them.

With their black, reptile eyes they stared back at him, and long tongues flicked swiftly from their mouths while their flat heads bobbed from side to side.

Ben shuddered in revulsion. He wasn't afraid of snakes, but there was something uncanny about these creatures; they seemed to be driven by one mind, for when one serpent moved the others mirrored the movements exactly.

"Those things would frighten anyone," he mumbled. "No wonder the birds aren't happy."

"What is it?" Nelda's voice called up to him.

He edged further along the rock and away from the nest before answering.

"Snakes! They've been eating the gulls' eggs!"

Below him Nelda raised her hands to her mouth but said no more.

Ben prepared to climb down again. "Well, I'm not touching them," he muttered. "They might be poisonous for all I know. Yeuk! The daft birds'll just have to find somewhere else and lay more ..."

His words vanished, for as he glanced along the nesting ledge he noticed for the first time the sprawled bodies of many seagulls. Their wings were spread open as though they had struggled and tried to take to the air before they died, and as he looked closer he saw that a vicious and bloody ring was cut around each limp neck.

"What can have ...?"

Amidst the bodies there came a movement and at first Ben thought that one of the gulls was still alive – then he knew.

Twined tightly about the creature's neck was a snake. Spasmodically constricting and loosening its coils the serpent made the broken corpse twitch and jerk until finally the bird's spine gave a hideous *snap*.

"They've strangled them!" Ben gasped. "The snakes have throttled the poor things!"

But the worst was yet to come. Within one of the nests a single egg lay whole and undamaged, and even as the boy turned his eyes from the gruesome spectacle of the strangled corpses he saw the shell judder and splinter.

The nest was empty of snakes but as the egg began to move, every sharp head turned and the tongues flicked out more rapidly than ever. At once a deadly stream of serpents flowed towards the nest, rearing up in expectation. With silent intent they surrounded the egg, swaying like reeds before its jarring, rocking movements as the chick within struggled to free itself.

"No!" Ben whispered, "This is awful." Yet he knew there was nothing he could do.

A piece of the eggshell fell into the nest and the waiting hunters swirled around it. Then a small hole appeared, followed by another.

Ben grimaced and clenched his teeth, screwing up his face in anticipation of the cold murder that was about to take place. But what happened next made his heart cease beating and he let out a petrified howl that silenced the squawking gulls around him.

Down the cliff face he scrambled, hurrying as fast as he safely could.

"What's the matter?" Nelda cried, sensing his panic and growing fearful. "Are you bitten?"

In a moment he was at her side but even that was

not enough. The boy jumped from the boulders and hurried over the shore to be as far from the shadow of that ledge as possible.

Nelda hastened after him. "Tell me!" she yelled. "Ben! Let me help you – show me the wound!"

The boy turned to her and she saw that the blood had drained from his face. He had not been bitten – he had been terrified.

"The egg!" he panted. "When it hatched! It was vile! Oh, Nelda! The snakes – there was no chick inside! It was full of snakes! They came out of the gulls' own eggs! They were actually inside them! How can that be?" He paused for breath, trembling in disbelief.

"The birds must have been sitting on them when the first clutch hatched!" he wailed. "And those filthy things wriggled out to strangle them – it's horrible! How could snakes come from birds' eggs? It isn't possible!"

Nelda stepped back and lifted her eyes to where the gulls were still zooming about the ledge.

"'Tis a jest of the Deep Ones' devising," she uttered coldly. "Thus are other mothers destroyed by their offspring. It is a grim sign to warn me of their displeasure, a terror to reveal unto me how mighty is their power – as if I needed the reminder."

"They did that?" Ben cried. "It's sick!"

"It is, though I doubt if that shall be the last sign. I fear there will be many more. Who next will suffer for me and my unborn child? Who else am I placing at risk?"

"What are you going to do?" the boy asked, recovering slightly from the shock. "Will you come and stay with us? You can't stay here. It just isn't safe – who knows what they'll do next?"

A strange look clouded Nelda's face. "No Ben," she replied mildly, "I shall be quite all right for at last

I have decided for myself." She gazed at him briefly then picked up his schoolbag and handed it over. "Time you were returning home," the aufwader told him. "Go now."

"I'm not leaving you here!"

"Please, it's what I want."

Knowing there was no arguing with her, Ben swung his bag over his shoulder. "Shall I see you tomorrow then?" he asked.

"Perhaps."

Giving the cliff one final dubious and scared glance, Ben bade farewell and began the return walk over the shore towards the town.

When she was quite alone, Nelda took from her pocket a disc of polished green glass and held it close to her chest.

"Tonight," she whispered.

* * *

High over the church of St Mary the crescent moon shone cold and milk-white. Its pale beams glowed over the long grasses that rustled before the midnight airs and ringed the edges of the headstones with frosty haloes.

Through the dismal graveyard Nelda made her way, and though this time she did not have Old Parry to spur her on, she was not afraid. Engulfed by the huge black shadow of the church her pace neither quickened nor faltered – a grim determination was upon her and no vague fears would stop the aufwader that night.

Clasped firmly in her hands was Old Parry's lens, and when she reached a grim yet familiar spot she put it to her eye and began to search.

The churchyard was still and silent, yet upon that raw and exposed clifftop, Nelda was not alone.

Some distance behind her, following the precise route she had taken between the tombstones, a figure came. It was tall and wreathed in shadow, dressed in flowing black robes which merged into the gloom and made the stranger almost invisible. Like a swirling shred of the night's own fabric it stole stealthily after the aufwader. Its footfalls were as noiseless as a cat's and beneath a deep cowl, two eyes watched the small foraging shape intently.

Nelda was too wrapped up in the dim green world of the glass disc to realize she had been followed. Her anxiety to find what she sought drove out every other concern, so she failed to notice the shadow that flitted over the graves, stealing closer with every moment.

Impatiently, she parted the dense growth of weeds but the object of her frantic searching was nowhere to be found. Lowering the lens, she cast around the cemetery to see if she was indeed at the correct grave. Yes, it was smaller than the rest, but that repugnant and sickly little herb was not there.

Desperately, she peered through the glass again and dragged the obscuring grasses aside, tearing them up by the roots – and then she found it.

Beside the weathered headstone and hidden by the large thorny leaves of a thistle, she saw the ugly, grey growth. Nelda was filled with the same loathing but she reached out her hand and without a moment's hesitation plucked the bitter weed from the ground.

The stem of the hideous plant was cold to the touch, and whether it was the breeze or some uncanny force all its own she could not tell, but the thing moved in her fingers. The spiralling creepers unfurled and fluttered about her hand as the repellent flower raised itself and the two clattering stamens began to wag madly, diffusing the nauseating scent which polluted the night more than ever.

"It's as if it's glad I took it," Nelda muttered. "It

wants me to taste the infernal juice. Oh, Deeps take me, is all the world ranged against this child? How witless I have been, to think I could be the bearer of new life. I should have put your petals upon my tongue when Parry led me here before, and smacked my lips in gratitude for your deliverance of me. Oh, how I wish that I had."

Her hands shaking with apprehension and dread, Nelda lifted the vile herb to her mouth. "Forgive me, my unborn babe," she sobbed. "There truly was no other way."

Nearby, concealed behind the crumbling slab of a tombstone, the robed figure stirred.

Nelda's trembling fingers moved to her lips and she closed her eyes as the flower touched her tongue.

"NO, LASS!"

A stern and forceful voice barked out at her and from the dim shadows a dark shape sprang and knocked her hand away, wrenching the foul plant from her mouth.

With tears rolling into his whiskers, Tarr Shrimp flung the weed to the ground and crushed it beneath his feet.

"Grandfather!" Nelda cried. "What are you doing? Stop!"

Tarr looked at her, his face a tormented confusion of anger, shame and pity.

"Oh, Nelda!" he blurted, throwing his arms about her. "Can tha ever forgive such an old fool?"

"I've missed you so much!" she wept. "I felt so alone I didn't know what to do."

"Hush now, Ah'm here now. We ain't beaten yet; theer must be a way. Ah'll not let owt take thee from me, not while theer's life in my bones."

"But the curse – I cannot escape that."

Tarr hugged her forlornly, then his tears dried and his despair was replaced by a fierce resolve. The leader of the aufwaders drew back from his granddaughter and stared defiantly out to the dark vastness of the sea.

"Only one hope have we now," he murmured. "At the time of the next full moon ah shall summon the herald of the Lords of the Deep."

Nelda buried her face in his shoulder and the two fisherfolk clung grimly to one another.

Retracing its footsteps, the robed figure slipped silently through the dismal gloom. It had witnessed all that had occurred and a serene smile appeared beneath the deep hood of its robes.

7

THE BALLAD OF MOLLY WERBRIDE

It was a week of excitement and revelations in Whitby. With the aid of two walking sticks, Miss Boston began hobbling about the town and ordered that the wheelchair be returned to the hospital as she no longer required it. Gleefully she tottered into shops and renewed those old animosities which had once been so vital to her. Everyone was pleased to see the progress she had made and Mrs Noble in the fish shop even gave her two free kippers.

Aunt Alice revelled in her joyous reception wherever she went. Those dreary months of hard work and intensive study were worth that first morning alone. Jutting her chins in the air, she held her head with unashamed pride and carefully made her way to each familiar battleground. Now the whole town could see that her illness had not conquered this independent, strong-minded ninety-three-year-old, and people hailed her in the streets with friendly smiles and words of encouragement. Even Doctor Adams was pleased to have been mistaken about his most troublesome patient and congratulated her enthusiastically.

At the end of that first day of successful roaming, Miss Boston glowed with satisfaction but wondered how long it would be until she could manage with just one stick and then without any assistance at all. In fact she was so engrossed in this matter that when Edith Wethers told her she and the doctor were planning to retire to the Isle of Wight and would spend their honeymoon there to look for a suitable property, the old lady hardly showed any interest whatsoever in this most absorbing news. Edith left her to 'brew her potions' and departed to continue organizing and drawing up numerous lists for the impending wedding day.

She and the doctor had decided that a short engagement would be best, for he had tactlessly said that there was no point in hanging around at their age. The date they had fixed however was galloping closer at a frightening speed and Edith started to suffer from dreadful attacks of blind panic and was forced to take a pill in order to sleep at night. In the daytime she would spend long, indecisive hours fretting about the slightest problem, working herself into such a tense jangle of nerves that she had to go for long walks to calm down.

Miss Boston seemed blissfully unaware of her friend's daily traumas and spent unending hours contorted in weird positions as she exercised and strengthened her leg muscles.

One evening as she lay on her back with a bunch of freshly picked herbs and flowers held close to her nose, Ben confided to her all that Nelda had told him.

The old lady inhaled deeply, raised her left foot off the ground, lifted it as high as she could, then lowered it again before taking another great breath and repeating the process with her other leg.

When Ben had finished the tragic tale, Aunt Alice waved the posy around her head three times then tore off a handful of leaves and rubbed them vigorously on her knees.

"Dear, dear," she tutted, "the poor creature. What an iniquitous business it is. And you say there is nothing the other fisherfolk can do? How unjust and undeserving – she is but a child herself. Those Lords of the Deep must be infamous beyond belief to allow such cruelty."

"At least she's made it up with Tarr," he said. "I don't know about the rest of the tribe."

Miss Boston's eyebrows perked up as a new thought struck her. "Nevertheless," she whispered, "perhaps this has something to do with Prudence's warning. Is this to prove the danger which we are to face? Maybe, maybe."

Putting the now straggly bunch of flowers and herbs aside, she said, "Thank you, Benjamin. Would you kindly keep me informed of any further development?"

The boy agreed but he left the room feeling disappointed. In the past Aunt Alice would have stormed straight to the caves and demanded to involve herself in the matter, whether the fisherfolk wanted her help or not. It was as if she didn't really care what happened to Nelda and the baby unless it directly affected her. Scowling with this new and uncomfortable opinion of the old lady, Ben left the cottage and went to seek his aufwader friend.

* * *

On the Friday before the wedding, a bored Jennet trailed over the swing bridge and wound her way through the West Cliff. The girl had nothing to hurry back to the cottage for, and if Dithery Edith asked her to try on that appalling bridesmaid's dress one more time she would tell her exactly where she could stick it.

Miss Wethers had paid no attention to her protests that she was too old to be dressed up like a china doll.

"Don't be silly," the oblivious bride-to-be had commanded. "You'll look so pretty."

In despair Jennet had looked to Aunt Alice for support, but the old lady had been too busy to take any interest in the matter and decided that it was better to leave it all up to Edith.

The girl's cheeks still burned when she thought how ridiculous she looked in that monstrous, sugary creation – decked out in yards of pink satin. She was sorely tempted to take a pair of scissors to the ghastly outfit, snip off the rippling frills which fringed the neck and shoulders, and turn up at the registry office in her jeans and a T-shirt.

At least Ben had not escaped, and indeed would be made to suffer such a humiliating indignity that Jennet vaguely thought the entire fiasco would be worthwhile. For her brother, Edith had chosen a kilt, and the girl was looking forward to seeing his mortification in front of the whole town.

Standing beneath the great whalebone arch, she gazed down at the harbour and across at the ragged pinnacles of the abbey on the opposite cliff, with a sullen and dismal expression clouding her face.

Jennet positively hated it here now. She felt as though the town was smothering her and she longed to be in some distant place, far away from small minds and petty attitudes.

If she had the chance she would leave tomorrow and forget this dreary shrine to tedium that was perpetually locked in a bygone and backward age. Away from here she felt sure she would be able to forget, and the yearning dreams would fade completely.

"I just can't help but remember *him* here," she murmured. "God – when will I be free?"

Flicking her hair over her shoulders, Jennet descended the steps and began walking back towards the bridge.

At the quayside she halted and let the fresh salty air wash over her and lost herself in the sight of the sparkling water. The flashing sunlight was hypnotic and the rebellion was lulled within her. Of course she wished Miss Wethers every happiness and was pleased that at last she had found someone who would cherish and adore her.

"If only that had happened to me," she whispered with regret.

With her eyes half closed, letting the vibrant, dazzling patterns shine through her lashes, she contemplated her young life and wished it belonged to someone else. It was a warm afternoon and Jennet blinked drowsily – was she dreaming or could she hear music?

Very faintly, brief snatches of a lilting tune were carried to her on the river breeze and it was so delicious that the girl hardly breathed, in case she lost the sound forever.

The music appeared to be coming from the East Cliff and, filled with curiosity and the desire to hear more, Jennet hurried over the bridge.

In Market Place a crowd of tourists were gathered, and when Jennet hastened up Sandgate she squeezed her way to the front and let the delightful music flood through her.

Encircled by the appreciative onlookers was a small female folk band. One of them breathed sensual life into a wooden flute, and her joy at the glorious earthy tones that it oozed was sculpted on her ecstatic face. At her side a younger but much more serious woman concentrated on the fiddle that was wedged firmly beneath her chin, and when the bow flew across the strings, the notes made Jennet's heart leap and she tapped her toes unconsciously. The third musician possessed one of the most beautiful faces the girl had ever seen. She was both graceful and delicate, dexterously playing a sweet-sounding concertina, her elegant fingers nimbly moving over the ivory buttons as her lovely face nodded to the rhythm. Her long hair hung in a great corn-coloured sheaf that glinted with veins of deep gold when it caught the evening sunlight and, aware of this, she stood a little apart from the others to remain within the slanting rays.

They were all dressed in richly-coloured and flowing clothes, with tiny mirrors sewn around the full skirts and bright tapestry waistcoats with tie-dyed scarves and bandanas knotted loosely about their hips, and, joining in with the instruments, a multitude of bangles, necklaces and bracelets chimed and rattled against one another.

Together the women weaved a harmonious display of melody and brilliance and Jennet was enchanted. It reminded her of those first happy weeks when she and Ben had just arrived in Whitby and explored the town during its annual folk festival.

With a combined shout, the trio ended their music and bowed as the audience showed its approval. Each woman handled the enthusiastic applause differently. The flautist went quite red in the cheeks and glanced at the ground bashfully, whilst her friend with the fiddle was too busy retuning to take much notice of anything. Grandly stepping forward however and basking in the adulation, the golden-haired beauty laughed and shook her burnished mane. With a flamboyant sweep of her arm, she took up a tambourine and beat it to focus everyone's attention solely upon herself.

"Shall we play you one more before we finish for the day?" she asked.

The people nodded keenly and clapped in time with the beat of the tambourine.

"What shall we give them?" she called to her

companions.

Brushing her own mousy and rather neglected hair from her flushed and freckled face, the flautist in a shy voice muttered, " 'Bobbing and Ducking'?''

" 'The Moon in her Eyes','' suggested the fiddler.

Dismissing both of these, the beauty unleashed her ravishing smile upon the crowd and every man gawped and yearned for her.

"No, no,'' she said huskily, "I've a mind to bring in my daughter on this one. Pear! Pear, where are you?''

On the opposite side of the audience from Jennet, a girl not much older than herself had been sitting cross-legged on the ground, but at her mother's summons she skipped into the centre of the area and took the tambourine from her.

She was as raven as her mother was fair. The girl's hair was sleek and dark and the two contrasted starkly with each other even though she was attired in the same hippy fashion. Tiny Indian bells tinkled around the hem of her purple cheesecloth dress and beneath them a pair of grubby, dusty feet tripped lightly over the stone flags.

"What is it to be?'' the fourth member of the troupe cried, playing up to the crowd.

" 'The Ballad of Molly Werbride','' her mother answered, taking hold of the concertina once again.

At a signal from her the other musicians began to play and her daughter waited for the cue.

This tune was different to the one that had gone before. It was a slow, haunting lament and the flute whistled faintly like the wind over the moors as the strings of the fiddle began to moan, suggesting a human voice wailing in despair.

Then the concertina introduced the main theme and the girl called Pear opened her mouth and started to sing.

She had a fabulous, throaty voice which at times

mirrored the high notes of the flute and soared up to the sky entwined with its purity. Abruptly it then merged with the resonant chords of the fiddle – matching it until the two sounds were impossible to separate.

Jennet listened to it spellbound. The ballad was a dark and cautionary tale of a young maiden who went "a-roaming" over the moors and was seized by the hunting spirits of the wild, never to be seen again.

The singer performed it marvellously and no one in the audience made a sound. Even the children in pushchairs were dumbfounded, and as the sublime music carried into the streets the milling traffic of shoppers and trippers were so moved that they caught their breath and momentarily forgot about postcards and the price of souvenirs.

When the song was over, the applause was tremendous and lasted several minutes with much ringing of the change that was tossed into the upturned and clattering tambourine.

"That's all for today," the girl's mother told everyone, "though we will be here tomorrow if you fancy a second helping. I thank you!"

With admiring glances, and making mental notes to return the following day, the clot of people around Market Place began to break up.

Jennet leaned against one of the pillars of the old town hall and lingered to watch the folk band pack away their instruments.

Hopping over the ground, collecting the stray coins that had missed their target, the young singer drew close to Jennet and with a merry grin stared at her.

"What's this then?" she asked pertly. "Glued to that pillar, are you? Did you like the performance so much you can't tear yourself away?"

Jennet smiled shyly. "I thought it was excellent," she said, "only I missed most of it."

"Well, there's always tomorrow if you can bear any more of my warbles. Some think the old ballads are too long-winded and one exposure is quite enough."

"No really, I thought that last one was – well, perfect. I understood everything that was happening and why she went off like that."

"I must admit of all the pieces we do that one is a real favourite with me too. It's got a bit of everything, don't you think? Passion and cruelty, excitement and misery, fear and dread – but that's the way of things. I think if I was tied down to drudge in the one dismal spot for too long I'd go raving mad and run off as well. I don't blame Molly Werbride in the slightest – good on her!"

Jennet agreed readily. She liked this strange girl, with her bare feet and the ready laugh in her voice that threatened to erupt into explosive mirth at any moment.

"They call me Pear," she said. "It's actually short for a great mouthful, but what can you expect from a mother who used to be a teacher but expects to be treated like the Queen of Sheba?"

"Is that your mother – with the fair hair?"

"Oh, you mean the really ugly one," she nodded sarcastically. "Yeah, it's a shame – she can't help it. Still, her boils and scabs aren't too noticeable today. Urgh! Did you see those letchy old dads in the crowd before? I thought they were going to start slobbering – I almost hit them with the tambourine! Lusting after my mum indeed and her born so deformed! Quite disgusting."

The girls laughed and the sound made Pear's mother turn and advance towards them with her fine eyebrows raised quizzically.

"What's all this?" she inquired. "Who's your new friend? Are you plotting something together? Were you talking about me?"

Now that she could see her more closely, Jennet was certain – the woman was truly beautiful. Every feature was perfectly modelled and the few lines that marred the otherwise smooth and lustrous skin only served to accentuate the exquisite symmetry of her face.

"Don't you listen to a word this vagabond tells you," she advised. "I'm afraid my daughter has no sense of what's polite or acceptable. No shoes again I see, Pear."

The girl folded her arms obstinately. "Meta's always nagging at me to wear bits of dead cow on my feet," she complained, "but I keep telling her that shoes are for horses. I want to feel the sand in my toes and the grass under them. I won't eat meat so why should I wear it?"

"I bet you do in winter," Jennet teased.

"No I don't, I put my placky wellies on."

"See what I mean?" her mother groaned. "She's so stubborn – I just know she'll do something really awful one day to shame me."

"Thought I already had," Pear smirked. "Have to try harder, won't I?"

The woman gave her a gentle shove then looked back at the others. "Well," she said, "we're ready for the off. Are you coming, you savage?"

"No," Pear told her. "I'll hang round here for a bit, see you after."

"All right, I'll leave you and...?"

"Jennet."

"I'll leave you and Jennet in peace. Lovely to have met you, catch you later – ciao."

The two girls watched the trio pack up the instruments and set off down Church Street towards the one hundred and ninety-nine steps.

"I like your mum," Jennet said. "Is she always so laid back?"

"Yeah, Meta's cool I suppose, never gives me any hassle. Terminally vain though – the time she spends brushing her hair and looking beautiful, I couldn't be bothered."

"Funny how you call her by her name," Jennet said thoughtfully. "My mum would've killed me if I'd done that."

"Why?"

"She just would've, that's all."

Pear tied the tambourine to a yellow ribbon around her waist. "That's dumb," she remarked. "Meta would laugh her socks off if I started calling her 'Mummy'. How old is yours? She sounds like a real crumbly."

Jennet hesitated then replied, "Both my parents are dead."

"BONG!" Pear howled and promptly enacted a routine where she mimed cutting her tongue off.

"It's all right," Jennet assured her. "It was a few years ago. I didn't say it to make you feel awkward."

"Oh, I don't," Pear chirped. "In fact my dad's six foot under too so we're halfway equal. Now, if I could only bump gorgeous Meta off we'd be square!"

Jennet giggled and realized that she had not felt so relaxed and at ease with anyone for a long time.

"So where are you staying?" she asked. "Is it in the Youth Hostel up by the abbey?"

Pear pulled a painful face. "Come off it," she cried. "No, we're parked behind that ugly church on the cliff."

"Parked? So you're staying outside Whitby?"

"No, our van's up there. Caroline – the one with the fiddle – owns a camper and we all pile into that."

And so she told Jennet of the nomadic life the folk band led, drifting all over the country performing their songs and living from day to day – not knowing where they would be from one week to the next.

Intrigued, Jennet listened and pangs of jealousy rankled within her. It all sounded so marvellous. They were free to do whatever they wished and she felt that her own life was completely drab and uneventful in comparison.

The two girls talked together for nearly an hour. Pear was a unique character; she was nearly sixteen and despised conforming to convention and the ridiculous rules of society, flouting them whenever possible. She loved to puncture snobbery and regaled Jennet with hilarious stories of life on the road. She had never been to school but had learnt everything from her mother – except how to behave in a "decent and responsible" way.

Ambling leisurely through the streets, the impudent girl would pull all manner of faces at those who obviously found her gypsy-like appearance startling, and Jennet cracked up to see how quickly they hurried away.

Yet for all this, Pear was also an excellent listener and Jennet revealed more to her in that short time than she ever had to either Aunt Alice or her brother. Deprived of a real friend for so long, she spoke of her innermost fears and dearest longings.

"Look," Pear eventually said, "we've been gassing for ages and I'm starved. Why don't you come round and have something to eat with me and the others?"

Jennet eyed her doubtfully. "Oh, I don't know," she began. "I mean I don't want to intrude..."

"Rubbish," Pear told her. "You're dying to see the van and it's Liz's turn to cook – the things she does with a packet of lentils and a few herbs! You can't refuse that, now can you?"

Jennet was intrigued and longed to join them, but she really should have returned to the cottage over an hour ago.

" 'Course, if you've something better to do...?"

That decided it. "Nothing!" she replied at once.

Behind the wall of the churchyard, overshadowed by the stately ruins of the abbey, was a large car park. In the winter months the place was deserted except for the steamed-up vehicles of courting couples but in the summer it was choked and congested by many different kinds of transport, from motor bikes to small lorries, and that evening was no exception.

Pear led Jennet through the maze of cars, chatting amiably as they went. "We were lucky when we arrived this morning," she said. "Someone was just pulling out of a space near the edge and we nipped right in. That's the van over there."

She pointed to where the corner of the churchyard wall met the cliff edge. A cream and orange camper van took up a generous amount of space, and sitting outside it upon the hummocky grass were Pear's mother and the other two members of the folk band.

They waved in acknowledgement as the two girls approached and Jennet saw that the woman who had played the flute was busily cutting up vegetables and throwing them into a huge pan which bubbled above a primus stove.

"Hi!" Pear called when they were close enough to be heard. "I've brought Jennet back to try some of your grub, Liz."

The freckle-faced woman gave a self-conscious smile and mumbled inaudibly.

"Liz never has much to say for herself," Pear told Jennet, "but she says all she has to in her music; she plays the guitar as well as the flute. Real talent she has."

The girl's mother rose to greet them. "Hello, you two! How lovely to have company. I'm glad it wasn't my turn to cook tonight."

"I wouldn't have brought Jennet if it was," Pear uttered bluntly.

171

"Sit down," Meta told them, making room on the blanket which was spread over the grass. "You don't mind eating vegetarian do you, Jennet? None of us are carnivores, are we? No dead flesh for us; slabs of fear pumped full of poison, that's all it is – revolting."

"All right, Meta," Pear interrupted, "get off the soapbox, not enough people are watching."

At first Jennet felt uncomfortable amongst the other women and looked cautiously about her. She had never met anyone like this strange group before and could not begin to guess how they had met and decided to travel together. A more unlikely collection of people was difficult to imagine.

The one called Liz was painfully shy and hovered about the primus, not once lifting her eyes in their direction. Nearby, sitting cross-legged, with her nose buried in a book, was Caroline. Politely yet making it obvious she did not want to join in any conversation, she said hello to the girls then returned her attention to the pages of her novel.

Jennet found Pear's mother to be the most unsettling of the lot. Her beauty was so radiant and intense that she felt horribly plain beside her, like a candle flame held against the harsh brilliance of the sun. She could understand why Liz was so quiet and timid – no one could ever be noticed in that luminous company, except perhaps Meta's own daughter.

Beside her mother's lambent beauty, Pear's jet black hair was a welcome balance to the eye and her irreverant backchat held Meta's overwhelming personality in check.

The handsome woman loved the sound of her own voice. It was obvious she adored the limelight and being the centre of attention. Her laugh was always the loudest and lasted just that little bit too long. She was undoubtedly the driving force behind the group, and Jennet slowly discovered that she didn't really like this lovely yet domineering beauty. Meta was queen of them all and she knew it. Her constant and tenacious control of any conversation swiftly became tiresome, yet in Pear's mocking company her glamour was just bearable.

From the simmering pan a tantalizing scent floated, and Jennet's mouth watered as she realized how hungry she was.

"Will it be much longer, Liz?" Pear begged.

The woman gave a meek shake of the head and went to fetch some plates from a cupboard in the van.

Presently the dishes were passed around, heaped with a rich smelling mixture of nuts, rice and chick-peas. It was delicious and Jennet ate it quickly.

Caroline laid her book down and chewed thoughtfully whilst Liz went to sit by herself in the camper – as if to be seen eating by a stranger was a most horrendous prospect. Assuming elegant poses with a fork in one hand and the plate in the other, Meta managed to look ravishing even with her mouth full. At her side, Pear chattered in garbled bursts, telling Jennet more of their lifestyle, and soon it was as if the girl had known them all her life and though she still found the blonde woman tiresome she was perfectly willing to remain in their company for as long as she was welcome.

The group's lifestyle sounded extremely attractive; they had no cares and the only money they needed was for petrol and food as they made most of their own clothes. Not once did Jennet think of Aunt Alice or Ben, and found herself wishing that she could stay with the band forever.

"So," Meta said, "tell us about yourself and this place. In all our years together we've never been to Whitby, have we? It looks a fascinating little spot and there's a good health food shop. I had to drag Liz out of it, didn't I Caroline? Do you like it here, Jennet? Is it really as full of mystery and legend as it seems?"

She raised a shapely hand to the abbey ruins and assumed a dramatic and fearful pose. "I am trying to imagine how it will look when the night comes," she said in hushed tones, "how spooky it will be for us all in the camper van. Have you ever been here at midnight, Jennet, when the moonlight shines upon those ancient, broken stones and weird noises carry upon the wind?"

The girl made no reply; there were certain memories she would rather not recall.

"I see you have," the woman persisted. "What adventures were yours? Were you terrified or did a lover's arms embrace you?"

"Shut up, Meta," Pear rapped, coming to Jennet's rescue. "You're talking garbage again. You only do it to hear yourself – shame you don't realize how boring it is."

Meta smiled and sat once more. "My daughter is always chiding me," she confided. "I pity her having me for a parent – it must be awful to have such a dreary mother who's always seeking attention."

"You're doing it again!" Pear gasped, throwing a cushion at her. "Hey, Jennet, do you want your palm read? Caroline's really good at it. Caroline, come and do the old clairvoyant bit for her."

"I don't know about that," Jennet muttered, shoving her hands beneath her knees. "I don't believe in that kind of nonsense; there's enough of it at home."

"Oh, it's just a laugh," Pear cried. "Go on, don't be dull."

Dutifully, Jennet raised her upturned palm and the woman called Caroline came over to peer at it.

Taking the girl's hand in hers, she stared and frowned, following certain lines with her fingernails.

"This curve here is your Head Line. It shows that

you're sensitive but not very creative – you probably get depressed quite easily too."

Jennet squirmed. Did she have to be quite so blunt?

"Mmm, your mount of Saturn says that you're an extremely practical person, a good organizer, like me, with no time for fantasy or ludicrous notions. The Heart Line here isn't very pronounced – that's not very common."

At this, Meta gave a lusty sigh. "Perhaps Jennet's surpressing a secret passion – maybe you did come up here with a lover after all. Is he an uncouth yob or a dreary artisan who'll end up an accountant?"

"Don't be vile," Pear scolded her mother. "Go on, Caroline."

"There are a lot of broken paths here," she breathed. "You've been through many upheavals, haven't you? It's levelled out recently but it still isn't steady. And look, that is interesting – hmm." She gave the hand a dismissive pat then twisted her mouth to one side.

"Radical change," she summed up. "No doubt about it, very soon your whole life will alter. More upheaval, I'm afraid, but it might be for the best."

"What ... what sort of change?" Jennet stammered.

"Oh, your life will take an entirely new direction," Caroline said, returning to her place and retrieving the novel.

Jennet stared blankly at her palm, then became steadily encouraged and much happier. "I was hoping for a change to happen," she said. "Maybe it will after all."

"Oh it will," Pear affirmed. "Caroline's never been wrong yet."

"If only it'll happen soon. You are lucky. I wish I could go wherever I wanted to and not be told what to do all the time."

"What's stopping you?"

"Well, school for a start and then my brother and Aunt Alice – oh, lots of things."

Lounging on the grass like a contented cat, Meta let out a sympathetic groan. "Excuses," she murmured. "If you really wanted to change you'd do it. There'll always be something to blame for your inertia."

"We can't all be carried away from our humdrum lives by a dashing stranger," Pear interrupted. "Stop measuring others by your own shameful youth. Do you know, Jennet, my mother was just out of college and had only been in her first teaching job three weeks when she was whisked off by my father. She just upped and left everything behind – friends, family, everything. Completely mad, don't you think?"

Jennet shrugged. "I don't know," she breathed. "Depends on who the man is, I suppose, and how much he loves you."

"There you are," Meta declared, wagging a finger at her daughter, "Jennet understands, don't you, honey?" She reached over and stroked the girl's hair then added, "Would you like a drink? I've got a bottle of wine in the van – I can think of nothing better than to sit with friends and enjoy a glass or two."

Before Jennet could answer, Pear's mother was already ferreting in the van for the bottle.

"I'm not really allowed to drink alcohol," she murmured. "I don't know if I should."

Pear sniggered. "Why not? I was brought up on beer and wine, wasn't I, Meta?"

"Only way to keep you quiet, Lambkin. Does wonders, some stout in the baby's milk – I would've gone quite berserk otherwise. Here we are."

She passed the glasses around and uncorked a large bottle of dry white wine.

Jennet held the glass nervously as Meta filled it and gingerly sniffed the clear fruity liquid.

"Here's to your radical change," Meta announced, raising her own glass, "whatever that proves to be. Hoi, Liz – what about some music?"

From the camper the timid woman emerged and in her arms she carried a guitar covered in fading stickers. Very softly she began to strum the strings and a babbling tune drifted around them. As Jennet sipped the wine, the music mingled with the taste, and it was so lovely that she closed her eyes to fix this moment forever in her memory.

* * *

As the light failed and the sky gradually turned a hazy deep blue, Sister Frances swayed uncertainly and rubbed her eyes.

Disorientated, she looked around and found that she was standing in the abbey grounds.

The venerable remains of the holy building were dark, and high above her – silhouetted against the louring sky – the skeletal frames of the east windows cast violet shadows over the confused nun as she tried to remember what had brought her to this place.

"Here I am again," she declared to the ancient columns before her. "Come on, Frances, get a grip on yourself. They'll come to take you away if you keep blacking out like this. Oh Lawks! What can the time be?"

Charging through the grounds with her head at a tilt and her great long legs marching in determined strides, she left the abbey behind and headed for the church.

When she was skirting the edge of the car park, Sister Frances brought herself up sharply and turned this way and that as though she had lost something.

"How divine," she gushed, listening to the strains

of a slow, peaceful melody. "What a pretty tune. Wherever is it coming from?"

Following the delightful sound with child-like curiosity, she gravitated towards the cliff edge where, amongst other vehicles, a camper was parked.

Small glass jars containing night lights burned beside the van and the nun was charmed by the glimmering scene. Gathered in a semi-circle, five figures were talking in low voices and one of them played a guitar so well that it brought tears to Frances's eyes.

Silently, her large feet crept closer and an enraptured expression appeared over her face and she put her hands together as if in prayer.

The guitar player happened to glance up and the music faltered when she saw the tall figure peeking around the side of the van.

"Oh, please don't stop!" Frances implored. "I only wanted to listen for a teeny moment. It was all so heavenly, a perfect tranquil scene, with all you chums sitting around on a jolly evening ..." Her voice trailed away. One of the figures had turned quickly and was trying to hide her face. Sister Frances recognized the girl immediately.

"Jennet!" she cried. "What are you doing here? Shouldn't you be at Miss B's? And what have you got in your hand? No, I don't believe it is lemonade! Oh, how beastly of you! It's white wine – I can see the bottle! Come here at once!"

Striding between Pear and Meta, she took hold of Jennet's arm and wrenched the girl to her feet.

Pear giggled at the sight of the outraged nun but Frances was indignant and she berated the other women for leading Jennet astray. "It isn't the slightest bit funny," she warned them. "I intend to tell a policeman!"

Meta drained her own glass and looked at her

steadily. "You're right of course," she said in all seriousness. "I think you had better return home, Jennet."

"I don't want to!" the girl cried. "Oh, why don't you mind your own business?" she snapped at Frances.

"This is for your own good Jennet, dear," the nun declared, leading her away from these dangerous intoxicators. "Do stop struggling."

Jennet strained and tried to pull her arm free but the ridiculous woman was stronger than she seemed.

"Let her go!" Pear called.

"Be quiet!" Meta growled. "Don't interfere!"

But her daughter leaped up to bar the nun's path and Meta reached out to drag her backwards. "Did you not hear me?" she growled.

"Who does that freak think she is?"

Meta glared at the girl and hissed, "Must I say it a second time? Do you need a lesson in obedience? Let her take Jennet back."

Pear took one look at her mother and sat down again instantly.

"How did you get involved with those disreputable people?" Frances asked, dragging the miserable Jennet through the car park.

But the girl was not listening. Looking over her shoulder, she could see that Pear was as unhappy as she was. "I'll see you tomorrow!" she shouted.

Pear made no sign that she had heard, and before Jennet could call again Sister Frances had pulled her into the churchyard towards the one hundred and ninety-nine steps.

"You'll do no such thing!" the nun told her. "It's the wedding tomorrow and you'll bally well be there!"

Jennet trotted wretchedly behind her. Pear was the first friend she had had for as long as she could remember and the others had treated her as an equal. Now here she was being patronized like a child again. She hated Sister Frances and she hated Whitby.

Sitting before the camper van, Meta stared harshly at her daughter. "We must hope that the police are not informed," she said. "We dare not risk their involvement."

Pear lowered her eyes. "I'm sorry," she whispered, "I wasn't thinking."

"Perhaps I ought to train you a little more thoroughly."

The girl cringed and nervously put her hands to her throat.

Nearby, Caroline began to tidy up the dishes and said tersely, "Hillian won't like this."

"Don't worry about that," Meta sneered. "I can handle her."

* * *

Much later, at the closed premises of The Whitby Bookshop, two women tapped lightly on the door and were ushered quickly inside. Into the darkness, past the neat and ordered shelves they went, talking in rushed whispers until they reached the spiral staircase. Up the winding way each of them climbed, up to the first floor which brimmed with mellow candle-light and the smell of melting wax.

Miriam Gower had arranged the area as before; the books and display bins had been pushed against the walls and in the centre of the cleared space the wooden box was carefully positioned.

The formidable owner of the bookshop showed her guests to their places and seated herself upon the carpet with as much grace as her hulking frame permitted.

With the deep warm glow of the candle-light curving over her round face, she looked at the other two members of the coven excitedly.

"You are sure the time has come?" she asked, a little out of breath after mounting the staircase. "Only two chances remain, remember."

Hillian Fogle clicked her tongue in annoyance. "Question don't!" she yapped. "When the rest of the sisters are assembled it said, then we were to call it up again. Now the others are here so we must speak to it tonight."

She nodded to the third figure who now sat in the place once occupied by Susannah O'Donnell. So far the newcomer had remained silent and Hillian scrutinized her through her spectacles. "Went today successful?" she asked.

The third witch was idly admiring the way the candle flame glinted in her golden hair as she held it up to the light, and took a moment before answering.

"Oh yes," Meta murmured, "the first seeds were sown. The girl is definitely one of us – how can she fail to be? Was *he* not the most commanding man? Given more time the young fool will be under our control."

Miriam's pointed tongue licked her garishly painted lips as she regarded the bitterly beautiful woman before them with envy and mistrust sparkling in her almond eyes. "For your sake I hope that is true," she commented.

"If there's one thing I know how to do above all else," Meta returned with equal archness, "it's how to ensnare."

"Oh, we know that," Miriam said. "That's how you trapped *him*."

Meta let that pass. "With Pear's help the girl's ultimate co-operation is assured," she said with a forced smile, "so you can waddle off and worry your bovine head about something else, can't you? How to shed a few stone perhaps?"

"Sisters," Hillian tutted, "old quarrels have no place here. Let us begin; lift the lid."

Miriam leaned forward and the immense shadow cast by her top-heavy bosom threw one half of the room into utter darkness. Carefully she took from the box the wizened fishmonkey, and Meta gave a low whistle at the sight of the shrivelled creature.

"Charming," she remarked.

"Fine looks aren't everything," Miriam replied tartly.

"Is that the voice of experience speaking?"

Hillian took out the second bag of incense and poured the contents on to the burner. When the fishmonkey was placed on the lid of the sea chest she lit the powder and waited.

The pungent smoke threaded about the scaly form and flowed into the withered nostrils to work the magic once more.

Bleating like a new-born lamb, the repulsive creature gasped and stretched its puny arms.

At each woman in turn it blinked those yellow eyes and twisted the large head upon the emaciated neck.

"You have waited overlong to summon me," it hissed. "You ought to have acted sooner."

"The rest of the coven only did arrive today," Hillian said. "There was no point to waken you before now."

"Then they should have journeyed with more haste!" the fishmonkey snapped. "My master is impatient – time has grown short. Events have moved onwards, events you are ignorant of."

"What events is these?" Hillian asked. "How are they concerning us?"

"When the sun hangs low in the sky at dusk tomorrow," it told her, "a complication shall arise. If we are not careful and cunning it shall undo us."

"What must we do?"

"The boy," the creature spat, "his destruction is still uppermost. He must be killed this night before it is too late."

Hillian nodded quickly and Miriam gave a wide grin.

Staring in mild amusement at the peculiar little monster, Meta cupped her chin in her hand and asked, "And how are we to do that? I have been led to believe this child is no ordinary boy. He already suspects something is happening. Did Hillian not tell me he has put a charm upon his window that we may not enter that way again?"

The fishmonkey ground its brown teeth and wormed about to face her. "This time the human must be lured into the open," it commanded. "Out to the wild where we can deal with him."

The owner of the bookshop sniffed haughtily. "Just how are we to accomplish that?" she demanded. "What possible bait would bring an eight-year-old from his warm bed in the middle of the night?"

The creature swivelled its head and the papery skin crackled at the swiftness of the movement. "Do I not recall that on the first time of my awakening thou wert keen to prove thyself worthy?"

Miriam shot Hillian a superior glance. "That is so," she admitted readily.

"Doth thy eagerness still hold true?" it asked.

"It most certainly does!" she retorted. "If I were the one to rid your lord of his enemies then I should be chosen to wear the ring of amethyst and lead the coven."

The fishmonkey tapped the lid of the box thoughtfully then bared all of its needle-like teeth. "So be it," it barked. "Thou art selected."

The large woman's head was split in two as an

enormous smile divided her face. "You may count on me, oh mouthpiece of the Allpowerful – I shall not fail you." And she leered triumphantly at her coven sisters as though she had beaten them both in some rivalling contest.

"You have still not answered the question," Meta remarked. "Just how will you draw the boy from his home?"

A wheezing laugh issued from the creature's parched lips. "Fear not," it muttered, "the lure will prove too tempting to resist." And it gave a rasping cackle before instructing Miriam in what she would have to do.

* * *

Ben slept fitfully. Images of Nelda interrupted his dreams; horrible visions of the aufwader writhing in pain as her skin bubbled and began to weep salty water. Tarr was at her side and he grasped his granddaughter's liquifying hand whilst shaking his fist at Ben.

"Tha's done this!" he raged. "Her death lies on thee alone. Tha could've lifted the curse but no – tha were weak! A curse on thee, landbreed. May tha rot, Benjamin Laurenson!"

His angry cries were taken up by the rest of the tribe who had gathered behind him and they damned the boy's name with all their might and sorrow.

"Benjamin, Benjamin – Ben."

The boy stirred unhappily. The voices had melted into a single whispering chant and there was no escape from its insistent calling.

Suddenly he was awake and his eyes gazed sleepily up into the darkness.

"Benjamin," the voice breathed again.

Ben's scalp tingled and his heart fluttered. He was

no longer dreaming – yet it was impossible he should hear that familiar voice.

"Benjamin," it said again.

Trembling with fear and excitement, the boy lifted his head from the pillows and stared past the foot of his bed.

With a kind and loving smile traced over her face, a petite figure stood in the centre of the room, watching him adoringly.

Standing in the dim ray of light that slanted through the curtain, a silvery aura flickered about the female form. It shimmered over the curling hair and the clothes she had worn the day she had died, and as a tearful sob burst from Ben's mouth, she raised her hands to him and wept.

"Benjamin," she said again, "don't cry – I'm here."

The boy drew his pyjama sleeve over his streaming eyes and in a joyful voice murmured, "Mum!"

The ghost of his mother looked just the same as he remembered her and she tilted her head to one side to look at him admiringly.

Ben hardly dared to move in case his "visitor" vanished into the ether again.

"I miss you," he eventually cried, "and Dad – Jen does too."

The phantom made no answer but put a finger to her lips and took a step backwards to the open bedroom door, beckoning for him to follow.

Ben hesitated. Once, during a seance that Aunt Alice had held downstairs, he had been frightened by hundreds of spectres and he had no wish to repeat the experience.

A look of understanding passed over Mrs Laurenson's face. "Don't be afraid, Benjamin," she whispered. "I shall be with you."

Reassured, the boy cast back the bedclothes and pulled on his slippers.

"Where are we going?" he asked quietly. "Should I get dressed?"

The shade shook her head and glided through the open door to the gloomy landing beyond.

Ben followed her quickly. His mother was already floating down the stairs as he left his room and he called to her softly.

"Shall I wake Jen?" he asked.

But the glimmering form of Mrs Laurenson made no reply and he hastened after her into the hall.

The front door of the cottage was wide open and the chill night airs filled the ground floor of the normally cosy building and transformed it into an icy tomb-like place. Ben shivered and looked for his mother but she was nowhere to be found.

"Please don't go yet!" he begged. "Please, Mum!"

Then he saw her, waiting for him in the courtyard, bathed in the unearthly glow of the street lamps that flooded through the alleyway.

Quickly Ben pulled his coat from the hook and scurried into the night after her.

Down Church Street the silent ghost led him, and as Ben struggled into his coat a thousand questions burned inside. Yet his mother was always just ahead of him, and though he ran to catch up she seemed to drift before him like a leaf snatched away by the wind.

Along Henrietta Street he hurried, the soles of his slippers slapping over the cobbles, and he clawed his toes to keep them on his feet.

As he ran by Fortune's kipper house, the silvery figure was already waiting by the cliff edge, where the ground dropped steeply down to the crashing waves that now covered the rocky shore. For a few moments his mother remained there, then she moved towards the footbridge that linked the cliff to the stone pier far below.

"Mum, wait!" the boy wept as he saw her disappear down the sloping and narrow pathway.

One of his slippers flew from his feet but Ben did not wait to retrieve it. Over the dry and stubbly grass he ran and leapt on to the wooden boards of the perilously high bridge.

Into engulfing darkness the boy hurtled, dashing headlong down the immense throat of night. Like a huge and impenetrable tunnel it surrounded him, and above and below there was only blackness. No stars pricked the heavens and no light was reflected over the vast open sea. Only a pitchy void lay ahead, except for a single silvery shape that gleamed coldly where the bridge joined the pier.

The sound of the hungry sea rose up from the deep reaches, as though it was eagerly waiting for him to falter and fall the dizzying height to his death. Keeping his thoughts trained solely upon the frosty spectre in the distance, the boy tried to shove all such frightening ideas to the back of his mind, but the relief which bubbled within him once his bare foot touched the cold stone of the pier was overwhelming.

The ghost of his mother smiled at him, then like a flickering will-o'-the-wisp she turned and floated further away.

Ben let out a dismayed whimper. "Please wait!" he wailed. "Wait for me."

Over the huge sandstone slabs he ran, along the old stone spur that jutted defiantly into the sea to shield the harbour of Whitby from the ravages of the merciless waves.

Through the bleak night he raced, forever chasing the shining figure who was always just out of reach.

By the disused lighthouse, where the pier stopped abruptly and the wooden extensions began, the ghost paused and the folds of her clothes swirled about her like the misty shreds of a shimmering fog.

"Oh Benjamin!" she called, turning her face gladly upon him as the boy approached breathlessly. "Now at last I can speak."

Ben panted and leaned against the rail. They were totally cut off from the world now, wrapped up in the darkness of the shadowy sea that stretched around them on all sides, and Whitby seemed a twinkling series of golden stars many miles behind them.

Mrs Laurenson smiled as she looked longingly at her son and hugged herself tightly.

"The grave is an empty place," she muttered with a bleak and ghastly expression forming on her dead lips, "an empty vacuum devoid of light and love. Oh Ben, I have been so lonely – the endless hollow night has swallowed me and desolation is all I know now. In the cold, suffocating earth I have missed you so much my darling, so very, very much."

The boy shuddered and wished she had not told him that. Reaching forward he tried to draw closer for comfort, but the spectre pulled away sharply.

"You cannot touch me," she lamented. "I am only a vapour and if you try then I shall vanish like smoke."

Ben understood and sniffed forlornly. "We've both missed you, Mum," he said. "Jennet's always looking at the photo album."

"Ah, Jennet," the phantom echoed plaintively. "If only my pretty daughter were blessed with the same gift as you. How I long to speak with her and share the things a mother ought to. I know she is unhappy – I see this from beyond the solemn eternity of my mouldering dust. How it grieves me to witness her tears. What sins were mine that I am compelled to suffer this misery in death?"

Ben thrust his hands into the pockets of his coat as the bitter cold that blew from the surrounding sea pinched and chilled him.

"Why have you brought me here?" he asked.

A patient smile spread over his dead mother's face. "The lights of the town confound and dazzle me," she answered, whirling around in a slow circle and staring into the fathomless night. "There are fewer disturbances here, out in the still darkness. When the vibrations are strong they hinder the passage from one world to the next and weaker souls cannot break through."

"But you did."

"I did, yes."

"Oh Mum, I wish you hadn't left us, I wish you and Dad were still alive ..." The tears rolled down Ben's cheeks and the phantom knelt upon the ground, wringing her hands that she could not hug and comfort him.

"Oh Benjamin," she uttered, "listen to me. Do you wish to see your father?"

Ben looked at her hopefully. "Dad?" he cried. "Is Dad here too?"

"Not yet," she said, "but this is where he shall pass through. Here the ether trembles and the veil is but a thin and meagre membrane. If we call to him he will follow our voices."

"Dad!" Ben shouted. "We're here!"

His mother floated forward, over to where the pier railing was buckled and the stone around the steel posts was cracked and hazardous. Orange warning tapes had been strung across the perilous spot like the web of a huge bright spider, but the phantom pointed past them and out into the pitch dark.

"Over here, Benjamin," she said. "That is where he will come through. Call to him now, summon his shade from the insensible grave. Let him know you still love him."

The boy darted to her side and yelled into the blank sky.

Below them the sea churned against the pier wall, sluicing and roaring above the din that Ben was making as he howled for his dead father.

"I can't see anything!" he cried. "Nothing's happening – where is he?"

"Trust me," his mother smiled, "he will come. He has waited so long for this moment – we are both so alone. Where are you, darling? Can you hear me? Our son is here – he desperately wants to see you. Please, for Ben's sake."

The cold wind rushed around her and the ghost reacted as though she had heard an answering voice.

"Yes, my love!" she cried. "I can hear you."

Frantically Ben stared hard at the empty sky but could neither see nor hear anything.

"Was it him?" he wept. "Is he there?"

"Oh yes," she replied, "your father will soon be with us. Look out there. Can you not see the faint mist? He is very close now."

"Where?" Ben cried, pushing against the orange tapes till they stretched and he leaned precariously forward.

"There!" she shrieked. "I see him!"

The tapes snapped and boy held on to the mangled rail to keep from falling, yet still his eyes hunted anxiously for a glimpse of his dead father, oblivious to the awful danger.

Mrs Laurenson stepped aside to let her son have full command of the pier edge and silently she glided behind him.

"Where are you, Dad?" he yelled. "Where are you?"

Beneath his feet the loose stones moved and tiny fragments rattled into the boiling waves below.

A cruel and ruthless smile twisted the phantom's face as she raised her hands.

"Dad!" he screamed. "Dad!"

Suddenly Mrs Laurenson seized Ben by the shoulders and gripped him fiercely.

The boy teetered on the edge, his remaining slipper spun through the night and was snatched into the deep thrashing waters.

"Mum!" he cried, startled and bewildered. "You can touch me ...!"

Her savage fingernails bit through the material of his coat and pierced deep into his skin.

Ben shrieked and struggled to free himself; losing his balance on the terrible brink he almost fell and pulled her with him.

"Mum!" Ben shouted. "What's happening? I don't ... I don't ..."

"Keep still!" the ghost bawled and she slapped him savagely across the face.

Ben yelled in terror as the evil vision of his mother laughed like a demented demon and forced him to look down at the dreadful waters below.

"You're not my mum!" he screamed. "Let go! Let go!"

"That's enough!" she snapped, hitting him brutally over the head. "Be quiet, you little runt," and she hauled him off his feet.

"No!" he cried, lashing out with his hands. "Get off!"

The boy tore at the imposter's clothes and at once the illusion was shattered as the spectre wilted and crumpled.

An expanse of velvety fur slithered to the floor and the towering frame of Miriam Gower was revealed in all her Goliathan and heavy-boned malevolence.

Ben stared in disbelief at the enchanted seal skin that he had wrenched from her. Silvery sparks still glittered over the sleek hide and two blank eyes appeared to stare sadly up at him.

"Into the waters you go!" Miriam snarled, dangling

him over the edge with her ogre-like hands.

Ben clung to the rail and kicked out at her.

"You're the cow in the bookshop!" he spluttered. "You're mad!"

"Oh, I am," she agreed, "but it is an insanity borne of love and devotion. Soon my beloved will return to me and I shall feel his warm embrace and writhe beneath his supple weight."

With her masculine strength, she ripped the boy's hands from the rail and spat in his face.

"They say drowning is an extremely horrific and painful way to die," she gloated, her bright lips gaping in a foul, gratified smile. "How lucky for you that your head will probably be dashed against the wall before your lungs are filled."

Ben glanced at the black water swirling and crashing beneath him. Vainly he clawed at her, but the woman was too strong and with a last snigger, she let him fall.

Ben screamed.

Miriam was thrust aside and a slender hand flashed out.

A sudden pain bit into Ben's neck as the coat tightened and choked him.

A straining shriek bellowed behind and at once the darkness flew over his head and the next the boy knew he was rolling over the stone floor. In a tangled ball, he smashed into the solid bulk of the lighthouse and fell on to his face.

Miriam staggered against the rail and whirled around, incensed at the interference.

"Who's there?" she screeched, the lights of the town sparkling in her eyes and blinding her to the one who had saved her intended victim.

Ben groaned and rubbed the back of his head where it had bumped against the stones. Then he heard laughter.

Miriam was hooting raucously.

"You!" she shrieked, her bosom quivering with scornful mirth. "Get out of my way! How dare you interrupt this! How ..."

Her derision dwindled and was replaced with a terrified squeal. As she rocked with murderous glee, beneath the heels of her feminine yet oversized shoes more of the crumbling brink collapsed and the broken railing was torn from the pier then plunged into the sea.

The woman's petrified scream boomed over the harbour. Too late, the one who had rescued Ben rushed forward to save her. Miriam Gower lost her footing and her imposing frame plumeted backwards.

Down she toppled, her massive arms flailing the night, and a shrill screech blistered from her chest only to be quenched when she hit the waves.

Into the foaming sea the owner of the bookshop crashed and it seized her with vicious greed.

Ben hid his face, and even though his fingers were thrust into his ears he could still hear her frenzied voice howling amid the churning, drowning water. And then there was only the sound of the sea and Miriam Gower had been silenced forever.

Timidly, he opened his eyes and ran over to the brink. But there was no sign of her. Spinning around he searched for the one who had saved him and there, running back towards the town and blurred against the golden lights, he saw a tall figure swathed in black robes. Then the mysterious stranger vanished into the distance, and drained of any further emotion, Ben began to walk back the way he had come.

In the bookshop the fishmonkey let out a frustrated whine and slapped the wooden box angrily.

"Failure!" it raged. "The boy still lives – he lives!"

Hillian looked across at Meta. "Then Miriam ...?" she ventured.

"Dragged into the deeps!" the creature snapped. "Swallowed by the sea! Your coven is useless! You are defeated at every turn! My master did choose unwisely!"

Hillian stared at the empty space where her coven sister had been sitting earlier and touched the necklace about her neck.

"What are we to do now?" she whispered hoarsely.

The fishmonkey lashed out at her. "Only one further time can I aid you!" it snarled. "The boy will be doubly on guard henceforth. The next attempt must not fail – the hand that strikes must be one that he trusts implicitly!"

Ferociously it turned to Meta and pointed an accusing webbed claw at her. "Now the fate of us all lies with thee!" it warned. "You must make certain the girl joins the sisters – she is now the only key to all our goals."

Meta bristled. "At the close of tomorrow," she stated firmly, "the irritating child will be with us."

"May that not be too late!" the creature growled. "For the morrow may bring its own nightmares for us all."

8

THE FLEDGELING

Jennet awoke early but discovered that Miss Wethers had already been up for quite some time and was scuttling from room to room in her panic to be ready for the great occasion later that afternoon.

Her incessant squeaks of indecision brought Miss Boston from her room and she scowled at her old friend. "Do sit down, Edith," she cried as the woman blundered into her a third time.

"I can't!" she whined. "There's so much to do still! Oh Alice, am I doing the right thing? It's such a huge step to take at my time of life."

Miss Boston groaned and settled down to eat her kippers. "Personally I think the man's a complete dunderhead," she muttered, savouring the smoky scent of her breakfast, "but then so are you – you'll make a magnificent couple I'm sure."

When Jennet entered the kitchen Edith pounced on her.

"Have you tried the dress on today?" she simpered. "I think you'd better just to be sure it fits properly."

The girl pouted. "I've only just got up!" she protested. "And I refuse to put that hideous frock on until the last minute."

Aunt Alice waved a fork at her whilst chewing a morsel of kipper. "Now, now," she said, "don't be uncharitable – it is Edith's special day. We must humour her, no matter how aggravating she becomes."

"The cake!" Miss Wethers squawked. "I must nip round to Cicily Drinkwater's to see if it's ready to be taken to the hall."

Miss Boston glanced at the clock. "Isn't it rather early for that, dear?" she asked.

"I've got to do something!" Edith babbled. "Oh, my tummy's all upset – I feel quite quite dreadful."

Jennet buttered a piece of toast and fled the kitchen quickly.

"Where are you going?" Aunt Alice called after her.

"For a walk," she shouted on her way out. "I won't be long."

Hearing the front door close, Miss Boston lay down her knife and fork and clucked wearily. "Really, Edith," she chided, "if you're like this now how will you survive till the afternoon?"

Miss Wethers gave a pathetic whimper then hurried upstairs to make sure her hat was still in the box.

*   *   *

Upon the clifftop, Jennet hurried through the car park and made for the camper van.

"Hello!" she called. "Pear – it's me!"

There was no reply and as she drew up to the cream and orange vehicle she realized that no one was inside.

"They've started early," she mumbled. "They can't be playing already – I'd have heard them."

The girl waited several minutes more then decided to go and find her new friends.

Down the abbey steps she clambered, always

listening for the cheerful melodies of the folk group, but that morning only the seagulls were singing.

Through the lanes and narrow streets she searched, yet there was no sign of the women and Jennet barged through the ranks of early shoppers crossly.

At Market Place she halted and wondered if she ought to wait there – even though it might be hours before the band were scheduled to appear.

Dejected and downcast, she moped around and leaned against the same pillar as the previous day. Staring into Church Street she saw that a queue of disgruntled-looking people were standing outside the bookshop and peering through the window, impatient that it was still not open.

"That fat woman's probably had enough at last," she grumbled to herself.

Turning her head she scanned the other shop fronts; the baker's was busy as always, small children were staring hopefully into the toy shop, the health food store had attracted its usual mix of serious corduroy-covered cranks and intrepid gastronomes. Jennet drew herself up – inside that shop a timorous, purple outline was hovering uncertainly.

"Liz!" she exclaimed, running across the street and darting inside.

Within the dimly-lit premises an aromatic and treacly fragrance rose from the many barrels containing dried and sugared fruits and a warm, nutty smell was drifting from the restaurant at the back. Standing awkwardly by a row of baskets containing dates, sultanas and raisins, the modest figure of the flautist checked the list in her hand and inspected the sweet-scented wares.

Abruptly, the shy woman whisked around when Jennet called her name and a scoop full of raisins fell from her hand in surprise.

"Mornin'," she greeted the girl, casting her eyes down to the floor.

"Do you know where Pear is?" Jennet asked.

The woman fidgeted with one of the strings of beads around her neck and shifted uneasily. "No," she burbled under her breath, "she left early."

"To look round town?"

"Don't know."

Jennet thought it best to let her resume her bashful, mouse-like shopping. "I'll see if I can find her then," she said moving towards the entrance.

Furtively, the woman shambled over to the window as the girl disappeared down the street and a secretive, coy smile appeared on her freckle-covered face.

When she had scoured the whole of the East Cliff and satisfied herself that her new friend was nowhere to be found, Jennet crossed the swing bridge and searched along the quayside.

Midday approached relentlessly and having roamed the steep lanes from Baxtergate to Pannett Park without seeing any sign of Pear, the girl began to make her way home.

Meandering through the oddly-named Khyber Pass she emerged by the bandstand and rambled along the Pier Road. A colourful multitude of tourists were enjoying the sun, tucking into doughnuts and ice-creams and feeding the slot-machines in the buzzing amusement arcades. Idly, Jennet continued to peer around her as she headed homeward but it was no use.

And then, when she was wandering down Marine Parade, she saw a strikingly tall woman whose cream and golden hair blazed in the noonday sun as she sauntered through the countless, goggling men.

Pear's mother wore a scarlet kaftan embroidered with dandelion-yellow silks. She walked with an accomplished swing of the hips and her head tossed from side to side laughing at the silly faces that turned to feast their eyes on her.

"Hey, Jennet!" Meta hailed waving a hand and jangling her many bracelets.

The girl hurried towards her and as the crowds parted, she stopped and stared at the animal that padded by the woman's side.

Restrained upon the tightest of leads, Meta had by her a magnificent jet-black dog with a panting pink tongue and round brown eyes that rolled in their sockets as Jennet came forward. The beast's shaggy tail wagged immediately and it pulled on the leash, rearing on to its hind legs whilst pawing at the air with the others.

Jennet took a step back warily.

"Down Seff!" Meta commanded, yanking on the leash until the dog yelped and slammed its head against her leg. "Don't worry," she told the girl, "Seffy won't bite – just needs to be taught obedience."

"May I stroke her?" Jennet asked.

"Of course. Seffy's a soppy thing – a bit too much so, in my opinion."

Jennet knelt down and scratched the animal behind the ears. The tail thrashed madly and it pushed its snout forward to lick her face despite the collar which cut into the muscles of its throat.

"Poor thing," Jennet cried, "the collar's too tight!"

Meta gave a tug on the lead that dragged the dog from Jennet's hands and smacked it smartly across the glistening nose. "The brute needs to learn," she said. "It must be trained properly."

Jennet flinched at her treatment of the animal but she bit her tongue and groped for something else to say. "I didn't see it at the van yesterday," she eventually uttered.

"Oh, Seffy isn't ours," Meta grinned. "Oh no – she belongs to a friend here. Unfortunately he is unable to give her the exercise she really requires, so whenever possible I do what I can. But you're right, she is a fine specimen and with such an impressive pedigree that it would astonish you."

Jennet's eyebrows twitched uneasily as an uncomfortable doubt tingled and nagged at the back of her mind. No, whatever it was she could not recall it.

"Do you know where Pear is?" she asked.

Meta tossed back her head and stared across at the East Cliff. "Isn't she over there?" she declared. "I thought she went out with Liz and Caroline this morning to do some shopping."

"I've looked there, and Liz hasn't seen her – I haven't bumped into Caroline."

"Oh, she's probably in the library. Caroline loves a good book."

"But what about Pear?"

Meta shrugged. "If she's not with her then I don't know. I am certain that she will be back at the van by four o'clock this afternoon however. Is that a help?"

"Can I come round then?"

"Of course you can, honey, you'll always be welcome amongst our little group. Look, I'm just going down on to the beach to give Seffy her exercise. Do you want to join us?"

Jennet declined. She was not sure about this flamboyant woman, and though the prospect of throwing sticks for Seffy appealed to her she knew that a more pressing appointment was waiting.

"I can't," she said. "I've got a wedding to go to, but as soon as I've escaped from it I'll see you at the camper."

" 'Escaped'?" Meta roared with laughter. "How very amusing! Oh yes, that's what marriage is all about – an institution to flee from. Ha ha ha! So droll!"

Jennet had no idea why the woman was laughing, but as usual the performance was too loud and too long.

"I ... I'll be off then," the girl muttered.

Meta calmed herself and with a flourish waved her farewell. "Till later, my pet!" she called and spun on her heel dragging the dog closely by her side.

Jennet watched them trail on to the sands but instead of letting the animal off the leash once they had left the road behind them, Meta kept it pulled on a tighter rein than ever.

"Some exercise!" Jennet observed and then her brow creased into a frown as she realized what had troubled her before.

"How come Meta knows Seffy's owner and takes her for walks? She said she'd never been to Whitby before!"

* * *

That afternoon the happiest woman in the entire world was Mrs Edith Adams. In the space of twenty minutes all her years of loneliness were finally dispelled and she emerged from the registry office flushed and excited – content and overjoyed for the first time in her life.

"Congratulations, the pair of you!" Miss Boston chuckled leaning on only the one walking stick.

With her arm linked in that of her husband, Edith waggled her hand and let the ring sparkle on her finger. "I can't believe it!" she squealed. "Oh Conway!"

The doctor gave his wife a gentle squeeze and kissed her on the cheek.

"Jubilation!" gushed Sister Frances as she stomped

gawkily up to them. "Simply top class ceremony, who would have thought it? You two really are an inspiring lesson to us all."

The new Mrs Adams was not sure how to take this. "I beg your pardon?" she twittered.

"I mean to say," the nun gabbled on, "if people of your senior years can tie the knot then it gives hope to everyone – doesn't it, Miss B?"

Both Edith and Miss Boston looked away from the tactless and absurd nun.

"Come now, Frances," a small woman with tiny black button eyes broke in with an apologetic cough. Peeking over the rims of her spectacles she gave her charge a belligerent look and led her out of harm's way.

"Oh Mother Superior," Frances suggested, "can we pop in to the bunfight? I do so love a party!"

"You most certainly cannot!" was the indignant reply. "Have you forgotten the last party you gatecrashed? I refuse to let you anywhere near the place!"

Sister Frances grumbled under her breath and buried her chin into her chest sulkily. "Rotten old killjoy," she murmured.

Clutching her bouquet, Edith peered round for the children and squeaked for them to stop hiding and have their photograph taken.

Without saying a word, Ben left his hiding place behind a plump woman in a navy blue dress and stepped forward.

The boy had said nothing of his horrific experience the night before. It had all been so eerie and bizarre that he had difficulty believing it himself and tried not to bring the memory of Miriam Gower's drowning screams to the forefront of his mind.

At that moment, however, his cheeks were rosy and pink, having been pinched and tweaked by all the cotton-gloved and behatted ladies who had flocked to the wedding. Cooing and pecking at him they shrilly pronounced that he was "as cute as can be" and ruffled his hair after planting their dry, beaky lips upon his shrinking forehead.

The lamentable outfit which elicited these unwanted attentions consisted of a frilly white shirt, silver-buckled shoes and, worst of all, a kilt that was too short. Glassy-eyed and not daring to look too closely at the amused crowd which had gathered before the steps of the registry office, he assumed a fixed expression for the photographer and wished the ground would open up.

Jennet was having similar difficulties. Not only had Edith made her wear the most hideous dress ever to be rejected from a doll factory, the ghastly woman had also compelled her to tie a massive pink ribbon in her hair.

Aunt Alice looked at them both and shook her woolly head at what her friend had done to them. "Perhaps I should have interceded," she chortled. "Oh well, it's too late now."

The confetti rained down like pastel-coloured snow and with a mad impulse to conform to old traditions, Mrs Adams swung her arms and flung the bouquet over her shoulder.

"Great heavens!" a startled and delighted voice cried. "How simply spiffing! Look, everyone!"

Blushing a deep crimson, the Mother Superior gazed to heaven for divine strength as Sister Frances twirled the bouquet above her head in gleeful triumph.

When the hired car departed to take the newlyweds to the reception, Jennet unravelled the ribbon from her hair and walked over to Aunt Alice.

"Quite unnecessary!" the old lady commented, watching the car turn the corner. "The place is only two hundred yards from here!"

Jennet nibbled her lip nervously. "I don't feel very well," she lied, holding her stomach.

"You poor dear," Aunt Alice cried, putting her arm about her. "Probably nerves, added to the fact you haven't eaten much today. No doubt you'll feel much better with a bridge roll and some tinned salmon inside you."

"I couldn't," the girl refused. "I really would like to just go home and lie down."

"But the reception!"

"I know. I'm sorry, apologize for me."

Miss Boston gazed intently at her and the girl averted her eyes. "Would you like me to accompany you?" she asked kindly. "I never did care for fruit-cake, and cheap champagne always gives me wind."

"No you must go!" Jennet cried. "I mean, she's one of your oldest friends – how would it look?"

"Yes!" Ben piped up behind them. "I don't want to miss the food!"

"Very well," Aunt Alice consented, "if you're sure you'll be all right, Jennet dear?"

" 'Course I will."

"Come then, Benjamin, would you care to escort this old spinster to the function that awaits us?"

Jennet lingered until they had departed, the old lady barely leaning on the walking stick and her brother holding her free hand – his silver buckles winking as he walked.

When they were out of sight, Jennet checked her watch and hurried off in the opposite direction.

Straight up the one hundred and ninety-nine steps she hurried, the voluminous folds of her pink satin dress tangling around her knees and tripping her up many times before she reached the summit.

Pear was sitting on a stool outside the camper van

when the girl came rushing from the cemetery. The spectacle of this bright, fluttering apparition brought her leaping to her feet and doubling in two with laughter.

"Which Christmas tree did you fall off?" she wept. "Have you seen yourself?"

"Don't be horrible," Jennet blurted, leaning against the van. "I'm supposed to be a bridesmaid."

"Who got married, Mr and Mrs Candyfloss?"

The girls giggled and Jennet threw herself upon the grass. "With any luck the foul frock'll turn green," she sighed. "I looked for you this morning."

Pear tore a clump of weeds from the soil. "I know," she muttered, "Meta told me."

"Where did you get to?"

"Oh ... just around."

"Well, I couldn't find you."

"Hey!" Pear cried. "I bought you a present."

"A present? For me? What is it?"

The girl foraged inside the van and brought out a small brown paper parcel.

Jennet took it and gave her a puzzled look. "Smells like old Hot Cross Buns," she said, "and it's all crumbly."

"It's Henna."

"What's that for?"

Pear flashed a mischievous grin. "I'm going to colour your hair."

Jennet put the packet on the ground. "Oh, I don't know ..." she demurred.

"Don't be boring," the other insisted. "You were only saying yesterday how you wanted to change your life – this is a beginning. The power of change is within us all but only the truly free know how and dare to use it."

"Yes, but to dye my hair ..."

"Don't worry, it'll wash out."

And so the two spent a hilariously messy afternoon. First they mixed the henna powder into a thick paste and daubed it over Jennet's hair, massaging it well into her scalp. But much of the gritty stuff went astray as they larked about and flicked it at one another and it was not long before the pink satin dress was speckled and stained a ruddy brown.

When the other members of the folk band returned, they found Jennet with her clogged hair plastered flat against her scalp and hanging in dripping hanks about her shoulders like seaweed.

All of the women were pleased to see her and Meta teasingly remarked that Jennet was like a caterpillar in a cocoon and she was impatient to see the butterfly that would emerge.

When it was time, Pear poured a pan of water over her friend's head to rinse out the henna and Jennet dried her hair with a towel, then borrowed a brush from Meta.

The women sat down around her and looked on the transformed girl with sincere admiration.

"You look a hundred times better," Meta told her. "What a difference – quite like 'The Ugly Duckling'."

"Don't listen to her," Pear said. "You were never ugly. Meta's just scared you'll be prettier than she is."

"Mm," Liz nodded, "very nice."

Jennet drew her fingers through her hair and longed to see how she appeared. "Have you a mirror?" she asked.

"Only the ones on the van," Meta answered. "Go, take a peep – see what you think."

Jennet rose and walked apprehensively to the side of the camper. Crouching, she gazed into the wing mirror and stared at the image within.

She hardly recognized the face that looked out at her. The henna had inflamed a lustrous, coppery fire in her drab dark hair and when it moved the rich colours rippled and gleamed. Jennet could not believe the change, she seemed older and more assured and after staring at the reflection for several minutes, she whirled around and gave Pear a delighted hug.

"It's better than I ever hoped!" she cried. "I even feel different. It's marvellous, thank you!"

Caroline took her fiddle from the van and as the others complimented the girl, began to play a gentle melody.

"I predict that our fledgeling is going to blossom into a great beauty quite soon," Meta crooned. "What a frightening woman she will be. Imagine all those hearts that will turn to her – will she spurn them and be a cold destroyer of men? Or will she have one great passion in her life and be dominated totally by it – forsaking all else and consumed utterly by its ravaging flames? Which would you prefer?"

Jennet sniggered. "I shall choose only millionaires," she told them gravely, "and make them buy me lots of expensive jewellery."

"Jewels for M'lady Jennet!" Pear announced and she removed from around her neck several long strings of glass beads. "There you are, your ladyship, your crown jewels."

Jennet swung them round in her fingers and looked haughtily from side to side. "Not forgetting lovely clothes," she added.

From the van Pear brought a sequin-covered shawl and wrapped it around her friend's neck. "There you are, Your Highness – cloth of gold from the far-off Indies."

"But what will you do if his wealth runs out?" Meta asked. "Will you stay by your bankrupt millionaire and sell all your finery?"

"No chance!" Jennet answered. "I shall leave him and find another."

"How deliciously wicked," Meta purred, "but what about love? Millionaires are always fat and bald and their breath stinks of cigars – you must have a paramour."

"A what?"

"A lover of course – the special one to whom you always return and who visits your dreams."

The smile faded from Jennet's face, and she pulled the shawl from her shoulders. "I don't think so," she muttered. "I did think that at one time perhaps – but I was stupid. It was only infatuation, a silly crush and besides, he was a horrid man."

Meta smiled disarmingly. "Why are we drawn to the wrong men?" she drawled. "It's never the reliable and faithful ones – always the beasts who treat us like dirt. Bewitched moths to brutal flames, that's what we are."

She stretched like a feline and took a deep breath. "It's another ravishing evening," she remarked, "and there just happens to be another bottle of wine waiting to be opened. Would you like a glass, Jennet?"

The girl hesitated.

Meta watched her and put her hand to her brow, peering around the van as if searching for something. "I may be wrong," she said, "but I don't think there are any stray nuns on the horizon. You're perfectly safe, child – or did that overgrown penguin make you sign the pledge? Do you think you have to be saved from our terrible influence?"

"No," Jennet rallied, "I'd love a drink."

It was not long before they all held a glass of wine in their hands and Meta led them in a toast.

"To the flowering of our new friend," she declared. "May her tinted tresses be but the first of many changes in her young and vital life."

To prove that she didn't care what Sister Frances or

anyone else had to say, Jennet took a great gulp of the wine and pulled the shawl over her shoulders once more.

Gradually the rest of the women took up their instruments and joined Caroline in the wonderfully soothing tune. Jennet listened to them happily but the sound was so enchanting that it began to lull her senses and before long she was yawning and blinking.

"I'm sorry," she apologized, "it's been a long day – what with the wedding and every ... oh dear, I am tired."

The women smiled at her and continued to make the melodious music until the battle to keep her eyes open grew more and more hopeless for the girl and, in the end, the incredible weariness overcame her.

Without warning, Jennet fell back on to the grass and lay as still as death.

Pear leaned over her and gently pushed one eye open. The pupil was large and stared unflinchingly upwards.

"Has it worked?" Meta asked, putting her concertina down.

Pear nodded, "Yes," she said sorrowfully, "she's out cold."

"Then let us go at once!" her mother hissed to the others.

Immediately, Liz and Caroline ceased playing and as one they rose to put their instruments into the camper van.

"Now pick up the girl," Meta told them, "and put her inside."

"Carefully!" Pear added.

"Just be quick!" snapped Meta, glancing warily around the car park.

Hastily, Jennet was bundled into the vehicle and when the two women had climbed in after, Meta pulled the large side door shut with a loud slam and hurried to the front where she jumped into the driver's seat.

"Pear!" she called. "Get in!"

Her daughter had wandered to the cliff edge and hardly heard her.

"What is it?" Meta barked. "Hurry! We must waste no time!"

Reluctantly Pear clambered in beside her. "Did you hear it?" she asked.

"Hear what?"

"The music. It was unlike any I have ever … you must have heard it. It was floating up from the shore far below – it was so sad."

Meta sneered. "Those loathsome wading creatures!" she spat. "They must have assembled and begun already. Now there is no time to be lost – your annoying little friend must be initiated tonight!"

Pear wriggled on her seat to look into the back of the van and gazed thoughtfully at Jennet.

"You won't hurt her, will you?"

Meta turned the key in the ignition and grappled with the gear stick. "Don't bother about her!" she shouted above the splutter of the engine. "Fill your mind with our great cause. What is she to you? Just some fool of a girl the High Priest hardly gave thought to!"

Pear stared glumly out of the window and with a lurch, the camper van lumbered from the car park and sped down Abbey Lane, leaving Whitby far behind.

9

THE BRIDES
OF CROZIER

With his fist wrapped tightly about his staff, Tarr stood stiffly upon the rocky shore, his wind-burned countenance grim and resolute. Gathered around him in a large semi-circle that faced the outgoing tide, the rest of the tribe were sitting upon boulders and gazing in subdued silence at the impassive leaden sea.

Every face was set and grave, for that night was a solemn and melancholy occasion and their hearts quailed within their breasts when they thought of what their leader had taken upon himself to do.

The aufwaders were dressed in ceremonial finery and even the older members had washed and scrubbed themselves until their leathery and lined skin glowed ruddily. Beards had been brushed free of twig and shell and all heads were bare in honour of the expected guest.

At her grandfather's side, Nelda had clothed herself in the bridal dress she had worn when Esau had claimed her, but now the blue-green garment was tight about her middle and the stitches gaped at the seams of the richly-embroidered fabric.

With a heaviness of spirit, she looked around at the

213

other fisherfolk but drew no comfort from their sombre faces.

"We waste our time, grandfather," she said hopelessly. "The Triad beneath the sea will not choose to hear us. Why should they after all this time and the cries of every mother who has gone before me?"

Tarr's bristly eyebrows knitted together and a fierce scowl creased over his face. "They'll hear me, reet enough!" he snarled, glancing up at the darkening sky. "The hour grows near – the moon is rising."

Low over the horizon, the round disc of the full moon appeared faint in the fading blue of the evening and at a signal from Tarr the aufwaders began to sing.

Very faintly at first, each of the fisherfolk commenced the chant. They were old words handed down from mother to son, a song that stretched back into the early days of the Earth when the many tribes crowded the shoreline and dealt freely with the three powers of the waking world. Not once in living memory had the remaining aufwaders assembled to perform the litany, but it was so deeply anchored within their being that no one faltered and the words of the ancient chorus rose before the cliffs, borne upon the twilight breeze.

Only Tarr and Nelda remained silent, and as the dirge-like music burgeoned about them they stared resolutely out to sea.

Early stars pricked through the cobalt sky which grew gradually dimmer until the shore beneath the cliffs became swamped in a dismal gloom. Yet still the funereal chant continued and as the moon climbed higher, Tarr beckoned to Eurgen Handibrass who was crouched at the front of the semi-circle and the elderly aufwader rose creakily to his feet. In his gnarled hands he carried a bulky object covered by a cloth of fine muslin decorated with intricate embroidery and, treading carefully, he took it over to the leader of the tribe.

Eurgen bowed and uncovered the sacred artefact that he bore. There in his hands was the ceremonial conch. Its lustrous interior mirrored and revelled in the bright silver moonlight, reflecting a pearly sheen up into Tarr's unwavering face.

Staunchly, he received the shell from Eurgen and curled his fingers about its smooth surface.

Raising it above his head he held the conch aloft and in a bold and authoritative voice called out, "Behold the Horn o' the Deep! Ever has it summoned the herald o' the mighty Triad and let this night be no exception! Yet ah would'na call down their fury on any save messen – fer the sake of my son's bairn I call to them this neet and if wrath is all they offer then let it fall on me alone!"

Throughout this stout, defiant speech the fisherfolk had continued to sing and showed their approval of his actions by rocking to and fro. Even Old Parry joined them in this, for the time had indeed come when all resentments must be put aside. Her cracked voice chanted loudly as Tarr put the great shell to his lips and blew.

A single blaring, sonorous note blasted over the waves. Nelda's grandfather had never sounded the conch before but now he put all his strength into that one bugling roar. Every pent-up bitter memory, every wretched and grief-filled fear was poured from his soul and hurled in a tormented scream out under the stars.

When his lungs were spent and long after Tarr had given the shell back to Eurgen, the awful, piercing note continued to echo and ricochet around the encircling seas and he put his trembling arm around Nelda's shoulders.

"What now?" she murmured.

"We wait, lass."

The hours deepened. The heavenly field of stars blazed with glacial fires in the velvet blackness, and soaring high above at the pinnacle of its ascent, the cream-coloured moon radiated an ethereal splendour over the slumbering world.

Upon the shore, the aufwaders had grown silent and a small number, goaded by Old Parry, began to complain that they were wasting their time – the Deep Ones had ignored the age-old summons.

Sitting on the ground, with his granddaughter asleep in his arms, Tarr kept his weary eyes trained upon the darkness, where the far distant rim of the sea had faded into night. The damp slowly crept into his bones but he made no movement to ease his discomfort and, like a figure rendered in stone, remained silent and motionless.

And then his fatigue disappeared and the hope which had dwindled to cold ash inside him revived.

"Nelda!" he cried, shaking his granddaughter. "Look! Behold, all of yer! See what glimmers yonder!"

The tribe stirred and raised their dozing heads at this excited outburst.

Upon the invisible horizon a tiny pulse of light gleamed, sailing ever nearer out of the darkness towards the shore.

" 'Tis the herald!" Tarr yelled. "He comes! At last he comes!"

Everyone staggered to their feet and waited with refreshed vigour as the dim glow drifted closer, and only those with the sharpest sight could discern its origin.

A small rowing boat was floating over the water, at its prow a lantern swung gently and its pendulous beams threw a sweeping blue light over the craft's single occupant.

The herald of the Deep Ones was a hunched and hooded figure, whose cloaked form remained motionless throughout the long journey to the water's edge.

"Grandfather," Nelda whispered, "what if he has only come to scorn us and cast a further doom upon our heads?"

"Dinna tha fright so," he muttered. "Ah've a bargain to strike wi' thattun," and he patted the flap of the satchel that was strung over his shoulders.

Steadily an uncanny, unseen force propelled the wooden vessel through the waves, and when it was just in reach of the shore, the boat drifted to an abrupt halt.

The huddled form within the boat made no move but Nelda could feel that it was staring straight at her, glaring at her swollen stomach, and she caught the briefest glimpse of a glittering cluster of eyes beneath that deep, sea-green cowl.

Leaning upon his staff, Tarr strode to the edge of the tide and raised his hand in dignified salutation.

"Ah welcome thee, most noble guest," he began, reciting the courteous words of greeting, "as sole leader of the aufwader race, the keeper of the ..."

"Peace, Tarr Shrimp," interrupted an unearthly, strident voice from the depths of the herald's hood. "Thou art known unto me and so too the plight of thy bantling. Hearken to me now, for the pleas and entreaties which bite at thine tongue are known also to my masters. Thou wouldst beseech of them mercy and compassion – is that not so?"

"It is," Tarr gruffly answered, "an' ah will'na be ..."

"Speak no more," the herald commanded, "but know this – well do the rulers of the fathomless waters comprehend thy despairings and well also the weight of the curse that has hounded thy kind unto near destruction. But no pleas or entreaties shall they hear."

"They must!" Tarr demanded, and he dragged from the satchel a strange and hideous object. It was a carving wrought in jet, depicting a cruel and evil serpent that twisted about the trident symbol of the Deep Ones.

Nelda stared at it in horror. "The Guardian!" she cried. "Grandfather – no!"

"Aye!" he bellowed, and fiercely shook the carving at the figure in the rowing boat. "Tha knows well enough what this be! Irl did make this in the distant long ago – afore thy masters dragged him into the drink! 'Tis this which keeps the dreaded worm tethered in slumber beneath the cliffs."

The herald stirred and the many eyes gleamed out at the last Guardian of Whitby. "I know it," the voice rang, only now it was laced with sorrow, "and too well. Why show the precious thing to me?"

"Because if'n thy black-hearted masters are set on letting my gran'child and her bairn perish, then by all that's deadly ah'll take this bauble an' dash it to bits wi' mine own hands."

"Even knowing the cost of such rashness?"

"Aye! Let Morgawrus awake again – ah'll not weep fer it. That unholy devil is the only threat the Deep Ones fear – an to make them quake, theer ain't nowt ah wouldna do!"

Nelda gripped his hands. "You wouldn't!" she implored him. "Oh Grandfather, it would destroy everything!"

Grimly Tarr gazed down at her. "Without 'ee, lass, ah dinna care about owt else."

The hooded figure turned and stared out to the blackness of the sea as if communing in thought with his powerful lords. When he returned his gaze to the fisherfolk he said bitterly to Tarr, "Unwisely dost thou gamble. To incur the wrath of the Most High is a rash and perilous game – I would beg of thee to renounce thy impudent threat and repent swiftly."

"Nivver!"

"Then this am I instructed to tell thee – not thy voice alone shall the Lords of the Deep and Dark hear."

The aufwaders murmured to one another and Tarr peered curiously at the herald, wondering what he was up to. "Who else then?" he cried. "For as leader ah'm the tongue o' the tribe; the Deep Ones need listen only to me."

But the figure in the boat ignored him. "Two voices shall they hearken to!" it exclaimed. "Thine and one other."

Tarr scowled doubtfully. "Then who else?" he asked.

The herald leaned forward. "Despite the prime laws which were given unto thee," he muttered, "thy race hath mingled with the landbreed and one of their number is known to thee."

"Ben," Nelda whispered.

"I speak not of the human child, but the aged female who dwells with him. Only when she – Alice Boston – stands upon this shore shall the Lords of the Deep and Dark hearken to thy pleas, Tarr Shrimp."

Nelda's grandfather narrowed his eyes suspiciously. He could sense that the herald was withholding something, yet he had no choice other than to obey him. Turning, he looked at the rest of the fisherfolk and called to Old Parry.

"Tha knows wheer the Boston lives?"

"What if I do?" the crone answered.

"Get thissen over theer now – and be quick."

Parry sniffed but thought better of the viperish words she wanted to spit at him. The herald was staring in her direction and before this agent of the

Deep Ones her vinegary spirit was utterly quelled. Without grumbling another word, she set off towards the town and was soon lost in the silvery shadows of the moon-glimmering night.

* * *

Jennet let out a dismal moan. Her head was swimming and felt as though it was filled with squiggling tadpoles. Blearily she opened her eyes but found herself enveloped in a fuzzy darkness in which she floated dizzily, and a drunken titter issued from her lips.

Through the hazy gloom, she groped with her fingers, touching the cold linoleum of the camper's floor and the low cupboards to her right. She was lying upon a narrow, padded seat, and when she reached out further with her hand, the girl rolled off and collapsed in an undignified bundle between a suitcase and a cardboard box containing groceries. Jennet giggled and spent the next few moments waiting for her claustrophobic world to stop spinning and snap into dim focus.

Alone inside the van she remained still as her drugged mind drifted in a groggy fog and then, gradually, she became aware of voices.

Filtering through her clouded senses the sounds were indistinct and distorted. Jennet listened in blank amusement to the weird warbling and smiled stupidly as she tried to clamber back to the seat. After falling headlong into the box and splitting a bag of lentils, she hauled herself up and pressed her nose flat against the side window.

Outside the camper van was a wild and barren unearthly landscape which in the bright moonlight appeared all the more ghostly and desolate. Cut off from the rest of the living world, it was a lonely waste of rolling moorland, where the very skeleton of the earth projected from the soil as outcrops of cold and immovable stone.

Jennet's distracted and wandering thoughts briefly pondered on the mysterious and melancholy place. Nowhere could she see any sign of civilization, no friendly lights glittered in the distance and only those low and garbled murmurings disturbed the eerie stillness. It was a sepulchral isolation where ancient terrors might lurk beneath the undisturbed heathered hills and go stalking through the forbidding night.

Then she realized that she was not alone. Indistinct shapes were moving in the pools of deep shadow and the girl watched the figures drowsily. They were as busy as ants, absorbed in the building of a tall wooden framework in a level clearing a safe distance away from the camper.

Jennet grinned – the people did look silly. They were dressed in loose-fitting robes of billowing black and she waved gleefully as one of them paused and stared across at the face framed in the van window.

Purposefully the figure strode towards the vehicle and when it drew close, Jennet saw that it was Pear.

"Hah!" Jennet honked, as the side door was heaved open. "What are you supposed to be?"

Pear smiled at her. "I'm glad you're finally awake," she said kindly. "You do like me, don't you, Jennet?"

The girl sniggered. "Sure," she nodded, "you're my best friend."

"Good," Pear responded. "That's good, because you're mine too and friendship's a marvellous, unexpected thing for me. You're not afraid, are you? There's nothing to worry about."

"'Course not. Oh, but I've spilled lentils all over the floor."

"That's all right. Now just remember nobody's going to hurt you. In fact, at the end of tonight we'll be sisters."

The drugged girl sighed. "I'd love a sister," she burbled, "someone like you."

"Do you want to come out of the van now? Come join us."

Taking her by the hand, Pear led Jennet over the springy ground towards the others.

Jennet plodded after her, throwing her head back to squint up at the vast expanse of the starry heavens. "It's so big!" she cried. "Look how big the sky is – wow, it's huge! Aren't the stars enormous and bright out here?"

She looked at her companion and then beyond to the figures building the near-completed timber structure.

"Pear! Pear!" she chuckled. "That's the one who wears the posh clothes in the nicknack shop – and there's the miserable Neugent thing from the café. Don't know those other two! Oh look! There's Meta and Caroline and Liz – coooeee!"

As she staggered past them, every one of the robed women smiled at Jennet and warmly greeted her with words of welcome.

The girl laughed, they seemed so serious, but it was all so ludicrous and she exploded uncontrollably – pointing at their poker-straight faces and earnest sobriety.

With her fake smile withering from her face, Meta stepped next to Hillian. "I can't believe this idiot is the one hope we have left!" she muttered impatiently.

"Be quiet," Hillian hissed at her. "She have enough wit to be performing the part set out for her."

Standing before the tall, finished bonfire, Jennet swayed woozily and clung on to Pear. "This is funny," she babbled, "so very, very funny."

"That's right," Pear confirmed, "it's only a daft dream. Just remember that none of this is real."

Hillian clapped her hands together for attention and ushered the others to form a circle.

Around the bonfire the women gathered, their obedient faces turned towards Hillian Fogle, their acting High Priestess.

"Pear," Jennet gurgled, "look, I'm wearing that horrible bridesmaid dress, hah, hah! You'd think I could think up something better, wouldn't you? Why haven't I got one of those groovy black numbers like the rest of you?"

Meta threw her an irritated glance but Jennet was too giddy to take any notice.

Hillian grinned indulgently then stepped into the circle. "Sisters!" she called suddenly. "Tonight we are being assembled together for the first time in many months and a griefing commemoration it is also. Another of our sisterhood did pass over last night. Miriam Gower – is lost to us. Thus are we only eight in number – first we lose Roselyn, then Judith Deacon, little Susie betrayed our cause and now Miriam. She will be very much missed."

The expressions on the women's faces displayed no outward sign that they mourned for the owner of the bookshop. In fact one of the two that Jennet did not recognize had difficulty suppressing a glad smile.

"Yet," Hillian continued, "we must never despair, for this night a new sister is to be joining us. She is already halfway to being one of our dwindling number – for when *he* was alive she was in truth known to him. The priest's charm was on her and is even now still at work within her soul."

Spinning around, Hillian raised her arm and pointed directly at Jennet.

"Greetings, sister!" she declared loudly. "Welcome, Jennet!"

Suddenly the other women, including Pear, began to chant Jennet's name, repeating it over and over with fervent intensity.

Spluttering with mirth, the girl fell against her friend. "Hellooo," she sang back at them.

"Everyone here," Hillian shouted above the chanting, "does share a common bond – a shared devotion that is uniting us all and makes us strong. When the coven is assembled nothing is beyond our grasping, no one can be safe from our glorious purpose."

"So mote it be!" everyone yelled. "So mote it be! So mote it be!"

Hillian walked over to Jennet and took her head in her hands. Then she bent forward and kissed the girl's brow.

"Does your heart not still long for *his* embrace?" she asked. "Even as we, did you not love him with each gramme of your body and was there nothing you would not have done in *his* exalted name?"

She gestured at the other members of the coven who were all breathless with mounting excitement, and even the painfully shy and timid Liz was flushed and eager with anticipation.

"See, their hearts already beat the faster just to think of *him*. We are all tethered to that most gratifying and unparalleled man. By blood and by soul are we his and the delicious shackles of his influence are felt even beyond the grave. Never shall we forsake his memory and always shall he protect us."

Jennet blinked at her. The effects of the drug that had been put into the glass of wine were beginning to wear off. The girl sagged against Pear as she pressed her fingers to her temples and the turgid, obliterating mists of drunkenness started to disperse.

"This is the collar of the sisterhood," Hillian proclaimed, holding up a string of wooden African beads. "By this mark are the brides of Crozier known and under its restraint were we kept in check by his governing hand. Yoked to him, subjugated to his will, enslaved to his bidding."

The other women reached to their throats and pulled down the black robes to reveal identical necklaces which each of them wore, and Jennet gaped at them in dumb bewilderment.

With great ceremony, Hillian lifted the threaded string high over Jennet's head and fastened it about her neck.

The girl grimaced – the necklace was uncomfortably tight.

"Now be the new link in *his* impenitent chain," Hillian called, and with the nail of her thumb, she scored a small circle in the soft skin of Jennet's throat.

"Now you are his forever!" the woman declared and she whirled round to face the others. "The initiate is joined!" she cried. "Coven of the Black Sceptre, we have a new sister – our number is grown to nine again!

At this, the witches cheered and they hailed Jennet as one of them.

Pear squeezed her friend's hand. "Now we are sisters," she said, kissing her upon the cheek.

Jennet grunted. Her head was throbbing and she stared about her with a growing sense of unease and fear. What madness was this? The nonsensical dream was becoming a waking nightmare.

Hillian returned to her place between Liz and Gilly Neugent and nodded to Meta.

Pear's mother stepped forward with a box of matches and crouched before the bonfire. At the first attempt, a heap of dry bracken flared into flame and soon the whole of the wooden framework was leaping with yellow fire.

Jennet backed away from the scorching heat but Pear's guiding arm drew her back and the girl gazed at the faces of the other witches, unable to understand what they were all doing here.

The eyes of every woman were filled with the reflection of the flames, and the sizzling light shone red and gold over their excited faces, making them appear unclean and depraved. With frenzied and feverish expectation, they stared deep into the bonfire's crackling heart and began to murmur to themselves a name that they relished, a name that brought intense pleasure – the name of their cruel and magnificent master.

"*Nathaniel*," they whispered, "*Nathaniel, Nathaniel.*"

"No!" Jennet cried as finally the vile truth dawned and a sickening horror swept over her. "This isn't happening!"

She pulled her hand from Pear's grip but the older girl caught hold of her again.

"Don't be afraid!" Pear assured her. "You're one of us now. Come – dance with us around the flames."

As the other witches began to move about the bonfire with slow and careful steps, Pear pulled Jennet after them. Nathaniel's name was still pouring from their mouths and gradually the whispering mounted as the movements grew swifter until everyone was shouting at the top of their voices.

"Let me go!" Jennet begged.

Pear tugged and dragged her, spinning the girl in the terrible reeling dance. Around and around the roasting fire she stumbled, the passionate shrieks of the others deafening and terrifying her.

"Relax," Pear cried, "this is your great chance! You said you wanted to change your life – well, this is it! This is the ultimate freedom. Nathaniel has given us the means of our deliverance. We can cast aside the cares of this miserable world and unleash the full ferocity of our inner selves. That dark corner which we keep hidden and secret can be embraced and released."

"No," Jennet implored, "stop this!"

Pear laughed. "Don't struggle," she told her, "seize hold of your destiny and run beneath the moon with me. Come tear through the grass and bound over the moors."

"Never! You're all raving mad!"

As though attuned to the essence of the bonfire, the witches were now leaping like tongues of flame. Their heavy black robes whipped about them, their arms stretched up to the hollow sky and their gaping mouths screamed for their beloved.

It was an infernal scene. Sweat streamed down their maniacal faces and each of them grasped the primitive necklace at their throats.

"Tonight!" Pear shouted deliriously. "Tonight the brides of Crozier will be unchained!"

Even as Jennet stared, a hideous change crept over the others. The faces that shone in the bloody firelight twisted and stretched. The flames were no longer mirrored in their eyes for now a brighter, hellish blaze was burning there. Within each of the witches a supressed, barbaric nature was struggling to break loose, and the whoops of delight that issued from the transforming mouths degenerated into gutteral howls. Before the flickering, broiling light, their forms blurred as all that was human was cast aside and the untame wildness of their profane, wanton souls took control.

The witches' hair shrank into their skulls, and hackles bristled down their necks as their backs buckled and they fell to the ground as hips snapped and curved inwards. Flesh rippled and bulged into tough sinew and bitter claws spiked from shrivelling hands. The hindering black robes were thrown down and, naked in their growing fur, the contorted creatures pranced about the circle, baying at the moon.

Jennet tried to scream, but her own voice was choking and to her terror only a yammering whine came out. The necklace of beads constricted and though she tore at it with her fingers the thread could not be broken. The blood pumped fiercely through her veins, throbbing violently in her ears like the harsh beating of pagan drums, and she felt her willpower drain and seep away.

The dense, burning woodsmoke filled the girl's nostrils and, as if that was a trigger, a dark memory flashed into her panic-stricken mind. It was the Fifth of November and Nathaniel was telling her of heathen times and chilling sacrifices, taunting her brother with heinous threats and controlling her absolutely. Before her wild, round eyes, a vision was forming, rising from her subconscious, and she howled as the image took shape in her thoughts.

The bearded face of Nathaniel Crozier was mocking her from the past and his commanding control came stabbing out at her. Jennet tried to drive the sinister man from her mind. She knew it was fatal to remember the sound of his compelling voice and the deadly force of those glittering, murderous eyes and yet it was impossible not to.

A searing pain sliced through the girl's stomach as all over her body the skin stung and needled. Throwing back her head, Jennet let out a shriek of pain and horror, for the transformation had begun.

"That's right," Pear encouraged, "give yourself up to it – surrender your will, let the beast free."

In her strange new voice, Jennet howled and her cheek bones melted into a new and different shape. Her long hair was already dwindling and her ears becoming silken points when suddenly and with a tremendous effort, she wrenched herself from the fiery ring and fell backwards on to the spongy ground.

"I can't!" she managed to yelp. "I can't!" and before Pear could reach her, Jennet sprang to her feet and fled the lurid scene as fast as possible. Over the moor she dashed, pelting blindly through the heather, too frightened to glance round, too terrified to hear the angry cries of the coven behind.

"Jennet!" Pear called. "Don't! You must come back – you'll put yourself in terrible danger!"

Pear looked to Hillian who alone amongst the others was still partly human.

Retaining much of her true shape, Hillian Fogle was a ghastly spectacle. Her face was a hybrid jumble: a great slavering snout protruded from her brows, yet her spectacles were still balanced precariously across the furry muzzle. Her short dark hair still curled behind her ears but they were huge and alert, listening to the sounds of the night and following Jennet's frantic movements through the darkness.

Before her voice became lost in the rabid snarlings of the savage animal she was rapidly becoming, Hillian growled at Pear and snapped, "Get you after her – bring the fool back ... gggo nooooww!"

The witch shuddered and fell on all fours, shaking with the horrible power of change.

Pear looked at her, then at the others who were now almost completely mutated into immense and ferocious black dogs whose great rolling eyes were ablaze with a harsh scarlet glow. The coven barked and shrieked, tearing around the bonfire and biting at the heat haze that pulsed from the flames. In the mad scramble of fur and teeth, the girl could not even identify her mother and she stepped back cautiously. Then, catching sight of Jennet's shimmering dress in the moonlight, she tore after her.

Jennet ran swiftly, driven by her abject terror of the fiends she had left behind. As soon as she had abandoned the frenzied circle, her bubbling bones had settled and reformed within her face and her tingling skin was soothed by the cool breezes.

She had no idea which direction to take but found herself heading for the camper van and then beyond into the wildness of the vast moorland. Through the bracken she crashed, desperate to put as much distance between herself and those evil, monstrous women as she could.

The satin dress which in the daytime had been so sickeningly pink was a ghostly grey in the moonlight, and its voluminous folds flapped madly about her ankles. Jennet grasped great swathes of it in her hands to keep from tripping and, like a scared and hunted rabbit, over the rough and bleak terrain she raced.

Closing on her, with her bare feet flying through the grass and heather and the black robe streaming behind like the great dark wings of a swooping predator, came Pear.

Calling for Jennet to stop, the witch girl bore fleetly down on her young friend. Her legs streaked ever faster, lessening the gulf between them until she could hear the breath rattling in her quarry's lungs and the large gulps of air she gasped and swallowed.

"Wait!" Pear shouted. "You must wait!"

Without turning around, Jennet bawled back at her, "Keep away from me! Get back to those disgusting filthy ... things! Help! Help!"

But Pear had caught up with her. She clutched and tore at the satin dress and leapt at Jennet – throwing her off balance and hurling her sideways. The girl screamed and pushed the other away but Pear pushed her to the ground and jumped on to her stomach.

The breath wheezed from Jennet's windpipe and she squirmed beneath Pear, clutching her belly, unable to speak or cry out.

"Where did you think you were going?" Pear demanded. "Why did you run?"

Coughing and spluttering, Jennet choked in sheer disbelief. "You're ... you're crazy!" she sobbed.

"Me?"

"Oh please," Jennet cried, "let me go, just let me go."

"Hey," Pear exclaimed in concern, "there's nothing to be scared of." She leaned forward to put her arms about her but Jennet pushed her off and scuttled over the ground to escape the embrace.

"Don't touch me!" she yelled.

"Jennet! What have I done? I thought you understood – you're one of us. You knew Nathaniel, you loved him the same as the rest."

"I didn't!" Jennet screamed. "He was an evil, foul man! I'm glad he's dead! He cared about nothing but himself!"

Pear scrambled after her. "That's not true!" she hotly denied. "Nathaniel was the most wonderful man I have ever known. He liberated us all. Most of those women back there were dying in miserable, dreary lives before they met him."

"Women?" Jennet snorted. "Didn't you see what happened? They're just like Rowena!"

"We're a family!" Pear shouted. "Nathaniel gave us a purpose and united us – you don't know how happy we've been. To run free beneath the moon, pursuing the wind and bounding over fields, it's a feeling unlike any other – the ultimate achievement and his great gift to us."

Jennet shook her head. "Don't be stupid, you're not free – it's an illusion. He used and repressed you and he's still doing it. Can't you see that you were just his slaves like I was once? At least I discovered what he was like in time."

Pear pulled at the beads around Jennet's neck. "You're wrong," she said, "and you know it. You don't really hate him or this wouldn't be so tight. It's your cherishing of him that keeps it there – bound close to your skin."

"That's rubbish."

"Oh no, I'll tell you what's rubbish. It's this game you're playing – denying what you know is right for you. You're not really happy. How could you be, living with an old cripple who hardly notices you and a brother who's always had all the attention. How much longer do you want to be trapped in that drab existence where you don't fit in? If you come back with me you can belong to a real family again."

Jennet turned her face away. "Stop it!" she snapped angrily. "You're trying to trick me. Well, it won't work. I'll never listen to you again. I thought you were my friend but you weren't. You only pretended to be to lure me into this! I hate you!"

"That isn't true," Pear insisted, dismayed by the accusation. "I am your friend, honest. I only wanted us to be sisters, I never ..." She broke off and lifted her head. The night was filled with the vicious baying of the coven and the sound was growing nearer.

"No," Pear whispered anxiously, "they're coming this way."

"I won't join them," Jennet declared, "ever!"

But the other girl's face was troubled and almost fearful. "You don't understand," she mumbled. "Hillian should've stopped them, kept them by the fire."

Jennet listened to the fierce clamour of the approaching pack and turned ice cold with dread. "What ... what will they do?" she stammered.

"When the primitive half is in control," Pear muttered, "there is no reason, no sanity. Savage instinct spurs them – it's too late for you now, Jennet.

If they catch you they'll tear you to pieces."

"What can I do? I can't outrun them!"

"I wish you'd been ready," Pear wept. "Oh Jennet, listen to them. I know their voices, they're howling for blood. The dancing was too intense, they won't be satiated until they've killed tonight. They're hungry for flesh. I'm sorry – so sorry."

Great tears splashed down Pear's face and the riotous uproar of the pursuing, snarling dogs came blasting towards them.

Thinking quickly, the witch girl gave the petrified Jennet a desperate hug and whispered, "I am your friend, please believe that. I'll draw them off, lead them on a false trail."

"You?" Jennet breathed. "How?"

"Don't argue, just run and keep on running – I mightn't be successful but it's the only chance you've got. The road lies over there – hurry."

Jennet staggered to her feet. "What about you?" she asked. "Won't they kill you?"

"Just go!" Pear raged. "And if you make it safe home, and I pray to your god that you do, then don't speak of this night to anyone."

"But ... but ..."

"Quickly! Get out of here!"

"I don't know how to thank you."

"Just go!"

Jennet stumbled forward, yet she could not resist glancing round to take one final look at Pear. But the girl was already running towards the baying hounds and as Jennet watched, the black robe fell from her friend's body and her human shape vanished as she too transformed into a sleek black dog that sped away into the distance to lead the others away.

"Oh God! Oh God!" Jennet cried, tearing through the scrubby grass of the desolate moor.

To her relief, the frightful yammering began to

recede into the distance and she silently thanked Pear once more, but after only a few moments the sound changed and the fury of the pack was terrible to hear. Louder and louder it grew and Jennet realized that the witch girl had failed.

Over the undulating ground the foul brides of Nathaniel dashed. They had caught Jennet's scent on the air and it thrilled and tantalized their questing nostrils. Hot was the blood that pumped through their altered veins and hot was the tender meat that they desired and lusted after. Their steaming breath billowed around them in a rank vapour and their glaring red eyes shone balefully into the gloom, searching for their prey.

The smallest of the vicious and growling hounds ran reluctantly at the rear of the pack. With Pear's mournful tears running down the creature's snout and a cruel and savage bite bleeding on the animal's flank, it whimpered as it followed the others.

Flying before them, Jennet's heart thumped and quailed against her ribcage. She couldn't run much further, yet the horrendous noise of the witch beasts grew louder with every passing second. She knew that it was only a matter of time and a grim thought told her that she was probably giving them splendid entertainment by fleeing. What better sport than a chase? Soon they would be biting at her heels, snapping at her calves and tearing the dress to shreds to feast upon her. The hellish fiends would leap from the darkness and drag her down where those mighty jaws could rend and crunch.

Despairingly, she remembered Rowena Cooper and the old friends of Aunt Alice that the evil woman had murdered. These witch creatures were unbeatable and as her legs became ever more weary and aching, she realized there was absolutely no escape. Here in the wild, in the dark vastness of the

empty moor there was nowhere to run to and no one to help her.

Pushing herself onward, she cursed the day she heard the folk band and damned herself for listening to their lies and believing they were different to anyone else.

The pack was very close now. Soon she would feel the first panting breath upon her and then it would be nearly over. Jennet could not stand it any more and she screamed.

"Aunt Alice! I'm sorry! Oh Ben, forgive me!"

Bracken and gorse scratched her legs and shredded the satin but still she fled and then, when her lungs were near to bursting, she lurched through a low, straggly hedge and abruptly the soft springy ground disappeared beneath her feet.

Blinking in confused astonishment, Jennet found herself upon the tarmac of the wide road, yet her instant relief was swiftly curtailed.

The road stretched for miles in either direction but no cars were travelling upon it and no headlamps glimmered in the distance.

"Then I'm done for!" the girl cried. "I'm as good as dead!"

The barking tumult was horribly close now. Soon the savage dogs would burst through the hedge to pounce on her. Forcing herself to lumber on, Jennet tried to run but it was all in vain and her exhausted muscles finally gave way and she collapsed on to the hard surface of the road.

Suddenly a bright light clicked on and the girl's prostrate form was caught in a wide, dazzling beam. Jennet lifted her head but the light blinded her.

"Help me, please!" she cried. "You must!"

And then, to her amazement, she heard a familiar voice which she had always ridiculed. But the mere sound of it in that desperate and bleak spot brought an overwhelming sense of joy and salvation to the girl and her pounding heart leapt.

"Don't just stand there gasping like a goldfish! Jolly well climb aboard."

There, straddling Miss Boston's old bicycle, with one large foot on the ground and the other raring to go on the pedal – was Sister Frances.

Jennet did not hesitate, and rushed over to her.

"Quickly," the nun urged, "sit on the handlebars. I used to give my brother Timmy rides like this – 'course he was only five and yours truly twelve. Do hurry, Jennet. Oh sweet Lord, listen to those fiends!"

From the hedge the first of the hounds came charging. Bursting on to the road, its sharp claws clattered and slithered and the huge dog slid and tumbled, unable to stop itself careering into the hedge on the opposite side. But immediately it sprang up and scrabbled towards the two defenceless humans, preparing to leap at them.

"Hang on!" Frances shouted, pushing away with her foot and pedalling like mad.

With her legs dangling either side of the front wheel and her hands gripping the handlebars for dear life, Jennet felt the nun's head press into her back as Sister Frances strained on the pedals.

Behind them the rest of the pack came spilling over the road and furious growls and barks filled their ears as the infernal beasts gave chase.

The wheels of the bicycle whirred and hissed over the road as the nun's woollen-stocking legs revolved and pumped at an astonishing rate. But jostling and loping swiftly behind, the brides of Nathaniel unerringly came.

Their foaming jaws snapped, lunging for the rear wheel, and the demonic fires of their malevolent eyes shone in the reflector on the mudguard and made the whirling spokes shimmer with a red blur.

"Get thee jolly well behind me!" Frances puffed. "And stay there!"

But the pack's endurance seemed limitless and down the winding road they tirelessly pursued the zooming bicycle.

Jennet's hair streamed in the wind and when Frances raised her head to see where she was going it blew into her face and she had to peer around the girl's side to see anything at all.

The bicycle wobbled and suddenly the dogs caught up with it. Running alongside, they snarled and jumped up to snap at the nun's pedalling legs.

Jennet wailed and screwed her eyes up, expecting the bicycle to be dashed aside, but Frances' face was stern and she put on an extra spurt of speed that shot them clear of the pack and she crowed with triumph at the top of her voice.

"Don't worry, Jennet," she shouted right in the girl's ear, "I think we're going to be all right. Look, there are lights ahead. I'll warrant those nasties won't chase us through the villages."

She was right, for as they hurtled along the road, the old bicycle soon began to leave the yowling dogs way behind. Snarling and full of unspent malice, with a final frustrated bark the brutes turned their massive heads and the gleaming eyes vanished in the darkness.

Lingering for a moment in the middle of the road, the smallest member of the pack watched the speeding figures of Jennet and the nun fade into the distance amidst cottages and parked cars, and a pink tongue lolled from its jaws. Then, with a toss of its head, the creature hurried after the others and the dark instincts she had kept under control for so long at last took possession of the sleek midnight dog and Pear howled as viciously as the rest.

Eventually, when the lights of civilization shone

around them and Sister Frances could pedal at a more leisurely pace. Jennet was consumed by shock, and her horror at what she had seen engulfed her.

The bicycle came to a juddering halt as the girl's despairing sobs threatened to completely overturn the contraption and Sister Frances held her tightly.

"You let it all out," she advised. "Do you the world of good, but don't overdo it. The danger's over now so no moping or you'll get maudlin. Got to pick yourself up and start all over again, as the song goes."

"I'm okay," Jennet sniffed, wiping her tears on the frilly sleeves of her devastated dress, "but it was so awful – if you only knew – I don't believe it myself, the things I saw."

"If you don't believe it, then there's no point thinking about it, is there?"

"You don't understand."

"Don't I? Well, look, if you don't stop blubbing we'll never get home this side of Christmas – buck up, there's a good girl."

As Frances resumed her pedalling, a curious thought occured to Jennet. "What were you doing out there with Aunt Alice's bike?" she asked.

Looking casually at the buildings of Ruswarp as they sailed sedately by, the nun replied, "Well, I haven't got one of my own. I had to borrow it, didn't I?"

"That's not what I meant," Jennet said, "and you know it. Why were you out riding at this time of night in the middle of nowhere?"

"I might as well ask what you were doing out there," the nun answered blithely.

Jennet was too tired for Frances' renowned playfulness. "All right," she muttered, "if you don't want to tell me, I won't go on about it."

The bicycle trundled on and soon the lights of Whitby shimmered in the distance.

"Here we are, Jennet," Frances told her, "this is

your home. You don't belong with those poor misguided wretches. I think that today you should be glad that you were always the bridesmaid and never the bride. You have a real family here who cares and loves you – never forget that."

"How did you …?" Jennet began, but the nun had started to hum to herself and refused to listen.

When they came to Church Street they dismounted and Sister Frances escorted the girl to the alley entrance that led to the cottage. "Here," she said, "I'd best entrust you with the return of this worthy steed to its rightful place."

Jennet took the bicycle from her and looked into the nun's serene face. "Thank you," she said simply.

Frances smiled, then she shook herself and gave the girl a puzzled look. "Cripes!" she groaned. "Mother Superior will really have my guts for garters this time – whatever can the time be? Oh Jennet, you do look dreadful. Whatever happened to that swanky frock? It's all ruined. Well, I can't stay here, can I? Up to my neck in hot water again – oh dear!"

And with that she hurried away, leaving a stunned and bewildered Jennet gawping after the nun's retreating figure.

10

THE LORDS OF THE DEEP AND DARK

Miss Boston and Ben had only just returned to the cottage from the wedding reception, and had not even had time to look into Jennet's room to see if she was feeling any better, when an angry knock rapped on the front door.

"Gracious! Who can that be?" Aunt Alice cried, nearly pricking herself with the enormous pin she was carefully removing from her hat. "Could you answer it for me Benjamin, dear? If it's Edith returned having decided wedding bliss is all too much, then I'm afraid she'll not be getting her old room. I'm moving back in there tonight – and the place can return to normal at last."

She sucked her teeth disagreeably and shook her quivering chins. "I don't know where Cicily Drinkwater gets her unpalatable marzipan from, but it isn't the highest quality, that's for sure. The cake was rather dry too – though I imagine the reason for that was Edith's parsimony, too mean to put more than two drops of…"

The old lady frowned and wondered where the boy had got to. Hobbling on her walking stick, she followed him into the hall. "Who was it at the door, dear?" she called. "Upon my word!"

Holding the front door open, Ben turned to stare and began to say something, but Miss Boston was too fascinated by the slightly out of focus shape she saw stamping on the step.

"You should have said, Benjamin," she gently scolded. "Don't let your aufwader chum remain out there. Where are your manners? Let Nelda in."

Old Parry spat into a flower pot. "Is she barmy?" she croaked. "I ain't that trollopy Grendel!"

Aunt Alice peered at her closely and apologized for the mistake. "I beg your pardon, I'm afraid my perception isn't as gifted as Benjamin's. Don't be offended, come inside."

"I won't never set foot inside one of these poxy smell-holes!" Parry snorted. "What do you take me fer?"

"A very rude and disagreeable personage indeed," Aunt Alice muttered under her breath.

"Gar!" Parry scowled. "Just get a move on and be quick about it!"

"Get a move on where?"

"Is the old bird feeble in the head?" Parry hissed, jabbing Ben in the ribs. "Where else does yer think you'd be a trottin' off to at this hour? I've been sent to fetch yer. The messenger of the great Triad is wantin' a word an' I would'na keep him waitin'."

Aunt Alice let out an impressed whistling breath. "How thrilling!" she clucked. "Whatever can he want with me?"

But Old Parry had accomplished her errand and was already shuffling through the courtyard.

"Wait a moment!" Miss Boston called. "Quick, Ben, my hat and cloak."

"I'm not going to see the fisherfolk in this getup!" the boy protested.

The old lady tutted at the kilt and buckled shoes. "I'm afraid you'll have to," she told him. "There isn't time to change – just put your coat on."

"What about Jen?" the boy asked, glancing up the stairwell. "Should I go and tell her where we're going?"

"Good heavens no. She's probably fast asleep by now anyway – we can tell her all about it in the morning."

Jamming her everyday hat down over her woolly head, she twirled a tweed cloak over her shoulders and hurried Ben out of the cottage.

"Come on," Aunt Alice urged, "that unpleasant character is way ahead of us."

Limping slightly, the old lady left the courtyard and, with the silver buckles of Ben's shoes glinting as he ran after her, they made their way to the shore.

In the short span of time that had passed since Old Parry's grudging departure, neither Tarr nor the huddled figure in the boat had uttered a word. Yet the leader of the aufwader tribe remained ever watchful and wary of the herald. Why had he insisted on seeing Miss Boston? It made no sense whatsoever – the fate of his granddaughter had nothing to do with her.

Old Parry's cracked and grumpy voice broke in on his troubled thoughts.

"The landbreed cripple's a-comin'," she told the herald, ignoring Tarr completely, "and that plaguey nuisance of a brat too."

"Ben?" asked Nelda, turning to see two familiar figures emerge from the gloomy shadows of the rocky shore.

"Well met! Well met!" Miss Boston cheered, stopping to wave the walking stick boisterously. "How splendid this is, and what an honour to be sure!"

Waddling into the semi-circle of fisherfolk, she nodded a greeting to everyone and they, in respect for all that they owed her, bowed.

The old lady beamed and, as she drew level with Tarr and Nelda, gazed at the water's edge where the small craft bobbed silently upon the languid waves. The blue light of the lantern shone over the herald of the Deep Ones and Miss Boston took a further step forward in her enthusiasm to get a better peep at him.

"Your Excellency!" she cried, attempting a clumsy curtsy. "I am deeply touched and gratified to be invited here."

Behind her, Ben eyed the figure cautiously. He had seen him once before, when the herald came to ban the marriage of Nelda and Esau. The boy had not liked the look of him then and he certainly didn't like it now. Without thinking, he moved close to Nelda and she turned a worried face to him.

"What's happening?" he whispered.

But before she could reply Tarr struck the rocks with his staff.

"Reet!" he shouted at the herald. "The Boston's 'ere now an' I demand to be heard. Too long have we paid for the mistake of Oona these many years. Too many wives and mothers have perished 'neath the cruel might of the curse an' too many bairns have gasped an' died afore they've had chance to breathe. Now, are them three what dwell in the deeps gonna let my Nelda go the same way? Am I nivver to hear the first cries o' her babe or must I smash this contrivance and wake old Morgawrus?

"Look at us!" he bellowed. "This paltry few is all that's left of the many tribes which once thrived along this coast. Must every black boat be burned afore them nazards o' the brine see how cruel they've been? A foul damnation on 'em, ah says – an' ah'll bring that about if'n it's the last I do!"

Throughout this impassioned and volatile speech, the messenger said nothing, but when Tarr had finished and stood quaking with rage, comforted by

Nelda and Miss Boston, the figure in the boat stirred.

"Verily", he intoned, "the time has indeed come for the grievances of thy race to be taken before the Lords of the Deep."

"Then do it!" Tarr roared. "Tell 'em of our sorrows and what'll happen if the curse isna lifted!"

The herald crouched forward and in a hushed voice answered, "No, I shall not."

"But you just…"

"I shall not take thy haughty and proud ultimatum before the thrones of my masters! If thou wishest to be heard, then thou must deliver the message thyself!"

The fisherfolk drew their breath and stared at one another in shocked amazement. No one since the days of Irl had ventured down to that cold and deadly realm.

"Dare you accompany me into the fathomless waters, Tarr Shrimp?" the messenger asked. "Hast thou the valour to face the dread powers of the world and speak as thou hast done to me?"

Tarr's face fell. He had not expected this and his spirit balked at the very thought.

"What sayest thou?" murmured the herald. "Is the leader of this meagre tribe as craven as he is overbold and rash?"

Disconcerted, Tarr lowered his eyes and gazed at Nelda. The contours of his granddaughter's face were graven with fear and dread.

"Don't listen to him," she said. "You mustn't go."

Tarr stroked her leathery cheek with his aged hands and the angry resolve returned to burn in his heart.

"Aye!" he snapped back at the herald. "Ah'll come! What new torture can them divils contrive we ain't already sufferin'?"

A low chuckle issued from beneath the seagreen cowl. "Much," it whispered. "As yet thou knowest naught of the torments my masters can devise. Yet forewarned of this, art thou still set on stepping into this vessel with me?"

"I am."

"No, Grandfather!" Nelda wept, flinging her arms about his neck and clinging to him despairingly. "I won't let you go! I won't! They'll destroy you!"

Tarr pulled away from her and placed her hands into Ben's. "Ah mun, lass," he said simply, "'tis the one chance we've looked fer down the years – what leader'd throw that aside?"

"Please don't leave me – you're all I have left!"

"And tha's all I've got," he said sadly, "and that's why it mun be done. Here – take the guardian and keep it safe. Ah'm not daft enough to take that down theer wi' me. If I dinna come back by dawn, smash the thing to bits. Swear now."

"I swear."

"Reet," Tarr announced, glaring back at the messenger and stepping towards the water's edge. "Ah'm ready."

"Stay a moment," the herald commanded. "Did I not say that thy voice alone would not be heard?"

Tarr's brow corrugated with irritation. "Nay!" he shouted. "Ah'll not let Nelda to come!"

"And neither would I wish it," the voice snapped back from the hidden depths of the hood. "One of thy race is quite enough."

"Then who?" Tarr mumbled.

For an instant the light of the lantern was mirrored in the messenger's clustering eyes and everyone saw that they were staring straight at Miss Boston.

Astounded, the old lady clapped her hands. "Do you mean to say," she began hesitantly, "do you honestly mean that I too am to journey with you both – all the way down there to have an audience with the ruling Triad?"

Amusement was in the herald's voice when he replied, "Such is mine offer; travel the ancient paths and stand at the feet of the three thrones, Alice Boston."

Her face was a rapturous picture of elation and, leaning on the walking stick she gave an exhilarated jig of rejoicing.

"Happy day!" she grinned. "Oh Benjamin, isn't this exciting?"

But Ben was as unhappy at the prospect of her leaving as Nelda was about Tarr's departure. She seemed to have no regard for the terrible danger she was placing herself in and behaved as if she was simply going for a boat trip around the harbour. He tried to tell her not to go but Aunt Alice would not listen, her mind was made up.

"Use your intelligence, Benjamin dear," she said. "The Deep Ones wouldn't have asked to see me merely to keep me prisoner down there or something worse. Besides, they bear me no grudge, I've never had any dealings with them. This is a mighty honour. If I refused then I would regret the decision for the rest of my life and that would be intolerable."

The hooded figure of the herald called out impatiently. "Hurry," he said, "we have far to travel this night – far away is the realm of my masters. Step into the boat."

Miss Boston raised her eyebrows at Tarr and held out her hand to him. "Shall we go down to the water together?" she asked. "I should really have brought my wellingtons."

Tarr glanced back at Nelda. "Remember thy promise," he told her. "Dawn tomorrow."

Tearfully she nodded and drew closer to Ben as both her grandfather and Aunt Alice waded out towards the boat and clambered aboard.

When they were seated opposite the strange

messenger, the small wooden craft spun around and pulled away from the shore.

"Good fortune go with you!" Nelda shouted.

"Take care," Ben cried.

Tarr held up his staff in farewell and with a sudden notion Miss Boston cupped her hands around her mouth and yelled, "Benjamin! Don't forget to feed Eurydice!"

Then the boat picked up speed and it sailed swiftly over the open sea.

"That's the last we'll see of them," Old Parry's spiteful voice mewled. "None of us'll ever see their faces again in this world. They've gone to meet their doom."

* * *

Over the immense cold sea the rowing boat flew, slicing through lazy waves – cleaving an ever-widening wake in the great grey waters.

The cliffs of Whitby and the lights of the harbour had long since vanished over the rolling horizon and Miss Boston settled down to enjoy this fascinating and rare opportunity to the utmost.

Beside her, with his staff placed across his lap, Tarr stared impassively past the crouching shape of the herald and out into the distance beyond.

No muscle twitched on his face to betray his thoughts or feelings and with his arms folded, he endured the journey without saying a word.

All around them, the bright moonlight shimmered and danced over the moving surface of the water. Wobbling stripes of milky light were reflected over and into the little craft and Miss Boston craned her neck from side to side in childish amusement. It was all so marvellous, she wanted to drink in and remember everything – she still couldn't believe what was happening and tiny chortles of pleasure quaked inside her bosom.

Suddenly Tarr stirred and he lifted his hand to his brow as he peered into the far horizon.

"Nine times bless me!" he murmured. "What be that yonder?"

The old lady followed his concerned gaze and her wrinkled eyes grew wide with delight and astonishment. "Stupendous!" she cried. "What a spectacle!"

Upon the rim of the wide salty world, a tremendous tumult was churning and thrashing the waters. As they watched in stunned silence, the sea erupted and enormous spouts burst high into the night, glittering beneath the moon like a blizzard of cascading frosty fire.

The ferocity of the explosions boomed over the rumbling ocean, and gigantic shock waves sped outwards in massive rings of foaming water that tossed the little boat like a cork in a storm.

Miss Boston and Tarr gripped the sides of the vessel desperately as freezing spray stung their faces and the aufwader yelled his fury at the herald. "We'll be drowned!" he raged. "Ah should 'ave reckoned theer'd be no parley wi' the Triad! Well, they'll not be laughing when the serpent is loosed."

"Fear not!" the cloaked figure shouted above the seething din. "The way is merely being prepared for us – we shall not be harmed."

"Does tha mean we're headin' straight fer yon tempest?"

"Into its very heart."

Towards the crashing waters the wooden craft sailed, smashing through the walls of froth that stampeded against them and riding the rampaging, tormented surf.

Miss Boston scrunched up her face as the salty

deluge battered her, but keeping one eye half open she saw in the distance a most incredible and awesome sight.

Towering in the night sky, forming from the insane, lashing sea, was one colossal wave. Slowly and horribly the immense mountain of brine grew. The north wind raged against its horrendous and shimmering bulk, whipping the surrounding waters into the air and hurling them upon the vast glassy slopes of the monstrous, thundering vision.

Higher it soared, its terrible peak rearing into the starlit sky until the snowy, foam-capped crown vanished from sight.

Before its huge and deadly magnificence, the boat was like a minuscule insect. The titanic wave filled their entire vision and an icy gale blasted about them. Yet even as they watched in dread and disbelief, the incredible nightmare trembled and shook. With a deafening roar that ripped through the night, the sheer wall of water toppled and fell.

Tarr threw his hands before his face and Miss Boston prayed silently as they waited for their destruction.

The fierce thunder mounted and the freezing gale tore and plucked at them, but the violent doom that they expected failed to happen.

Cautiously, Tarr lowered his hands and stared. "By Gow!" he whispered incredulously.

The titanic wave had curled in upon itself and was even now spinning over the sea. But the spiralling, vertical whirlpool maintained its position in the water, diminishing neither in bulk nor height and as Tarr watched, a dark circle appeared directly in the rolling centre.

"Deeps take us!" he breathed as the wheeling fissure widened and became a huge black mouth.

The herald mocked him coldly. "That is exactly

what will happen."

Miss Boston gazed at the great, churning vortex that loomed ever closer and the rush of the reeling waters beat against her ear-drums.

"Behold the gateway to their Majesties!" the herald laughed above the squall. "Now does the peril truly begin!"

Caught in the unescapable pull of the whirling nightmare, the little boat flew into its ominous shadow and the yawning cavern of the rumbling gateway reared high over their heads.

All other sounds were lost as the spiralling tunnel sucked the twisting gale into its throat. Up to the whirling threshold the boat sped, and the rolling curves of the monstrous wave closed around them.

The vessel rocked and jerked and the lantern swung madly at the prow, its light glimmering in sapphire streaks over the surrounding spinning gloom.

Then with a lurch the sea dropped and the boat teetered on the brink of oblivion. For an instant, Tarr and the old lady glimpsed only a black void, and then the craft shot down into the darkness beneath the waves.

Into the cold realm of the Triad the little boat travelled, the spiralling tunnel created by the limitless power of the Deep Ones drawing it swiftly further into the uncharted reaches of the sea.

It was a mad, bouncing ride. Miss Boston's stomach turned over a dozen times as they descended and though at first she had been mortally afraid, gradually she began to look curiously about her and actually started to relish the bone-jolting, nerve-jangling journey.

Beyond the twisting walls of the spiralling vortex, strange sights were momentarily illuminated by the boat's lantern and the old lady marvelled at the wonders that were revealed to her.

Dim wrecks of ancient ships flashed beyond the coiling water – old galleons teeming with colourful fish that glinted with rainbow brilliance as they darted into the sweeping beams of light.

Then they were lost far behind and beneath the wooden boat a bottomless chasm opened in the ocean floor.

In a great swooping arc, the swirling tunnel plunged downwards and the sides of the drowned canyon raced above them. Deeper the boat hurtled and in the gaping trench hideous creatures swam in the darkness. Within the crevices gnawed into the chasm wall, sickly green lights glowed and bulging eyes glared at the snaking pathway that frothed and boiled through their dismal territories.

Miss Boston clasped her hands before her – enchanted at the unfolding spectacle. Bloated, distorted shapes passed overheard, weird undiscovered monsters of the deep that no human eye had ever seen – ghastly submerged islands of coral-encrusted blubber, grown vast and terrifying in the absolute dark.

As the boat shot through the writhing channel, a huge barnacle-covered fin broke through the round churning walls, slicing the foaming water in half. Miss Boston and Tarr were drenched and glanced up at the immense calamitous shape uncertainly.

"Fear not," the herald assured them, "the watch-dogs of my masters are inquisitive – nothing more. We shall not be harmed."

The great, malformed fin withdrew into the blackness once more and the boat skimmed forward undamaged, although the old lady and the aufwader were soaked to the skin.

Abruptly the tunnel emerged from the chasm and the dim, deep green of a warm ocean now spiralled about them. Travelling parallel to the reefs below, the boat's jarring jolts subsided and swiftly but steadily it journeyed.

Miss Boston removed the sopping hat from her head and wrung it out over the side. About them she began to see broken fragments of ancient architecture lying amongst the coral, and corroded columns of marble rose upon either side of the churning passageway.

Between the great, stately archways of a forgotten civilization they sped. Fallen statues of primeval gods sprawled on the ocean bed and ruined temples choked with waving weed reared in the distance. Throughout this decaying country wound majestic colonnades, high bronze towers speared from the murky verdigris of their crumbling desolation, and palaces that were once the residences of vengeful kings and proud princes now appeared grim and forbidding – the abodes of many-eyed monsters.

"Fascinating!" Miss Boston declared, staring at the eerie, deserted kingdom. "What was this place? What happened here?"

In a chilling, whispering tone, the herald answered, "Once 'twas a populous city, mightiest upon the earth. Before even the first of the aufwaders set foot on the shores of Whitby, this place flourished. Learned were the scholars and fearless were the conquering kings. Held in high favour with the Lords of the Deep were they and much wisdom did they teach these nobles of early man."

The ruins were left behind as the boat careered along and Miss Boston glanced back at the disappearing city sorrowfully. "How was it destroyed?" she asked.

"The serpent came," the cloaked figure replied darkly. "Morgawrus laid the continent to waste and drowned it in the deeps. Thus did the fell dragon of the ancient world incur my masters' wrath and they marched against it unto the very coast of thy home."

"Morgawrus did that?" Miss Boston repeated, and she looked dubiously at Tarr, but the aufwader's face was set and he made no indication that he had seen or heard anything.

Further through the seething tunnel the boat sailed and, deep in thought, Miss Boston waited for the journey to end.

Around them the sea grew darker, yet ahead, rising from the ocean floor, a midnight blackness began to take shape.

As the old lady stared, she saw that they were speeding towards a gigantic mountain of rock. Its sheer sides were almost vertical and she could see that the spinning pathway was winding unerringly towards it.

Faster the boat raced until only the massive crags and cliffs of the mountain filled her vision. Ever onward the vessel rushed, tearing at a breakneck speed, and the old lady was sure they would be smashed against the cruel slopes.

Enormous boulders rocketed closer, then at the last moment, there was an opening in the rock and into this the whirling tunnel swept.

Suddenly the boat lurched and trembled as it shot into a series of dimly-lit grottoes. The enveloping, spiralling vortex began to revolve more slowly and abruptly the glimmering walls came splashing about the sides of the wooden craft as huge bubbles burst against the prow.

Drifting now upon the swirling eddies within a rocky tunnel, the boat floated lazily forward.

"Are we nearly there?" Miss Boston asked. "It would appear we are slowing down."

Even as she said it, they were propelled into a cavernous chamber whose vaulted roof was lit by hundreds of lanterns. The pillared walls and lofty ceiling were embedded with quartz and mother-of-pearl and the lustrous surface rejoiced in the sapphire lights and made the chamber blaze like a cloudless sky. Yet beyond the farthest archway, the whole of one gigantic wall was completely black, no lamps flickered there and no reflected gleam pierced the engulfing gloom.

Miss Boston had the distinct impression that they had entered a kind of cathedral and she blinked at the sheer, ravishing beauty of it. From every corner, there echoed a constant music of flowing crystal water and the very air was sweet and wholesome.

Into the centre of this wondrous cavern the boat sailed and the old lady knew where they were headed.

Rising from the lake of clear, cold water was a tall finger of rock and winding about the column's girth was a flight of roughly-hewn stone steps.

Gently, the boat bumped against a wide ledge at the foot of the stairs and the herald bowed. "This is your journey's end," he murmured. "It is bidden that you alight here."

Tarr gave the figure a stern glance, then climbed expertly on to the bottommost step, his feet sploshing in the water that sluiced over the edge. The aufwader's back was aching and his legs were cramped and numb but he said nothing and leaned upon his staff, waiting for Miss Boston to join him.

"Thank you so much," she clucked to the herald as if she was merely dismounting from a bus. "You took it a little brisk at times but I wouldn't have missed a second!"

The old lady rose uncertainly and the boat tipped to one side as she scrambled for the firm safety of the ledge. Holding on to Tarr's outstretched hand she managed the feat at last, then realized that she had left her walking stick in the boat.

"Botheration!" she uttered, stooping down to retrieve it.

Unexpectedly, the hooded messenger leaned towards her and in a low, warning voice hissed, "Beware my Lord of the Frozen Wastes."

"I beg your pardon," she cried in astonishment, "what do you mean?"

"Too late!" he whispered fearfully. "*They* are with us!"

The water around the boat foamed and boiled and to Miss Boston's consternation, the craft began to sink.

"Quick!" she called. "Get out, man, whilst you can!"

As the water spilled over the sides and poured into the little craft, the hidden face turned to her. "Be not afraid for me," the messenger said. "I am commanded to leave thee now." Down he plunged and the frothing waters closed over the sea-green hood.

Alone with Tarr upon the central column of rock, Miss Boston gaped but the aufwader was unconcerned about the fate of their guide.

"'Ims a being of the deep," he uttered gruffly. "Come – we'd best climb these steps."

Around the pillar of rock they cautiously ascended until finally they were standing on the wide, flat summit and gazing down at the smooth surface of the lake far below.

"Easy!" Miss Boston exclaimed. "That's nothing compared to the abbey steps. Before my illness I used to climb them every day, you know."

Tarr ignored her and stared tetchily around them. "Wheer are they?" he mumbled. "Wheer are them divils hidin'?"

"Mr Shrimp," the old lady urged, "I think you should be more careful. Discourtesy never pays."

"Bah!" Tarr snorted, stamping his staff upon the rock. "Ah'm fed up wi' waitin'! If'n the Deep Ones wanna hear what ah've got to say then why don't they show thesselves?"

Immediately the cavern began to tremble and from beyond the furthest arch where the wall was dark and smothered with shadow, a fabulous radiance suddenly welled up. Into the immense chamber flooded a rich and glorious golden light that mingled with the azure beams of the lamps and bathed everything in warmth and splendour.

"Moonkelp!" Tarr murmured, squinting into the beautiful, scintillating glare.

Miss Boston shielded her eyes, but when they adjusted to the delicious brightness, she saw that the far wall was not made of rock but was a solid sheet of water, held back by the grace of the almighty Triad.

The huge, quivering barrier was a blaze of magical light, which gradually dwindled, and then through the rippling liquid, three monstrous shapes shimmered into view.

Miss Boston wished she had brought her binoculars with her. She suspected that she and Tarr were looking on a scene that was in reality far removed and profoundly remote. Yet slowly the blurred and indistinct outlines became clearer and assumed the forms of three gargantuan thrones.

They were tortuously wrought in towering branches of blood-red coral and great gnarled shells clustered over the minarets that thrust high into the wild seas. But seated upon them and silhouetted by the light of the moonkelp which now bloomed continually behind the majestic thrones were the shadowy, writhing figures of the Lords of the Deep and Dark.

The old lady lowered her eyes humbly but the leader of the aufwaders stared with stubborn defiance at the terrible powers of the world, undaunted by their ghastly and horrific aspect.

Never in all his long life had Tarr imagined that one day he would actually stand before the Triad, and though his mind reeled at the awesome spectacle, his courage did not fail him.

The mass of tentacles stirred upon the central throne. Within the aufwader's and Miss Boston's thoughts, a rumbling bass voice reverberated and blasted, forcing them to stagger backwards as if struck by an unseen blow.

"Hail to thee Tarr, son of Athi!" the compelling and painful greeting echoed in their heads. *"Descendant of the line of Mereades, thou art most welcome here. It is good to look once more upon the noble countenance of thy kind. Too long have my brethren and I been deprived of thy honourable company."*

Tarr and the old lady recovered from the unexpected invasion of their minds and peered through the crystal waters at the Lord of the Circling Seas who addressed them.

"Glad were the days before the breaking of the laws," the vision continued. *"Venemous was that time when Eska was born in the drylands and we were sundered."*

At this Tarr grew angry and he stamped his foot to be heard. "Aye!" he cried, "and the poison of tha curse still blanches us. Ain't it time fer the wrongdoing to be forgiven? Does ycr know how many o' my kind – how many o' them 'noble countenances' – have been blighted unto death and gone screaming to fritful agonies 'cos of one misguided blunder? In your own hallowed names can tha not see what ruin tha've brought about? Are the seas not girt enough – mun they be made the fuller by our uncounted tears?"

The three immense shapes listened gravely to his embittered and furious outburst, yet as she watched in stupefied silence, Miss Boston saw that the shadowy figure on the left-hand throne stirred restlessly.

"Much love was there betwixt the waders of the shore and the Triad," began the Lord of the Roaring Waters. *"In those blessed days thy race were true to their words and stout of heart."*

"Mebbe!" Tarr shouted. "But of the paltry few that are left, theer's still heroes and warriors amongst us!"

Then the impatient form of the Lord of the Frozen Wastes writhed and finally he spoke.

His voice, when it blistered into the minds of Miss Boston and Tarr, stabbed and sliced like inummerable razors, knifing icily through their thoughts.

"Hearken to the white-haired fool!" he scorned. *"Those he speaks of do no more than net fish and search the waters for flotsam. Brave and doughty indeed were the tribes of old, yet remember my brothers how they did prove faithless. The punishment he grumbles against was a just reward for Oona's unpardonable transgression."*

Miss Boston shuddered. Having that voice hiss and wheedle inside her head was a loathsome experience.

"Even so," the Lord of the Circling Seas lamented, *"grievous indeed would be the day that announced the end of the stunted folk of the shore. I would not wish all traces of their kind to be forever lost."*

On his right, the second shadow agreed. *"Could not some way be contrived to spare the few that remain and save them from this doom we have laid upon them?"*

"Never!" shrieked the Lord of the Frozen Wastes. *"The crawling maggots are not to be trusted. Ever have they bitten at our divinity. Did not Irl trespass amongst us? And, using knowledge learned at our own halls, he did steal and carry off our most prized treasure, which he secreted and concealed for many years."*

"Irl has paid his debt," the central member of the Triad uttered. *"Must we condemn all for the actions of the few?"*

"Then what of Esau?" the Lord of the Frozen Wastes seethed. *"Hast thou forgotten the haughty words he did rail at us when we forbade the union? That dotard did nearly bring about our destruction. Did the serpent not wake again? Was he not unfettered? For that treacherous act alone the last of the filthy tribes should be doomed into oblivion!"*

His brothers considered all that he had said and in turn they regretfully nodded their agreement. *"The creatures are too perfidious,"* sighed the voice of the Roaring Waters. *"What further catastrophes would they bring about if we lifted the mother's curse? No, the time of their great numbers is long past and though I hold those blissful days dear I shall be content to let the memories be glad ones. The race must disappear from the world."*

"Then a foul damnation on yers all!" Tarr yelled, shaking his staff at the shimmering wall. "Ah didna come hither to beg fer the lives of me granddaughter an' her bairn – just to say this. Listen well and listen long, tha black-hearted fiends! Tha knows nowt! Down theer in tha cosy dark, a-hoardin' that glisty moonkelp and throwin' tha weight about – well, we doesna need yer any more an' never did!

"Does tha really not know why Irl stole that accursed shinin' weed in the first instance? To finish off the task tha bungled! Aye, the enchantments which yer placed on Morgawrus to keep him snorin' for eternity wore thin and so the most cunnin' an' artful of my kind took it on himself to make it reet. Yet all he needed were a bit o' that stuff yonder and he knew tha were so greedy yer'd nivver part wi' the merest scrap. So he up and steals it from under your very noses and goes on to fashion a charm of his own devising to keep the villain asleep under them cliffs. Then what does yer do, eh? Tha drags him under and drowns the very one what saved yer.

"And now my Nelda, her what helped find the

blasted moonkelp after all this time and her what helped find Irl's missing guardian, is gonna perish. Her sweet briny blood'll be on your crow-black souls! Well, before that happens know this – if'n tha don't lift the stinkin' curse, that charm of Irl's is gonna be dashed to smith'reens and then old Wormy'll come to get yer!"

The aufwader's torrent of hate and abuse ended with a final pounding of his staff and his eyes shone beneath the wiry brows, daring the Lords of the Deep to strike him down.

Beside him Miss Boston stood with her hands behind her back and wondered what the Triad would make of the passionate tirade.

The indistinct forms upon the thrones remained silent for too long and the old lady suspected that Tarr's threat had not shaken them as much as he had hoped.

Then the Lord of the Frozen Wastes stirred and inside their minds he coldly said, *"Thus are the ungrateful wretches revealed. For the sake of a few miserable, noisome lives would this vile knave release the destroyer upon the world. Is there no base treason his race is incapable of perpetrating?"*

"Ah'll go to my grave the happier knowin' the serpent has got thee as well," Tarr called defiantly.

"Morgawrus shall stay tethered in sleep," the central figure rumbled, *"for if thou wert to break the last guardian then thine own doom and that of thy granddaughter would be hideous beyond imagining."*

"It's that already," Tarr snapped impatiently. "Tha canna threaten me no more, tha'll not wriggle out of this!"

"Wouldst thou really submit that child to unending pain and suffering?" the resonant voice asked. *"The fate that does await her now would be a blessed release compared to that which thou wouldst inflict upon her."*

Tarr scowled and he looked at the figure with less confidence than before. "What does tha mean?" he asked.

At the foot of the column on which they stood, the water surged and bubbled and the familiar shape of the wooden boat rose swiftly to the surface. Still seated within the craft the herald turned and bowed to his masters, the sea-green cloak dripping with weed and brine.

Laughing insidiously, the Lord of the Frozen Wastes muttered in a sharp and malicious tone. *"Behold, oh leader of the wading rabble. See what horrors the urchin Nelda can expect. Is this, our messenger, not the most reliable and trustworthy of slaves? Doth he not perform his duties well? Dost thou know how long he hath been chained within that craft to do our bidding?"*

Tarr stared down at the herald who now sat with his head down, abashed and afraid.

"Didst thou not think him a being of the deep?" the repulsive voice persisted. *"Yea, that is the way of it now, but 'twas not always thus. Once this cringing baseness walked amongst thy kind – in truth he was one of thy greatest warriors and wisest craftsmen."*

"No," Tarr gasped in horror.

"Yes," the mocking friend answered, *"thy trusty guide who brought thee hither this night – is none other than Irl himself."*

"Still alive?" Tarr cried. "After all these ages?"

"Oh yes, we have many ways of extending the span of thy flickering lifetimes. Yet to live forever would be no punishment; there is always a price to be paid. Irl – show him."

The herald refused to move and the voice grew harsher and more repellent than ever.

"Show him!" it commanded.

Very slowly, and shivering with his head cast downwards, the herald unclasped the cloak and removed the hood from his head.

Miss Boston uttered a cry of dismay and Tarr staggered against his staff.

Sitting inside the boat was the most disgusting, unnatural mutation of scale and clammy flesh they would ever see. Pale green was the deformed monster's slimy skin and it stretched in sagging, ulcerous swathes about the crippled frame. Five tentacles snaked out from beneath the grotesque bent body, three spiky gills twitched and flapped around a parrot-like beak, and covering the horribly swollen head were two clusters of compound eyes that glittered under the light of the lanterns and the glow of the moonkelp.

Tarr turned away and his pity went out to the frightened, tortured creature below.

"*A fine pet hath Irl made,*" the Lord of the Frozen Wastes declared, "*though he refused to reveal to us where our treasure lay hid, no matter what we did to him. Is he not comely to thine eyes, Tarr? Yet his every movement is an agony and the very touch of his own flesh is abhorrent and fills his waking hours with despair. Canst thou not see thine own grandchild arrayed thus in the raiment of the deep? How shall she fare in the eternal night if thou release Morgawrus? Better than us no doubt, but couldst thou consign her to such an existence? There are many other diverse forms she could wear – Irl's handsome mantle is but one. Wouldst thou like dear little Nelda to be even as he and suffer forever?*"

"No," Tarr wept, "dinna cast that at her – please, I beg of you!"

The voice laughed at him and Miss Boston shook her head sadly as the aufwader broke down and slumped to his knees, craving their forgiveness.

"The guardian shall not be smashed!" he wailed. "Leave my Nelda be – ah beseech you, oh mighty lords. Ah'd rather she die under the curse than exist as such a nightmare!"

"Then we do accept thy entreaty," the central figure murmured sorrowfully. *"The widow of Esau shall perish swiftly and the infant with her, and to show that we are compassionate, by our mercy shall her time come soon. I perceive now that only woe and strife hath come about when the landbreed and thy kind have dwelt side by side – it will be best for all this way. Alas thy race will be doomed to extinction. Hast thou anything more to say?"*

But Tarr could not answer. His anguish was unbearable and he blubbered like a baby himself helpless upon the floor with his head in his hands.

"He might have nothing to say," Miss Boston suddenly shouted, brandishing her walking stick imperiously, "but I most certainly do!"

Flinging her tweed cape behind her, the old lady drew a deep and vehement breath then berated the Deep Ones vigorously.

"Is this your great and vaunted wisdom?" she demanded. "Will you stand aside and let a mother and child die because of some stupid law which you made up in the first place? By all that's holy I have never heard such utter balderdash! You are nothing but meddling cowards – mountebanks the lot!"

The shadowy figures writhed at her furious attack but Miss Boston would not be quelled. "If you are as mighty as you pretend," she bellowed indignantly, "then what are you afraid of? What warped and twisted pleasure do you enjoy from the misery of others? It isn't tears that flow into your precious waters but the blood of innocents! How much have you spilled to muddy your precious realm and cover your despicable tracks? Fie upon all three of you if you spill more! And remember this – you may indeed be the powers of this world, but beyond your reach there is a higher authority and it is to Him you shall answer!"

"Enough!" roared the Lord of the Circling Seas, and the violence of his thundering thought as it broke

into her mind sent Miss Boston stumbling back.

"Never before has an audience been granted to one of the lesser breeds of man – thou, old crone, art the first and last. Yet if thou dost not put a guard upon that garrulous and incautious tongue then I shall let the waters roll over thy insolent head now."

Miss Boston pursed her lips and gazed at him truculently. "Would it, pray," she began sarcastically, "be too much to inquire exactly why I have been brought here? Or do you simply like showing off? In my day there was only one deterrent for a bully – hit the perisher soundly with a slipper. I only wish I had one big enough."

"Alice Boston," the shadowy form said curtly, *"it is for thee to tell us why thou art here."*

The old lady waggled the stick at him. "What are you blabbering on about now?" she cried.

"By small degrees thy strength hath returned to thee," he continued in a strange and almost admiring tone. *"Day after day thou hast cast thy petty spells and laboured over what clumsy remedies are in thy puny power. But what then? Once thy ailments are defeated and thou art restored, how much further wouldst thou press?"*

Then the Lord of the Roaring Waters took over. *"Curious were we,"* he said softly, *"much have we desired to look on the one who put the final chain upon Morgawrus. None save we can remember the desolation the serpent wrought in the early morning of the world. Gone are the peoples of the kingdom he despoiled and their noble blood is thinned with that of baser creatures. Thus are we grateful to the one who returned the destroyer to the prison which we fashioned in those forgotten days."*

"So," Miss Boston remarked, "I'm here for a pat on the head, is that it? Well, I don't want your congratulations, thank you very much! If you hadn't botched the job in the first place Nathaniel Crozier would never have been able to awaken the brute."

A deadly silence descended and the figures sat motionless upon the towering thrones. Then in a sneering, malevolent whisper, the voice of the Frozen Wastes said, *"The serpent may indeed be at rest – yet for how long?"*

The old lady tutted. "You don't have to go over that again," she barked. "There's nothing to fear, the guardian is safe."

"Yet the hand which invoked the forces locked within that mighty charm may also undo them."

"Don't be ridiculous!" she cried. "Why should I do that?"

"With the aid of the guardian thou wouldst be able to control the serpent and bind it to thy service – is that not the reason for thy recovery?"

Miss Boston spluttered speechlessly. "Absurd!" she eventually blurted. "I refute that ludicrous accusation absolutely!"

"Then why hast thou cheated Death?" the Lord of the Circling Seas demanded. *"The date was set down but the hour appointed has come and still thou livest. Thrice now hast thou evaded the angel – why hast thou dared to survive?"*

"What are you saying?" she cried in bemusement. "I haven't the faintest idea…"

"No?" The Lord of the Frozen Wastes' stinging hiss whipped into her mind. *"See how the lies drip from her tongue, my brothers! The witch hath flouted our design and refuses to pass over – she conspires against us!"*

"Nonsense!" she laughed. "I'm most awfully sorry if I haven't popped my clogs, but I have no intention of doing that for some time."

"Then what is thine intent? Art thou indeed determined to regain all thy former vigour?"

"I am!"

"And once that is achieved – what then? Art thou to pursue this dubious cause? Is it thy desire to dispel utterly the chains of age and never fear them again? What deeds

wouldst thou perform to attain that, I wonder. Is there naught thou wouldst not do? Are there things thou hast already done which thou wouldst never have dreamed of before this obsession gripped thee?"

Miss Boston frowned. "I've done nothing to be ashamed of," she answered.

The voice dwindled into a prying murmur. *"Really?"* it oozed. *"Is neglect not a crime – is that not a matter for guilt and shame?"*

"Neglect?" she cried. "I haven't neglected anything!"

"What of those in thy care? 'Tis they who have suffered."

A look of understanding passed over the old lady's face. "The children?" she muttered. "But how have I neglected them? I love them both dearly!"

"Thy constant striving to regain thy strength hath made thee blind to their needs and wants. Too long hast thou pored over thy sorceries, too many hours have they been alone. Yet was it not for their sake that this laborious task of misguided self-healing was undertaken – or hast thou forgotten that also?"

"Of course not!" she denied passionately. "I am pledged to protect them – Jennet and Benjamin are my only concern! I don't care what happens to me, all I want is to be able to defend them when the time comes!"

At this, the shadowy figure upon the middle throne said, *"If that is true, then consign the boy into our care. As the one who returned our treasure to us, he has our favour and thus are we committed to guard and watch over him."*

"Proclaim thy devotion to the child," urged the voice of the Roaring Seas. *"Reveal to us the meaning of compassion. Make the ultimate sacrifice, Alice Boston, and we shall look after him."*

"Beware, my brothers!" the Lord of the Frozen Wastes interrupted. *"The Witch is not to be trusted. Do not put your faith in this ambitious female – for is she not*

already tutoring the boy in the ways of her feeble craft? How else could he have thwarted the angel? Verily I warn you, the hag is no fool – she is nurturing a dangerous power within that human whelp and to what evil purpose will this lead?''

Miss Boston shook her head in disbelief at all they had said. "I'm not tutoring anyone!" she announced. "Least of all Benjamin. Why, the very idea is totally preposterous."

Moved by the words of his wheedling brother, the Lord of the Circling Seas angrily replied, *"Not so! The child has been studying thy Book of Shadows, and his knowledge of things best left hidden increases with every moonrise!''*

"Benjamin!" Miss Boston said crossly. "I had no idea – I'm sure it's all perfectly harmless."

"Harmless?'' the bitter voce raged. *"The child was brought to Whitby for one purpose alone. To aid the aufwader girl and discover the moonkelp! That he hath done – we cannot permit him to develop his gifts any further!''*

Hearing these words, Tarr raised his head sharply and rose to his feet.

Miss Boston opened her mouth to say something but could only splutter as she realized what had been said.

"What ... what do you mean by that?" she murmured. "You did not bring Benjamin to Whitby – he came with Jennet because..."

Her voice failed as finally she understood and Miss Boston's horrified outrage boiled and flared within her breast.

"The children", she began, struggling to control her contemptuous fury, "came to live with me because their parents were killed. They drowned when their car plunged into a river. My God – were you so desperate for your precious weed that you committed murder in order to manipulate one little boy and his sister? You disgust me!"

She closed her eyes and turned away from the sight of the three thrones, too appalled to speak any further.

At her side Tarr's face was drawn into a horrible expression of hate. "Now ah know", he snarled, pointing an accusing finger at the powers of the world, "why, out of all others, my Nelda was allowed to live after she were born. She were only a puppet fer tha to use in tha greedy search. Tha needed her to be ready to meet a human child wi' the sight! That was all she were good fer! Her whole short life were leadin' up to that one moment when she'd help the lad find your poxy treasure – ain't that so?

"Well, now her part's been done an' theer's naught else tha got planned fer her, so she might as well die. Good thing too, eh? Makes the whole nasty business that much tidier!"

Shaking with rage, the aufwader strode to the edge of the high platform and spat as far as he could. "Damn yers all!" he yelled.

Miss Boston watched him approvingly, then stared back at the shimmering wall of water and spoke up in a clear and strident voice. "A curse on you!" she said. "I pray long and hard that you shall get what you deserve. Do you honestly expect me to surrender the children into your care? You must think I am mad! I am now more determined than ever to protect them from your unholy influence and shall do so unto the last breath in my body!"

Behind the thrones the light of the moonkelp dimmed as the sea grew dark.

"*Silence!*" commanded the Lord of the Frozen Wastes. "*Hag! Thou hast asked why thou wert summoned to this place – for one purpose only was the audience permitted. Know now the judgement of the almighty Triad!*"

"*The boy child has indeed done us great service,*" the central figure boomed. "*Our coveted prize is returned to*

270

us, yet still he associates with the aufwaders. Henceforth this must cease!"

Tarr laughed grimly. "Tha can't do nowt to stop the lad," he growled. "He's more than welcome in our midst – an' more so when I tells the rest what I've 'eard this night. The boy can come a-visitin' whenever he chooses. Alone amongst humans he has touched the moonkelp and so is under tha protection. Theer's nowt tha can do to stop 'im."

"Is there not?" the voice echoed mysteriously. *"We believe a solution has been found and our oath of protection need not be broken. Look to the water."*

Miss Boston and Tarr glanced down as the smooth surface of the placid lake was pierced by thousands of bubbles. From the black depths, an object resembling a small stone came floating upwards.

With a mild splash it burst into the air, then rolled and spun in the water as it drifted towards the pinnacle of rock.

Miss Boston descended the winding stair as the curious object came to rest against the bottommost step, and with the handle of her walking stick she fished it out.

Glistening in her palm was a round earthenware jar no larger than a tennis ball, and she examined it cautiously. The container was glazed a deep swirling green; around the base weird characters and symbols were inscribed and removing the wax that sealed the lid, she warily looked inside.

A pale, almost luminous cream filled the jar and the old lady sniffed it tentatively.

"And what might this be?" she asked.

In a soft, mellifluous voice the Lord of the Circling Seas replied, *"In thy hands is the answer we have sought. Take the salve and with it anoint the boy's eyes."*

"Why?" she demanded.

"We cannot permit the child to continue mingling with

the aufwaders. That singular ointment will remove his special sight. Never again shall he see the folk who dwell by the shore, nor the shades of those who have passed through the veil."

"How dare you ask me to do such a dreadful thing!" the old lady shouted. "Benjamin's sight is a wondrous and most marvellous gift – I would not dream of stealing it from him!"

Upon the left-hand throne, the Lord of the Frozen Wastes swelled with anger and his enormous shadow whipped and thrashed in the icy waters.

"Behold the ignorance of mortal kind!" he thundered to his brothers. *"Let us destroy these two now and send the herald back with fierce words of warning to those who wait upon the shore."*

"Peace," the voice of the Circling Seas called. *"The leader of the aufwaders must return to make certain the guardian remains unharmed, and who can measure a human's heart? Perhaps our words shall weigh upon thee, Alice Boston, and thou shalt use the salve ere long."*

"I rather think that is highly unlikely," she replied.

Without warning, the Lord of the Frozen Waters let out a wrathful shriek that shook the cavern.

"Then begone from this place!" he roared, rising from the throne, thrashing his snaking limbs. *"Thou art dismissed!"*

At once the glimmering images behind the wall of water were engulfed in darkness and Miss Boston gazed grimly at Tarr.

"It would appear the audience is over," she observed.

A rush of froth and foam signalled the return of the small rowing boat and it floated back to the surface. Still crouched within, the tortured remains of Irl gazed at Miss Boston from beneath the hood of his cloak and he spoke urgently.

"Quickly – thou must make haste. The way back to thy world will soon collapse!"

THE LORDS OF THE DEEP AND DARK

Miss Boston and Tarr hurriedly clambered aboard the boat but as soon as they were seated, the immense barrier of dark water trembled, and with a tremendous rending crash, the might of the Deep Ones was withdrawn and the freezing torrent came flooding into the chamber.

The pinnacle of rock was thrown down and the seething tides hammered into the quartz-covered walls, snatched the lanterns from their huge iron hooks, and smashed against the vaulted ceiling.

But the small wooden boat was already tearing through the dimly-lit grottoes beyond. Carried on the racing currents, it soared wildly through the passages hewn into the mountain and pitched uncontrollably as the incredible forces of the whirling vortex clutched and seized it.

Out into the cold deeps the little boat shot, hurtling back along the spinning tunnel, but the journey was faster than before and Miss Boston was thrown from side to side as the craft darted wildly forward.

The eyes of the herald sparkled in alarm as he stared behind them and saw that the spinning walls of the enchanted way were closing. Violent surges thrust the boat onward as the tunnel snapped out of existence, unravelling with a furious turbulence that tore apart the ocean floor, leaving a path of foaming destruction in its wake.

Over the drowned continent the vessel rampaged, but swiftly the decaying cities vanished from sight as the tunnel convulsed and buckled, threatening to dash the boat to pieces at any moment.

"Hold on!" the herald yelled and his voice rang with fear. "Save us, oh masters! The way fails too swiftly – we shall be torn apart!"

Only the savage, screaming waters answered him as they stampeded malevolently and raced for the boat. The spray of the collapsing vortex blasted into

Tarr's face as he glanced round and saw that the terrible, churning cataclysm was only metres away. Beyond the roaring confusion of the unwinding tunnel, the murderous pressures of the deep were waiting, eager to crush and kill.

Tarr wrenched his eyes from the horrendous sight and stared anxiously at the herald. "We'll not make it!" he bawled.

"Have faith, Mr Shrimp!" Miss Boston cried. "They wouldn't dare let anything happen to us, otherwise Nelda will destroy the guardian. This is just a show of bluster."

Suddenly her hat was plucked from her head and sucked into the darkness behind. The old lady snorted tersely. "Steady on!" she shouted into the storm.

At a breakneck speed the boat flew through the cold reaches, rocketing ever upwards until, with a sickening jolt that rattled its timbers, the little craft was hurled from the sea and flung out beneath the fading stars.

The waves lashed and the wind tore at Miss Boston's cloak as the mouth of the gigantic whirlpool toppled and came raging down, smiting the waters and splitting them asunder in its ruinous downfall. A tempestuous cauldron steamed and foamed within the sea, its choking vapours hissed into the air, obliterating the heavens with billowing clouds of thick white mist.

Wraith-like, the rowing boat sailed noiselessly through the mist and its occupants took great glad gulps of the cool night air, relieved to be above the waves once more. Neither Tarr nor Miss Boston ventured to speak; they were both thinking about what they had learned and the vile knowledge angered and depressed them. As they drifted towards the distant shores of Whitby, their spirits sank ever lower and with downcast faces they floated into the night.

Finally it was the herald who broke the forbidding silence.

"There is fear in the Deeps," he said in a soft and conspiring voice. "For only the second time in the history of the world the cold regions are filled with dread – the Triad is afraid."

Miss Boston was startled out of her despondency and Tarr stared at the huddled figure keenly.

"Messages and rumours spread swiftly beneath the waves," the herald continued. "Many are the frightened tales spreading from the bitter realms. 'Tis said that the Lord of the Frozen Wastes is especially fearful and has despatched many spies to watch the shores of my ancient home."

"Theer's nowt to see theer," Tarr said sourly, "save misery and hopelessness."

Leaning across to Miss Boston, the tormented remains of Irl whispered to her anxiously. "Cruel and devoid of compassion are my masters," he began, "yet they are wise beyond all others. Use the thing they have given to thee, rub the salve well into the boy's eyes. His sight is a curse and only woe shall befall him and those he loves."

"I'm afraid you cannot persuade me," she answered stubbornly. "I swear here and now as God is my witness that I will never use their despicable ointment."

So adamant was the old lady that she took the jar from her pocket and stretched out her arm ready to throw it back into the sea, but the herald called for her to stop and the command in his voice was so compelling that Miss Boston wavered.

"I beg thee not to cast it aside," he cried. "The gifts of the Deep Ones should not be lightly surrendered."

The folds of the sea-green cloak stirred as the

hideous shapes within uncoiled and a putrescent, snaking tentacle emerged – creeping towards Miss Boston.

For a brief second she feared that the creature was going to strike her, then she saw that bound about the tapering tip of the extended limb was a piece of carved jet, suspended on a fine gold chain.

"Unto thee do I now give this," Irl said gravely. "I fashioned it in the young long ago, when I was a leader of my tribe and resolved to quest for the moonkelp."

Holding the carving high above the tendrils of mist which still clung to the boat, the herald gazed on his craftsmanship sorrowfully, then gave the amulet to Miss Boston.

The old lady received the dark jewel silently and peered at the intricate detail. In her hands, the bright moonlight curved over a tiny squat figure whose face was hidden beneath a veil embroidered with the ancient script of the aufwaders, and emblazoned over the back of the black, glimmering gem was the symbol of the Triad.

" 'Tis the very charm I devised to conceal me from the vigilance of the Lords of the Deep and Dark," Irl told her. "When it is worn around the neck it renders my masters and their countless agents insensible to thy presence. Without it I could never have stolen the shining treasure and wrought the guardian to keep Morgawrus entombed."

"I cannot accept such a precious gift," Miss Boston said, reaching out to return the ancient pendant, "but if anyone has a claim to it then surely it would be Mr Shrimp and the rest of the fisherfolk?"

The herald shrank from her and the hood shook from side to side. "The last tribe is doomed," he said flatly, "and I fear that thou mayest yet have need of the charm's properties – the spies of my Lord of the

Frozen Wastes are ranged about the town. May this assist thee in evading them."

"I am most grateful," Miss Boston breathed, "though I pray it won't be necessary."

Irl's tone grew cold and ominous. "I assure thee it will," he uttered, "yet its power to withstand the piercing gaze of my masters doth wane after a time. Use it only in the direst need and remember that they are capable of anything. Nothing is beyond their reach – do not forget that. They do serve only their own ends and thou knowest already how merciless are their punishments."

Tarr stared at the cloaked figure and could not stop a look of revulsion creeping over his face. The herald noticed it and gathered the cloak tightly about his grotesque form.

"Do not provoke them further," he told the aufwader. " 'Tis better for thy granddaughter to die sooner than be damned to eternity as I."

Guiltily Tarr lowered his eyes and not another word was spoken for the rest of the journey.

* * *

Upon the shore beneath the cliffs many of the fisherfolk were asleep when the blue light of the boat's lantern reappeared in the distance.

Ben and Nelda were sitting upon a coarse blanket and wrapped in two more, struggling to remain awake, when the aufwader on watch leapt up and called to the others.

"They're here! They've returned!"

Rubbing the sleep from their eyes, they lurched to their feet and waited in fearful silence as the vessel sailed closer.

"Are Aunt Alice and Tarr all right?" Ben asked.

"They are," Nelda replied, but her hopes

plummeted as she realized how still and quiet her grandfather seemed. Even before the boat came to rest at the water's edge she hung her head and murmured, "The Deep Ones have denied his pleas."

Tarr glanced across at her forlorn figure and a large tear trickled down his round nose. "Ah dinna know what to tell her," he wept.

Miss Boston put her arm around him. "Be honest with the girl – she deserves that."

"Aye," he sniffed, "and a 'ell of a lot more that I canna give."

"May her ending be swift and without torment," the herald said gently, "and may courage be granted to thee, Tarr of the Mereades, for the full face of doom is staring at thy kind. A ninefold blessing upon thee and fare as well as thou art able."

Tarr looked at the herald and bowed his head in respect. "Ah would ask tha to join us," he said. "A mighty honour would it be for Irl to come amongst the descendants of his folk."

"No," the cloaked figure refused, "and if thou dost indeed honour and revere my old name, then forget this meeting. Irl died an age and more ago – let not his esteemed memory be clouded with the horror I have become. Go to thy people, Tarr, but mention me never."

The aufwader understood and with a quick nod, he clutched his staff and clambered from the boat.

"Thank you for all you have done," Miss Boston said.

"Heed my warnings," the herald urged her, "for thy peril is mounting. My masters will not be content until thou hast done their bidding. I say to you, Alice Boston – beware."

"Where will you go now?" she asked.

"Back to them, back to the world of darkness and cold – such is my punishment."

The old lady made to scramble from the boat, but at the last minute she reached forward and before the herald could stop her, reached into the shadows beneath the hood.

"Goodbye," she said warmly, as her hand caressed the scaly flesh hidden within.

A strangled cry broke from the herald's mouth as the unexpected and unlooked for touch pierced his heart.

"Go now," he murmured thickly.

Miss Boston smiled and with Tarr's help alighted from the boat.

With the water lapping about their knees, they waited until the wooden vessel had turned and sailed into the distance before wading on to dry land and speaking to the others.

Nelda needed no explanation. She could see from her grandfather's sombre expression that she and her unborn child were going to die and she staggered into his outstretched arms.

"Come, lass," he croaked, "let us return to our cave."

The fisherfolk covered their faces as they too understood and one by one they trailed back to the cliffs.

"Wouldn't they listen?" Ben asked in dismay. "Aunt Alice, what happened?"

Miss Boston stooped down and hugged him fiercely. "Oh Benjamin!" she murmured. "I think we should return home too. At this moment I want to feel safe and surround myself with my familiar clutter – a strong cup of tea wouldn't go amiss either. It won't be long before dawn, why don't I tell you everything over breakfast?"

With her tweed cloak hanging heavy and wet from her shoulders and the boy's arm wrapped around her waist, Miss Boston wandered over the gloomy shore into Whitby.

11

OVER TEA AND CHEESECAKE

The early crying of the gulls jolted Jennet from an uneasy sleep. Nightmare visions of the coven had pursued her throughout the night and, looking into the bedside mirror, she saw that dark circles rimmed her raw, swollen eyes.

When she had returned, the girl had found the cottage empty, and thinking that Aunt Alice and Ben were still enjoying themselves at the wedding reception, Jennet had gone straight to bed. But she had spent most of the night weeping into her pillow and the feelings of betrayal, horror and isolation were just as strong in the bright sunshine of the morning.

Slung over the end of her bed were the tattered remains of the bridesmaid dress and the girl quickly snatched at them and stuffed the ripped mass of satin into a drawer.

Mechanically, she pulled on her clothes – wincing as her jeans dragged over the yellow bruises and scabbed scratches that covered her legs. Then, yawning, she opened the door of her room and went downstairs.

In the kitchen she found that her brother and Miss Boston had already eaten their breakfast and the old lady was busily recounting her astounding experience beneath the waves, with many wild sweeping gestures of her hands.

Aunt Alice paused as the girl entered and greeted her profusely. "Jennet dear!" she exclaimed. "I do hope you're feeling better this morning – help yourself to toast and there are some scrambled eggs in the pan, if you feel up to them."

The girl hastily recalled the lie she had told to excuse herself from the reception. "I'm fine," she lied again, "but I'll just stick with the toast, thanks."

Taking a seat at the table she thoughtfully chewed her breakfast and was so preoccupied with her own worries that it was only after several minutes that she noticed the circles around Ben's eyes were larger and darker than her own.

"Are you all right?" she asked. "Ben, you keep nodding off."

With his head resting on his hand the boy gave a weary grunt and Jennet looked to Miss Boston.

The old lady poured herself another cup of tea then folded her arms upon the table. "I'm afraid neither of us has had any sleep," she said.

Jennet put her toast down and a dreadful thought struck her – what if she had cried out in the night about what had happened? "Why ... why was that?" she stammered. "Did something keep you awake?"

"That's putting it mildly," Aunt Alice replied, eager to tell her all about the Lords of the Deep.

"I'm sorry," Jennet said hastily, "I had a nightmare, that's all."

"Did you, dear?" Miss Boston clucked. "You poor thing, I thought you looked a trifle peaky – and have you done something with your hair? Anyway, let me tell you what happened to us!"

The girl listened in astonishment as the old lady gabbled about the Deep Ones and what they had said – she did not however disclose what she had learnt about the children's parents.

"And this", Aunt Alice announced, slamming a small green jar on to the table, "is what they gave me to anoint Benjamin's eyes – can you believe such a thing?"

After her own terrifying ordeal Jennet thought that she could believe anything. But she merely shook her head and let Aunt Alice continue.

Yet it was Ben who spoke first. Staring thoughtfully at the jar and peering at its contents, he said, "Why don't they want me to see Nelda again?"

"Is she really going to die?" asked Jennet. "Was there nothing you could do?"

Miss Boston shook her jowls regretfully, "Alas no," she muttered, "I'm afraid the fisherfolk are doomed."

Ben pushed his plate away and stared at the floor.

"Why don't you go to bed?" Aunt Alice told him. "You must be shattered. I'll wake you this afternoon and if you feel any brighter you can go and call on Nelda."

When the boy had risen from the table and shambled out of the kitchen, Miss Boston tutted. "It'll be a most difficult time for him when Nelda dies," she said. "She's the only young friend he's got."

"He's got me," Jennet murmured, but she knew that was not true for her recent unkindness had driven Ben away from her and now they hardly ever talked to one another. Swilling the toast down with a gulp of tea, she said in an apologetic whisper, "Aunt Alice, I've been a pig lately – I'm sorry."

The old lady smiled at her. "Don't be silly, dear," she said, "I haven't noticed ..." Miss Boston faltered as she remembered one of the accusations the Lords of the Deep had charged her with. "Neglect ..." she whispered, "yes, perhaps I have been guilty of that."

Shaking herself, she snapped out of the unpleasant memory and took hold of the girl's hand. "Don't you worry," she cried, "it's going to be very different around here from now on. Jennet dear, I've been so preoccupied with my ailments that, to my shame, I haven't made any time for you. Is there anything you'd like to tell me? How are you getting on at school? Wasn't there some talk of your work slipping – is that because of me?"

"No," Jennet quickly replied, "that's all sorted out – it was my fault but I'm going to try harder from now on."

"So what have you got planned for today? It's another beauty. Am I mistaken or did that fool of a nun mention you'd made friends with a group of musicians? Will you be seeing them this weekend?"

Jennet shivered. "I don't think so," she said. "In fact I'd be quite happy to stay in until school on Monday."

"As you wish," Miss Boston muttered clearing the breakfast dishes into the sink.

"I'll do them," the girl offered.

Mildly surprised, Aunt Alice stepped back and allowed Jennet to take over. "Goodness," she grinned, "we are eager to please this morning."

"I just want to make up for the past few months," Jennet shrugged. "If there's anything else I can do…"

"Well, if you really want to help, I was going to turn that sickroom back to how it was before my illness. Heaven knows where Edith put half the stuff I had in there. At least a dozen of my ornaments and corn dollies are missing – I bet she threw them in the loft or put them in the church bazaar. Do you remember what she did with Prudence's African souvenirs – the ones she left me in her will? You know, the moth-eaten zebra skin and the Zulu shield with the spear? Why, Jennet, wherever did you get that necklace?"

The girl's hands flew to the beads around her throat as Aunt Alice stepped forward to admire them.

"They appear to be most awfully tight," she

observed. "Isn't that terribly uncomfortable? Here, let me adjust the ..."

"No!" Jennet snapped. "It's all right, honestly."

The old lady blinked at her in astonishment – the girl's mood had changed drastically.

"Well, if you're certain," she relented. "Is that what all the youngsters are wearing now?"

"Only the select few," Jennet replied grimly.

Miss Boston's eyebrows twitched quizzically and for the first time she realized just how much Jennet had changed. She was no longer a child and, unsure of what to say to her, Miss Boston took herself off to the sickroom and turned on the radio.

Alone in the kitchen, Jennet leaned against the sink and buried her face in her sud-covered hands. She had tried to remove the beads before she had come downstairs, but the necklace seemed to sense her intention and had almost strangled her. Was Pear right? Was she really the same as the rest of the coven?

"Please no," she whispered. "I'm not like them, I'm not."

When Aunt Alice returned, Jennet was busily drying the dishes, and hoped the old lady would not realize that she had been crying.

"Most distressing," Miss Boston declared. "There never seems to be any good news these days – I've a good mind to take the plug off that instrument. You only ever hear about earthquakes or air disasters – why don't they broadcasting something chirpy for a change?"

"You should tune into the local stations," said Jennet, trying to sound cheerful. "They're good for tame, heartwarming stories."

"But I did. That was Radio Middlesbrough, and very nasty it was too."

Jennet took another plate from the rack and wiped

it with a dishcloth. "What was it today?" she asked, "Naughty vicars or crooked landlords?"

"Oh, it wasn't anything like that – something quite grisly and downright vicious. A flock of sheep have been slaughtered on a remote farm."

"Isn't that what they're reared for?"

"That isn't what I meant. No, the poor creatures were slain in the fields – the farmer found them this morning and very horrible it was too, by his account. Too dreadful to be the work of vandals or hoodlums. The police believe a pack of wild dogs is responsible. Can you credit it, in this day and age!"

The plate fell from Jennet's hands and smashed upon the floor.

"Jennet!" Miss Boston cried. "You're white as a sheet!"

* * *

For the rest of the weekend the girl refused to leave the cottage and filled her time doing those chores which she normally loathed. No job was too dull, whether it was weeding garden borders, helping Aunt Alice sort out the front room, or washing the windows – so long as it took her mind off Pear and the coven that was all that mattered.

The girl's unexpected enthusiasm for these mundane household duties disconcerted Miss Boston, but Jennet absolutely refused to be persuaded to step outside the front door and the old lady began to suspect that she was avoiding something.

"Perhaps she has fallen out with her new friends and doesn't want to bump into them," she surmised, brushing all too near the truth.

Ben however was hardly at home and spent long hours with the fisherfolk. Nelda had grown very weak and when Miss Boston learned this she became grave, knowing that the Deep Ones had accelerated the aufwader's time.

On Sunday afternoon, the old lady went to the cliffs herself and was saddened to see how poorly Nelda had become.

The youngest member of the tribe could no longer walk and she lay upon the floor of the cave suffering from painful spasms.

She and Tarr exchanged mournful glances, but they spoke encouragingly to the child though they knew their words were hollow. Miss Boston wished there was something she could do for her and when she returned home, searched through The Book of Shadows for a salve or lotion that would at least ease the aufwader's pain. But there was nothing and the old lady tossed the volume aside, then threw herself vigorously into the housework.

Ben stayed at Nelda's side for most of the day and grew ever more dejected and morose. He could tell that she did not have long, yet could not imagine his life without her. Eventually, when the shadows deepened outside the cave, Tarr instructed the boy to return home and in a trembling voice, Ben bade them goodnight.

On Monday morning, the atmosphere in the cottage was one of glum despondency. Jennet did not relish the thought of walking to school, afraid that the coven would be waiting for her to step outside the front door and snatch her again. But she couldn't lock herself away forever, so she put on her uniform and waited for her brother.

Ben, however, was too upset to go anywhere. He refused to leave for school and would not touch any breakfast until Aunt Alice assured him that as soon as he ate something they would both visit the caves.

Jennet watched him sorrowfully swirl his spoon

around a bowl of cereal. His strange friendship with the fisherfolk was a mystery that she would never share, but she could understand and feel his grief as surely as if it were her own.

"Give my love to Nelda," she said to him. "I'll see you this afternoon."

Ben continued to brood over his breakfast. "I will," he muttered, "if she's still alive."

Miss Boston had given up attempting to be jolly and, following Jennet to the door, whispered, "If she still lives then these will undoubtedly be her final hours. The poor mite was failing fast yesterday; you could almost see her deteriorate before your eyes – a dreadful tragedy."

"I'm glad you'll be with him," the girl told her. "I've always been there for Ben before, but this is something beyond me and I can't help him. We're so lucky to have found you."

Aunt Alice was lost for words and could only wave as Jennet left the courtyard and disappeared into the street beyond. "Surprising girl," she mused as she returned to check how much Ben had eaten, "she really is behaving most oddly."

A faint drizzle had soused the early morning; in Church Street the cobbles glistened and awnings dripped on to the unsuspecting passers-by. Cautiously, Jennet headed for school, peering with suspicion into the lanes and doorways on either side, for the sisterhood of the coven could be lurking anywhere.

When she reached Market Place, where she had first met Pear, Jennet's pace increased. She was still turning around to glare dubiously at the pillars of the old town hall, when in front of her a voice abruptly called out her name.

Jennet spun around and there, standing by the entrance to the closed bookshop, was Pear.

"Jennet!" she cried. "I've been worried sick – where have you been hiding? I thought you'd come and see me!"

"You thought what?" Jennet spluttered incredulously. "After what you and your friends tried to do?"

The witch-girl stepped into the drizzle and the anguish on her face was unmistakable. "I'm so sorry for what happened on Friday!" she swore. "It all went wrong, the others are sorry too – when the beast takes command there's nothing you can do!"

"Is that why you killed those sheep?" Jennet snapped angrily. "If I hadn't escaped it would have been my body that was found all torn to bits."

"Please!" Pear implored. "We should have explained properly – we thought you were ready. Let me talk to you …"

"Get lost!" Jennet shrieked. "I don't want to hear any more of your lies. I can't believe how stupid I was. If you and your friends don't leave me alone I'll tell the police! I should have done that in the first place!"

She stormed past the witch-girl but Pear ran after her. "There's no escape," she told her. "Jennet, none of us can be free of Nathaniel – he is part of our souls. Stop denying it to yourself."

"Rubbish!"

"Then why are you still wearing the necklace?"

Jennet made no answer and, flustered, she hurried towards the school.

"You must listen to me!" Pear shouted. "Your old life is over – you belong to *him* now. Why won't you let me explain? Wait, please!"

Furious at both herself and her former friend, Jennet roughly pushed Pear away and screamed at her. "I'll never listen to you again!" she shrieked, and all the browsing tourists turned to stare at the two girls. "You're a liar and a coward! If you really wanted to get away from those filthy witches nothing could stop you! I saw your face as you dragged me round that bonfire – you were revelling in it. You disgust me – just stay away!"

Pear clutched at the girl's coat but Jennet pulled it free and strode away.

Standing alone in the middle of the road, Pear broke down and wept genuine tears. "Jennet!" she wailed. "Don't leave me! You don't understand! I can never be free of Nathaniel – or the others."

"Course you can!" the other shouted, not bothering to look round.

"No I can't!" Pear snivelled. 'You see … you see – Nathaniel Crozier was my father!"

Jennet halted and turned slowly around. In spite of her anger she suddenly felt an overwhelming sense of pity for the older girl, and without thinking, said, "Meet me after school."

Pear nodded quickly and Jennet hastened away.

* * *

In the Walrus and the Carpenter Café, later that afternoon, the two girls were sitting at a small table by the window, each with a cup of tea and a piece of cheesecake.

An awkward and uncomfortable silence had prevented them saying much of anything and they half-heartedly picked at the dessert, both waiting for the other to speak first.

Finally Jennet could stand it no more and came straight out with it. "Is it true then?"

"What?" asked Pear.

"About Nathaniel being your father, or was that another lie to get me to talk to you?"

The older girl looked away and slowly moved the

crumbs around the plate. "It's all true," she confessed. "I am his daughter."

"I thought he was married to Rowena."

"Don't be naïve; she was his legal bride but in a sense he was married to every member of the coven."

Jennet eyed the other customers and lowered her voice so that they couldn't hear. "Why did they want me to join them?" she hissed. "What would be the point? Why are they still clinging to his memory? Why don't they go back to whatever lives they had before?"

"If you'd let me explain," Pear told her, "then you'll understand why they – we – have done what we have."

Jennet folded her arms. "Go on then," she said bluntly, "tell me."

With her elbows on the table and her chin in her hands, Pear began. "You have to realize", she said, "that to us Nathaniel meant everything – literally. He was our High Priest, the very reason for our existence – mine especially. He only had to make the vaguest hint and we would rush to do whatever it was. You must know what that feeling is like. You were under his influence – was there anything you would not have done for him?"

Jennet bit her bottom lip and remembered how foolish she had been. "No," she admitted.

"And you only knew him for a short time," the other continued. "Can you imagine how forceful that power would become over the years? Poor Liz got so dependent on him that she couldn't eat or drink without his permission; she was like a ... like a ..."

"Pet dog?"

"Worse than that," Pear answered, ignoring the sarcasm, "and then – then he died."

She stared out of the window at the people passing by and her dark eyes glittered with tears. "No one

can ever know how terrible that was for us," she said huskily. "The same instant Morgawrus killed him, each member of the coven felt a sudden ... desolation as he was wrenched from us. We thought it was all over, there was nothing more to live for, no driving purpose in our lives – Liz almost took her own life. First Roselyn, the one you call Rowena, and then him, who we all worshipped."

"What did you do?"

Pear shuddered, recalling the insane and bloody actions of the coven in that ghastly time. "We were too distraught to care what we did," she murmured. "A madness was upon us. It wasn't just livestock that we butchered, no – far, far worse. There are voices that I can still hear – terrible screaming cries that will never be stilled and will hound me forever."

She lowered her eyes and fidgeted with the napkin before continuing. "Then, when we were gorged on carnage and the raving hysteria left us, it was Hillian who decided we should attempt to contact my father on the other side. So, we performed certain ... rites, yet the message we received exceeded anything we had anticipated.

"Through that contact we learned much. Nathaniel had been the unwitting agent of a greater power. When he followed Rowena to Whitby he was merely pursuing the pattern set down for him. He was like a rat in a maze."

Pausing, Pear absently stirred her tea and watched the waitress hovering near the other tables ready to take down their orders.

"Do you mean that someone else wanted him to free the serpent?" Jennet asked. "But why? It would wreak havoc and destroy everything."

Pear shook her head. "No, it wouldn't," she stated proudly. "You see, my father really was a master of domination. There has never been anyone like him in the whole history of the world – he was unique. The weary, sluggish mind of Morgawrus would've presented no difficulties for his arts. The monster would have been enslaved to his will as surely as you were.

"What Nathaniel didn't realize was that he was only an instrument playing another's tune. All along a darker, ancient mind had been at work, bringing the strands together and weaving the web that we are now enmeshed in."

"Are you trying to tell me", Jennet interrupted, "that Nathaniel was innocent, that I've misjudged him? You really don't give up, do—"

"I'm not saying anything of the sort!" Pear denied. "My father was certainly never 'innocent'! Look, do you want to hear the rest or not?"

"Go on. If waking Morgawrus was never Nathaniel's idea, then whose was it?"

Pear looked around warily and gave the other customers doubtful glances. Then, in a hushed and fearful voice, she whispered, "Meta hasn't told me but I've heard her and Hillian talking. Have you ever heard of the three beneath the waves – the Lords of the Deep and Dark?"

"Yes," Jennet answered slowly. "What about them?"

"That's who was behind it all! One of the great Triad!"

Jennet stared at her, then snorted with derision. "That's nonsense!" she said. "Aren't they the ones who put the serpent under the cliffs in the first place? Why would they want to release him?"

"I said only one of them," Pear insisted. "Think about it. Nothing comes close to rivalling the power of the Triad, nothing except Morgawrus."

"So?"

"Well, it stands to reason – one of them wants to get

rid of the other two, he wants to rule alone."

Bewildered, Jennet rubbed her forehead. "And you're saying he can't do that by himself, he needs the serpent to kill his brothers?"

"Of course! And using my father he could have done it too, except—"

"Except it didn't happen that way. Aunt Alice stopped him."

"She interfered," Pear spat, "and my father's control was shattered."

"Good!" Jennet said, finishing off her cheesecake.

"But that isn't the end of it," Pear muttered. "Morgawrus was entombed again but then the evil member of the Triad became fearful that his brothers would discover his murderous intentions. Using the moonkelp he looked into the future and saw his own destiny."

Leaning across the table, she whispered, "What the Lord of the Deep saw there chilled his black heart. For it was written that his own end was near. One of the three mightiest beings in the world felt threatened as never before – not since the serpent first rampaged over the land and sea. Now a new, more terrible danger was taking shape, something so deadly that his death is practically assured."

Jennet felt the air in the café grow cold as she tried to imagine what could possibly be more horrific than the Lords of the Deep. "What sort of nightmare is this new threat?" she asked nervously. "It must be really horrendous to scare one of the Triad."

Pear gave her a long and steady look before answering. "You really want to know?" she murmured.

"Course I do!"

"You won't like it."

"Tell me!"

Pear gently put her hand over Jennet's and in a

level, sincere voice said simply, "It's Ben."

The girl stared at her, then picked up her schoolbag ready to leave.

"It's true!" Pear swore. "Don't go, sit down!"

Jennet's eyes were filled with contempt. "I really am stupid!" she fumed. "I was actually starting to believe you. I don't know who's madder, you or me!"

"Somehow," Pear told her, "one day, your brother will bring about the destruction of the Lord of the Frozen Wastes. That's why the coven is here, don't you see that?"

"Come to watch then, have you?" bristled Jennet. "Come to see the mighty one who tricked your beloved father get his just rewards?"

"No!" Pear cried indiscreetly. "We're here to kill Ben!"

The rest of the customers in the café looked up from their tea and stared at the two girls in surprise. Pear cursed herself for shouting so loudly then made a rude gesture to each of them in turn. On the seat opposite, Jennet had sat down again.

"If you or that dirty coven so much as go near my brother ..." she began, "no, even better, I'll go to the police right now."

"Don't do that!" Pear said quickly. "Even if they believed you they couldn't do anything. Jennet, you don't know the others; they don't care how many they kill to get what they want. If you mention this to anyone you will only be responsible for many more deaths. What the coven has been promised in return for the boy's life outweighs any risk. It's all they are concerned about."

Angrily, Jennet asked, "So what is the price of my brother's life? What are you going to get out of it?"

"As soon as Ben is dead," Pear shamefully replied, "the Lord of the Frozen Wastes will give Nathaniel back to us. He will live again – that is the bargain

Hillian has made."

Appalled and speechless, Jennet felt sick.

"Oh, the Deep One can do it," Pear said. "Nothing is beyond them."

Jennet had had enough. She wanted to go home at once and tell Aunt Alice everything, but one question still remained unanswered. "Why are you telling me all this now?" she asked bitterly. "Wouldn't your mother and the others be furious if they knew?"

Pear looked straight into her eyes and shrugged. "I wanted you to know that I am your friend," she breathed. "I've never had one before. I was raised in the coven and brought up in their society alone. Things that you would consider good and beautiful were denounced as ugly and wrong. The only love I knew was the devotion the others felt for my father, and Meta was too busy trying to keep his attention to be bothered with me. I was never allowed to mix with other children and if I tried to wander off on my own, well – the coven was very skilled at thinking up new punishments. Sometimes, when Nathaniel was away from us, the others would encourage me to annoy Meta or blame me for something they had done. It was a favourite game of theirs to see who could come up with the most original and humiliating chastisement – Rowena was always good at that, and Miriam.

"I've always had to do exactly what they tell me. You think it'd be easy for me to escape from them but it isn't. It might be a cruel and hard life but it's the only one I know – I really don't think I could survive outside the coven. Oh Jennet, I loathe what they make me do, yet I have no choice. When we first came here to ... to do what we must, they told me to get you on our side, but it wasn't like that – not for me.

"I really did like you, Jennet, that first day when we

talked – I realized we had so much in common. I know what it's like to be lonely amongst a crowd of others. Please believe me when I say how sorry I am for all that's happened and what will happen. It'll be difficult for you to accept it at first, but you'll grow to understand, and remember that when your brother is dead you'll still have me to talk to."

She reached out to touch the other girl's hand but Jennet shuddered in revulsion and pulled herself away sharply.

"I'm not like you!" she cried. "You're as bad as all the rest – worse because you pretend to be something kind and ... oh, I despise you!"

Quickly, Jennet fled from the café, slamming the door behind her.

Alone at the table, Pear's raven hair cascaded over the cloth as she bent her head and great desolate tears splashed into the dregs within her teacup.

The door of the café opened again and the girl hastily wiped her eyes as her mother sat down to join her.

"Well?" Meta demanded. "Did you do it?"

Pear nodded.

"How?"

"In her tea when she wasn't looking."

A wintry smile crept over the perfect symmetry of the beautiful woman's face. "Thank you my pet," she drawled. "I'll go and tell the sisters."

12

A BARGAIN
SEALED WITH BLOOD

Through the narrow street Jennet pushed, but by the time she reached the cottage her temper had been replaced by a chill dread. What if Pear had purposely drawn her away from the place, whilst the rest of the coven ...

Jennet fumbled with the key, threw open the front door and at the top of her voice shouted "Ben! Ben!"

A muffled thud sounded in the front room and the girl barged inside with her fists clenched.

"Why, Jennet dear! What on earth is the matter? I nearly jumped out of my skin when you bellowed like that and look – you made me drop Prudence's shield."

Standing before the mantelpiece, with one hand clutching at the empty air, the other holding a rusting spear and her face a picture of astonishment, was Miss Boston. At the old lady's feet and looking totally incongruous, the elliptical shield was still rocking on the carpet, and draped over the armchair was a moth-eaten zebra skin. The scene was almost comical but Jennet's anguish forbade any frivolity and she stared about the room before leaping away to look in the kitchen.

"Where's Ben?" she cried. "Where is he?"

Throwing down the spear and taking up her walking stick, the old lady hurried after her. "What's happened?" she called. "Jennet?"

The girl dived into the parlour and was about to race upstairs when Miss Boston caught her arm.

"Benjamin", she declared, "is in his room."

"Are you sure?"

"Of course I am! He's been with Nelda all day, but Mr Shrimp sent him home to get something to eat. The poor boy is worried sick. We'll both be going out again later so I suggested he had a lie-down first. Now, tell me what has occurred to make you go charging around like an outraged Amazon."

Drawing the girl into the front room, Aunt Alice removed the remains of the zebra and bade her sit down on the armchair. Then, with her hands clasped behind her back, she assumed the posture of an old-fashioned and overbearing school mistress as she waited for the explanation.

Jennet didn't know where to begin, but slowly she related the whole dreadful story of how she had been ensnared – guiltily averting her eyes when speaking of the wedding day and how she had lied to slip away. But Miss Boston did not scold her and when she looked up she saw that the old lady's face was pale and strained.

Jennet paused, uncertain whether to continue. Then letting out a heavy sigh of pain, Aunt Alice sank into a chair as the full horrible knowledge dawned on her. That one of the children in her care could have been so unhappy as to even contemplate joining the coven was an awful realization and she shivered hopelessly.

"How could I have been so blind?" her cracked, aghast voice whined. "God's grace, I might have lost you to those evil creatures! Oh Jennet, I've failed you. I was so full of myself and too pleased with my own victories that I completely trampled over your needs and drove you away. The danger that Prudence warned me of has already come and I was found wanting. You might have been killed that night on the moors – I didn't even check that you were here. Oh, forgive me."

The extent of Miss Boston's self-condemnation startled the girl and she struggled to calm her.

"Don't blame yourself," Jennet begged. "It was my fault. You didn't drive me anywhere, I ran there all on my own. I've been spoilt and selfish and couldn't see who my real friends were."

"No," Aunt Alice uttered, "I'm the one who's been selfish. All these months I've done nothing but think of my own health and welfare. What a ridiculous joke that is."

Seizing her walking stick, she lumbered to her feet and a fierce, determined expression glowered on her face. "I'm not having this," she roared. "Where are these evil women?"

"Wait!" Jennet cried. "I haven't finished. I met Pear just now and she told me … she told me that they're going to kill Ben."

Miss Boston could hardly believe it. "But why?" she wailed. "He's only a child!"

"Because they think once he's dead, Nathaniel will be given back to them. I know it's crazy but they're totally obsessed and stark raving mad. They really believe it and there's nothing they won't do."

A sudden noise from upstairs signalled that Ben was awake and Jennet stared at Aunt Alice fearfully.

"What are we going to do?" she whispered.

"We must tell the lad," the old lady decided. "It's only fair he knows the danger he's in. Listen, he's coming down. In here, Benjamin!"

The boy entered the former sickroom and gave the faintest of nods to acknowledge his sister's presence before turning his attention to Aunt Alice. "When are we going to the cliffs?" he asked.

"The cliffs?" she repeated. "Benjamin, we've got something to tell you."

Ben shook his head wildly. "She's gone, isn't she?" he wept. "Nelda's died!"

"No!" Aunt Alice assured him. "This is nothing to do with her."

"Then it can wait!" he shouted, running for the front door.

Jennet sprang from the chair and rushed after him. "You mustn't go out there!" she yelled, wrenching his hand from the door handle. "You've got to stay in here!"

"Let go!" he cried. "I've got to see Nelda!"

"You can't!"

"She's dying! Get off me – you don't care about anyone but yourself! Leave go!"

"Benjamin!" Miss Boston's voice trumpeted authoritatively, "Listen to us! Jennet is right – if you step outside you might never reach the caves."

The boy stopped struggling and sensed the deadly earnestness in her voice.

"It's Nathaniel," Jennet told him. "His followers are here. They … they want to kill you."

"I know that!" he snapped at her. "They've already tried twice!"

Jennet stared at him blankly and Aunt Alice put her arm about him. "What do you mean?" she asked, stunned. "Why didn't you tell us?"

"Don't know," he mumbled. "Jen's been horrid and I didn't want to worry you – 'sides, I can handle it."

Miss Boston groaned in dismay. "What have I done?" she grieved. "I've alienated both of you. That's too dear a price to pay for my recovery. I wish … Oh, I don't know what I wish any more."

Ben took hold of her hand and squeezed it gently. "I want to see Nelda", he repeated, "one last time."

"Don't let him go," Jennet urged.

But before the old lady could stop him, he had pulled the door open.

"Good evening, Ben," called a light, silvery voice.

The boy started and behind him Jennet cried out in alarm.

Standing alone in the courtyard, with a supremely confident smile on her lovely face – was Meta.

The witch grinned at him and tossed her golden hair over her shoulders. "How fortunate for me," she gurgled. "I was just going to call on you, but I see you're already on your way out. It's a fine evening, there'll be such a ravishing sunset later – all red and bloody."

"Come in, Benjamin," Miss Boston commanded. Then, glaring past him at the witch, "Don't step over the threshold."

Meta hooted with derision. "The threshold?" she sneered. "You old fool, that barrier was broken by my loved one long ago. I can waltz into your dingy little hovel whenever I choose."

Aunt Alice placed herself in front of the children and barred the doorway.

"Begone from this place!" she demanded. "I'll not let you harm them."

Casually, Meta admired the bangles on her slender wrists and hardly took any notice of the old lady. "It's only Ben we want," she replied as though Miss Boston was being petulant and unreasonable, "I'm afraid Jennet just isn't worthy to join us. Sorry, honey, but that's the brutal truth."

In the hallway Jennet's skin crawled and she hurried into the front room to escape the sight of Pear's hateful mother.

"I'm not leaving," Meta promised, "and I'm

302

extremely patient – we all are."

Behind her, filing calmly through the alleyway, came Liz and Caroline, and shambling reluctantly after them was Pear. The witch-girl glanced at her mother with reproach burning in her heart and she gazed into the cottage, vainly trying to catch sight of Jennet.

Behind the net curtains of the front room, Ben's sister regarded Pear with contempt, but unconsciously her fingers reached for the necklace at her throat. With a jolt, she realized what she was doing and dragged her hand away.

Aunt Alice eyed the assembled witches uncertainly. Here, cut off from the main street, there was no one to help her.

"Reinforcements?" she asked drily. "One old woman and two children too much for you on your own?"

"Why don't you send the boy out?" Meta's syrupy voice treacled. "It'll be easier on you in the long run, and so much more convenient for us."

Controlling her anger and dread, Miss Boston tutted in the most irritating way possible. "My, my," she admonished, hoping she sounded mildly amused. "We are getting desperate, aren't we? Forced out into the open and in broad daylight too? Whatever happened to skulking about the shadows and frightening youngsters in the dark? Rowena did it so much better than you – she had the most marvellous flair for this kind of thing. I'm afraid you haven't quite got the talent for it, have you? You see it takes a lot more than a good hairdo and wacky clothes to follow the old ways. But then I don't expect a baggage like you to be interested in the correct path – you've never graduated from toad-boiling and doll-pricking!"

"Take care, old cripple!" Meta shrieked. "You'll

answer for that!"

"Not today, thank you!" Miss Boston returned and with that she slammed the door.

"That was rash, Alice," she scolded herself. "We're in scalding waters now!"

Ben hurried into the front room and ran to the window. "Look," he muttered nervously, "there's more coming through the alleyway."

Jennet stepped up behind him. "The rest of the coven!" she said in dismay. "We won't be able to stop them! We're trapped in here!"

"I've still got a few tricks up my sleeve!" Aunt Alice called, dashing into the kitchen and returning with the salt-cellar in her hands.

"I could climb over the back fence", suggested Ben, "and get help."

"You'd never make it," Jennet told him, remembering the yammering chase over the moor. "Don't you see, that's precisely what they want you to do! They'd love it for us to panic and split up."

In the hallway Miss Boston was busy reciting words of protection, invoking forces to defend them – all the while scattering salt around the doorway.

Ben stared miserably at the scene in the courtyard, repelled yet fascinated.

Hillian Fogle had been the last one to join the others. Immaculately dressed as usual, she strode between Meta and Liz and held up a large bulky object that was covered in a black cloth. Carefully she unwrapped the material and there in her hands was the fishmonkey.

Aiding the coven for the third and final time, the servant of the Lord of the Frozen Wastes blinked in the failing light of day and tapped its shrivelled webbed claws together.

Within the cottage Ben instinctively drew away from the window as a pair of yellow eyes gleamed at him.

"What's that?" he cried.

The fishmonkey squirmed in Hillian's grasp and raised its spindly arms, barking instructions to the coven.

"It's horrible," Jennet murmured. "Come away from there, Ben. All they have to do is smash the glass and they're in."

At that moment Aunt Alice rushed into the room and threw salt everywhere as she called out spells of challenge. Then she hesitated and peered at the solemn gathering outside, scowling in consternation.

"Why haven't they done anything?" she mused aloud. "What are they waiting for?"

"Maybe they're going to send that hideous thing in after us," Jennet muttered.

Then, as they watched, the fishmonkey craned its gruesome head and gave Hillian a snarling command. At a nod from her, the other members of the coven joined hands and, to Miss Boston and the children's utter surprise, they began to sing.

"Great Glory!" Aunt Alice exclaimed. "What do they think they're doing? It's like an infernal parody of Christmas with demonic carol singers!"

Low and whispering, the weird chanting of the witches filled the courtyard. It was an ugly, monotonous discord, and as the scarlet rays of the setting sun bathed everything in a lurid hellish glare, their faces were vivid masks of excitement and cruelty.

Stealthily, like the relentless creeping flow of water, their voices rose and penetrated through the windows until the front room of the cottage echoed with their jarring music.

Ben pressed close to Aunt Alice and she put her arm about him protectively.

"I don't understand," he muttered. "What does it mean?"

The old lady shook her head. "Haven't the foggiest

idea," she replied worriedly, "but those are desperate people out there and that makes them more deadly than ever. It might be one last malefice – a black spell from the dark path – although what they hope to achieve is … I really don't know. We must be certain the house is secure. Benjamin, you stay here with Jennet while I make sure the windows are locked upstairs."

"You're not expecting them to climb up the walls, are you?" he cried.

Aunt Alice's eyes opened wide. "I expect everything!" she stated grimly before trotting into the hallway and up the stairs.

Ben kept a close watch on the figures outside. Yet his gaze was constantly drawn to the deformed and malignant shape of the fishmonkey, and the hairs on the back of the boy's neck tingled when he saw that the foul creature was smiling straight back at him.

Behind Ben, in the shadows of the darkening room, Jennet shrank against the wall and felt the oppressive music of the coven close around her as the drug began to take effect. The girl's face was beaded with cold sweat and her flesh was trembling as wave after wave of fear and control beat towards her. Like a terrified and cornered rabbit her eyes rolled in their sockets and she opened her mouth to scream – but only a parched whimper crossed her lips.

The noise of the song was unbearable – how could Ben stand it? Why didn't he hear the terrible drumming in his head and the shrill goading that devoured her energy and conjured up repugnant images in her mind?

About her throat the necklace constricted and she gasped as it bit into her skin. "No," she whined, sinking forlornly to the floor. "Keep away from me!"

Concealed beneath the armchair, Eurydice stared at Jennet and her ears flattened against her skull as she arched her back, and with a frightened mewling cry, the three-legged cat darted from the room and raced up the stairs.

Ben had heard his sister's strangled gasp but he did not turn to see what the matter was, for in the courtyard something weird and awful was happening – the women were changing.

"This night shall be your final chance!" the fishmonkey shrieked in Hillian's arms. "Fail in this and your dream is dashed! Concentrate now, oh followers of the Black Sceptre. Put forth your joined might and destroy this base worm!"

With renewed vigour, the coven spat out the eerie, strident song, and as their lips parted to form the mysterious words, they drew them back over their growing teeth and their jaws pushed forward to form ravening snouts. The spine of each woman, including Pear, stretched and snapped, and dark fur sprouted and bristled around the large dog-like ears that tapered from their growling heads.

Ben gaped at them in horror as they assumed terrifying new forms, nightmarish half-creatures – part human, part animal.

The song changed into a bestial chorus as the witches barked and snapped out the words and the boy called fearfully to Miss Boston.

"Aunt Alice!" he shouted. "Come here quickly!"

His voice died in his throat for suddenly he became aware of a wheezing, grunting noise directly behind him and with a sickening terror clutching at his stomach, he slowly turned around.

"Jen!" the boy cried. "What's the matter?"

The girl was gagging for air as the beads pressed against her windpipe and her eyes bulged from her skull. She stared horribly at her brother, then clawed at her throat, fighting to breathe. As she struggled a name formed upon her cracked lips and she was powerless to resist. Finally she surrendered to the terrible might of the chanting coven and throwing back her head, the girl screamed.

"NATHANIEL!"

Ben fell backwards. A frantic light shone in his sister's swollen eyes and her body jerked and flinched as she tried to regain control but the coven had her now – she belonged to them completely.

In despair, she watched as her limbs began to move, driven by a will stronger than her own and though she screeched and wailed there was nothing she could do.

"Help me!" she wept to her brother. "I can't stop them! Oh Ben, help me!"

Dominated wholly by the combined wills of the coven, Jennet took a prowling step closer to the boy whilst outside the clamour of the witch hounds mounted feverishly.

"Jen!" Ben murmured, backing away from her. "Don't mess about!"

"I'm not!" she cried as her feet dragged over the floor towards the fireplace. "I really can't stop myself!"

At that moment her eyes fell on the objects which Aunt Alice had dropped and a hideous panic gripped her. "Ben!" she cried, her voice high with fear. "Run – get away from me! Can't you see what they're trying to do?"

Jennet's voice choked as she realized the evil truth and her legs buckled beneath her, forcing the girl to stoop down. Like a spider her hand leapt out and seized hold of the rusted African spear and, with tears streaming down her face, she lifted the ghastly weapon and aimed it at her brother.

Ben let out a petrified yell then whipped round and fled into the hall where he ran straight into Miss Boston.

"Benjamin!" she declared. "What ...?"

Her gaze passed beyond him to where Jennet stood framed in the doorway with the spear gripped tightly in her hands.

"Jennet?" the old lady asked in dismay. "Is that you? Put the weapon down, please."

"Aunt Alice!" the girl sobbed wretchedly. "Make them stop! Make them stop!"

"This is monstrous!" Miss Boston roared. "Leave the child be!" Flinging open her arms she drew a holy symbol of exile and banishment in the air but the coven's control over the girl was absolute.

Jennet cried piteously as she was compelled to stumble on and the point of the spear came slicing and stabbing towards the old lady and Ben.

"Avaunt!" Miss Boston bellowed as she stood her ground.

"Get away from me!" Jennet beseeched them. "They'll make me kill you!"

Muttering one last spell Aunt Alice shoved Ben up the stairs out of danger then called the girl's name over and over.

"Cast them out, Jennet!" she urged. "Free yourself – Jennet, listen to me!"

The blade came sweeping down and the old lady only just dodged aside in time.

"I've tried!" Jennet wept. "Look out!"

Again the spear thrust out and Miss Boston knew her efforts were in vain. Nothing could save the girl from the coven's influence.

"Benjamin!" she cried. "Go to my room – hurry!"

The boy darted upstairs but on reaching the landing he stopped and stared over the banister at the awful scene below.

In a savage attack, Jennet dived at Miss Boston but the old lady made a grab for the spear and tried to wrench it from her.

Into the kitchen they crashed, slamming against the sink, and the dishes were thrown to the floor as they fought with each other.

The girl possessed an unnatural strength and Miss Boston was no match for her, yet Jennet slithered on the broken crockery and, seizing her chance, Aunt Alice pushed her away.

Still clutching the spear, the girl slid into the table and Miss Boston headed for the kitchen door locking it behind her.

Breathless after the struggle, she shouted through the barrier, "Are you injured, Jennet?"

Inches from her face the wood splintered and flew into the hall as the spear came punching through the door and Jennet's terrified voice rang throughout the cottage.

"It's no good!" she howled. "Forgive me, Aunt Alice – forgive me!"

Miss Boston stepped back from the quivering door as Jennet pounded upon it and the frenzied assaults of the spear tore and gouged great rents in the crackling panels.

The old lady edged towards the stairs. The hallway became littered with sharp shards of shattered wood and the broken door quaked in its frame as Jennet struck it one last time.

With a thundering crash the tattered remains flew off the hinges and smashed into the opposite wall. Screaming in abject terror, the girl leapt over the debris and came charging up the stairs.

Fleeing before her, Miss Boston sped over the landing, shoved Ben through into her bedroom and slammed the door in Jennet's anguished face.

"There's no key for this lock!" Aunt Alice cried, putting her weight against it as the girl pushed and kicked. Desperately, she looked about the room. "Benjamin!" she called urgently. "The dressing-table, try to bring it over here!''

The boy heaved at the old oak dressing-table. It was incredibly heavy and he jumped in alarm as an angry miaow issued from beneath it.

"Get out of the way, Eurydice!" he yelled and the cat scooted around the room, searching for a new hiding place. Grunting, Ben managed to waggle and pull the dressing-table close enough for Miss Boston to help him.

Together they pushed it against the door handle and Jennet's insane hammering ceased, only to be replaced by the vicious blows of the spear.

"She'll get through!" Ben wept. "There's no escape from here – we're cornered!"

Aunt Alice watched impotently as the blade came snapping through the wood – the boy was right.

In the courtyard the fishmonkey's amber eyes blazed with fiery malevolence. "Louder!" he screeched, inspiring the coven and spurring them on. "Give the child your strength, slay the insolent boy! In the name of my almighty master – kill him, kill him!"

The witch hounds were bawling the abhorrent song now, their fiendish muzzles furrowed with rage and their long teeth dripping with frothing saliva – anticipating the murder they were impelling Jennet to commit.

Dark shadows gathered around the cottage as night settled over the town. Revelling in the evil tension, his eyes bright as lamps, the fishmonkey let out a high-pitched, reedy laugh. In a fever of black rejoicing, the foul creature pulled himself up Hillian's plump arm and scrambled to her shoulder to get a better view of the window above.

Clinging to the lapel of her expensive jacket, the fishmonkey cackled and squawked shrilly.

"Destroy him! Plunge the weapon deep into the

whelp's gullet! Hack and chop! Disembowel the enemy of the Allpowerful – let there be but offal and gore! Strew his entrails over the sea!"

Balancing on the witch hound's shoulder he threw back his ghastly head and tittered wildly, clapping the webbed claws, thrilling to the discordant sorceries that bludgeoned and blasted into the cottage.

In her bedroom, Miss Boston and Ben cowered against the wardrobe as Jennet lunged through the ragged hole she had made in the door and clambered over the dressing-table barricade.

The girl was almost fainting in despair but the incessant will of the coven propelled her on and she could only splutter and scream as she stalked over to the old lady and her brother.

"Jen!" Ben whined. "Snap out of it – you can do it!"

"I can't!" she cried pathetically.

Girding herself one last time, Miss Boston raised her hands and in a forceful voice proclaimed, "In God's holy name! I do evoke the hallowed strength of all the Seraphim, Cherubim, Witnesses, Thrones, Principalities, Dominions, Powers, Angels and Archangels! Aid us in this dark hour, drive out the bewitchment. Let the strings that tie this child be cut!"

For an instant Jennet wavered as the cruel enchantments yielded. But the iron resolve and ferocious tenacity of the coven snapped back around her as their howling screeches yammered to a crescendo outside and with a mournful whimper the girl pounced at Aunt Alice.

Valiantly, the old lady wrestled with the spear that came plunging for her. With all her remaining strength she tried to tear it from Jennet's grasp but it was no use. The girl punched and kicked and with an agonized cry, Miss Boston was knocked to the floor.

"Aunt Alice!" Jennet shrieked, and she leaped over her body towards Ben. "Stop me, someone!"

The boy cringed in the corner as his possessed sister crept up to him with the deadly weapon poised in her hands.

"Don't do it, Jen!" he begged through his tears. "Please!"

Jennet's torture disfigured her features. Her livid face was drenched with sweat and tears, and though she tried to scream as her arms raised the spear over her head, only a throttled moan came out.

Ben pressed into the corner and his round eyes stared in mortal dread at the blade which reared above him.

"Jen!" he wailed for the last time.

Sprawled over the floor, Miss Boston lifted her aching head just as the weapon plummeted towards Ben.

"No!" she shrieked.

Outside the cottage the coven gave a tremendous shout, then their savage voices were drowned by a hideous scream. Ben's voice blistered over the courtyard and the witch hounds held their breath expectantly. Abruptly the boy's shrill cry ended and the fishmonkey sucked the air through his needle-like teeth, widening a ghastly smile.

"Is it done?" he cackled to himself. "Is it over?"

From the upstairs window Jennet's distraught howls rose to an insane yell and through her raving shrieks Miss Boston's appalled voice spluttered.

"Benjamin! Benjamin! He's dead. Jennet – you killed him!"

The girl's torment was terrible to hear, yet the members of the coven lapped up the hideous grief and their tongues came lolling from their foaming jaws.

Only one of the witch hounds turned away in

disgust. The smallest of the misshapen women covered her face and the bones shrank inside the malformed head until Pear regained her human form. In revulsion and shame she lowered her moist eyes and stepped back from the others.

"I must be certain," the fishmonkey hissed anxiously. "I must know the landbreed maggot is dead."

Closing his glinting eyes, the creature stretched out his bony claws and searched the cottage with his mind.

"The girl is descending the stairs," he sensed "How lame and shaken she is – yet up in that room what shall we find?"

Emitting a triumphant gurgle, the fishmonkey writhed upon Hillian's shoulder and his breath came in gulping wheezes as he cackled and sniggered.

"Only one other presence is within!" he screeched. "One of great age – and the reek of death overshadows her. The wormling is no more! We have accomplished the task. My master is victorious!"

The front door of the cottage opened slowly and upon the threshold Jennet stared out at them.

Blood stained her hands, and patches of dark crimson were smeared and spattered over her school uniform. Her blank face was drained of all colour and expression and her eyes were dull and glassy, as though it was she and not her brother who had perished.

Suddenly, as if even to stand was too much for her, the girl swayed and she slumped against the door.

Quickly Pear rushed over to her. "Jennet!" she called, putting her arms about her. "Let me help you – come with me."

Like a zombie, Jennet allowed the girl to lead her towards the coven. As if in a dream, Jennet saw the frightful witch hounds gather about her, but at her side Pear whispered reassuringly and supported her when she stumbled.

"Ben ..." Jennet muttered thickly. "Ben ... I ... I killed ..."

Lifting her shaking hands she gazed at the sticky blood, but her emotions were utterly drained and she looked up in confusion as Hillian Fogle assumed her human shape once more.

"I'm one of you now," Jennet breathed. "There's nothing left for me here."

Hillian beamed at her. "Again I do welcome you, sister," she said. "You have done your work well. The coven of the Black Sceptre has a new and loyal disciple."

Pear gave Jennet a joyful hug. "I told you we'd be sisters," she sighed. "Don't worry – you'll forget this, I promise. The nightmares do end – I know. Oh, there's some nasty scratches down your neck here, do they hurt? They look deep and painful."

"Your brother did not die without protest, I see," Hillian commented, then she instructed Pear to take care of her and regarded the fishmonkey sternly.

"So," she declared, "our part of the bargain has been kept. It is the turn of your master now to be fulfilling his half. He must not betray us!"

"Fear not, bride of Crozier," the creature answered. "The Allpowerful doth intend to reward thee. Let us repair to the place appointed."

Hillian removed the monster from her shoulder and he suffered to be covered in the cloth once more as the witch hounds melted back into their ordinary selves and headed for the alleyway.

"Hillian!" Meta called, running after her. "That old hag is still alive in there – she might yet cause difficulties."

The owner of the curio shop glanced back at the cottage. "Then she must die," she uttered calmly.

"Elizabeth! See to it this instant, then join us as swift as you can!"

Liz looked at her rebelliously. "But Nathaniel!" she whined in protest. "I don't want to miss ..."

"At once!" Hillian demanded. "Obey me or you shall never set eyes on him again!"

The timid woman gave a fearful nod then bounded towards the cottage, and as she ran her face transformed to its previous half state. Snarling, the witch hound stormed through the open door and went ravaging up the stairs.

* * *

Tarr placed his hand on his granddaughter's forehead and withdrew it hastily.

"The lass is burnin'," he mumbled dismally.

Old Parry dipped a rag into a bowl of cold water and dabbed it over Nelda's brow.

"She'm fadin'," the crone observed. "Won't see the night out. I've seen it afore – too many times."

Tarr staggered to the entrance of the cave and smote the rocky wall with his fist.

Since the setting of the sun, Nelda's condition had declined rapidly. Her temperature soared, racing to an unbelievable heat, and the fevered brain of the young aufwader began to deceive her senses with fanciful and rambling delusions.

Visions of the mother she had never seen drifted before her misted eyes until they were dashed by the wrath of the sea, and then her late aunt was sitting by her side.

Perched upon her head was the familiar battered oilskin hat, and jammed about her waist that ridiculous cork lifebelt. In the shadow of the hat's brim her large eyes glittered kindly and a gentle smile broke over the pickled walnut face as she looked at her niece.

316

"Take heart, Little One," she whispered, "you'll be with us soon."

"Hesper!" Nelda mumbled deliriously as the vision shimmered. "Have you come for me?"

Old Parry's face twitched and grimaced. "Garn, Shrimp!" she huffed. "Now she thinks I'm yer daughter!"

With his spirit broken, Tarr gave Nelda a woebegone glance and, unable to stand the sight of her distress any longer, he shambled from the cave and into the night.

"He were always squeamish," Parry snorted. "Menfolk – ain't got the stomach for watchin' on death!" and she nibbled a morsel of salted fish appreciatively.

A jet black darkness had engulfed the shore below the cliffs and the creeping tide was invisible as it moved stealthily over the rocks.

Desolate and crushed beyond endurance, Tarr limped down towards the water's edge then fell to his knees. His racking sobs squalled over the sea while behind him, emerging from their caves, came the rest of the fisherfolk.

In sombre silence they watched their leader lamenting and heard his keening wails float on the heavy air. Then, one by one, they trailed down to join him at the brink of the rolling, sable waves.

Upon the horizon a jagged streak of brilliance suddenly lit sky and sea and a peal of distant thunder rumbled ominously. For an instant the crowd of aufwaders were caught in the stark glare, then everything was swallowed by the darkness once more.

Yet the remote brewing storm mounted steadily and bolts of energy crackled from the troubled heavens. Assembled about Tarr, the tribe lifted their weary faces and felt the wind turn as rumour of the tempest spread inland. Long, shell-entwined hair stirred in the growing, buffeting breeze and the languorous waves began to race over the flat rocks of the shore.

Stricken with grief, Tarr wept for Nelda and her unborn child until his eyes were stinging. Then as the thunder roared closer he raised his ashen face and his anger flared within him.

"Growl all tha can!" he bawled, shaking his fist at the lightning. "Ah know it's tha in theer. Showing off agin, are tha? Well, it don't impress me. Come on – blast me yer divils!

"Narr!" he ranted. "It's the lass that tha's come fer! Her an' her bairn – well, she'm almost ready! Not much time left to them!"

Clambering to his feet, he turned bitterly to the tribe and roared in a voice to match and challenge the thunder. "Bring out the black boat!" he boomed. "An' bear my Nelda out here also. I want them three nazards to see what they've done to her! I want them to look on her agonies and hear them fretful screams. If theer's any shame in them sour hearts then I hope it burns 'em. Stir thesselves! Get her, I says!"

The fisherfolk looked at one another doubtfully, then as one they hurried to obey him.

* * *

With her claws raking over the flowered wallpaper and scoring deep tracks in the plaster beneath, the grotesque witch hound climbed the shadow-filled stairs of Miss Boston's cottage.

Her nostrils gaped as she savoured the scintillating fragrance of fear that still hung on the air, and on to the landing the apparition stepped.

One old woman was an easy and boring kill, and in this daunting form Liz expected no retaliation from the irritating nuisance. A swift slash with the claws across the throat and the job would be done and she could hasten after the others to greet *him*. It was all too incredible and fantastic, but that night she would look on his features again, hear his voice – perhaps even feel his embrace.

Desperate for that yearned-for moment, she threw open the bedroom door and with a smack of her talons, the obstructing dressing table beyond was hurled against the wall.

"Don't you believe in knocking?" called a peremptory voice.

The witch-hound snapped her jaws and her eyes gleamed in the gloom, then suddenly the light was switched on and a startling figure leapt before her.

There, robustly weaving her walking stick through the air as though it were a sword – was Miss Boston.

The old lady's countenance was grave and fierce and she lashed the weapon expertly from side to side.

A raging growl bubbled up from the witch hound's throat as she stared at the idiotic spectacle, and tensing her muscles, she prepared to spring.

"On guard!" Miss Boston yelled, hopping forward and striking the fiend's snout with the stick.

Liz barked in outraged amazement that anyone could be so stupid.

"Ho, ho!" Miss Boston cried, swiping the stick across her opponent's leg. "Nice doggy want some exercise?"

Enraged, the beast snarled and lunged violently at her. Miss Boston threw up her weapon to defend herself and deflected the ripping claws.

"Come on!" she taunted, thwacking Liz on the head. "I'm only a feeble old woman!"

Driven berserk by this infuriating torment, the witch-hound roared and charged at her. The two clashed brutally, toppling against the wardrobe, and after the briefest of struggles Miss Boston was thrown to the ground.

Down swooped the rapacious jaws, snapping for the ample folds of skin around Miss Boston's neck.

But the old lady was not beaten yet. Fumbling with her hands, she strained to reach a bottle that had fallen from the dressing table, and just as the long teeth came to rip out her throat she seized the perfume and sprayed it right into the witch hound's face.

Yowling, Liz reared back and clawed at her burning eyes. Immediately Miss Boston scrambled to her feet, and snatching up a vase from the window ledge, brought it smashing down upon the creature's skull.

Her attacker let out a frightful shriek of pain, but was not defeated and the blood which trickled down her muzzle served only to enrage her all the more. With the murderous glow from her shining eyes casting a hellish light upon the old lady, Liz rose and flew at her.

But Miss Boston had already reached beneath the bed and with a tremendous "CLANG!" struck the witch hound with a large porcelain vessel that sent her reeling across the room.

"One for the pot!" Aunt Alice yelled, unable to resist the unforgivable remark.

A feeble groan burbled from Liz's canine lips as she tried to raise her head, but a mass of black stars was crowding around her and she collapsed senseless to the floor.

"Pity," Miss Boston announced, rolling the figure over with a shove of her shoe, "I was just getting into my stride!" And she whirled the walking stick two or three times, thrusting and parrying and feeling mightily pleased with herself.

Stepping over the unconscious Liz, the old lady gazed sorrowfully at the corner of the room where a

glistening heap of gore was spreading over the carpet.

"Tragic," she muttered. "If only I could have prevented it."

Turning aside, she waddled to the wardrobe and rapped three times on the door.

"It's all right," she promised. "You can come out now."

The wardrobe creaked open and a frightened face peered out at her.

"Was it too stuffy in there for you, dear?" she inquired. "I'm most awfully sorry but I knew those wretches would send someone in for me. I do hope you weren't too alarmed when we slammed into the door."

Grinning cheekily, she helped Ben out from amongst her clothes and the boy stared at the witch-hound on the floor.

"Is she dead?" he asked doubtfully.

"Good Lord no!" Aunt Alice returned. "But I think she might have distemper and also a touch of mange by the look of her. Still, it'll be a long time before she feels up to going for a walky."

Ben shifted his attention to the bloody corpse in the corner but Miss Boston clucked and told him that he could mourn for Eurydice later.

"A most marvellous feline," she commented. "I'm beginning to understand what Tilly Droon saw in the species. Was it really sheer fright that made Eurydice jump out like that and scratch your sister's face or did she indeed sacrifice herself for you? I don't suppose we shall ever know. It cost the unfortunate animal her life, but otherwise Jennet would never have been jolted from their influence. Come, we must make haste; the coven have still got your sister and I'm going after them. Pass me that cloak please, Benjamin. Goodness knows the girl must be terrified. Is the amulet secure around your neck?"

Ben fingered the pendant that Irl had given to Aunt Alice and nodded.

"Good," she said, throwing her tweed cloak over her shoulders. "Now we haven't a moment to lose; the herald warned me that its power to conceal you from the Deep Ones and their agents does not last long."

Striding towards the door, she paused to look at the walking stick in her hand and with a hearty, jubilant chuckle cried, "I don't think I need you any more!" and she hung it on the door handle before marching determinedly down the stairs.

"But how do you know where they've taken Jen?" Ben called.

"There's only one place that'll do for their hellish purpose this night!" she answered, hurrying through the wreckage of the hallway. "Come on, child – to the Abbey!"

13

BORN IN THE FIRES

Black, blanketing clouds had coursed in from the sea, covering the face of heaven and pressing low over the cliffs of Whitby – heralding the approaching storm.

The first fine drops of rain drizzled from the midnight sky but the brash wind scattered and whisked the mizzling shower, hurling it wildly about the crumbling dignity of the ancient Abbey ruins.

The grounds of the holy, broken building had been locked at six, many hours ago, but above the noise of the gusting wind a sharp metallic snap echoed over the Abbey plain as chains were cut and padlocks forced. In the darkness the gates hung from their hinges and the breathless, impatient intruders passed through, smashing the doors of the shop beyond and hurrying out on to the wet grass.

High above the anxious figures of the coven, the imposing majesty of the Abbey rose. Dipped in the unlit gloom of the greedy dark it seemed a boundless place without end. The gothic arches curved far into the weeping night and the weathered columns of the nave and south transept merged with the looming clouds.

Still holding on to Pear, Jennet staggered through the teeming blackness, staring timidly at the shadow-filled shapes that reared around her. The corroded stonework took on a sinister aspect as if indistinct forms lurked within deep recesses and watched her with resentful eyes – incensed at this disturbance.

In zealous, craving whispers, the witches spoke of their longing and Jennet could sense that Pear too was captivated and ached for the culmination of their dreams.

Squawking amidst the voracious babble, the cracked voice of the fishmonkey directed them behind the majestic ruins. Between the truncated pillars of the presbytery and over the excavations of shallow graves, the coven proceeded eagerly.

With the great eastern window rising behind them, they hurried to where a large, dark pool stretched into the farmland beyond, and gathering in avid anticipation at the water's edge, their yearning faces gazed at it covetously.

In former times the monks had fished there, but since the Dissolution the pond had diminished and now only the neighbuuring cows visited the marshy banks.

The surface of the black water sizzled and spat as the rain pelted from the turbulent heavens, and with an exulting cry, Hillian Fogle raised the fishmonkey over her head.

"Hear me!" she yelled. "The Coven of the Black Sceptre has done its work! The boy threat is no more! Our part in the bargain has been kept – now bestow upon us that which was promised!"

The mummified creature in her hands lifted its head and with a screech called to his master. "Lord!" he squealed. "The followers of thine agent have in truth succeeded. Draw aside the curtain of Death – send back the one they worship!"

Jennet shook with nerves as the witches held their breath and the atmosphere became tense and charged with feverish excitement. The rain had bedraggled them, but the girl noticed that Meta was already grooming her dripping hair for when their beloved returned.

A branching fork of lightning suddenly split the night and the Abbey flared beneath it as an almighty burst of thunder blasted over the cliff.

The plain trembled and at Jennet's side, Pear gave a glad shout. "It's started!" she cried. "Look!"

The surface of the pool was shimmering. As the lightning crackled overheard, and before the coven's adoring eyes, a faint glow flickered about the muddy banks and smouldering wisps of smoke curled up into the drizzle.

"Send him forth!" the fishmonkey squealed, madly waving his puny arms. "Knit again the sinew and clothe the unclean spirit in the raiment of flesh so that he might live again!"

Abruptly, a tongue of green flame leapt from the water, and with a flurry of sparks the pond ignited. The lurid glare of the emerald fires shone over the witches' faces and they began to mutter their high priest's name.

"Nathaniel," they hissed, "Come to us! Come to us!"

The flames danced in Meta's captivating eyes and she felt a delicious joy burn within her breast, nourishing and sustaining her very soul. *He* would soon be with her again and the very thought of his rapturous presence flushed shivers of exquisite pleasure down her spine.

"My love," she murmured lustily, "return to me."

Dazzling flames blazed furiously over the water, leaping ever higher and spiralling round, forming a twisting pinnacle of light that roared upwards. High above the cliff the shining beacon of green fire soared, spiking up past the ruined Abbey and piercing the seething clouds.

With a deafening clap of thunder, the towering flames stabbed into the heart of the storm and for an instant blinding needles of snaking energy illuminated the whole sky as they radiated through the tormented night.

Her face uplifted to the dazzling and frightening spectacle, Jennet stared as the massive clouds pulsed and throbbed and the booming roar of the sea trumpeted around her.

"It's fantastic!" Pear bawled. "Oh Jennet, it's actually happening – I'll see him again!"

Within the rearing coils of flame a shape was forming. Steadily it grew and Jennet's mouth fell open as a familiar silhouette began to stir in the whirling furnace.

Surrounded by the life-giving fires stood the figure of a man, and from the mouth of each witch issued a sensual and joyous breath.

Pear's attention was fixed solely upon the face now forming in the rippling flames and she stepped forward, disregarding the fierce heats of the fire. Into the fizzling mud she trod, opening her arms in greeting, and her wet clothes steamed before the blistering column of light.

"Father!" she called. "Father!"

Behind her, Jennet shielded her eyes from the harsh glare, then the cliff shook as a mighty clap of thunder resounded from the sky.

At once the flames dwindled and sank back into the pool and the plain plummeted into darkness.

Incredulously, and as a tempest of confused emotions curdled inside her, Jennet stared at the figure that was standing knee deep in the black water.

The most evil and callous outcast from virtuous humanity inhaled the damp air of the summer night and tilted his head arrogantly as a triumphant smirk spread across his bearded face.

Nathaniel Crozier, warlock, High Priest of the Black Sceptre and destroyer of vulnerable souls, appeared exactly the same as when Jennet had last seen him.

Glinting in the deep shadows beneath his brows, the sparkling, raven eyes glittered at each of his motley brides and a venomous chuckle left his lips.

"Father!" Pear sang, floundering through the water to meet him.

"Persephone," his compelling voice declared, "come to me my little succubus! Let all my hellhounds come to me!"

His command jolted the other women from their blissful amazement and with shrill, intoxicated whoops they splashed into the pool to touch and embrace the lord of their lives.

"Nathaniel!" they cooed, pawing at him, vying with each other and grovelling in the mud to gain his attention, "Praise to you!"

Clinging to his waist, Gilly Neugent gazed up at her reason for living, but he ignored her completely and she loved him all the more.

Fighting the others to reach the warlock, Meta threw her arms about his neck and kissed him fiercely.

"Choose me tonight!" she pleaded in his ear. "Let me serve you."

An irritated sneer curled over the mouth of the reborn fiend and he shrugged her off coldly, gazing past the desperate women at the two figures who had remained on the bank.

With the fishmonkey still in her arms, Hillian bowed to her high priest.

"Hail to you – darling man," she called breathlessly. "My heart is alongside itself with cheer. The road to this much happy moment was fraught with many dangers. Alas, we did lose Susannah and

Miriam but to venerate you again is worth a thousand deaths."

Nathaniel's teeth flashed as he grinned. "Bravo, Hillian," he thanked her. "You have proven yourself the most worthy of all my cattle. To you will the ring of amethyst go – you shall be priestess over them. Together we will accomplish much."

Meta threw the plump, bespectacled woman a despising glance but the decision had been made and she pulled at his frayed jacket, trying to make him look at her.

"Enough!" Nathaniel icily demanded and immediately the witches recoiled as he began trudging through the water towards the marshy bank.

In the new priestess's arms, the shrivelled fishmonkey raised its webbed claws in salute.

"Thus hath my master fulfilled his portion," he shrieked. "The bargain is complete. Behold the might of the Allpowerful, his strength reaches unto the very shores of the hollow void."

Nathaniel gazed at the ugly creature in disdain and said in a cold and deadly warning, "No one – no man, woman, demon or god – uses me, not even the Lord of the Frozen Wastes!"

"Disclose not his exalted name!" the fishmonkey screeched. "There are many spies eager to hear it!"

"What do I care?" the warlock spat defiantly. "It was my will that controlled the great serpent and I shall do so again. Then let the Triad quake! I shall repay the Lord of the Frozen Wastes for using me – his repentance will be sung unto the furthest reaches of heaven!"

The creature gnashed its teeth and flapped its arms as it squawked in protest. "Twice now thou hast uttered that name. Desist from this folly – or we are all damned!"

Nathaniel ignored the ranting curiosity and his roving eyes glared into the gloom.

"What's this?" he murmured. "Are our ranks increased by a further member?"

His penetrating stare pierced the shadows where Jennet stood rooted with fear and his malevolent power cut into her.

The girl wilted before the intensity of those horrible eyes – yet at the same time a glorious thrill tingled in her heart.

"Janet," the leering man said in velvety scorn, "has the lamb finally come to wear the wolf's mantle? You ought to have embraced me long ago, child – I invited you to, remember?"

Unable to speak, she nodded faintly and swayed with uncertainty as her head pounded. She knew that she hated this foul and hideous man but could not recall why. He seemed so enchanting and charming and she felt the necklace grip her throat as her old devotion to him awakened and welled up in her breast.

In Hillian's arms, a puzzled frown stole over the fishmonkey's grotesque face and the creature stretched out a weedy arm in the direction of the town as it muttered vexedly under its stale breath.

Leaping from the water, Pear rushed to Nathaniel's side and cried joyously, "This is my friend, Jennet. She's one of us now, Father. Without the sacrifice she made you would never have been returned to us."

"Then I have much to thank her for," Nathaniel purred. "You have reedemed me from a most ignoble end, my little maiden. Won't you embrace me now and seal your fate with us?"

Jennet made to rush at him. All she wanted was to feel his caresses – nothing else mattered in the whole world. Then the voice of the fishmonkey sliced through her insane longing.

"WAIT!" he screamed, writhing madly in Hillian's grasp. "All is not as it should be – there are forces at work here. I feel them beating out a charm of concealment and blindness, yet even now they fail. The shadows they weave are dispersing – Ahhh! I have been cheated and deceived! The threat to my master is alive!"

Turning his ferocious face to Nathaniel, the fishmonkey clawed the air and screeched, "HE LIVES! The boy is not dead!"

The power of Irl's amulet had waned at last.

"Treachery!" the fishmonkey raged. "The Allpowerful has been betrayed!" He twisted his hump-backed body to stare accusingly at Jennet and pointed a menacing claw at her. "Thou hast done this!" he shrieked. "The lies did pour off thy poisonous tongue! This duplicitous wretch did murder no one! Her reviled brother still breathes! What dissembling guile is born in humankind!"

Jennet swallowed nervously as the coven stared banefully in her direction while the mummified creature ranted and squealed with outrage and fury.

Before her, Nathaniel's harsh eyes narrowed and she shivered in the malignance that beat out from them.

"It isn't true!" Pear shouted, springing to the girl's defence. "Father, Jennet did kill him, there was blood – we all heard the scream. Jennet, tell them."

But Jennet could say nothing and the witches drew closer around her.

"Unwise was my master to put his faith in such as you!" the fishmonkey cried at them. "So much for thy boastful claims, high priest. Thy feeble conjurations are not even capable of dominating one wilful child! What over-reaching hope hadst thou of being the governing force behind Morgawrus?"

"Be silent!" Nathaniel demanded.

But the creature would not be stilled, "Verily did the Allpowerful overvalue thy vaunted abilities a thousandfold! Thou art as sand on the shore, a witless fool amongst moon-calved mortals!"

Nathaniel bared his teeth at the fishmonkey then turned on Jennet and struck her viciously.

Wailing, she clutched her stinging face and Nathaniel reared over her.

"You pathetic idiot!" he growled. "You jeopardized the entire bargain! I might have been locked in the abyss for eternity!"

Furiously he spun on the fishmonkey and in a horrible voice proclaimed, "This is how I deal with the disloyal and faithless!"

"Father!" Pear cried, hanging on his arm. "No! Don't – Jennet's my friend!"

The warlock brushed his daughter off. "Be still, Persephone!" he roared. "You have no need of this wretch – she is not a member of our 'family'!"

Pear fell back, her eyes filling with bitter tears.

"Now," Nathaniel hissed at Jennet, "step forward!"

At first the girl refused and cringed away from him, but then as his eyes burned away her will she lurched over the sopping grass.

The warlock gave a brutal smile. "Now kneel," he commanded.

Jennet wept as she fell into the mud and prostrated herself before him.

The other members of the coven giggled in ghastly amusement at her humiliation. Meta tossed her head and hooted too loudly as usual, but with her cheeks streaming with pitying tears, Pear turned away.

"Now you shall see how Morgawrus would have submitted to me even as this child has done," Nathaniel declaimed, "for I am a master of control and my will reaches out into the innermost depths of the mind. See how easy it is to dominate! The girl is powerless to resist, she must obey me and so shall she die! Meta – give me your athame!''

The woman unfastened the ceremonial dagger at her waist, and with a sickening flutter of her lashes that made Pear's stomach heave, she handed it over.

Nathaniel snatched it roughly then dangled the blade before Jennet's face.

''See the bright steel!'' he murmured. ''Take it in your hands and put the blade against your ribs.''

Pear shuddered as her friend received the dagger and silently pressed the point to her chest.

''And so shall the serpent be mine,'' the warlock boasted. ''Now, dear little Janet, push the blade in.''

The girl gripped the handle tightly.

''STOP!'' bellowed a fierce voice behind her.

Jennet wavered as Nathaniel glared beyond her to where two figures came charging from the shadows of the Abbey.

A wooden smile lit the warlock's face as he recognized Alice Boston and the boy at her side.

Fuming indignantly, the old lady raced up to the girl and knocked the dagger from her grasp. The blade spun in the air then speared harmlessly into the mud.

''The boy!'' shrieked the fishmonkey furiously. '''Tis he – destroy the whelp! Kill the maggot!''

Ben eyed the creature in disgust and kept close to Aunt Alice as she tried to rouse his sister from Nathaniel's power.

''Jennet!'' Miss Boston cried, peering into the girl's eyes and shaking her. ''You're safe now – return to us!''

A low, mocking chortle came from Nathaniel as he regarded his old adversary with undisguised scorn. ''Well, well,'' he muttered. ''Still interfering and tampering in schemes too great for you? You're wasting your time with her, you know – she's besotted with me. Once they've tasted my charm, my dainties can't escape.''

Miss Boston scowled at him. ''What devilment is this?'' she stormed, undaunted. ''I saw you perish before the might of Morgawrus! The world was a gladder place for your passing – creep back into your unholy grave! You and your infernal brood ought to be wiped from this earth, damn you all! This has gone on for far too long – I won't permit it to continue a second longer! Jennet, in the Name of the Father I release you!''

Aunt Alice's hands grabbed the wooden beads at the child's throat and with a strenuous yell, she tore them free.

Jennet fell against her as the warlock's influence was wrenched away, then she cried out and cowered from him in terror.

Miss Boston patted her mud-clogged hair. ''Don't you worry,'' she consoled, ''he can't get at you now – his dominion over you is gone forever.''

Behind Nathaniel the coven murmured at this unheard of defiance and the fishmonkey cackled shrilly.

''A sorry display hath this demonstration been thus far!'' it squealed. ''Slit the boy's throat and be done – these others are unimportant.''

The look on the warlock's face equalled the grotesque ugliness of the fishmonkey. The old lady and the girl had made him look inept and his wrath boiled behind those glittering eyes.

''That was the last time,'' he rumbled, ''the last time you meddle in my affairs. The hour of your death is long overdue, harridan! I will take great pleasure in settling that account.''

Raising his hand he pointed at Miss Boston and the children, but she gave an impudent laugh and reached swiftly into her cloak.

Into the driving rain she flourished the tattered pages of the Book of Shadows and, as a crackling spiral of lethal magic came battering from Nathaniel's outstretched fingers, she held it before her like a shield.

The loose binding melted under the savage attack, Aunt Alice stumbled backwards from the terrible forces that blasted against the book and black sparks flew in all directions. The lifetime's work of Patricia Gunning was burning in her hands; all the spells of healing were devoured, the blessed formulae were rapaciously consumed and, with a pitiful splutter like a damp firework, the charms and incantations fizzled and were quenched.

Miss Boston sucked her cheeks in worridly then, shouting out a string of Latin words, flung the dissolving volume straight at the warlock's head.

In a blinding explosion of silver fire, the Book of Shadows erupted and a ball of brilliant flame cannoned into Nathaniel Crozier, dazzling and singeing his eyes. Then, as the fiery stars sputtered and perished, he stared at the place where the old hag had stood. Both she and the children had vanished.

Wintry hatred froze on the warlock's face and the fishmonkey screeched its derision.

"It was but the simplest of conjuror's tricks!" the creature bawled. "The crone is already escaping from this place and heading for the Abbey steps. Stop her and bring the boy child to me before it is too late – my master's wrath increases."

Nathaniel snatched the ceremonial dagger from the ground and gave it to Meta.

"Get after them," he snarled. "I don't care what you do – just kill them all."

The golden-haired woman brandished the knife

proudly and with a lingering look at her beloved, raced through the ruins.

"Meta!" Pear shouted in dismay. "No!"

"Persephone!" Nathaniel barked, but the girl was already tearing after her mother.

In Hillian's arms the fishmonkey waggled its repulsive head and, in a condemning tone, muttered, "Thou hast failed, thou and thy rabble have reneged on the bargain. Thy part has not been honoured, the boy lives still."

"Not for much longer!" the warlock retorted vehemently. "Meta excels as an assassin."

"Empty words," the wizened creature denounced. "Too often hath much been promised and all for naught. Thou wert given new life, yet you have dared cheat the Allpowerful."

Nathaniel had heard enough from the ugly monster and made no reply. Instead, Hillian gazed at the deformed object in her hands and laughed dismissively.

"What matter is that to us now?" she scoffed. "The Lord of the Frozen Wastes has given us our High Priest – that is all we ever wanted. I pray the boy does indeed grow to bring about the demise of the Lord of the Frozen Wastes. I am sick to my teeth of his demands and your constant puling squeaks!"

The fishmonkey glared up at her, then with a raging screech it wrested free of her grasp and launched itself upwards, shrieking in a frenzy of hate.

Hillian's spectacles were thrown to the ground as the webbed claws tore into her flesh and the witch screamed in alarm and pain.

Gouging deep into her skin, the creature squawked and slashed out bloody rents. "A curse on the day thou wert contacted!" it cried. "Thou hast used my master for thine own ends – fie on you, Drab of the East!"

The needle-like teeth lunged for Hillian's neck but they snapped only the rain as Nathaniel dragged it from her and threw it to the ground.

"I think we can dispense of your services now," he muttered in a threatening voice filled with menace.

The fishmonkey wormed and bolted through the mud, dragging itself by its emaciated arms, but Nathaniel came stomping after and with a vile laugh he brought his foot fiercely down upon the creature's humped and bony back.

A piercing squeal blared from the gaping mouth as the brittle body shattered and the scaly, papery skin burst into a flurry of tiny fragments.

"Master!" it gibbered, writhing and twisting like a headless snake.

Grinning, Nathaniel crushed the creature's limbs, snapping the bones until they hung pathetically from the shoulders, twitching helplessly. Above the splintered remains of its misshapen body, the domed head gasped its last and the yellow eyes stared balefully upwards.

"Dost thou ... thou truly believe ...?" the servant of the deep rasped, "Didst thou think my ... my mighty Lord would be so ... so unwise?"

The light dimmed behind the eyes but the fishmonkey managed a final sneer and with a cackle gurgling in its broken neck, scorned Nathaniel and the rest of the coven with consummate loathing.

"No ... no trust did he have in thee and thine!" it wheezed. "Ha! The Lord of the Frozen Wastes shall not be chea ..."

The ugly head rolled to one side and the flimsy eyelids closed as a rattling breath groaned from the gawping mouth.

Nathaniel kicked the shattered fragments aside and turned to the others. The witches had gathered about Hillian, who was whimpering from the agonies that seared her flesh.

"My face!" she howled. "My face!"

From the ragged wounds her blood was flowing freely but the warlock looked at her without compassion. "Be quiet," he rebuked. "The scars will heal – I didn't recruit you for your beauty."

Obediently Hillian stifled her cries and the others stood away from her.

"Time to leave this place," he snorted. "Heel!"

The witches trailed after him but suddenly the night was torn asunder as a blinding bolt of lightning forked from the churning clouds and flashed over the surface of the pool behind them.

For a brief moment a layer of livid flame blasted across the dark water, and when it dispersed and only the smouldering gloom remained, Nathaniel stared back suspiciously.

"Miserable weather for such a long-awaited reunion," observed a pert, arch voice.

The warlock stepped forward and his face fell.

From the rain-splashed water a figure was rising. Her short, strawberry-blonde hair was held back by a black band, accentuating her fine-boned features, and a seductive smile played over her thin lips.

Dumbfounded, Nathaniel stared at the newcomer, whilst around him the witches muttered in surprise and through her bloody tears Hillian felt her new position as priestess slip hopelessly away from her.

The woman in the pool stretched her lithe frame and straightened the black robes that covered her. Then she gazed steadily at her speechless husband and with a mocking, girlish laugh, asked, "Have you nothing to say, darling Nathan? Am I so unwelcome?"

"Roselyn!" the warlock growled, his rising anger dispelling all bewilderment. "Why are you here?"

Wading through the pool, with her garment

billowing around her, the woman who had lived in Whitby as Rowena Cooper spoke in soft, treacherous tones and her face was wreathed in a dangerous, deceitful grin.

"Surely you must know by now," she murmured darkly, "that wherever you go, my dearest heart's blood, your wife must follow. I too have torn through the veil! We are united at last!" And she strode stealthily towards the bank, with faint derisive laughter trickling from her lips.

*　*　*

Down the one hundred and ninety-nine steps the children and Aunt Alice tore. The driving rain pelted in their faces and over the wet, slippery stairs they slithered and scrambled. Far below them the drenched rooftops of the town glistened and the streets rippled like rivers as the rushing deluge gushed from the drain-pipes and flowed over the cobbles.

Clinging to the dripping handrail, Ben hurried as fast as the perilous, glass-like steps allowed, while just behind, Aunt Alice lumbered with Jennet still clutching on to her cloak.

"Hurry," the boy called, too busy concentrating on the hazardous way to turn around. "They'll be coming after us!"

"Come along, Jennet!" Miss Boston cried. "Exert yourself, child!"

Still in shock, the girl blundered aimlessly after her. Half stumbling, half falling, she was beyond caring what would happen to them. The loss of the necklace and Nathaniel's malevolent influence had left a ghastly hole inside her. It was as if she had suffered a tragic wounding that left her bereft and empty within.

"We're not even halfway down!" Aunt Alice blustered, pulling her by the hand. "Quickly!"

Jennet skidded to a defeated standstill and leaned heavily against the rail. "I can't," she protested wearily, "there's no point."

"No point?" Aunt Alice repeated furiously. "At any moment that devil and his harpies will come charging after us!"

"I don't care," the girl insisted. "Can't you see? I've had enough – I just want it to end."

Miss Boston gripped Jennet's muddy uniform and scolded her furiously. "You listen to me, madam!" she cried. "It's time you stopped thinking about yourself! Was there ever such an ungrateful and selfish child?"

Jennet flinched before Aunt Alice's withering scorn, but before she could respond the old lady pointed down to where Ben's sopping figure was hastily descending.

"Look at him!" she rapped. "Your brother needs you – he always has. Are you going to abandon him now? If we escape this night there are worse dangers in the world."

Jennet blinked the rain from her lashes, and as she listened to Aunt Alice's tirade she began to emerge from the apathy that the shock had wrought.

"Ben!" she called suddenly. "Wait for us!"

The girl darted down the steps and a pleased grin lit Miss Boston's face as she hurried after.

At the summit of the Abbey steps two points of hellish light shone in the darkness, glaring through the slanting rain at the three figures fleeing below. With a wild snarl, Meta tucked the dagger into her belt as her jaws trembled and formed a ravaging snout.

The witch-hound's golden hair streamed behind her as she bounded in pursuit. Her elegant hands tapered into bitter talons and she dragged the sharpest claw over the railing until the metal squealed and screeched.

Nearing the bottom, Miss Boston and the children heard the dreadful clamour and they glanced hurriedly upwards.

"Meta!" Jennet exclaimed.

The frightful squealing grew louder as the misshapen woman raced towards them. Her gleaming eyes blazed with malice and hatred, and from her transformed head she let loose a terrible, bestial shriek.

"Quick!" Aunt Alice shouted. "Don't turn round, don't look at her. We still have a chance."

Baying into the squalling night, the witch-hound chased her prey. Galloping like a gusting wind, she could smell their fear, and the scent heated her blood as the savage side took absolute control and she slobbered with evil greed.

In some remote region of her barbaric mind a familiar voice called her human name – but it was too late now.

Coarse fur was already bristling down her neck as her hair shrank into her skull and her claws came clattering over the stone. In a tangled knot of cheesecloth and cotton, her clothes were cast aside and on all fours Meta stampeded down.

Hearing the awful yammering blare behind them, Miss Boston and the children flew into Henrietta Street and the old lady threw herself against the door of the nearest house.

"Help!" she bawled, hammering with her fists. "Open up! Help us!"

Holding on to her brother, Jennet turned as the great black hound with fiery eyes came leaping and she screamed in terror.

"Open up!" Aunt Alice demanded, punching and

kicking the front door.

Ben heard the muffled sound of footsteps within the house and the lock turned, but his attention was fixed upon the monstrous creature which came prowling towards them. The great jaws lolled open and a row of jagged teeth were revealed as the lips curled and the hideous beast uttered a guttural growl.

Abruptly the front door opened a chink and an irritated man peered out at them. But his face fell as he beheld the fiendish hound and with a scared whimper of panic he slammed the door again and drew the bolt across.

"Wait!" Miss Boston trumpeted. "You must help us!"

Closer to the doorway the huge dog stalked and the hot breath steamed from its flaring nostrils.

Cornered, Aunt Alice turned to face it, pulling the children behind her.

"Begone from this place!" she commanded, but her voice was thin and woeful and the infernal eyes became evil slits as the muscles tensed and the hell hound crouched, preparing to spring.

"Meta!" a voice cried anxiously. "Stop!"

Hurtling down the one hundred and ninety-nine steps came Pear. In her hands she clutched a bundle of clothing and she scurried over frantically, just as the immense apparition flew snapping at Miss Boston.

"No!" Pear yelled, snatching hold of the wooden beads about the dog's neck.

With a throttled yelp, the creature was dragged off balance and went toppling to the ground, tearing its claws over the cobbles. Still gripping the necklace, Pear was hauled after and for several confused moments they were a tangle of legs and talons.

The beast's powerful limbs raked the air and, mad with rage, it struggled back to its feet, gnashing its

terrible jaws and twisting from side to side, trying to bite the hand which held grimly to the beads.

"No, Meta!" Pear shouted, heaving on the thread until the brute choked and the burning eyes bulged. "The killing must stop!"

Quickly she stuffed the clothes into the gaping maw, glanced at the huddled figures on the doorstep, and with a desperate plea to Jennet cried, "I might not be able to hold her – fly now! Go to your aufwader friends! Don't worry about me!"

Miss Boston needed no further prompting and she and Ben jumped from the step then headed for the shore.

Jennet hesitated before following. The two girls stared at one another. "Thank you," she said.

Pear opened her mouth to speak but an almighty yowl issued from the hound's jaws as it spat the gagging cloth on to the floor and the animal brought its teeth snapping for her arm.

"Meta!" the girl shrieked. "It's me! Come back! Meta, come back!"

Snatching up the cheesecloth dress, she threw it over the brute's head, and as it strained and scrabbled for release she called her mother's name. The hackles beneath the necklace became a rich golden colour and the sprouting hair flowed finely through Pear's fingers as the glare faded in the monster's eyes.

The witch-girl looked up from the dwindling form but the street was empty. Jennet had run after the others and with an aching heart she watched as her mother assumed her human shape.

Naked in the pouring rain, Meta grabbed her wet clothes then struck her daughter angrily.

"You little fool!" she yelled. "I had them!"

Pear touched her smarting cheek gingerly and winced at the pain. "But it's wrong!" she answered. "All this is wrong!"

"Quiet!" Meta roared, slapping her a second time. "Do you want the others to know about this? Do you know what your father will do? Just because you're his daughter doesn't give you the right to disobey his demands. You know as well as I what happens to those who fail him!"

"But Jennet ..." the girl wept.

Meta pushed her roughly against the wall and in a low, threatening hiss said, "If he hears of your betrayal, Nathaniel will not balk at murdering you – what will happen to me then?"

"You?" Pear sobbed. "Don't you care about me?"

Her mother leered and spat on the ground. "You'll endure an eternity of torment," she muttered, "but you'll only have yourself to blame. You know what he's capable of – how he delights in torture. Why didn't you think of that before you let those wretches go?"

Pear sank to her knees. "What can I do?" she blubbered desolately.

With a cold, harsh expression malforming her beauty, the witch looked down at her. "Atone for your disobedience," she demanded, "show your devotion to the coven, let there be no doubt of your submission."

"H ... how?" Pear stammered.

A severe smile snaked over Meta's face. "Complete the task he set for me," she replied forcefully. "Kill those three and we shall take their hearts to him as proof."

"No," the girl murmured.

"You will do as I say!" her mother declared, pulling her up by the hair and sliding her fingers under Pear's necklace. "Must I beat the demon out from you? Scream your rage, daughter – do your father's bidding!"

Her strident voice rang in the girl's ears and the

wooden beads pressed into her skin as the tingling began and Pear let out a frightened whine.

"Don't make me!" she wailed. "Not Jennet!"

"You have no choice!" Meta barked, hitting her brutally. "Not when the primitive side has control – and I shall unleash it!"

The hellish glow welled up behind her daughter's anguish-ridden eyes and the witch sniggered horribly.

"I'll shake the beast out of you!" she snapped, but the girl was already lost as the power of change seized her. Pear's plaintive cries vanished and a chilling growl rattled in the throat of the black hound that now stood at Meta's side.

"Come, Seffy!" the witch laughed as the beast tugged impatiently on the restraining beaded collar. "Devour the enemies of your father!"

The hound bayed ferociously and together they rampaged down on to the sands.

* * *

Beneath the cliffs, where the rain lashed and the gale drove the white-capped waves over the shore, the tribe of aufwaders stood in a large and solemn circle.

Over the heads of the sea wives thick black shawls were draped, and from their murmuring lips they sang the dirge of the black boat.

In the centre of the lamenting circle a narrow vessel of ebony rested against the rocks. Its shapely prow pointed towards the open sea and beneath the great, fringed awning that covered the length of the craft, Nelda lay close to death.

The young aufwader moaned in distress, for the blood that pumped through her veins was gradually turning into brine and she cried in agony as it started to burn and blister inside her.

With the rain battering his uncovered head and flooding down his craggy features, Tarr stood beside her. Reaching into the black boat, his large hands closed tightly about his granddaughter's clenched fists and he watched as she drifted ever closer to that distant shore.

His grieving tears were washed and swept away by the storm and though it murdered his soul to look on Nelda's pain he could not leave her.

"Mother!" she screamed feverishly. "Forgive me! I killed you – Oh Hesper, why did I live and she did not? Speak to me, Father. What was she like? Will no one mention her name? Aaaaieee! A furnace is blazing within me! In the caverns there are eyes that watch – I cannot evade them. Is there none to save me from Esau?"

The fisherfolk hung their heads in shame and weeping. For the first time in many years, Old Parry's pitying tears overwhelmed her.

"Grandfather!" Nelda pleaded hoarsely. "Do not let them kill my baby! Spare me this doom – let me not suffer it alone!"

Despairing, Tarr clung to her, yet he could find no words to ease her torments and he gibbered impotently into the surrounding gloom.

Nelda's pinched, contorted face jerked from side to side as the brine scalded through her body and her glazed eyes saw only the void that awaited her.

Into this sorrowful scene Miss Boston and the children came blundering. Over the ledge beneath the towering footbridge they clambered, yet even as he jumped on to the boulders below, Ben let out a dismal cry.

For an instant as the gale tore the thick curtain of rain aside, the boy saw the tribe assembled around the black boat and knew that it could mean only one thing.

"Nelda," he muttered anxiously.

Aunt Alice peered at the grim tableau and caught Jennet's arm as the girl pushed on ahead of them.

"What is it?" she asked.

"The fisherfolk," Miss Boston replied sadly. "It would appear poor Nelda is dead."

"No," Ben cried and he dashed forward, barging through the crowd until he stood at Tarr's side.

In a croaking voice that was bleak with mourning the leader of the tribe uttered, "Ah knewed tha'd come, lad. She'm not gone yet but ... but theer ain't long."

The proud aufwader hid his face and his burdened shoulders shook as the weight of Tarr's grief crushed him.

Ben took up Nelda's hand that Tarr had relinquished and drew a sharp breath at the heat of the burning palm.

"Nelda," he said to her, "it's me, Nelda – it's Ben."

The large eyes rolled blindly in her shrivelling face but his voice cut through the fever and she managed a desolate smile.

"Ben," she gasped, "my human friend. So you are here at the end."

"Don't say that," he sniffed.

The aufwader shuddered as the pain convulsed through her then she coughed and in a distant, wandering whisper bade him goodbye. "Don't grieve for me," she wheezed. "Remember our friendship in happier days. When we trawled the coast for the moonkelp. Do you remember that?"

"Yes, me, you and Hesper."

"Hesper, yes, she will be there waiting for me. Oh Ben, hold my hand – it's so dark – hold me please."

The boy looked down at their entwined hands and as a further spasm racked her, Nelda gripped him fiercely.

"I burn!" she wailed. "It is eating me alive! Me and

my child are wasting out of existence!''

Respectfully, Miss Boston stepped forward to try to comfort Tarr, and the barren lamenting of the tribe rose around them.

Left behind, unable to witness the tragedy unfolding before her, Jennet waited uneasily. She watched as Aunt Alice consoled the empty air and saw her brother crying with his arms outstretched, but of the fisherfolk and the black boat she saw nothing.

Feeling awkward she looked away, turning her head back in the direction they had come, and a horrified breath rushed from her lips.

On the beach, loping over the sands, two figures were rapidly approaching.

Jennet stared at them in fear, then glanced quickly back to Aunt Alice and Ben. But as she opened her mouth to warn them, a strange resolve reared within her and a determined expression settled over the girl's face. Without a second thought, Jennet climbed back over the ledge and ran through the whirling rain to confront Meta and the black hound which bounded at her side.

Across the beach Jennet bolted, and holding up her hands she yelled, ''Get back! Don't come any closer.''

Meta pulled on the beast's collar and it barked in savage frustration as the witch slowed to a standstill.

''Patience, Seffy,'' Meta crooned. ''Let the fool come to us.''

Its eyes blazing, the hound strained to break free. But the witch held it firmly and spouts of wet sand were hurled into the air as frantic claws scrabbled to leap at the defenceless figure racing towards them.

Breathing hard, Jennet drew near and Meta chuckled loudly.

''I'm touched,'' she said. ''You simply can't get enough of our company.''

The horrific dog barked viciously, but the girl ignored it and looked the witch straight in the eye.

"It's over, Meta," she said flatly. "I'm not afraid of you or your precious Nathaniel any more."

"Then you're more stupid than I guessed," sneered the witch. "Do you know what could have been yours? Do you realize the ravishing life that you have spurned?"

It was Jennet's turn to laugh. "You're the stupid one!" she told her. "It's you who's chained to that vile man, not me. You can't see it, can you? I finally know how lucky I am. I have a real family, but that's something you'll never have."

"I have my beloved when he wants me," the witch cried, "and Pear."

Jennet glanced at the hell hound that snapped at Meta's side. "You have nothing," she said with a shake of the head.

"And neither will you," Meta retaliated, "when Seffy has torn out your brother's heart!"

The girl took a step backwards but no fear showed on her face – the coven had lost that power over her.

"I won't let you harm Ben," she said simply, "not this time – I'm his sister and I love him. I'll always be there to protect him."

"The boy must die," Meta spat, "and so must you. If you wish to make a futile gesture trying to save him, that will merely make it more ... entertaining."

Jennet chuckled and an odd, confident look lit her face. "Oh, I don't know," she muttered threateningly, "you might not find my efforts so futile after all."

The witch blinked, disconcerted to see a familiar red gleam rise in the girl's eyes, and she pulled the dagger from her belt.

"I'm not the same child who idolized you and your daughter!" Jennet declared with a hard, growling edge in her voice. "And I don't need your beads to give me strength. I warn you, Meta – go back to your pathetic friends."

Meta loosened her grip on the hound's collar and paced towards Jennet, holding the glittering dagger before her.

"I'm going to relish carving you," she hissed, "and your little brother!"

Jennet let out a defiant howl. "I won't let you harm my family!" she roared and with that she sprang. As the girl leaped towards the astounded witch, her shape blurred and suddenly a monstrous, chestnut-coloured hound was in her place.

Meta screamed and stumbled backwards, pushing Pear forward.

The black dog pounced on the other and the two ferocious creatures went tumbling over the sand, locked in a fearsome duel – snapping and snarling for each other's throat.

Savagely they wrestled and lunged, their terrible jaws striking and tearing out raw clumps of flesh and fur. Into the cascading night the brutal yammering echoed and they rolled headlong in a mass of claw and muscle into the thrashing waves.

Leaping out of their frantic path, Meta watched the deadly combat anxiously. In her hand the blade glittered ready to strike, but the confused jumble of tussling hide that bayed and splashed in the water raged so violently that she could not get close enough.

"Get her, Seffy!" she shouted as they clawed back on to the shore. "Kill her!"

Beneath the cliff face, the fisherfolk lifted their faces, amazed at the dreadful clamouring uproar, and Miss Boston gazed fretfully at the place where she had left Jennet.

"No," she breathed.

Leaving Ben and the aufwaders behind her, she

scurried hectically over the boulders and climbed over the concrete ledge to the beach beyond.

The terrible conflict was still churning the sands and the frenzied yowling filled the old lady with horror as she hastened towards the battling hounds.

As the snarling brutes vied with each other, Meta hopped from side to side. It was impossible to tell which of them was winning; both seemed evenly matched and the dreadful struggle bowled tempestuously around her.

Then, with a vicious snap of her huge jaws, Pear bit deeply into her opponent's flesh and Jennet yelped shrilly.

"Now!" Meta cheered, excited and enthralled by the gruesome outcome. "You've got her!"

The wounded creature fell back, whining forlornly as the other pinned it to the ground and the demonic eyes shone upon the exposed throat.

Saliva dribbled from the black snout and the teeth that were already stained with blood glistened as the lips drew back over the gums.

"Kill her, Seffy!" Meta urged, flushed with a delicious thrill. "Drink her hot blood and tear the tender meat from the bone!"

Her daughter growled menacingly at her prone, sprawling victim, but as she brought her powerful head down to rip and rend, the hellish glare dimmed in the beast's eyes.

"What are you waiting for?" Meta screeched. "Butcher her!"

Yet instead of slaughtering the other animal, the hound's pink tongue unfurled and tenderly it licked the whining dog's large brown face.

Meta shrieked in disgust. "Must I do it all myself?" she cried. "Get off, you disobedient fool!"

Harshly, she kicked Pear aside and her daughter gave a startled bark as she was pushed on to the sand.

Raising the dagger, Meta stooped over Jennet, whose glimmering eyes gazed up at her piteously. But the witch was unmoved and brought the blade swiftly down.

With a tremendous, baying cry, Pear sprang at her mother and Meta yelled in alarm as the huge black hound cannoned into her. The witch was thrown down, but in her astonishment and without realizing what she was doing, the dagger plunged deep into Pear's ribs.

The witch's daughter let out an agonized howl and collapsed on top of her. A fount of blood was gushing from the horrendous puncture in the beast's furry skin and it thrashed its legs, unable to stand.

"Seffy!" Meta shouted, dragging herself out from under the writhing animal. "Seffy, get up!"

But the hound could only whimper and as she watched, its panicky struggles became increasingly laboured. With a mighty effort, the stricken beast raised its head and its outline rippled and dwindled.

Upon the blood-stained sand Pear regained her human form, but her life was ebbing away and she looked imploringly up at her mother.

Meta stared at her in horror and disbelief. "Pear," she breathed, desperately putting her arms about the girl's naked body and trying to staunch the spurting blood. "What have I done? Oh, what have I done?"

"It had to end," Pear murmured. "The killing had to stop."

"Hush," the woman wept, cradling her in her arms. "Oh Pear – oh my baby. Help me, someone – God help me!"

Around Meta's neck the string of beads broke and with her dead daughter in her arms a grotesque and hollow scream issued from the woman's lips as she felt the full torment of what she had done.

"PEEEEAAAAAAAAARRRRRR!"

Shivering on the sands close by, a cruel bite bleeding on her shoulder, Jennet felt the tortured cry cut right through her and she buried her face in her hands.

"Jennet," a gentle voice said close by, "I'm so very sorry."

The girl threw herself into Miss Boston's arms and the old lady covered her with her cloak.

"Pear!" Jennet wept. "Oh Pear!"

Aunt Alice held her tightly. "That's it," she told her, "you let it all out."

"She ... she was ... was ... she was my friend!" the girl sobbed. "She was my best friend."

The old lady hugged her and looked sadly at Meta. The distraught woman clutched her daughter's limp body to her breast and sixteen years of wasted love came mewling from her broken heart.

"Come now," Miss Boston said gently to Jennet, "put on your clothes and we'll see to that nasty wound."

But from the direction of the cliffs Nelda cried out with pain and the old lady knew that the dangers were not yet over and that the night's sorrow was not yet complete.

14

AT THE END OF ALL THINGS . . .

With her head cocked insolently at the coven, Rowena Cooper stepped from the dark water of the pool and cackled hideously.

"I wasn't expecting a brass band and parties in the streets," she remarked sarcastically, surveying the witches with careless disdain, "but a glad smile or two wouldn't go amiss. Look at you all, gaping at me like dummies in a shop window! My, what a rag-tag bunch the coven is – I had forgotten.

"Hillian, dressing to impress as usual – how marvellously funny you still appear. But ah, your scarlet war paint suits you – let's hope the scars never heal, they give your drab olive face that certain panache it never had. And where is Snivelling Liz – is she scuttling around somewhere at the back? We do seem to be depleted, don't we? No Mannish Miriam or Potato Sack Judith? What, not even the stunning Meta – has the harlot deserted us at last? Has she found comfort in another man's embrace – or just his money? Whatever the case, I pray she has dragged that stinking brat with her."

Tossing her head dismissively, Rowena then turned her full attention to her husband. "And what of you, my dearest?" she crooned ironically. "Are you not overjoyed to see me back? So often have my despairing thoughts turned to you as I wandered in the lonely void."

A resentful sneer crossed Nathaniel's face. "If you thought about me at all," he said doubtfully, "it wouldn't be with affection."

Rowena pouted with feigned injury. "I haven't forgotten those early days in Nairobi," she drawled. "Do you not remember when it was just we two? Those were fine, adventurous times, in that Masai village where you took command and the tribe yielded the secret of change to you. How many infants did we murder that hot night? I know I slew three but you did enjoy it so, didn't you – I quite lost track. Do you know, darling, I think that must have been one of the happiest times we had together."

"That was a long time ago," Nathaniel said curtly. "We were both young, and you couldn't do enough for me. Oh, how things changed."

Rowena gurgled in mild astonishment. "Of course they did!" she laughed, stealing over the muddy bank. "I grew to despise you."

Nursing her bleeding face, Hillian Fogle eyed Rowena with hatred and distrust. "Beware, my Lord!" she called. "Artful and dangerous is she. Did Roselyn not betray you and pursue the Staff of Hilda for her own glory?"

"Really, Hillian," Rowena snorted, "your English still leaves a lot to be desired."

Nathaniel took a step backwards as his wife crept nearer. "What is it you want?" he asked. "You haven't cheated Death merely to indulge in nostalgia; that was never your way, my dear. Hillian speaks the truth; you did betray me, the staff was not meant for you to wield."

"Pooh," she purred acidly, stalking closer. "I never wanted the thing! I am here simply because you are still the keeper of my heart. Throughout the empty reaches of death, your image did haunt my melancholy soul and I have been sustained by the undreamed of hope of this one moment."

Rowena raised her arms to him and held them open, but the warlock knew his duplicitous wife too well to trust her.

"You could never lie to me, Roselyn," he snapped. "I always discovered the truth that lurked beneath your deceptions – have you forgotten?"

For an instant a vengeful light glinted in Rowena's eyes but she tittered and continued to advance towards him.

"Deny that the Lord of the Frozen Wastes has sent you back," Nathaniel challenged, "for my ears are well used to the sound of your subtle lies. Tell me what he hopes to gain by this."

"Are not the Deep Ones most merciful?" she answered. "Their power knows no bounds and to all of us here they have granted our dearest wishes. You, my fine Duke of the Darkness, baron of my heart, are restored to life and my coven sisters are reunited with their deity once more."

She threw her arms above her head and giggled wildly. "But I," she roared, "have been given the greatest gift of all, though the price to myself is costly indeed and from this awful pact I shall never be released. Yet gladly did I accept and never once, throughout the endless stretch of eternity, shall I regret it."

The warlock scowled as Rowena moved close to him. "What pact do you speak of?" he asked. "What has been promised to you?"

But she made no reply and the warlock began to feel unaccountably afraid. Raising his hand he summoned his powers and threw up a shimmering barrier of dark enchantment between them.

"Oh Nathaniel," she laughed, stepping leisurely through the seething spells which dissipated harmlessly around her, "are you frightened of me? How clever of you."

Her husband stumbled back and his black sorceries blasted before him, weaving a mightier wall of defence. Yet this also failed. Rowena breezed through it and her crowing voice sang his name gloatingly as she reached out and stroked his bearded face.

"Tell me you forgive the mistakes I made," she pleaded in a childish voice, wrapping her arms about him. "You know I never desired to wield Hilda's Staff to usurp you and rule in your stead. That was the last thing I wanted."

Rubbing her cheek against his, she pressed against him, savouring the delicious moments that would nourish her forevermore.

The warlock took hold of her wrists and tried to pull her away but the woman clung to him desperately. "Get off me!" he commanded but Rowena hugged him more tightly than ever.

"Kiss me," she begged, "just one last time."

Her lips pushed over his spluttering mouth and lingered there despite his struggling protests and then, laying her head on his shoulder, the woman sighed with satisfaction.

"It's done," she breathed, "and I am contented."

Nathaniel spat on the ground and again attempted to throw her from him.

"No, my wretched love," she muttered, "you cannot be rid of me now. This is why I am here. This is why the Lord of the Frozen Wastes has granted me this one, glorious moment."

"You're mad!" he cried, clawing at her arms to wrench her clear, but the woman's strength was incredible and her arms were locked like bars of iron about him.

Rowena shrieked with fey laughter. "Oh my fabulous husband!" she hooted. "Yes, I came here to steal the Staff of Hilda but for one purpose only – to be free of you! Yet even in death your despised memory plagued and tormented me."

"Let me go!" he yelled. "Roselyn, that is an order!"

"You don't understand!" she crowed. "I stopped serving you long ago. The Lord of the Frozen Wastes is my master. For many months now I have done his bidding and lain hidden in dark places, hoping beyond hope for such a chance as this. Now all bargains are void and I am to be the instrument of the Allpowerful!"

"Hillian!" Nathaniel called. "Help me – kill her!"

The other members of the coven rushed forward and their hands tore at Rowena but the woman whooped insanely and there was nothing they could do. "Too late!" she trilled. "I am beyond you now. My master has made me strong and given me life eternal – although in return I have sacrificed this human form."

Her wild eyes flashed triumphantly before the warlock's fearful face and in a low, condemning rattle she said goodbye.

"Now I shall be free," she breathed, "but you will be a part of me until the end."

And so Rowena Cooper abandoned her true shape and assumed the raiment which the Lord of the Frozen Wastes had decreed she must wear till the breaking of the world.

Without warning, from the wide flapping sleeves of her black gown, a mass of tentacles whipped and writhed and her arms melted into ropes of clammy muscle. The woman's face bubbled as her eyes ballooned into two great fragmented clusters and her flesh sagged into grotesque blubbery rolls of slime.

Nathaniel screamed as the wriggling, snaking

nightmare bound its coils tightly about him and the spy of the freezing deep gave a bellowing shriek.

"Save me!" the warlock screeched, his nostrils filled with the stench of rotting weed that beat from the apparition.

The witches wailed and struck at the bloated monster with their knives but Rowena's new form ignored their puny stings and with a braying rumble the pale underside of her deformed body flowed over her husband's frame and enveloped him just as it had Susannah O'Donnell.

"NOOOO!" Nathaniel clamoured as the acid began eating through his clothes. "Hillian!"

Horrified and flailing their arms against the quivering flesh of the monster in abject terror, the coven called to their beloved as the grey frills of glistening skin crept up to his chest.

The warlock's screams were terrible to hear. Into the vast bulk of the wobbling creature he slowly dissolved and a vile sucking squelch boiled up from the greedy innards as Rowena consumed him.

Hillian threw herself at the ulcerated hide, plunging her dagger deep into the putrescent jelly. But it was all in vain and the stab wounds healed as soon as she ripped the blade out.

"Lord!" she howled as the pale devouring fronds reached Nathaniel's neck.

But her anguished face contorted in despair as she saw the ghastly oozing mouth reach up and smother the man's head.

"Damn you, Roselyn!" he squealed as the liquefying juices swallowed him. "Daaaammnn yoooooouuuuuuuu!"

Within the massive, rippling body, his final tormented curse echoed and then was silenced.

A frightening calm settled over the Abbey grounds, disturbed only by the constant noise of the rain and the rapacious squidging sounds of Rowena's virulent digestion.

"No!" Hillian bawled, tearing at her hair. "Nathaniel! Nathaniel!"

But the warlock had vanished – every trace of him had been utterly consumed, and emitting a satiated, belching grunt, the loathsome apparition wriggled and dragged itself over the ground towards the pool.

Into the dark water Rowena Cooper retreated. Her one terrible ambition had finally been attained and now she had to pay the price. Imprisoned in this horrendous shape forever but contented at last, she sank beneath the splashing surface and disappeared in a rush of bubbles.

Upon the muddy bank, the remaining members of the coven screamed hysterically. All their plans, all their hopes had suddenly been dashed. Their magnificent high priest had been eaten alive and their minds recoiled from the evil memory. A dreadful madness seized them and they threw themselves on the ground devoid of reason. Now their lives were without purpose and they screeched until their throats bled.

Within the ruined Abbey a tall figure moved in the deep darkness. From the shadows it stepped and moved over the excavated graves towards the raving uproar until it was standing at Hillian's side.

The witch was rocking backward and forward and though her mouth gaped open, her screams had dried into a cracked, droning monotone.

Oblivious to everything except her overwhelming grief, she had not seen the stranger approach and when a hand was placed lightly upon her jerking head she was not aware of it.

"Peace be on you," the newcomer said with infinite grace and kindness. "The time of your servitude is at an end."

At once the beads about Hillian's neck broke and were scattered in the mud. The woman fell forward and her ranting terror subsided as the figure blessed her.

"No longer shall you be a slave to the memory of that evil man," the warm voice gently told her. "You are released."

Hillian gasped and she gazed around her as though shaken from sleep. "He ... he is dead!" she exclaimed.

The stranger left her and went over to where Caroline was weeping desolately. A second necklace snapped and the fiddle player collapsed in exhaustion.

Touching her scratched and wounded face, Hillian watched as her deliverer released each of the women in turn.

"Thank you," she sobbed.

Sister Frances smiled benignly and in a patient, inspiring voice addressed them all.

"Hear me now," she pronounced nobly. "Cast away your fears, for Nathaniel Crozier will never return. Henceforth rejoice and never more be troubled by the horrors of the past. Blessed are you, for the freedom of choice is returned unto you. Each one present has suffered much in the service of that black villain, but wounds can heal and if you are indeed repentant then your sins shall be forgiven."

The women listened to her dumbly and her stirring words brought them hope.

"What will we do?" Gilly Neugent asked. "Where are we to go? We lived only for *him*."

"Then you must begin again," the nun replied, "or pick up the threads of your old lives. Each of you has free will – shape your own destiny and let no other steer you. You have wandered too long in the darkness – come now into the light."

Uncertainly, the women rose to their feet. "Will you help us?" they begged her. "It's been so long, we don't know how to begin."

"You must help one another," Sister Frances answered. "Instead of striving for supremacy and indulging in petty squabbles, you must lend support and have generous hearts."

Bowing her head to them, the nun turned, but her attention was held by a livid light that glimmered out at sea.

"What is it?" Hillian muttered as the thunder blared over the cliffs and the rain hammered down more fiercely than ever.

"The end is near," Sister Frances said quietly. "The Lord of the Frozen Wastes himself is coming!"

* * *

Upon the shore, Miss Boston stared grimly into the tempest as a sickly green glow rose in the distance and beneath the waves the sound of a great bell began to toll.

"The Deep One!" she cried. "Is it he?"

Stroking her dead daughter's hair, Meta gazed at the pulsing horizon and nodded gravely. "All is lost for him now!" she shouted above the gale. "His designs are in ruin and soon his secret treason will be known to his brothers. He has nothing left to lose – for they will surely destroy him."

The sea churned and wrathful waves charged towards Whitby as the Lord of the Frozen Wastes rose from the fathomless regions. Leaving his icy realm, the waters boiled as torrents of black foam exploded to the surface and fountains of poison shot into the lightning-ripped sky.

Jennet peered out from under the old lady's cloak, staring in terror at the awesome tumult, and she realized that the evil power of the waking world was coming to wreak his vengeance upon them.

"Ben!" she cried. "I must be with Ben!"

The girl fled back to the concrete ledge and Miss Boston hurried after her.

Alone with Pear, Meta waited for the end to come.

Leaning into the ravaging wind, Jennet and Aunt Alice battled their way to where the fisherfolk defied the screaming storm and watched the calamitous rising of the mighty Lord of the Deep.

Beside the black boat, Tarr glared at the riotous seas, whose fearsome waves reached far into the crackling heavens while the lightning speared deep into the tortured waters.

Amidst the squall, and oblivious to the terror that encircled her, Nelda cried out and clutched Ben's hand despairingly. The boy flinched as the aufwader crushed his fingers, and when he stared at her he stifled a scream.

Nelda's skin was bubbling; huge blisters filled with salt water were swelling over her face and hands and Ben cried to Tarr in dismay.

Her grandfather looked down at her and wailed. "She's dyin'!"

A deafening thunderclap split the night and the jagged forks of blinding light smote the seething surface of the sea as the Lord of the Frozen Wastes reared up from the deep.

Into the shrieking blizzard the crown of his gargantuan head lifted, and, like the vast outline of a colossal mountain, his dark presence left the lashing tides.

About the immense brows a coronet of green stars blazed and the repellent countenance that was revealed beneath their lurid glare made the crowd on the shore recoil and call out in dread.

Through the insane waters, the unbounded god

rumbled towards Whitby.

"Ben!" Jennet shouted as she flung her arms around him. "Oh Ben!"

Looking up into the towering vileness that stretched into the yowling night, Miss Boston spread her tweed cloak about the children like a pair of protective wings and spoke to them hurriedly.

"My dears," she declared, "I've failed you – we cannot escape from the fiend that approaches. At least here, at the end of all things we are united."

From the black cloud that roared in the waters, a forest of tentacles came thrashing – like an army of gigantic snakes. Spreading before the immeasurable enemy the monstrous coils broke from the waves and reached through the sky.

Braving the spectral vision, Miss Boston stuck out her chins and stared upwards as the terrible shadow of the writhing demon fell over her and the children. A darkness deeper than the brumal night descended over the shore and the fisherfolk squealed in fear and panic, clinging to the boat as the sea charged towards them.

Blind to the chaos around him, Tarr sobbed over his granddaughter as the brine-filled blisters that covered her body began to weep and the hand that he held withered horribly.

"Nelda!" he bawled. "Nelda!"

Into the stone of the East Pier the first of the squid-like limbs tore and huge chunks were dragged down into the frothing water. The small lighthouse was thrown down and it toppled with a thundering crash as the tentacles smashed and drove into the solid foundations as though they were built of sand.

"Ben!" Nelda gargled, her voice choked with salt water. "Where are you? Stay by me, please!"

At Miss Boston's side, the boy looked wildly into the boat, then at the horror that reared from the sea.

A strange expression spread over his face and he suddenly pulled himself free of the old lady's arms.

"Benjamin!" she called as he ran towards the town. "Come back!"

"Ben!" Jennet shrieked. "Don't leave us!"

But the boy raced under the high quivering footbridge, made perilous by the shuddering violence of the Lord of the Frozen Wastes. As he fled over the sands and past Meta's huddled figure, the lofty narrow way buckled and with a splitting roar the footbridge dropped on to the rocks below – flinging clouds of concrete dust and twisted metal into the air. The noise boomed over the cliffs, but charging into the streets, Ben did not even glance back.

Jennet and Miss Boston peered in anguish through the swirling debris.

"Ben!" Jennet cried. "I've got to go after him!"

"No, child," Aunt Alice restrained her, "it's too dangerous – there's still rubble falling. He's gone, there's nothing you can do now."

The shore trembled as the full wrath of the Deep One was vented upon the harbour. Between the wreckage of the East Pier and the West, a host of writhing limbs sailed and with unparalleled fury they fell upon the fishing boats, dashing their timbers against the quayside.

Down came the harbour walls and death screams filled the night as the inhabitants of Whitby were shaken from their beds and buildings slid into the river.

From his supreme height, with the storm clouds gathered about his vast star-crowned head, the Lord of the Frozen Wastes surveyed the terrible scene with malevolent pleasure. A petrifying cackle blasted from his cavernous mouth as his gigantic lidless eyes fell upon the pinnacles of the Abbey perched on top of the cliff.

Into the sheer walls of shale his winding limbs pounded, and the rock thundered down as the twisting malice tore into the Abbey plain.

The stately ruins quailed as the Deep One grappled with its ancient columns, then with an idle flick of the serpent-like coils the broken stones of the holy place tumbled down the crumbling cliff.

Mercilessly he let out an exulting laugh. The sight gratified his malignant mind but there was still one act of vengeance before he could be truly triumphant.

Far below, cringing in his swamping shadow, he espied the minuscule figures gathered around the black boat and his ghastly mirth shook the coast.

*　*　*

Inside Miss Boston's cottage, Ben tore from his bedroom and leaped down the stairs. Under his arm the boy clutched a large bulky object wrapped up in his old duffle coat, and with his heart beating madly he flew through the hallway then out into the courtyard.

With a rattle of crumbling mortar the lintel of the front door gave an ominous crack and as hs sped out of the alleyway, Aunt Alice's home collapsed.

Into Church Street Ben ran, dodging falling masonry and hopping over trenches that gaped in the cobbled ground. The East Cliff was unrecognizable; heaps of debris had replaced the quaint shops, burst water mains gushed tall fountains over yawning pits and the first of many fires was already burning in the wreckage, broken gas pipes shooting rivers of dripping flame into the decimated night.

Through the devastation the boy carefully picked his way, forcing himself not to hear the desperate cries calling from beneath the rubble, and he scrambled down on to the sands.

In a mad dash, he headed back along the beach

while behind him, the town of Whitby was swept into the swollen river.

Yet upon the shore, Miss Boston, Jennet and the fisherfolk stared up at their doom.

As a great black mountain, the Lord of the Frozen Wastes loured in the hell-torn sky. The massive discs of his shining eyes pierced the battering rain and his branching hair whipped amongst the swirling clouds thundering through the blighted heaven. Around him his monstrous limbs reared in awful majesty. Not since the dawn of the unhappy world had a member of the Triad been unveiled in all his full black glory.

The faces of the insects that grovelled on the rocky shore, beseiged by destruction, were graven with terror. For this one moment of revenge, the Deep One had spared them from the cataclysmic upheavals and he savoured their raving fear.

"Now!" he bellowed hideously. "Go screaming into the abyss! For the hour has come for all of you."

Like an immense tidal wave, his vastness obliterated the sky and the tempest of his wrath plummeted through the gales.

In the deepening dark, Miss Boston squeezed Jennet tightly while at their side Tarr kissed Nelda's shrivelling hand.

Through the curling mists that had risen from the steaming sea, the Lord of the Frozen Wastes fell and the torrent of his anger stampeded before him, blasting from his evil, plunging countenance – tearing at those gathered beneath.

Fighting through the screaming storm, Ben clambered over the ruins of the footbridge and even as the mighty god of the waters avalanched from above, he cast aside his old coat and held aloft the thing he had taken from the cottage.

There in his grasp, swinging madly in the charging gale, was the Penny Hedge.

AT THE END OF ALL THINGS . . .

The flimsy fence of twigs and sticks that Ben had stolen and kept hidden beneath his bed these many months, tugged and pulled at his hands but he gritted his teeth and gripped it firmly.

In the black, freezing shadow of the Lord of the Deep, the boy glared up at the plummeting nightmare and a fierce snarl twisted his young face.

With his hair streaming in the shrieking wind and his drenched clothes flapping wildly about him, Ben threw back his head and in a loud, clear voice he yelled.

"OUT ON YE! OUT ON YE! OUT ON YE!"

Suddenly the Horngarth crackled and with a burst of fiery sparks the woven twigs became blinding white flames.

Up into the gaping maw the dazzling light shone, illuminating the grotesque contours of the infernal face and, as the age-old power to withstand one more tide beat out from the Penny Hedge, the Lord of the Frozen Wastes let out a deafening scream.

Thunder exploded around his massive head and a ferocious hail tore about his thrashing limbs as the sea was whipped into a demonic frenzy. But upon the Deep One's wrathful brow, the crown of stars dimmed and their baleful glow was lost in the searing brightness that flowed from the framework of sticks that the boy held over his head.

The ancient force of the magical barrier fell furiously about the evil member of the Triad. Chains of enchantment ripped at his titanic form, binding and holding him, until the terrifying apparition could no longer move, caught in a net of primeval magic.

With the Horngarth belting out the ensnaring spells of defence and challenge above his head, Ben glowered up at the motionless cliff of darkness and the boy bawled at the top of his voice, defying the Lord of the Frozen Wastes and crying down his destiny.

"Begone from the waking world!" the boy shrieked. "The powers of the Deep have no dominion here. The time of the gods is past!"

By the black boat, Miss Boston and Jennet peered fearfully over to where Ben ranted and they shuddered in disbelief.

The boy's voice was changing, it had become deeper than his own and was filled with arrogance. A hard bitterness crept into the severe words that tumbled from his lips as he shouted his scorn and Jennet shook her head incredulously.

"Gone are your temples!" Ben yelled with haughty derision. "Forgotten is your memory – slink back to your empty desolation for no more does the world need you. Humankind commands here now! It is Man who rules; he has succeeded your position and surpassed you in might! Return into the void of neglected memory and be a whisper on the wind!"

As he shouted these proud, insolent words a shadow crept over the child. Despite the blinding glory that blistered from the Penny Hedge, his face darkened and then, as Miss Boston and Jennet watched in horror, the boy grew.

His bones stretched and his features shimmered as Ben journeyed into his own future until standing beneath the Lord of the Deep was a swaggering, middle-aged man whose face was cruel and full of conceit.

"Ben," Jennet breathed, "what's happened to him?"

Miss Boston mumbled sorrowfully, "That", she replied, "is what your brother will become."

"Without us you are nothing!" the braggart continued. "I am Lord above the waters! Leave this place – crawl into your noisome holes and be glad that Laurenson is merciful!"

Jennet stared at the vain, boastful man. "It's

horrible!" she wept.

"That is why the Deep Ones fear him," Miss Boston muttered. "Look at that ruthless face. There is nothing that brazen villain would not do! There is no compassion in his eyes – great heavens, what have I nurtured?"

"But he isn't like that!" Jennet sobbed. "You know he isn't. He's just a boy!"

Running over the shore the girl called to the dreadful vision of her brother. "Ben!" she cried. "Ben!"

The man tore his eyes from the Lord of the Deep and glared down at her. A repulsive sneer flickered over his face and he regarded her with contempt and disdain. "Flee while you can, little sister!" he laughed and the foul sound pierced the girl's heart.

"You have no claim on me now!" he said sourly. "I have no need of a puling family. I am allpowerful – a master of control and domination! Run back to the old hag – you are nothing to me now."

Jennet fell back beneath the fierce hatred of his words. "Ben!" she wailed.

The man guffawed to see her pain, but then his face fell and he stared furiously up at the white flames of the Penny Hedge – they were dying.

"No!" he screeched.

As the light dimmed and the forces of the Horngarth were utterly spent, the man that Ben would one day become let out a terrible roar, then faded.

Only a charred skeletal framework remained of the hedge and, grasping hold of the brittle, torrefied twigs, an eight-year-old boy staggered in bewilderment, aghast at his evil destiny.

"Ben!" Jennet cried in relief.

But the power of the Horngarth had gone and as the wind blew a plume of black ash from the boy's hands, the Lord of the Frozen Wastes was released.

Yet raging in from the far distance, rampaging through the wild surf, came two immense towers of darkness.

From the distant reaches of the world the Lord of the Roaring Waters and the Lord of the Circling Seas came storming. Their brother's treachery was revealed to them and towards the devastation that had once been Whitby they raced.

Their wrath was more frightening than anything the survivors had yet seen. As black billowing clouds of doom they came and Ben leaped from the quaking rubble to be with his sister and Aunt Alice.

In a shriek that rocked the earth and sent the waters pounding over the despoiled land, the Lord of the Frozen Wastes quailed in terror.

The bed of the River Esk shivered and a wide fissure split across the ruined town. Into the chasm the sea tumbled and down into the gaping gulf the ruined town slipped.

Miss Boston held the children tightly and the fury of the Deep Ones lashed around them.

The Earth tipped and the shore buckled as the powers of the world did battle. Caught in the waves of destruction, Miss Boston wailed and down into the bottomless abyss she and the children were dragged. Spinning helplessly after plummeted the black boat of Nelda, and with her the sole remaining tribe of aufwaders was finally extinguished. The horrendous tumult rolled over the broken land, engulfing it beneath a foaming wrath and eternal night swallowed the world.

* * *

All was darkness, not a sound disturbed the eerie peace.

Ben opened his eyes but could see nothing in the

blind gloom.

"Jen?" he whispered. "Are you there?"

"Is that you, Ben?" the girl answered. "Where are you? I can't see!"

Aunt Alice's familiar tones echoed from the pitch black void. "Gracious!" she uttered in a small voice.

Very faintly, a pale radiance glimmered in the distance and a wonderful dawn edged over the rim of a placid, rippling ocean. Into the clear heavens the rejoicing light was thrown, bathing the cloudless canopy in rich golden beams.

Miss Boston marvelled at the sight and a fresh breeze ruffled her white woolly hair.

She and the children were standing upon a sandy shore. Behind them a curtain of shadow shimmered darkly but before them lay a stretch of sparkling water that shone like crystal.

"It's beautiful," Jennet breathed.

Suddenly an amazing sound cut through the sweet air and Miss Boston and Ben whirled round in astonishment.

There, sitting up within the black boat, with her head in her grandfather's arms was Nelda, and huge tears were rolling down her face.

Ben's heart leapt and he darted over to them, spluttering with delight, and the tears that Nelda wept were tears of joy – for in her arms was a new-born child.

The infant gurgled happily and its large grey eyes blinked up at its mother as a tiny mouth opened and it gave a chuckling yawn.

Nelda laughed and stroked the baby tenderly.

"It's a boy," she told Ben. "Look – isn't he perfect?"

Tarr grunted sagely, "Arr! He'm a Shrimp reet enough. That's my nose he'm got theer! A proper netter of fish he'll be – make tha proud 'e will."

Nelda gazed lovingly at the small wrinkled face

and smiled. "He already has," she whispered.

Around the black boat the hazy shadows retreated and the rest of the fisherfolk shuffled in a daze on to the gleaming sands.

"A bairn!" Old Parry squawked. "She's managed it – they both live!"

The aufwaders stared at the mother and child dumbfounded, then the seawives threw down their dripping shawls and they all clustered around Nelda to weep and fuss.

Miss Boston beamed at Ben as he ambled back to her.

"What's happening?" he asked. "Nelda was dying."

A mysterious smile twitched over the old lady's face and she looked into the swirling gloom behind them. "I'm not sure," she replied, "yet I have..."

"Be jubilant and banish your dread!" proclaimed a loud voice.

Everyone turned to see who had spoken and out of the shadowy curtain stepped a tall figure dressed in white robes that dazzled them in the brilliant sunshine.

"I don't believe it!" Miss Boston cried. "What are you doing here?"

Sister Frances strode to the water's edge. Gone was her ungainly gait and a strange tranquillity glittered in her large eyes. Gone too was the nun's gauche playfulness and when she addressed them it was with an air of supreme authority.

"Your time of sorrow has ended," she told the fisherfolk, "for the Mother's Curse has indeed been lifted. May that infant be but the first to bless your tribe in the days that are to come."

"How can that be?" asked Nelda. "What miracle has occurred?"

Sister Frances smiled. "The Lord of the Frozen

Wastes is no more," she replied. "His brethren have destroyed him. His evil has been purged from the world and his dark soul banished to the outer reaches of the void."

"Just one moment!" Miss Boston called indignantly. Puffing out her cheeks, the old lady clucked to herself then waggled a dubious finger at the nun's shining figure. "Are you trying to tell me," she began truculently, "that we have been returned – that this place is…?"

"You are where you were," Frances answered, "behold!"

She flourished her hand, gesturing towards the churning shadows behind them and as they stared, the darkness melted.

Rearing high into the clear sky was a towering wall of shale and jutting from the top of the cliff, like a jagged fang of rock, was the Abbey.

The mists receded further and beneath the glorious sunshine, the harbour flashed and glimmered. All around them the final shreds of shadow were uncurling and the gulls glided lazily over the rooftops as Whitby was restored.

Gazing at the wondrous sight, Tarr dropped humbly to his knees. "Praise the Lords of the Deep and Dark," he murmured reverently.

"This is the measure of their remorse," the nun declared. "In atonement for their brother's crimes they have laboured long and this haven by the sea and those who dwell therein are saved."

"Nine times bless me," Tarr muttered. "Theer ain't nowt they canna do."

"Not so," she replied, "for at the side of joy there runs also grief. See, they cannot undo what they have had no part in." Sister Frances pointed along the shore, where the figure of Meta still nursed Pear's body. "Never shall that unhappy soul be free of her torment," she said. "It will hound her always."

Jennet lowered her eyes and silently mourned her late friend.

"Are we really here?" Ben cried. "Are we really home?"

Aunt Alice stuck her tongue in her cheek and keenly scrutinized the figure that purported to be Sister Frances. "Who are you?" she asked. "What happened to that idiot with the Jolly Cheer Up Bag?"

"She is here," the white figure replied, "though her mind is at rest. Do not be startled, Frances has been most useful to me. You must know, Alice Boston, that not all possession is evil."

The old lady's face resembled a surprised frog and she spluttered in amazement.

"But now the time has come", the nun announced, "for many partings." She gestured to the sea and as the fisherfolk gazed out to the sparkling horizon they saw tiny shapes sailing from the distance.

"Grandfather," Nelda whispered, "what is it?"

With his whiskery brows knitted together, Tarr became solemn and around him the aufwaders uttered in dismay.

"The tribe has been spared," he snorted gruffly, "but at what cost?"

A fleet of small rowing boats was floating over the peaceful waves and standing at the prow of the foremost vessel was a figure arrayed in a tunic of bright silver.

It was an aufwader, but one such as Ben had never seen before. About his proud head was bound a circlet of purest gold, that revelled in the dancing sunlight and appeared to burn over his noble brow as a crown of flame. Around the stranger's shoulders, long sand-coloured hair streamed in the breeze and the face which it framed was etched with wisdom.

"By Gow!" Tarr exclaimed. "It isna!"

But all around him the aufwaders took deep excited breaths and shook their heads in astonishment.

"See the pattern twisted over yonder tunic!" Eurgen Handibrass shouted. "There's only been one wi' a crest like thattun! It were writted throughout the caves on all the works he did!"

Old Parry hopped up and down as she tried to contain herself. "Irl!" she blurted. "It's Irl!"

Miss Boston nodded, admiring the regal, legendary figure that sailed towards them. "So he too has been forgiven," she sighed. "Splendid!"

The boat which held the former herald of the Deep Ones floated to a halt at the water's edge, and Irl turned a great glad smile upon them.

"Hail to thee, Tarr of the Mereades!" he saluted.

Tarr bowed stiffly then Irl fixed his large green eyes upon Miss Boston. All the shifting moods of the sea were reflected within them and the old lady blushed coyly. "Hail to thee also," he greeted her, "Queen amongst mortal kind."

"Most gracious," she mumbled.

"The mighty ones are in truth merciful," Irl proclaimed. "They have repented of their anger towards our race!"

Many tears flowed from the fisherfolk, but as the other vessels glided to a halt, Nelda eyed them uncertainly. "Why are there so many empty boats?" she asked. "Who is to sail in them?"

Irl turned to her and in a lamenting voice said, "Compassionate the Deep Ones might be, yet they will not suffer thee to live alongside the humankind. I have been sent to guide thee away."

Ben rushed to Nelda's side. "You can't go!" he cried. "Tell him you're staying here!"

"Neither she nor any other can remain," Irl told him, "for the condition of their survival is that they accompany me."

"Where to?" the boy asked. "Can I still come and visit them?"

"No," Irl said sadly, "the Deep Ones have toiled unceasingly to raise an island in the far girdling waters and around it they have woven a mist which no mortal ship may penetrate. The race of the aufwader is passing out of thy world, child – their dwellings upon the enchanted isle will be forever beyond man's reach."

A lump formed in Ben's throat as the sobs welled up and a large tear rolled down his cheek as he looked at Nelda. "I won't see you again!" he sniffed.

"Oh Ben!" she cried as her own tears flooded out. "I'll miss you so much!"

Passing the infant to her grandfather, Nelda gave the boy a fierce hug.

"Don't forget me!" he blubbered.

"How could I do that?" she wept, disentangling herself from his arms and taking the baby from Tarr.

"Look at this child of mine," she cried. "Hold him in your arms before we part."

Ben held the infant gingerly and the tiny face gurgled up at him.

"He likes you," Nelda murmured. "See, my son – this is the one you were named after. Yes, my dearest friend, he too shall be called Benjamin."

Hearing this Miss Boston dabbed her own moist eyes and turned briskly to Tarr.

"So this is goodbye, Mr Shrimp," she said. "I can't say as I'm pleased. Whitby will be a sad place without you and your kind. It seems as if all the mysteries are fading and the world is becoming woefully dull and grey."

"Farewell," Tarr grunted. "If the tribe does flourish then tha knows theer'll be some young Bostons an' Alices amongst the tykes."

The old lady grinned, then walked up to Ben and

removed the amulet from around his neck.

"I really think we should return this to you," she said to Irl, reaching her hand up to him. "I don't suppose we shall be needing it again. Thank you so very, very much – we really are most grateful."

The noble aufwader received it thoughtfully. "Nay," he told her, "'tis my masters who are in thy debt. Much do they owe to thee, yet only one thing more is in their power to grant, for their labours have spent their strength and for many ages shall they sleep below the waves. So, I say unto thee now, has the time not come to trust in them? Dost thou recall what they said unto thee?"

Miss Boston withdrew her hand and looked at the children vaguely, but said nothing.

Irl shifted his gaze to the fisherfolk and in a loud, commanding voice declared, "Now is the hour of parting. View one last time your ancient home and step into the boats. A long journey lies ahead and this night you shall step upon a strange shore."

In mournful silence, the tribe waded into the water and boarded the small, bobbing craft, their eyes trained on the familiar contours of the cliffs, fixing the image in their hearts.

Tarr and Nelda were the last ones to leave the sands but eventually he put his hand gently on her shoulder and stepped into the waves.

With her baby in her arms, the young aufwader turned a pale face to Ben and slowly followed her grandfather.

"Wait!" the boy cried, splashing after.

"You cannot join us," she told him. "It is forbidden."

Ben shook his head and reached into the pocket of his coat. "I know," he said, "that isn't what I meant."

In his hands the boy held a small green jar. "The sight is too terrible a gift," he decided. "The glimpse of what I might one day become was enough to make me realize that. Besides, if you're not going to be here, then there's no point having it, is there?"

Removing the lid he stared at the ointment within and held it out to her. "Please," he murmured, "would you be the one to take the sight from me? I'd like it to be you."

With a sad smile that conveyed a wealth of unspoken emotion, Nelda dipped her fingers in the salve and tenderly anointed Ben's eyelids.

"You will always be with me," she whispered and when the task was complete she kissed him lightly on the cheek.

Miss Boston came to stand at the boy's side as Nelda passed the baby to her grandfather and clambered aboard their boat.

Ben blinked and his vision became hazy. The crowd of boats began to blur and already the fisherfolk were fading.

"Farewell, Ben," came Nelda's forlorn voice. "Farewell, my human friend."

A white mist rolled over the surface of the sea and the fleet of rowing boats turned gracefully in a slow circle to meet it. The dense fog curled around their timbers and the vessels were drawn from the water's edge. Soon only a low cloud could be seen drifting across the sea and it passed far into the vanishing distance.

Ben wept uncontrollably into Aunt Alice's cloak and the old lady patted him gently, whilst wiping her own tears away.

Throughout these sad proceedings Jennet had remained quiet, and though she could not see the fisherfolk she guessed what had happened.

"Are they gone?" she asked.

"Yes," Miss Boston nodded, "the old whalers of Whitby town have departed."

"Ben," his sister said awkwardly, "I'm sorry. I really am."

Aunt Alice entrusted him to her care as she turned to look at Sister Frances.

"They are a credit to you," the nun said warmly. "They are stronger now than when they first arrived. You have taught them much."

"Have I?" Miss Boston muttered. "I used to fancy myself as a wisewoman, yet at the moment I feel anything but."

"You are troubled," Frances observed.

Looking at the children, the old lady admitted that she was. "I have done my part in this," she murmured, "heeded Prudence's warning and came out valiantly once more – and yet ... I know that it cannot be forever. My age will catch up with me again; what will happen then?"

But the nun had turned away and was staring down the beach to where a small figure dressed in a gossamer nightgown played in the shallow surf.

The golden-haired child lifted his head to gaze at Miss Boston and the old lady gasped as the bright blue eyes shone out at her.

"What must I do?" she asked.

Frances shook her head. "I cannot advise in this. You will do as you have always done, Alice Boston – what is best for those you cherish – and may a blessing be upon you."

Miss Boston put her forefinger to her mouth as she considered, then finally breezed gladly towards the children.

"My dears!" she laughed. "What an adventure we have had. Won't there be a lot to tell Dithery Edith when she comes back from the Isle of Wight? She won't believe it, of course. My goodness, I could make short work of a hearty breakfast – would you be so kind as to run ahead and start cooking the kippers

for me, Jennet? You go with her, Benjamin – I'll be …
I'll be along soon."

The children began trudging up the shore towards
the town and in a broken whisper, Aunt Alice
breathed, "Goodbye, my dear ones, take care of
yourselves. I love you both so very, very dearly –
you'll never know how much."

"I assure you they will," Frances promised.
"Remember, the Deep Ones can do anything."

Miss Boston swallowed the choking sobs and
glanced back at the infant who was beckoning her.

"Come on, Alice!" she huffed, taking a deep, brash
breath. "Let's show them what we're made of!"

Flinging her cloak over her shoulders she marched
towards the small waiting figure, with her chins
flattened against her chest and a determined
expression fixed on her wrinkled face.

The shining form of Sister Frances watched as the
child gave a delighted chuckle and raised its chubby
hands to the old lady.

Miss Boston stole one final glance at the retreating
figures of Ben and Jennet then took the infant's
hands in hers.

"Now be at rest," the child beamed. "Your cares
are over."

With his merry laughter floating on the air, he
began to lead Alice Boston into the sea.

Sister Frances smiled faintly then her eyelids
fluttered and she put her hand to her temple as her
legs buckled beneath her.

Upon the cliff top, in the windows of the Abbey, a
beautiful radiance gleamed fiercely for a moment,
shining far into the clear sky – then was gone.

The sands appeared dull and chill and dressed in
her usual drab robes and black woollen stockings,
Sister Frances gawped about her.

"Lumme!" she gushed. "What am I doing here?"

Whirling unsteadily around in a doddery circle, the boisterous nun squinted at the shallow waters, where a dark furling shape swished beneath the waves.

"Sweet Lord!" she whinnied, galumphing into the sea, "I recognize that! Oh, don't let it be so – it's too, too awful!"

With her clumsy hands, she dredged a sage green tweed cloak from the water and inspected it with a horrified expression on her goggling face.

"Mis B!" she wittered, scooping through the waves to find her, "Miss B! Where are you?"

But Miss Boston was gone and in the ancient town of Whitby another bright and peaceful morning was unfolding.

* * *

Margaret Rodice eased herself into her chair and munched her way through half a packet of bourbons as she lost herself in the pages of her romantic novel. The lipstick prints around the rim of her fine china cup had almost obliterated the top of a shepherdess's head by the time she had sucked the watery tea down to the dregs.

Reaching the end of a heart-thumping chapter, she lay the book down and gazed out of the window at the leaden skyline of Leeds.

It had been a trying few weeks and her pride had still not recovered from having to take back that pair of difficult cases, the Laurenson children.

Oh, she had argued and protested, but the authorities had refused to listen and it was gallingly bitter to realize just how indifferent they were to her views and opinions.

Those children were the most unpleasant specimens ever to have passed through the doors of her hostel, and the discomfort at having to admit them a second time rankled inside her inflamed breast.

They had been back with her for almost a fortnight now and she had to admit that the change in one of them was not unappealing. That creepy little boy was no longer frightening her other charges and she hadn't heard him mention her late husband once. He spent most of his time moping about in the flagged garden or mooching sullenly in the recreation room. That was how it should be, a nice quiet child who didn't shout and didn't wet the bed.

Mrs Rodice's lips twitched, however, when she thought of the boy's sister. Whatever that barmy old woman had taught that girl it certainly didn't include good manners. Jennet Laurenson was the rudest and most insolent creature she had ever known. She watched over that brother of hers like a hawk and even the older thugs were afraid of her.

"Something must be done," the woman grumbled, nibbling her final biscuit and sucking the crumbs from her palm. "I wonder if that docile Adams woman who came to visit them last weekend would care to take them off my hands? She seemed malleable enough."

Her plottings were interrupted by the peeping of the telephone, and summoning her friendliest and most official-sounding voice, in case it was someone who mattered, Mrs Rodice snatched up the receiver.

* * *

The recreation room of the hostel was a poky place, just big enough to squeeze in a ping-pong table, but as one of the bats had gone missing and was never replaced, this facility was perpetually folded and jammed against one wall behind the television.

Sitting on two of the three reasonably comfy chairs,

Jennet and Ben played with a dog-eared and grubby pack of cards and whiled the afternoon away.

The past three weeks had been a miserable time for them. In the tragic absence of Miss Boston, Sister Frances had stayed at the cottage to care for the children, but this was only a short-term solution as the social services sought for a more permanent answer.

It was Jennet's fault that she and her brother had ended up back with "The Rodice". In an unguarded moment she had forgotten that the guileless nun had no comprehension of sarcasm and extolled the virtues of this establishment to the full. Unfortunately Sister Frances had believed every word and put a terribly misguided plan into action.

Jennet was mortified when she discovered that everything had been arranged but by that time it was too late. Bags were packed and they were shunted back under the auspices of Margaret Rodice.

Neither she nor Ben understood what was happening to them; everything they had grown to love had been taken away and they were back where they had started.

"Snap," the girl sighed in a dull voice.

"I'm bored," Ben moaned, flinging the playing cards across the room and stomping over to the window.

Jennet watched him press his nose against the glass and stare down at the road below. She wondered if he realized that it was exactly a year ago today that they had first set foot in Whitby and saw Aunt Alice's plump, clucking figure.

Ben slid his face across the window and gazed back at her. "Why did she do it?" he asked, proving that he too was thinking of the indefatigable old lady. "Why did she leave us?"

"I don't know, Ben," his sister replied, "I really

don't know. I was hoping that perhaps today … but no – nothing's going to happen. We've had our share of magic in our lives. You only get the one."

The boy sniffled and returned his doleful attention to the road outside.

Idly, his eyes watched a blue car veer from the road and glide up to the hostel gates.

Gradually, as the couple alighted from the vehicle below, Ben's mouth dropped open and he rubbed his eyes in wonder.

"Jen," he murmured feverishly, "Jen – the ointment! It's wearing off!"

Hurriedly, Jennet ran over to him. "Ben!" she cried. "Are you all right? What's the matter, what have you…?"

Her voice died, for she too looked down at the figures and she clasped her hands over her mouth as she burst into tears.

"You see them!" Ben shrieked, bouncing up and down on the chairs. "You see them! The Lords of the Deep and Dark can do anything! They can do anything!"

The children raced to the door and wrenched it open, just as The Rodice was tripping up the stairs in a state of great agitation.

"This is most irregular!" she exclaimed shrilly. "Most exceedingly irregular! I really don't understand…!"

Standing aside to let the visitors past, she stared at the ecstatic faces of the children framed in the doorway and shrugged.

Jennet and Ben gazed through their joyful tears at the man and woman before them, then with a happy yell – they ran into their parents' arms.

The Dark Portal
by Robin Jarvis

Book One of THE DEPTFORD MICE Trilogy

In the sewers of Deptford there lurks a dark presence which fills the tunnels with fear. The rats worship it in the blackness and name it Jupiter, Lord of All.

Into this twilight realm wanders a small and frightened mouse. Far from family and friends he perishes, and in doing so is the unwitting trigger of a chain of events which hurtle the Deptford Mice into a doom-laden world of terror and sorcery.

ISBN: 0 7500 0628 5

The Crystal Prison
by Robin Jarvis

Book Two of THE DEPTFORD MICE trilogy

An innocent young mouse lies murdered in a moonlit field, as the screech of an owl echoes across the ripening corn.

It is summer. Newly arrived in the countryside from the horrors of Jupiter's lair, the Deptford Mice find themselves embroiled in a series of horrible murders. At first the simple country mice suspect Audrey – but the truth is far more sinister …

ISBN: 0 7500 0574 2

The Final Reckoning
by Robin Jarvis

Book Three of THE DEPTFORD MICE trilogy

The ghostly spirit of Jupiter has returned, more terrifying than ever before. Bent on revenge, he smothers the world in an eternal winter of ice and snow.

Huddled around their fires, the Deptford Mice are worried: the mystical bats have fled from the attic, and underground a new rat army is being mustered. With food short, and no sign of spring, the mice know that a desperate struggle confronts them.

Few will survive.

ISBN: 0 7500 0272 7

The Alchymist's Cat
by Robin Jarvis

Book One in THE DEPTFORD HISTORIES series

It's the winter of 1664 and young Will Godwin, an alchymist's assistant, chances upon a mother cat and her three new-born kittens in a London churchyard. Taking pity on the freezing family, Will carries them back to his master's apothecary shop. And there, among the bubbling bottles and evil-smelling jars in Dr Spittle's laboratory, unfolds an extraordinary tale of sorcery, disease, villainy and murder.

ISBN: 0 7500 0890 3

The Oaken Throne
by Robin Jarvis

Book Two in THE DEPTFORD HISTORIES series

It is a time of magic, and a time of darkness. The fierce wars between the bats and the squirrels have been raging for many years, but tonight the battle for power takes an extraordinary new twist.

The Starwife, leader of the black squirrels, lies dying; before she can name her successor, she is betrayed and poisoned by her trusted handmaiden. As the vicious bat army launches a devastating attack on the Starwife's realm, the squirrel leader staggers to a window and calls for aid …

In different corners of the land, Vesper the young bat and Ysabelle the squirrel maiden are as yet unaware of the events that will sweep them into a nightmarish journey to save their kind from destruction …

ISBN: 0 7500 1393 1

The Whitby Witches
by Robin Jarvis

Book One in THE WHITBY series

Two children, Jennet and Ben, arrive at the seaside town of Whitby to stay with Alice Boston, a vigorous and eccentric 92 year-old.

Ben is gifted with "the sight" – he alone can see things hidden from the eyes of ordinary mortals. He sees the mysterious fisher folk of Whitby and he soon discovers that Alice Boston and her friend are not quite what they seem. Who are they? What are the fisher folk and why does a mysterious black hound stalk the darkened streets?

ISBN: 0 7500 0581 5

A Warlock in Whitby
by Robin Jarvis

Book Two in THE WHITBY series

The peace of an Autumn night in Whitby is disturbed when, high on the Abbey plain, something stirs. A scale-covered claw burrows out of the earth, and into the pale moonlight a hideous creature worms its way.

The next day, at the Whitby Railway Station, a certain Nathaniel Crozier steps off the morning train. Little do the other passengers know that he is the husband of the wicked Rowena Crozier, back in Whitby to avenge her death …

Miss Boston, Jennet and Ben are pitted against an even more deadly enemy, but can they succeed a second time?

ISBN: 0 7500 1203 X

The Whitby Child
by Robin Jarvis

Book Three in THE WHITBY series

In the depth of the night, a dark shape rises from Whitby harbour and crawls along the deserted streets, leaving a trail of slime in its wake. As Ben murmurs fitfully in his sleep, two glittering clusters of eyes stare keenly at the sleeping boy …

Along the windswept Whitby shore, Nelda the aufwader nurses a terrible secret. It is only a question of time before she must reveal the truth …

As Alice Boston lies paralysed by illness in her Whitby home, the ghost of a long-dead friend appears before her to warn of a great and impending danger …

ISBN: 0 7500 1581 0

The Dark Portal Audio Cassette

Abridged from the book by Robin Jarvis
Narrator: Tom Baker

Tom Baker's dramatic rendition of the first title in
THE DEPTFORD MICE trilogy, with its spine-
tingling blend of suspense, mystery and fantasy, will
hold both children and adults spellbound.

ISBN: 0 7500 1680 9

ABOUT ROBIN JARVIS

Robin Jarvis was born in Liverpool, the youngest of four children, and grew up in Warrington. His favourite subjects at school were Art and English and he went on to study Graphic Design at Newcastle Polytechnic.

His final degree show was full of goblins and river spirits that leered and dangled off the screen. After college he moved to London and put his design talent to good use creating characters for television and advertising.

His first book, The Dark Portal, developed from doodles of the Deptford Mice characters in a sketchbook. It was published in 1989 and became an instant bestseller, achieving the runner-up award for the prestigious Smarties Prize in the same year.

Robin now has three series to his name – The Deptford Mice Trilogy, the Deptford Histories and The Whitby Series. He won the Lancashire Library/National Westminster Bank Children's Book of the Year Award for The Whitby Witches and has widespread critical acclaim.

He still produces all of the artwork and illustrations for his books himself, working from home in Greenwich, South London.

For further information about Robin Jarvis and his books, please contact: The Marketing Department, Macdonald Young Books, 61 Western Road, Hove, Sussex, BN3 1JD.